Her Ruthless Warrior

The Syndicates Book 1

R.G. Angel

Her Ruthless Warrior

Cover: Fay Lane Cover Design
Editing: Silvia Reading Corner

By R.G Angel

Copyright © 2022 R.G. Angel

This book is a work of fiction. Names and characters are the product of the author's imagination and any resemblance to actual persons, living or dead is entirely coincidental.

This e-book is licensed for your personal enjoyment only. This e-book may not be re-sold or given away to other people.

If you're reading this e-book and did not purchase it, then please purchase your own copy. Thank you for respecting the hard work of this author.

WARNING: 18+ only. Please read responsibly. THIS NOVEL CONTAINS TRIGGERING CONTENT.

GLOSSARY

Ikigai – Japanese concept referring to something that gives a person a sense of purpose, a reason for living.

-Sama – is the most formal, and is very special.

-San – honorific neutral term, which most closely resembles "Sir/Madam".

Arigato gozaimasu – polite way of saying "thank you"

Orochi – Big Snakes of legends.

Gaijin – Japanese word for foreigners, specifically non-East Asian foreigners such as white and black people.

Oyabun – The head of the Yakuza

Bushido – A moral code concerning samurai attitudes, behavior and lifestyle

Yubitsume – Yakuza ritual: the cutting off of one's finger, is a form of penance or apology

Oji – Uncle

Nuhi – Slave/Servant

Wakagashira – A yakuza member ranking beneath the oyabun and responsible for seeing that his orders are carried out correctly.

Moushiwake gozaimasen – most formal apologies.

Hafu – half-japanese/mixed-race Japanese

Kanji – logographic characters

Sourumeito – Soulmate

Sōhei – warrior monk
Obāsan – Term of respect for grandmother/older woman you have affection for.
Shōwa – Shōwa era corresponding to the reign of Emperor Shōwa translate as "Bright Peace" in Japanese
Kyodai – A high-ranking member of the yakuza
Giri – Duty/Obligation
Shobadai – protection money
Kuchidomeryou – Hush money/bribe
Aishitemasu – I love you
Īe – No
Musuko – *Son*
Yome – Wife
Wafuku – Traditional japanese clothing
Haha – Mom
Suītohāto – Sweetheart

CONTENTS

Dedication	VII
Preface	1
Chapter 1	3
Chapter 2	17
Chapter 3	45
Chapter 4	57
Chapter 5	75
Chapter 6	95
Chapter 7	121
Chapter 8	139
Chapter 9	151
Chapter 10	171
Chapter 11	189

Chapter 12	207
Chapter 13	235
Chapter 14	261
Chapter 15	275
Chapter 16	289
Chapter 17	301
Chapter 18	313
Chapter 19	327
Chapter 20	337
Chapter 21	347
Chapter 22	371
Chapter 23	385
Chapter 24	397
Chapter 25	411
Chapter 26	425
Epilogue	439
About R.G. Angel	447
Also By	448
	449

To my Readers, thank you so much for taking a chance on my stories. You're changing my life.

To all women I've met and have yet to meet, you are the driving force in this world and I'm so proud of us (except you Amber, I'm not proud of you.)

To men with BDE, thank you for being a constant source of inspiration for my heroes (looking at you Chris, Henry, Idris, Tom, Simu...Basically most of Marvel and DC tight suits).

To coffee, thank you for being my savior, my unsung hero while writing this book, your contribution might be silent but never forgotten.

To my mother, nothing in this book is safe...*NOTHING*. So please just move along.

PREFACE

Koi No Yokan - The knowing feeling upon first meeting someone that you will inevitably fall in love with them.

CHAPTER 1

Violet

"I'm not sure I'm following." I breathed slowly as I fidgeted in front of Mr. Reynolds' desk.

He cleared his throat and leaned back in his chair, his round face much redder than usual. "Well, I'm not sure what there's to follow here," he snapped defensively. "This was a six-month training program. The six months are over, so you are not needed anymore." He pointed at the door behind him. "Turn around and leave."

Of course, he expected me to bow my head and leave. I was non-confrontational; I always followed every rule and every command to stay under the radar, to make sure I wasn't too much of a burden on my mother. I just remained like that, even after her passing.

He expected for me to just walk away because he was the marketing director and I was the assistant of his assistant, but it was time for me to put my foot down. It was time for me to ask why, once again, I was losing the little something I had worked so hard to get.

I had nothing left to lose.

Please, God, cut me some slack. I really need a win.

"Sir, I'm sorry to insist, but when we were brought into this apprenticeship program, we were told that the best performer would be offered a permanent position. I've been assured through the monthly assessments that I would be offered this position. Mrs. Taylor even asked me to come back this morning to sign my contract and start the permanent position."

His face grew redder as he adjusted his position on his seat, his imposing belly squeezing against his desk as he leaned forward. "Things change every day in the corporate world, Ms. Murphy. You would know that if you'd tried to educate yourself and didn't drop out of school at sixteen."

I inhaled sharply as I took the verbal blow. That one stung more than I expected, especially based on the reason I left school as young as I did.

It had never been my choice—no, it had been just another good thing life had stolen from me.

I blinked and looked down, having lost the small fire of injustice that had been burning—what had driven me to fight for myself.

He sighed. "Listen, companies are going through restructuring all the time—the position that once was to be filled doesn't exist anymore."

A flash of red in the corner of my eye attracted my attention, and I looked out the glass office wall to see Mr. Reynolds' niece sitting at what was my desk for the past few months.

"I see..." I trailed off, too defeated to even try. It was nothing I had done, nothing the company had really done; it was just a simple case of nepotism.

He followed my eyes and glared at his niece, who gave him a sheepish smile before she twisted toward the screen.

Should I feel better that he wanted to hide this from me? Was it to preserve my *tender feelings* or to make sure I wouldn't make a scene?

He sighed. "Listen, Violet."

Ah, it was Violet now, was it? He obviously knew I was bright enough to catch up on the situation.

"You were good, very good even, and you're not leaving empty-handed. We—" He looked around his desk and stopped on the leather-bound corporate checkbook. "If you'd let me finish before, you'd know that we decided to grant you a gracious, two-week bonus to thank you for all your hard work. Also know that should any entry position become available, your name will be at the top of the list."

I looked at him as he grabbed the book and wrote me a check. *Gracious?* This apprenticeship barely paid minimum wage, and I had to work a few nights a week at the dry cleaner down the street just to make ends meet.

I was supposed to start a job today where my salary would have been forty-five thousand dollars a year. Nothing to write home about for most people, but for me... it would have changed my whole life.

Instead, I would leave with broken dreams, wasted time, and a check for... I extended my hand to grab the white piece of paper he extended and read the amount. *$932.15?!* Was he serious? I looked up at him. That asshole even took out taxes!

"This experience is invaluable, Violet. You've spent six months working for one of the biggest real estate companies in California. It's not negligible, you know, and I'm willing to provide you with a stellar reference should you ever need one."

I knew what he was not saying. *Leave without making a scene, and I'll help you.*

I looked down at the check again. Lord, how I wish I didn't need the money. That I could just crumple it up and shove it so deep down his throat he wouldn't be able to breathe anymore.

I recoiled. *Where did that even come from?* I was not violent, never had been, but this compulsion...

It's in your genes.

I shook my head and blinked as tears burned the back of my eyes.

"I... Yes, thank you, sir." I was thanking the man who probably stole my only chance to make it out of my situation, just to give the job to his spoiled niece, who only wanted it as a whim or as a punishment.

"Don't mention it. I wish you all the luck in the world."

I nodded silently, completely exhausted and out of words, and turned around to leave.

"Violet?" he called just as I reached the door.

I turned my head toward him, hope blossoming in my heart against my own advice. Maybe he realized it was unfair, maybe he found a solution. Maybe he just—

"Don't forget to leave your badge with security downstairs."

My heart plummeted once again as shame at my own stupidity joined my other raging emotions.

I should have known better... When did life really cut people like me some slack?

I pulled the strap of my thrift store handbag higher on my shoulder and walked down the corridor with as much dignity as I could muster, trying to respond to the small, sad smiles people were giving me along the way.

Sandra, an assistant for the finance department, snuck into the elevator just as the door closed on me.

"It's bullshit!" she spat, her cheeks red and eyes shining with a self-righteousness that somehow made me feel both better and worse.

"What is?"

"Everything!" She made a wide gesture with her hands, forcing me to take a sidestep to avoid getting poked in the eye by one of her sharp, pointy nails. "That fucking old pervert once again fucked this company by hiring one of his backward relatives, and no one bats an eye," she huffed.

"I swear, that man knows something to get away with that much shit."

I agreed with her, of course. I had seen a lot of shit in the past six months, including the leering looks he had no place giving young women barely in adulthood, but I was not in the mood to fuel the fire. I was angry, yes, but mostly sad and tired, which all wrapped up in an overwhelming sense of defeat and doom.

"It is what it is." I shrugged, willing the elevator to make its way down just a little faster.

It is what it is... The story of my life.

"I'm going to be fine; I'm not worried." Maybe if I said that enough, I'll believe it. I sighed with relief as the elevator beeped, announcing my destination had been reached. "You better go back up now before you get into trouble. See you around," I added, quickly exiting the enclosed space, tightening my hold around the plastic pass in my hand, feeling it bite painfully in my palm.

I stopped by the white reception desk and met Reginald, who gave me the same sorry eyes as they did upstairs. He was from the same part of town as me, so he knew the extent of the opportunity that had been stolen from me.

"I'm sorry, little one," he said soothingly, resting his big hand on top of mine.

I looked down at his gentle gesture and my shaky composure cracked, letting a few burning tears escape.

Reginald was a gentle father figure who had been showing me nothing but kindness since my first day here and had managed to make me feel comfortable when I was on the verge of hyperventilating.

"You're twenty-one, baby girl; you'll get back on your feet. I know you will."

I sniffled, still keeping my eyes down, looking at my few tears shining on the white counter.

He squeezed my hand. "Let me call you an Uber; you deserve it. The company owes you this ride."

"Thank you." Normally I would have said no, fearing he would get into trouble.

But I didn't feel like making the thirty-five-minute, two-bus trip back home wearing an itchy dress and the uncomfortable heels I bought at the charity shop down the street to help me look professional.

I had felt like a fraud all the way here, and now, on top of a fraud, I felt like a failure.

"The car will be out in a couple of minutes."

"Thanks, Reginald... for everything."

"You're welcome, little one. Don't be a stranger."

I walked out, deciding to wait for the car outside, hoping the warm sun would help me feel a little better.

I got my phone out and called Jake. I needed my boyfriend right now. I needed him to make me feel better, even if he had warned me from the start not to get my hopes up.

The phone went straight to voicemail. He was probably in 'the zone,' working on some of his freelance projects.

I sighed, putting the phone back in my bag as a green sedan slowed and stopped in front of me.

"Car for Violet?"

"Yes, thank you."

I sat in the back and instead of giving him my address, I gave him Jake's. He lived much farther from the downtown area and somehow, the small pettiness of knowing this ride would cost them double to take me there, instead of my small studio apartment, made me feel a little better. I was sticking it to the man—even if it was for a meager thirty dollars.

Jake didn't live in my run-down neighborhood. He'd managed to escape and take a few steps up the ladder of life and live in an area with fewer guns than people. He 'made it,' as he loved to repeat every chance he had.

I was sure he could take a break from his current project and make me feel better. I closed my eyes and leaned against the headrest, letting the car vibrations lull me and relieve some of the stress.

I couldn't help but wince at the thought of going back to work at *Sunset Strip,* the supposedly 'high-end' gentlemen's club that was harboring the same type of perverts as cheap strip clubs had, except clients had thicker wallets... and blacker hearts.

I sighed, opening my eyes and meeting the driver's curious gaze just before he looked at the road again.

I could already picture Liam's smirk when I go back and ask for my barmaid job back. How he would give me part two of the speech he gave me when I told him I was leaving. He would tell me, yet again, that *Sunset Strip* was a family and you don't just walk away from your family. Then, in his *magnanimous* kindness, and in memory of his father and my mother, he would give me my job back.

I couldn't help the little grunt of annoyance that escaped my mouth at the thought.

"You belong here, Violet, like your mother. Why are you trying so hard to make it out?" Because I didn't want the same life she had; because she wanted nothing more than for me to make it out. Because I owed it to her to try my hardest.

"Hello? Miss?"

My eyes shot open and I looked out of the window, startled to have been nudged out of my thoughts.

I stared at Jake's small bungalow across the street, trying to regroup my thoughts and composure, at least long enough to tell him everything.

"Is it the wrong address?" he asked, not even bothering to hide the irritation in his voice.

"No, I'm sorry." I shook my head and opened the door. "It's right, sorry."

He mumbled something under his breath, and I'd barely closed the door behind me before the car had shot off.

I crossed the street and stopped on the sidewalk, frowning at the small red car parked just behind Jake's Volvo.

It was quite a popular little car, yet something made me take a few tentative steps toward it as a bad feeling settled in the pit of my stomach.

My frown deepened as I noticed the pair of mini red stilettos dangling from the rearview mirror. It might have been a very common car, but that keepsake? It wasn't.

This was Serena's car. Serena, my supposed friend and one of the most popular strippers at *Sunset*. Serena, who lived on the other side of town and who had only met Jake twice before.

I turned toward the house and walked slowly as the bad feeling turned into ice in my stomach.

The closer I got to the front door, the more I was hyperventilating, imagining the worst.

There must be an explanation. It could just be a coincidence.

Jake wouldn't do that to me, not after all the things I've been through. I told him I wanted to wait, that my virginity had value to me, and he said he was okay with that. He said he would wait as long as necessary, and despite being together for over a year, he'd never pressured me. I was scared to find out now why it might have been the case.

Bile rose in my throat as I reached the front door, unsure I wanted to face what could be happening or, if nothing sordid was happening, face my own unwarranted mistrust. I thought I was past my trust issues. I thought I was ready for the next steps in this relationship, but if a simple coincidence could shake the whole foundation of our relationship, then maybe I was not quite there yet.

I raised my hand to knock but thought better of it, and looked around, trying to figure out where he hid the emergency key.

I looked under the potted plants on his patio and under the door mat without any luck before I remembered he bought this stupid fake stone during one of our Target trips.

I looked around and, despite the worry brewing inside me, I smiled when I noticed it at the foot of the bushes brushing the wooden stairs.

I grabbed it and let out a little huff of relief when I found the key nestled inside it.

If nothing seedy was happening, he'll probably question my uninvited pop-in, but I was too concerned to think more of it right now.

I opened the door slowly and didn't have to question my decision as I heard a guttural moan of pleasure.

I tightened my hold on the key, feeling its ridges on my palm as I took one slow step after the other, trying to make sure he would not hear my stupid square heels *thunk* against his wooden flooring.

The closer I got to his room, the louder he became. I could also hear Serena call his name, asking him to fuck her harder with his big, fat cock.

I stopped, resting my hand against the wall as my stomach heaved violently.

I almost wished I could vomit right now and have him clean it after he sealed my horrible day with the worst betrayal.

I shook my head. I had enough! I couldn't continue to torture myself, listening to the sound of their pleasure. They needed to know that I knew.

The door of the bedroom was ajar, and I shoved it open, making it slam against the wall—the lovely yellow wall I'd painted for him last month.

How fucking stupid had I been! I wanted to help him have a nice home—where I thought I would move into one day, but clearly, not in the optic to have him fuck another woman.

Despite knowing what I was going to find, it was almost too much to see.

Her, on all fours, on top of the sunflower bedspread I had picked to match the room, and him, fisting her long ponytail as he hammered into her from behind, his head thrown back in pure abandon.

She shrieked when she saw me and fell face-first onto the bed.

He looked back and his face shifted from unadulterated pleasure to shock in an instant, and despite the ripping pain, I felt a little better knowing I'd ruined his pleasure—just as he'd just ruined a year of my life.

I would not become my mother!

I turned around and started to run when he shouted my name. I ran out and down the street, my vision blurry with tears and my legs wobbling, both from the painful turmoil inside me and the heels I was not used to wearing.

I heard him call my name again and realized he was following me into the street!

Fuck! I ran faster, despite my burning eyes compromising my vision. I took random side streets just to ditch him.

I crossed a street without looking—a mistake, one of many, really—but the one I realized was going to cost me my life as I saw the shape of a black car come racing toward me.

My ankle twisted as my heel met an unevenness in the middle of the road, and I fell heavily.

I heard the horn, the squealing of the tires, and closed my eyes tightly, bracing for impact.

Yep, I was going to die today, in disgrace and in shame... It was ironic how things had come full circle.

I was going to die the same way I was born.

CHAPTER 2

VIOLET

I held my breath but felt nothing. Was I dead? No, the painful stings on my palms and knees told me I was still very much alive.

Was I supposed to feel relieved of the fact? For a second, just a fraction of a second, I thought that maybe it wouldn't have been a bad thing if I was finally gone, if I could just stop fighting. It was all getting so exhausting.

I opened one eye and saw a pair of shiny black derby shoes. I opened my other eye and moved my head up slowly, taking in the pair of black dress pants, expensive-looking leather belt, white shirt, black suit jacket, and striped tie until I reached his face, which I couldn't see as I was blinded by the sun. It looked like a dark shape surrounded by a halo, like if he was my guardian angel.

I let out a broken chuckle at the thought. I could really use one of those right now.

The man crouched in front of me, and I could see his face—well, partially since he was wearing some dark, club-master sunglasses.

But despite my shitty feelings, I could see he was gorgeous, with wide shoulders, a well-defined jaw, wide lips, and a long straight nose. He was a fine specimen like you saw in the magazines. Ah, he was probably one of those male models here for some photoshoot. That was not so exceptional around here, either. We were close enough to LA for that to be commonplace.

What took me aback was the strand of long black hair that had escaped his man-bun. Somehow, I wouldn't have expected someone dressed like him to wear his hair like that.

"Me?"

I blinked at him, clearly missing what he'd said.

"Can you hear me?"

I nodded as the smoothness of his deep voice settled right at the base of my spine. He might have been an angel after all—nobody sounded like that in real life.

He sighed with relief.

"What got in your mind to run in front of a car like that?! You could have—"

"Violet!"

I winced as Jake's nasal voice made me want to puke.

The man glanced toward the voice and tensed. "I think I got my answer," he muttered darkly.

"Go away, Jake. I've got nothing left to say to you." God, did I have to sound so broken and pathetic?

"No, we need to talk, Violet."

"I had no idea your work project entailed fucking my friend. I'm sorry for being upset, Jake. How unreasonable of me!" I spat.

The man's lips curled up on one side, and I didn't need to see his eyes to know he was somehow proud of me.

"Let me help you up," the man said gently as he extended his hand toward me.

He reached around, helping me up, and wrapped his arm around my waist, pushing my face closer to his chest. Closing my eyes, I took a deep whiff of his expensive-smelling, woodsy cologne.

His touch and movements were surprisingly gentle for someone his size, and I almost didn't feel any pain as he pulled me up.

He steadied me, resting his hands on my hips. I was not a tall woman, but that man was particularly tall. I would say at least six-two or six-three, as even with these heels, I barely reached his pecs.

"Are you okay?" he asked again.

"Keep your hands to yourself," Jake threatened.

I just caught him balls-deep in another woman, and he dared to be territorial. After everything he just did? I'd almost let this stranger defile me in the middle of the road for what Jake did.

The image flashed in my head, and I blushed deeply—hoping they would take that for a wave of rage instead of shameful lust for this complete stranger.

The man kept his hands on my hips, tightening slightly as he turned his head toward Jake.

I followed his eyes and looked at Jake for the first time since his arrival, and it was not too difficult to see what he'd been doing before coming out with his T-shirt inside out, his jeans buttoned wrong, and bare feet.

"I said your hands," Jake repeated, glaring at where the stranger was holding me.

I opened my mouth to answer, but the man beat me to it.

"And I'm pretty sure she told you to fuck off... yet you're still here. I guess we're both not very good at listening to what we've been told."

Jake took a step toward us, assessing the man with weariness.

"Violet, let me take you home and we can talk." He pointed at my legs. "You can't take the bus looking like that."

I looked down at my knees, finally aware of the pain I'd felt when I fell.

"Oh." It was all I could say, looking at the bloody scratches on both my knees.

"I'll drive her home," the smooth-voiced stranger said with certainty, letting go of my hips.

Alarm bells rang as my head shot up with surprise, glancing at the stranger. I've listened to enough podcast and watched enough murder documentaries to know that going with him was probably the best way to get murdered.

"No, you're not." Jake protested.

I winced. In the state things were right now, I'd much rather take my chances with my potential murderer than be in a car with Jake for the next twenty minutes.

I looked at the man and nodded. "That'd be really nice of you."

He bent down to recover the contents of my bag on the ground as Jake took a step toward me.

I took an instinctive step to the side and bumped into the man as he stood with my bag in his hand. He shoved the bag into my arms. "Get in the car; it's unlocked."

I was still too shaken to listen to the warning bells in my head. I walked to the passenger door of the luxurious SUV before turning and looking at the man's back as he slowly walked toward Jake, a tattoo peeking out of his collar on the back of his neck.

He bent his head and whispered something into Jake's ear that made Jake take a couple of steps back as all color drained from his face.

"Clear?" the man said, and Jake nodded sharply before throwing me a helpless look.

The man sighed and turned before opening the door for me and helping me in.

That was not something that Jake or anyone ever did for me. How sad was it that a perfect stranger showed me more consideration than my boyfriend ever did?

I look at the leather seats and the wooden and chrome dashboard. How much did this car cost?

I looked at him as he settled beside me, his scent and presence comforting me against all odds.

"Are you okay?"

I nodded.

"I'd like to hear words, if you don't mind."

I looked down. "I-I'm fine." Was I? Would I ever be?

He sighed and brought his hand toward me.

"Oh, you're bleeding!" I let out as I noticed the cut on his forefinger and the droplet of blood that dripped onto the black carpet on the floorboards.

He looked down at his finger and shrugged. "It's nothing."

It was weird not to see his eyes; it really felt like he was hiding behind a wall, and I was only getting half the information.

"No, no. We don't want to stain your car." I rummaged through my bag for something to help with the bleeding when I noticed the broken coffee cup in it. It had been a present from Jake—all in all, it was a good thing that it was as destroyed as our relationship.

"It doesn't matter. This car has seen worse than a few droplets of blood."

"Seen worse?" I asked as I threw him a side look. He might have been a serial killer after all.

He let out a throaty laugh. "I meant messy passengers, no pools of blood."

I finally found what I was looking for in the side pocket of my bag and blushed at the pattern on the band-aid. I hadn't realized it was the one I had kept in there for emergencies.

"I'm sorry. This is all I have." I winced as I put the Hello Kitty band-aid on his finger.

"Ah." He looked at it for a second before letting out a low chuckle. "It gives me an edge, I think."

He turned the car on and started to drive down the street.

"I'm Violet," I offered after he made a U-turn down the street, and we passed a glowering Jake—not that he could have seen me through the dark window.

The man turned his head to throw me a quick look before concentrating on the road again.

"I'm sorry. I should have introduced myself before. I'm not used to people not—" He shook his head. "I'm Hoka."

"Hoka?" I tried, unsure I understood correctly. It was a name I'd never heard before.

He gave me a sharp nod.

"Hoka," I repeated once more with a smile. "I like it."

"I'm glad you approve."

I winced at how stupid it must have sounded, as if he cared whether I liked his name or not.

I was about to apologize when he turned left at the end of Jake's street to go downtown instead of the freeway, and I realized I had not given my address.

He didn't ask either, though, did he? I threw him a suspicious side look. This was really starting to turn out like an episode of *Dateline*.

"You're taking the wrong way. I live in Eastend."

Hoka looked toward me again, his eyebrows popping up out of his sunglasses—the only sign of his surprise at where I lived.

"I'm taking you to St. Mary's hospital. You're hurt."

I looked down at my legs and my scraped knees coated with drying blood and small black pebbles. It had not really hurt until now, probably due to the adrenaline rush caused by the whole situation but now that I looked at it, it started to sting.

"No."

He decelerated and turned his head toward me slowly. Um, that was quite a reaction for just a hospital trip. Maybe he thought I was crazy and regretted offering me a ride.

"I just... it's nothing I haven't dealt with before." I pointed at my knees and let out what I hoped was a derisive laugh, though it sounded broken and pathetic to my ears. *I have no insurance. I'm dirt poor and will not consider going to the hospital unless death is on my doorstep.* "Just drop me off at Fremont Clinic on Bellsway Street, it's fine."

"Fremont Clinic..." The way he let out the words, there was no need to explain that he knew exactly what it was and didn't approve.

He stopped at a crossroad, despite the road being empty, and stayed there for a few seconds as if he was thinking.

Maybe he didn't know where it was.

"If you—" I started as he put his blinker on and turned left. "Bellway Street is the other way."

"I know, but this clinic..." He shook his head. "I suppose you don't have insurance, but at least let me take you to my personal doctor. He's on retainer, so it won't cost me anything more."

I twisted my mouth to the side with incredulity. I hardly believe someone actually had a doctor on retainer, but at the same time, I didn't feel like waiting four hours just to see a doctor who would rather be anywhere than there.

"They're only scrapes; nothing to worry about."

"Maybe so, but I'd rather make sure it's nothing more. The road is a petri dish for bugs and bacteria. Who knows what might happen if it's not dealt with properly?" He gestured toward my feet, keeping his eyes on the road. "Your ankle is also getting a little darker. I just want to make sure nothing is broken."

I glanced down and sure enough, my left ankle was a little swollen and light blue. I threw him another side look as my questions about this man increased to another level. How did he notice that? He hadn't taken his eyes off the road.

I couldn't say I was scared of him, even if I should be, but I was wary and despite him showing me what seemed to be genuine kindness, I couldn't help that my level of wariness went up a few notches.

Maybe it was just who he was, but he was so commanding, so overwhelming with just a few words.

"Ah, I see. You wouldn't want me to die of sepsis on your watch." My voice shook despite my attempt at lightness.

He turned toward me, probably noting the stress in my voice. Was there anything this man missed?

He smiled brighter than before, revealing a small dimple on his left cheek. "I'm scaring you, I'm sorry."

"No, I—" I looked at my hands in my lap, feeling the apple of my cheek redden.

He sighed. "I didn't mean to. I'm used to taking charge; it's my job, and I sometimes forget that not everyone knows this." He let out a derisive chuckle. "I don't meet new people that often."

The admission somehow eased my apprehension. He had just shared something that was probably a little hard to admit.

"I'm just not comfortable being a charge for anyone," I admitted. "You clearly had somewhere to go, and you feel obliged to help when you're not to blame." It was only a partial truth, but I couldn't really say that his presence was overwhelming. He clearly had no control over that.

"I was going much too fast."

"Maybe," I conceded with a nod. "But I'm the one who crossed the road without looking, wearing deathtrap shoes."

"Okay, so we both did stupid things. What about we blame the cheating boyfriend instead?" he offered with a smirk. "He deserves nothing less."

"How do you know he's cheating?"

"It's textbook, really. How upset you were, his state of undress. The *audacity* of the man daring to stake his claim on you."

"He's a prick."

He laughed before turning serious again. "Something that needs to be said, though. I don't know the situation between you two, and I don't need to know, but you need to understand that no man, and I mean *no man* in the entire world, deserves you risking your life for him."

I nodded mutedly. There wasn't much I could have said because I knew that—it was something my mother had repeated to me since I was a little girl.

I looked out of the window as the houses morphed into mid-rise and then high-rise buildings as we got closer to downtown.

Hoka stopped his car in front of a white and silver, modern-looking building and the doorman rushed down the steps to open my door and let me out.

I stepped out and winced as my foot touched the pavement. Now that the adrenaline and anger had faded, I could definitely feel pain in my ankle.

Damn it, please don't let it be serious... I needed my feet if I wanted my job back.

I took a couple of steps on the sidewalk and winced, looking down at my open-toed shoes and pink-painted toenails.

What did trying to look pretty and girly do for me? Nothing. If I would have kept on wearing my combat boots, then I would have been just fine.

"You're in pain." Hoka pointed, coming to stand beside me.

His tone didn't carry any doubt, and I was sure my face said everything he needed to know. There was no point denying. "Yeah, but it's—"

I didn't get a chance to finish as he removed his sunglasses and reached down to carry me.

I let out a squeal when he lifted me bridal style, as if I weighed nothing at all, and walked up the stairs.

"What are you doing?! Put me down!" I shrieked as we entered the building and all the people in the lobby turned toward us.

"Everyone is watching," I hissed as he kept on walking with his head held high toward the row of elevators.

"They probably wouldn't have noticed if it wasn't for the shrieking and wiggling," he replied as the doors opened on a woman, who exited looking at him with so much hunger I couldn't help but blush at the intensity.

"It's ridiculous. I can stand now. Plus, I— Your *eyes*..." I whispered the last word, as I was hypnotized when he looked down and his eyes locked with mine.

I cocked my head to the side, forgetting that I was being carried in an elevator.

I was glad he'd kept his glasses on before, or I wouldn't have been able to stop staring.

His eyes were amber—not the light brown we sometimes called amber; no, his were eerie, like if gold had been melted just to be put in his eyes.

"Yes?" His eyes were searching my face, as if trying to find something. I wasn't sure what he was looking for, but they stopped on my lips only for a mere second. It was enough to make my heart jump.

The elevator pinged and the door opened, barely easing my racing heart.

The embarrassment and surprise I'd felt being picked up like that started to settle. I was suddenly very aware of his body against mine, the gentle scent of his fresh cologne, the hard, flat plane of his stomach against my hip.

I looked up as he walked to the reception desk, not even caring who was sitting there and how it may look. I detailed his chiseled jawline, down the column of his neck, to the edge of his shirt where another tattoo was barely peeking through.

"Ni-Nishimura-Sama." The urgency of her tone made me turn to look at her as the young woman stood briskly and bowed to him.

"My friend fell and hurt herself. I'd like her to see Dr. Mori, right now." He looked down at me with a small smile, and I couldn't help but wonder who he could be to justify such a greeting.

Like that would ever happen. A doctor dropping everything for—

"Yes, of course. Please follow me to room three, and I will send him in immediately."

Seriously, who is this guy? A prince or something? My eyes narrowed as his smile spread into a cocky grin.

I threw a look at the people sitting in the waiting room, who all shared various looks of annoyance, as we turned to follow the woman down a corridor.

"Dr. Mori will be right in," she said quickly, closing the door behind her as he set me down on the paper-covered black examination table.

"It was unnecessary, I'm fine."

He leaned against the wall, crossing his arms on his chest. "So humor me."

I was about to tell him that we might have to wait a while when the door opened, revealing a short Asian man with graying hair.

"Nishimura-San." He bowed to Hoka, who was still leaning against the wall.

Hoka gave him a little bow of his head and stood straighter. "My friend is hurt. I'd appreciate it if you could check her over and give her the total premium."

I cocked my head to the side about to ask what the total premium was, but Hoka waved and exited the room before I had the chance.

I let out a little sigh of relief; his presence was so overwhelming that it felt like I could finally breathe again once he left.

The doctor came closer, scrutinizing my face with detailed interest, as if I were a rare specimen.

"I'm Dr. Mori, miss...?" he asked, grabbing a chart on his desk.

"I'm Violet Murphy."

"What happened to you?"

"I... um, I fell," I offered, pointing at my knees, then showed him my right palm. I was just lucky my wrist seemed okay because I could kiss my job goodbye if it had been broken.

Wait a minute, I have no job right now, and nothing guarantees that Liam would give it back to me.

He nodded and brought a rolling stool in front of me. He sat and pulled down a round lamp that shone brighter than the sun, setting it right above my knees.

"Where did you fall?"

"On the road. Asphalt, I think?"

"I see, yes..." he whispered, pushing his glasses up his nose and reaching for a tweezer on a metal tray. "You did well to come. You have some residue in the wound."

We remained silent as he cleaned and bandaged the wounds, and I looked around the room. Once he finished cleaning my knees, he moved my ankle and I hissed in pain.

"Sorry." He glanced at me as he removed my shoe. "I have no X-ray machine here. I just want to make sure it is not broken." He moved my foot from right to left, causing a sharp pain, but I pursed my lips, trying to swallow any other hiss that would tell him of my discomfort.

"No, no it's fine. I'm sorry for taking your time... I'm sure you have a busy schedule."

He sighed and pulled back, his face softening. *So, he had been annoyed by the interruption.* "It's fine, Ms. Murphy. Helping Mister Nishimura's friend is an honor."

Hoka Nishimura. I loved the ring of his name.

He stood and grabbed a cream-colored roll from the small metal storage cabinet against the wall. "Your foot is not broken, just sprained." He sat back down. "I will tape it. Just try to keep to low activity for a few days."

I nodded. There was no point in telling him I couldn't afford a few days off. It would be a day, two at best.

"Can you remove your cardigan for the blood test?"

I frowned, tightening the cardigan around me.

"No need to be worried. Mr. Nishimura ask to give you premium care, which means a full checkup... including blood work. When was your last routine blood test?"

I looked down at my hands in my lap. I didn't think I'd ever had any. To be honest, I couldn't remember even getting a blood test before.

"I see." I guess my silence was answer enough for the doctor. "How old are you?"

I looked up. "Twenty-one."

He nodded and wrote something on his chart. "I won't force you to do something you don't want to do, but you really should consider it. It won't cost you or *him* anything more."

"Okay..." I trailed off, still unsure as I removed my cardigan.

It was all so strange. I was careful enough, but everything I'd just done was so unlike me. At the same time, I never had so much shit hit the fan at the same time before, either. I felt like my brain was shutting down, like it was going in overdrive due to all the shitty information that hit it at the same time. It had to be a lot for anyone really—being fired, finding out you were cheated on, and having a near-death experience, all in about an hour, was bound to do that to you.

I wasn't even sure why I was going through the motions, following every request from Hoka and the doctor. It was easier than thinking I suppose, easier than opening the door to the part of my brain that was trying to process everything, screaming for reprieve.

The doctor took the blood, tagged it, and I removed my other shoe as I gave him my contact details for the results.

He helped me down and I tried to press on my foot, gasping as a painful jolt went up my leg.

The doctor sent me a look that seemed to say, *'Seriously, what did I just say?'*

"I need to walk," I said defensively.

He sighed with resignation. "At least keep it to a minimum and avoid putting too much weight on it, and also," he pointed at my heels, "these won't do for a couple of weeks, minimum."

I frowned at the shoes on the examination table, as if they had been the one to blame for this whole ordeal and not my own impulsivity. I'd never wear stupid heels again.

I looked down at my bare feet on the cold floor. I would have to indulge in an Uber home, despite the state of my finances. I could not take public transportation barefoot.

Maybe it was instant karma. I decided to get an Uber to Jake's house—just to stick it up at *Sunny Valley Real Estate*—and here I was, paying for my own trip home.

"That won't be a problem."

"Very well, I will let you join your—" He stopped, detailing my face once again as if he couldn't compute Hoka and I being in some sort of contact.

"Friend," I offered, because somehow it sounded better than *'stranger who almost ran me over.'*

"Right." He looked at me for a beat longer before he tapped his finger on the chart. "I should have your results in a couple of days. We will call you then."

"Thank you again for everything."

I limped back to the reception and saw Hoka through a glass door. He was in a room talking on the phone.

When his eyes connected with mine, my stomach dropped at the intensity. Did anyone ever get used to his eyes? And I was not only referring to the color, but also the fierceness behind them.

He hung up and walked back, keeping his eyes on me and I was mesmerized, forgetting about the pain and everything that happened today for a few seconds.

"You're okay?"

When I nodded, he looked behind me.

"There's nothing too serious, just a few deep scratches and a sprained ankle." The doctor replied and I turned my head to find him standing right behind me,

What an ass! He needed to make sure I was not lying.

I turned back and glared at Hoka, making him chuckle.

"I've got the feeling you would rather set yourself on fire than admit you need help."

I opened my mouth, but closed it again. How could he know that? Was I really that transparent?

He looked back at the doctor and bowed his head slightly. "Arigato gozaimasu," he murmured before concentrating on me again, or rather, my bare feet.

The doctor said something I didn't understand before he called the next patient from the waiting room.

Hoka extended his hand toward the receptionist, and she gave him a small bag. "They just dropped it off," she clarified.

I looked at her curiously before turning toward Hoka.

"I suspected you wouldn't be able to walk on those today. Here." He extended the bag.

I hesitated before taking it. Who was this good Samaritan? My mother always said to never trust a man, especially one who seemed too perfect—and this one had been more than perfect from the moment we met.

I took the bag and pulled the small white box out. Carefully, I opened it and found a pair of tan leather-like ballet shoes.

"They adapt to the size of your feet,"" the receptionist explained. "I'm sorry, it's all I could find in a moment's notice."

"Oh, no, no. It's perfect." I made the mistake of standing on my injured foot and winced. I often fidgeted when I was embarrassed and here, I was getting an apology from a woman who went above and beyond for me. That was so unwarranted. "I really appreciate it, and I'm sorry for the trouble, really."

Truthfully, I was too desperate not to accept this charity. These shoes meant I could take the bus home and save at least twenty dollars—not a small sum for an unemployed idiot.

Hoka reached for the box, and I tightened my hold on it, not ready to let them go.

"No carrying," I warned him. Now that he knew it was not a serious injury, he could not put me through that embarrassment again.

"No carrying," he agreed with a low chuckle that caused an unfamiliar sensation to burst in my stomach.

He grabbed the soft shoes in the box, and I gasped in surprise as he kneeled in front of me and took my foot in his hand to slip on the shoe.

As his warm fingers traced the arch of my foot, I felt like my foot was on fire as a zing of another set of unfamiliar sensations caused a shiver of pleasure to zip all the way up my leg to the base of my spine.

He stopped, hesitating just for a fraction of a second, but it was enough to assume that he didn't miss how he affected me.

How much more embarrassment could I take in one day? How sad was it that the simple brush of his fingers on my foot made me react so viscerally? I hoped he would take this as a pained reaction from the injury and not what it shamefully was... pure attraction.

Be realistic, Violet, you're a charity case; nothing more than his good deed for the day. He's hot, much older, and obviously super rich. Get a grip... this can only mean emotional trauma, the little voice of reason, which sounded just like my mother, reminded me.

I looked at the receptionist, who was leaning over the counter, looking at him with wide eyes, her mouth slightly open as if she was witnessing the impossible.

He took a step closer as he stood, and he was standing so close that I could feel the point of his shiny shoes touching mine through the thin leather.

He towered over me, and when he looked down with a small smile on his face, I forgot how to breathe.

"You're extremely short," he murmured, still staying much closer than society dictated strangers should be.

I kept on looking up, so mesmerized by his amber eyes and the little specks of green in them that I'd momentarily forgot how to speak.

He raised an eyebrow, his smile morphing into a smirk, and I finally found my voice.

"I... um... I'm not that short. Not everyone is freakishly tall, you know."

"I'm six-four, it's not that uncommon."

"Sure... But it's obvious everyone will be short for you. I'm average size for a woman." I would not satisfy him by letting him know that I was, in fact, only five-foot-two—just below average.

"If you say so." He replied playfully as he extended his arm to me. "Will you at least agree for me to help you down?"

I nodded, resting my hand on his arm before glancing at the receptionist, who was still staring with such intensity, she completely ignored the woman in front of the counter.

"Thanks again," I told her before following Hoka's lead to the elevator.

As the elevator started its way down, I turned to him. "Thank you again, for everything. You went above and beyond for me."

"It was the least I could do."

It wasn't, we both knew that. The least he could have done was check I was still alive and be on his merry way.

"Are you going to be okay?" he asked as we exited the elevator and walked out of the huge hall, thankfully attracting much less attention on our way out than we did on our way in.

"Yes, I'm all better now. I feel like a new woman!"

He threw me a side look that was clearly skeptical. *Yeah, maybe I did oversell that one.*

My traitorous stomach chose that exact moment to growl embarrassingly loudly—loud enough for Hoka to look down at my stomach with an eyebrow raised.

"I'm hungry too actually," he commented, patting his flat stomach.

I highly doubted it was true, but I was way too embarrassed to say anything.

"I know a lovely little dim sum place right at the corner. It should be empty right now since the lunch rush has long passed."

"I've already taken too much of your time. I'm sure you have some places to be."

"Not anymore. Come on, let's go eat." He took a step down the stairs and extended his arm toward me again.

I took his arm with a defeated sigh.

Seriously, what did this man think of me? That I was a complete and utter disaster. It was such bad luck that I met him in these circumstances. Well, I was usually a mess, and I was a little lost, but nothing like the woman he saw today.

I opened my mouth to tell him that much, but closed it again, because what was the point? It was not like I was going to see him again after today.

But you'd like to, don't you? Obviously, I did. Any straight woman with eyes would.

"So, you're an expert in dim sum?" I asked, trying to make conversation.

"Are you asking because I'm Asian? I'm Japanese, not Chinese."

I stopped walking, completely mortified. God, could things get any worse?

"N-no. I asked because you knew exactly that there was a restaurant and—" I shook my head. "I," I looked up and saw his lips quiver. "Wait," I narrowed my eyes. "You're teasing me!"

He chuckled. "I am. Come on, let's go."

We walked in the mostly empty restaurant just as my stomach grumbled again.

"When was the last time you ate?" he asked as we took a table in the corner.

I shrugged. "Yesterday. I was planning on having breakfast, but today really was the worst day." For some reason, I hated the idea of him thinking that on top of being a mess, I was also reckless with my wellbeing.

I let him order the food, trying to think of what to tell him to correct his opinion of me and maybe get a step up from the charity case he probably thought I was.

I opened my mouth to simply tell him there was another version of Violet he had not met yet. A damaged version, yes, but not to the level of what he witnessed today.

But instead, the floodgates opened, and everything came out, starting from the godsend apprenticeship to the unfair dismissal this morning, to the lying, cheating scum of a boyfriend, to end up being almost crushed by his car.

I finally stopped as my throat was dry, and I looked down at the table and found that the steaming food was already there.

I looked around the restaurant and the waiter was not near the table. How long did I speak for?

I looked at Hoka, expecting him to look at me as if I'd completely lost it, but he was simply studying me, chopsticks in hand. "Let's eat," he said simply, reaching for a few different plates.

I nodded and silently copied him.

Way to explain that you're not crazy! I chastised myself, biting into a delicious shrimp siu mai.

By unleashing it all on him, I probably just sealed the deal... I could already imagine the conversation he would have with his girlfriend or wife about the crazy girl he'd met today. My eyes trailed to his left hand, and I felt somewhat relieved to find his ring finger free from any obvious commitment.

I let out a small grown at the absurdity of my thought.

He looked up, arching an eyebrow questioningly.

I waved my hand dismissively. "I just wanted to explain to you that I was not crazy." I sighed, reaching for another dim sum and dipped it in the sauce. "I realize I probably just made it worse."

He shook his head. "I don't think you're crazy. Reckless? Sure. But not crazy."

I looked up, mouth slightly agape with shock.

He chuckled. "You look more offended by being called reckless than crazy."

"I am! I did act a little insane, so the assumption was justified, but reckless?"

"You got into a car with a man you don't know."

I opened my mouth to reply but closed it again because it was true.

"I'm not usually like that, either." I shook my head. "Life taught me better than that," I added evasively.

He looked at me with that inquisitive look again. The one that seemed to see right through the darkest, most hidden part of me, and it made my heart skip a beat.

He reached into his suit jacket and retrieved a thin silver pen and a white business card. He turned it over and wrote something before sliding it toward me on the table. "This is my private cell number. Call me if you need anything."

I looked at the card and turned it over, but there were only two lines on it. One I assumed was his name as it was written in Japanese, and the second was a phone number.

I knew he didn't intend to, but this offended me somehow. "I don't need charity." I pushed the card back toward him.

He placed his hand over mine, stopping my movement. "I didn't think you did." He frowned, looking down at his hand on top of mine, though he kept it in place. "I'm not a very charitable man."

Right... I kept my eyes on his hand over mine. His hand was so big, it completely hid mine, and his skin was so warm and dry—it felt nice, even with the little calluses I could feel. I refused to move even a finger, fearing that it would make him break the contact. "What you did today proves otherwise."

He laughed, removing his hand and waving it dismissively.

I sighed, missing the warmth of his fingers and left the card on the table to eat some more.

"That's not in my habits, either."

"Then why did you?"

He cocked his eyes to the side, looking over my shoulders to the wall, as if he was seeing something that wasn't there. "I don't know."

The honesty of his reply somehow killed any subsequent question I might have had.

We finished the meal in silence, and Hoka spoke again just as the waiter left with a tip that was probably more than the meal itself.

"Take the card, please." He jerked his head toward it. "If not for you, then do it for me. I'll feel better knowing you have it."

I couldn't help but smile. "So basically, I'll do you a favor?"

A bright, wide smile filled his face, revealing a dimple on his right cheek. "Exactly."

Lord have mercy, why did he have to become more and more attractive?

We walked outside, and I blinked a few times, adapting to the bright sun after lunch in the dim restaurant. He gestured toward his car. "Let me drive you home."

I nodded, knowing it would be pointless to argue and also, I was so full from lunch that I would rather be home in a ten minutes' drive rather than a twenty-two minute bus ride.

"Thank you for the meal, it was delicious," I said as he opened the passenger door for me.

"Best you ever had, isn't it?" he asked, before closing my door and rounding the car to settle behind the steering wheel. "Where to?"

I gave him my address and didn't miss the tick of his lips when I told him, but there was no point defending where I lived. It was a dumpster fire, and everybody knew it. I would move in a heartbeat if I had any other choice.

"It was delicious," I replied quickly, fearing he would comment on the area I lived in. "But not *Loon Fung* delicious."

He threw me such a startled look, the car swerving a little.

"You know Loon Fung? It closed like, years ago."

I laughed but nodded. "Yes, my mother and I used to live in the small apartment on top of it when I was a little girl." I smiled despite the bittersweet memory. "It was a good time…"

"Things are often simpler when we are young," he replied, and we finished the trip in silence, both lost in our childhood memories.

I exited the car as soon as he stopped in front of my three-story building, fearing that he might offer to help me up to my apartment. I would have rather died than let him see the inside of the rabbit hutch I called home.

"It was nice to meet you, Hoka Nishimura. Thank you for making a particularly bad day a lot more bearable," I said just before closing the door, interrupting any reply he could have given me.

It took all my willpower to go up and into my place without looking back and seeing if he was still here or if he was already gone.

CHAPTER 3

Hoka

I watched as she walked up the stairs, wishing she would turn around but somehow knowing she wouldn't.

I didn't really understand why, but knowing she was here, in this neighborhood, didn't settle well with me. I had to use all my willpower to stop myself from telling her to come home with me.

It didn't make any sense. I didn't know her. She was nothing—nothing *important*, at least not in my life.

I had done so many unusual things from the moment I exited my car to see if the woman in the fetal position in the middle of the road was alright.

I shouldn't have given her my number. It was *not* something we shared widely, especially not with common people, yet she now had my card with my private cell number scribbled on it.

I'd also taken a risk—albeit a calculated one—when I decided to spend the day with her instead of doing what I was supposed to do. I had decided to leave behind my responsibilities, my obligation, just for a few hours.

I assumed it was because she didn't know who I was. She didn't know Hoka, the *mafia boss*, the man people pretended to like because they feared him. No, this woman liked *me*, at least, the part I showed her. She met Hoka, the *ordinary* man. It had been nice to banter and joke with someone who didn't know who I was, who didn't feel the obligation to agree and indulge me.

Just for a day, just for a minute, it felt good to be that man, but now was the time to go back to my life, back to the man I really was. Now it was time to be the mafia boss again.

I drove to the club, not really knowing what I would say to Jiro. I'd never had to explain not showing up, not owning up to my responsibilities. I was not used to being careless; I was not used to putting myself first. I should tell him about Violet... *Violet*. The girl with skin akin to porcelain, hair as black as a raven, and eyes such a unique turquoise, it felt like I was standing on the shore of Lake Bishamon.

Everything about her was a contradiction, both in her appearance and her attitude. She was broken, brought down, yet despite her obvious softness, there was a strength, a combativity that could rival some of my best men.

She was my secret, at least for now, an ephemeral dream. I felt good to have something just for me—something untainted by my way of life.

As expected, I found Jiro standing in front of my office door, arms crossed on his chest, his signature scowl firmly anchored on his face.

"What's the matter? It feels like I'm facing my mother after skipping school."

His scowl deepened. "Maybe I should scold you. You missed the meeting with the Triad. You know how important it was?"

I rolled my eyes. "It's always important with the Triad. What was it this time? Somebody peed in their cereal?" I opened my office door and sat in my overpriced leather chair. I felt safe in my space, in my universe. I could control everything in here, not like the insidious feelings that little woman caused in me.

"You're the one who said you wanted more responsibilities. You dealt with them, didn't you?"

Jiro stood in front of my desk, leg slightly apart, as if he was getting ready to go to war. Did he really feel like fighting me today?

"Of course I did," he snorted. "There was nothing special, but missing something like that is unlike you." Jiro arched an eyebrow. "Does it have anything to do with that silly band-aid on your finger? Is it a new mark of style?"

I looked down to my hand on the desk, realizing too late that I didn't remove the Hello Kitty band-aid Violet put on my finger. "What do you want me to say? I've got a soft spot for little kitties."

Jiro laughed. "Don't we all? Little kitties are the best!" He stated with a wink, as if I could have missed the innuendo.

I leaned back on my chair with a weary sigh. "What did they want?"

Jiro waved his hand dismissively. "They have a little territorial issue. Apparently, some Hispanics crossed the border into their territories to sell their drugs. They wanted to know if you would help them regain it in case of war."

I shook my head. "We don't meddle in other people's business." I tapped my forefinger on the desk. "We've got nothing to gain in this. Why did they think we would get involved? Because we are Asian?" I snorted. "Did they expect us to just have some kind of loyalty to the race?"

"Desperation can make you do stupid things." He shrugged, and I knew how right it could be. We had been on the verge of desperation once.

"What did you tell them?"

"I told them we couldn't do anything for them. I reminded them that we don't meddle in other people's affairs." Jiro sat in front of me with a sigh. "They were livid, at least until I reminded them of a time when we needed them and they decided not to help. I also reminded them that we didn't retaliate then, and it was in their best interest to do the same."

I nodded my approval of Jiro's decision. I would have done the same. We were very similar, him and I, which was the main reason I had picked him to be my right-hand man. He thought like me, which I wasn't sure was necessarily a compliment.

"See? You didn't even need me there. I wouldn't have done anything different."

He rolled his eyes. "I never doubted my decision. But your presence would have been crucial in case they refused to back down. Their boss could have been offended by your absence. It could have meant that you thought their meeting was beneath you."

I unlocked my drawer and retrieved my laptop. "Which I do," I confirmed, turning on my laptop. "It is not my problem if the Chinese can't control their business or territory. I am not a babysitter; I am the head of the *yakuza*."

I started to go through my emails, wondering why Jiro was still sitting here, staring at me.

"Who is the girl?" he finally asked, leaning forward and resting his elbows on his knees.

Ah, here it is. Somebody talked.

I smirked at him. "Who talked?"

He shrugged. "It shouldn't matter. You should have told me."

Since when did I owe you shit? I frowned, getting annoyed by the second. He seemed to have forgotten his place.

"And please, do tell me, since when do I owe you *any* kind of explanation?" I pointed at my chest. "I am the boss," I pointed at his chest, "and *you* work for *me*. Not the other way around. You better never forget that. Loyalty only gets you so far."

Jiro raised his hands in surrender. "I'm not questioning you. Well, maybe a little, but I mean no disrespect. Your safety is paramount to me. You entrusted your life and your business to me. We've been friends since before we could talk. You've never hidden anything from me. I just wonder why you would start now?"

I remained silent for a few moments, rubbing the band-aid Violet gave me with my thumb.

"I didn't tell you because there's nothing to say." I sighed. "I was driving too fast, not looking at the road, and I almost killed her." I flicked a dismissive hand toward the door. "She is just a girl in distress." I shrugged. "And it just felt nice to be the knight in shining armor instead of the bogeyman lurking in the darkness for once."

Jiro looked at me for a few seconds, scrutinizing my face, clearly trying to find any sign of deception. He wouldn't find any because it was the truth, even if partially.

"You're not the charitable kind," he insisted, and I almost laughed. That was exactly what I'd told Violet.

"I know, but I also have a certain code I like to uphold, and this woman was both literally and metaphorically on the ground. She was being chased by a psychotic ex-boyfriend." *A little bit of a stretch but...* "She honestly needed to escape, and you know what our rules are about women and children."

"Benevolence and mercy," he reluctantly said.

"Don't go searching for something that's not there, Jiro." I kept my eyes on the computer screen, not wanting to look at him full on in case he could see something I didn't really want him to see. "I have some work to do," I continued as I started to type—my not so polite way to dismiss him. I had other things to do, and I didn't feel like being studied like a bug under the microscope.

He stood with a nod and walked to the door. "Do you need anything else?"

I looked down at the band-aid and somehow felt like if I avenged the girl, maybe I could forget her.

"Do we have any dealings with *Sun Valley Real Estate*?"

"What do you mean by dealings? As in if we bought something from them?"

"Did we?"

He shrugged. "I guess so. It is the biggest company around here. We must have, but I can ask the accountant to look into it."

I nodded. "You do that, but what I want to know is if we own part of it. Do we own someone there?"

"Ah." He nodded. "That's a little trickier, but I'll have the answer by tonight. May I ask why?"

"I've got a petty little revenge to instigate." I replied evasively.

Jiro gave me a mischievous grin. "That's the best kind of revenge."

"You know it." I chuckled.

"Oh, I almost forgot, Aiya called when she couldn't reach you on your cell. She loved the flowers, and she accepted your dinner invitation for tonight."

My fingers froze on the keyboard, and I focused on him again, my eyebrows raised. "Funny, I don't remember sending her flowers or inviting her to dinner."

He winked. "You did. Tonight, at eight p.m. at *Le Trésor*."

My lips tipped down, unimpressed. Fuck, it had to be the overpriced, stuffy French restaurant, didn't it?

"It's her favorite. I told you a thousand times, you catch more flies with honey than with vinegar."

I shrugged. "And you'd catch even more with shit. I don't see your point."

He rolled his eyes. "You're welcome. She rejected you once, but she won't do it again. She'd learned from her mistakes. I'll get your answers about *Sun Valley* in a bit. Ring if you need me."

I sent a quick email to my private investigator—the one I used when I wanted things to be kept under the radar, even from Jiro. I asked him to do some basic research on Violet, something I would have rather asked him in person, especially since I was not a fan of paper trails, but I had no time today, not after Jiro committed me to a dinner with Aiya.

Le Trésor. I let out a groan and stood, walking to the tinted window, and looked down at the clandestine casino games happening down below.

Of course, it was her favorite. There was no one more elitist than Ayia Sato.

Yet I picked her as my wanted wife despite that.

Jiro's announcement would have satisfied me yesterday. I needed to settle down and conceive an heir, which would secure our line, but that was yesterday.

Today, today everything was different.

Today I met *her*.

I untied my hair, letting it fall down my back, and massaged my scalp, trying to get rid of the throbbing headache that had started as soon as I stepped into my office.

Violet Murphy.

I'd never really believed any of the bedtime stories my mother told me when I was a boy. They were always more incredible than the last. Full of *Orochis* and brave Samurai warriors who I descended from.

It was all stories and folktales; at least, that's what I thought until today.

I had been particularly annoyed this morning when that hysterical woman fell in front of my car, nearly causing an incident. I intended to tell her off and send her on her merry way, but then she opened her eyes and when they locked in mine... *Koi No Yokan.* This presentiment that is not quite about love at first sight, but more a trust in the *inevitability* of love when you first meet someone, and it happened right there, in the middle of a suburban street.

I rubbed at my chest, still feeling the echo of it.

I should not look back, I should not try to see her again.

That girl had enough problems as it was. Bringing her into my world would be both dangerous and pointless. It was not like we could ever have a future. She was a gaijin, someone who would normally be frowned upon just for stepping into our world. But a gaijin as the partner of the *oyabun*? No chance I could pull that one off, even with the potential of my feelings for her.

I sighed, burying my hands in my pockets, and I walked to the other side of the office, looking down through the other tinted window at the payday loan side of the business.

It was strange how her quiet desperation spoke to my soul. I had wanted to wrap her in my arms and soothe her when I usually fed from desperate people daily, without feeling a pinch of guilt.

I looked at the terribly thin man who extended his check under the parting glass with a shaky hand. He was clearly desperate to come here where the loans have over a fifty percent interest rate, yet I kept on making money off of them. Some were in the other room right now, playing in a casino they'd never beat.

What would she think of me if she knew what I was ruling upon? Would she still look at me like her hero?

No, of course, she wouldn't. She would probably look at me with the same fear I saw in most people's eyes, the fake reverence that made me sick.

I wanted to keep the image I had of her—the way she'd looked at me with both attraction and disbelief.

I could not see her again though, she had to remain my ephemeral memory. It was better for both of us if I stayed away and if she never called me.

But that didn't mean I couldn't avenge her from the shadows... Embrace my boogeyman nature and make them pay for the hurt I saw in her eyes, the scars, the cracks I could feel inside her.

I was going to rain hellfire on them, and then I would forget all about her.

Be ready because Hoka Nishimura, head of the yakuza is coming for you all. And I will enjoy the sweet taste of your fall.

CHAPTER 4

VIOLET

It took me two days to decide I was ready to face the world. I still felt some tenderness in my ankle, and I winced a little as I tied my trainers.

Okay, I was not completely ready to face the world but my bank account, with only two dollars and seventy-six cents, and the growing need to pay bills and buy food, told me that I was. The pity check had to be deposited today if I wanted to eat tonight and keep enjoying the luxury of electricity.

I sighed, reluctant to turn on my phone and face the music. I'd come home from my day with Hoka with no less than twenty miss calls from Jake and an insane number of texts.

I'd wanted to google Hoka Nishimura when I got home, but Mr. Scott, my pervy neighbor from 3C, had picked that day to change his Wi-Fi password, and I had no data left.

I had not been in the mood to deal with any of his messed-up requests to gain access to his Wi-Fi. Any research would have to wait. Not that it truly mattered; it wasn't like I was going to see that man again.

It was maybe for the best that I had no internet. I could just turn off the phone and forget everything during my two days of forced isolation.

When I turned my phone back on, my voicemail was full, and the numbers of texts were in the triple digits. I was surprised he hadn't shown up in front of my door. No, actually, I wasn't. Jake was much too proud to come here with the risk of being rejected in front of witnesses.

He was a catch, after all. I snorted. A chance to *'catch Chlamydia'* was more like it.

I shook my head with a sigh, slipping the phone into the back pocket of my black jeans. Jake would have to wait. I had my life to sort out, and he was now in my past.

I would not become my mother, I thought again and would keep repeating it if I ever thought about giving him a second chance.

I slid the key into the lock just as the pervert from 3C exited his apartment. Seriously, today of all days?

"Violet," he said with a frown, pushing his glasses up his nose. He was clearly not pleased that I hadn't begged for his new password over the weekend.

I forced a smile as I turned toward him. "Mr. Scott, how are you doing?"

He looked down at my feet, and I felt my stomach churn like it did every time he looked at them, even if I was wearing my trainers.

His Wi-Fi used to be free access, and one day he just put a password. I'd been stupid enough to be upfront and ask him for the password. I didn't have much money, but I'd offered him a couple dollars for it. He'd refused the money and only asked if he could take a photo of my socked feet in exchange for the password.

Did I find that weird? Immensely. Did I agree? Obviously! I was in the middle of *The Witcher* episode where Henry was in his bath! I was a virgin, but I was still a woman.

After that, he asked to take photos of my feet every time he changed his Wi-Fi password—which was becoming more and more regular. It made Jake laugh despite my discomfort.

"Your boyfriend made a scene this weekend," he continued, his frown deepening.

Jake came? Well, I'd have to thank the building maintenance guy for being the incompetent asshole he was and not fixing my buzzer. For once, his laziness really played in my favor.

"If this happens again, I will have to inform the building intendant," he continued, his annoyance still palpable.

I could have just laughed at that. The building intendant? It was the fancy name given to *Crackhead Jimmy* from 1A, and I would have loved to see him act on any complaint, regardless of the seriousness.

It seemed that Mr. Scott had forgotten which area of town we lived in.

Despite being a big fat man with a creepy foot fetish, I knew he was mostly harmless, but it was not necessary to fight him, not today anyway. I needed all the patience I had to face Liam.

I simply nodded. "It won't happen again." At least, I hoped Jake got the message and would leave me alone. "I'll give you my pair of socks when I come back, what do you say?" I knew he was selling them, along with the pictures he had taken of my feet—Mama Reynolds from across the hall told me about it, but again, I didn't care. Whatever rocked his boat.

He grunted and opened the door of his apartment, revealing he had nowhere to go and had probably been watching from his peephole, waiting for me to make a move.

"Just put them in a Ziplock bag and leave them in my letterbox," he said, as if it was a totally normal conversation to have. He started to close the door but stopped when there was just a sliver left. "The Wi-Fi password is ShelikeSit69. Capital S-es." Then he closed the door completely.

"Thank you," I called as I turned and grimaced. He really was gross.

I exited the building and stopped for a second, taking a lungful of fresh air before letting it out with a sigh.

Fresh air was a little bit of a stretch... There wasn't much *fresh* in this neighborhood, but after spending two full days holed up in my twenty-five-square-foot micro apartment, which I was positive used to be a storage room, in between the various food smells and other undefined odors I was trying to ignore, the air *felt* fresh.

I never realized how desensitized I really was until I walked outside and breathed actual air, no matter how polluted.

I didn't have much time to question anything as bus 19 rounded the corner and I had to sprint to the bus stop, hoping I would not damage my healing ankle any more than it was. I'd need my feet to be fully functioning if Liam gave me my job back.

He will, I reassured myself breathlessly as I slipped onto the bus just seconds before the doors closed.

I sat in the back and looked out the window, watching the changes of the urban scenery as we moved through the areas.

I've lived here since I was a baby, and I knew this town inside out. You could put me anywhere and I'd tell exactly where I was, just based on the color of the building, tags on the wall, and cleanliness of the street.

I stopped a couple of streets before Sunset Strip to cash in my meager pity check before walking there much slower than I should have, not only because of my ankle, but also because I was still reluctant to ask Liam for my job back.

It was still early, and the club didn't usually start to fill up until late afternoon, but I still sighed with relief seeing the almost empty parking lot and especially without Serena's car. I was not ready for her just yet.

Will I ever be? I shook my head. It was not like I had the choice.

It was one of the downsides of being poor, we couldn't always afford this type of qualm.

I walked to the back and smiled at the sight of Conor. He was one of my favorite bouncers here, and one of the first ones to tell me I was much too good for Jake. If only I'd listened then.

"Wee, V! What brings you here? Long time no see."

I waved dismissively. "Life, I guess..." I said with a laugh.

It probably sounded as fake as it was because Connor's smile dimmed, and he nodded as if he understood exactly what I meant.

"Is Liam here?" I asked, knowing full well he was after spotting his ostentatious BMW parked by the main doors of the club.

I only asked to assess if Liam would be receptive to my return. I knew how quick he was to blacklist people and the typical lies the staff had to give for him.

Connor nodded and moved from his spot in front of the door, opening it for me. "Yep, he's probably in his office. He'll be happy to see you."

I walked in the dark corridor, my steps a little lighter as I now expected a good outcome, despite having to beg for a job that was killing my spirit.

I was about to knock on the ugly green office door when my phone chirped in my back pocket.

I took a deep breath, knowing it had to be Jake again. I decided to ignore it, though I knew I would have to confront him eventually. It seemed that me, running away and getting in the car of an absolute stranger, rather than spending a minute more with him had not been clear enough to express my desire to take my distance.

Maybe I should take Connor with me when I decide to talk to him. He would probably enjoy scaring Jake away.

I shook my head and knocked. Now was not the time to think about that. I needed to get my old job back while keeping at least a little bit of my dignity, if it was at all possible.

"Come in."

Please don't be a dick, I begged Liam mentally as I opened the door.

He was at his usual spot behind his desk, in his big leather chair, wearing one of his trademark wide collar dress shirts, unbuttoned to the middle of his chest, revealing his red chest hair and oversized golden chain with a shamrock pendant. He was such a walking cliché for seventies kitsch.

"Well, well, well, if it isn't the prodigal daughter." He grinned, reaching for a cigarette and lighting it. "Come in." He gestured, blowing the smoke in my direction, making me crinkle my nose.

I hated the smell of cigarettes, especially when it was in such an enclosed space that also smelled like stale beer and old sweat.

I walked into the room and cleared my throat as the unpleasant smell seemed to be coating the back of it.

He pointed at the chair across his desk and kept his hazel eyes on me until I sank into the chair.

"What do you need, leanbh-cailín?" he asked with the faintest Irish accent, leaning back on his chair.

Little girl? Liam was cockiness personified, even if he had no reason to be. He was not ugly, but he was just ordinary. A shorter than average man who tried to compensate by spending too much time bodybuilding—making him look stocky instead of strong. It was also quite ridiculous to hear him use an Irish accent and wear everything showing Irish glory when he'd never even set foot in Ireland.

"I need my job back." I didn't need to beat around the bush with Liam. He knew from the moment I walked in what I'd wanted.

"Oh, do you now?" He nodded and stood, walking to the tinted window giving a premium view on the stage. "I thought you were better than that now."

I sighed. *Here we go...*

I also stood and went to stand beside him. A stripper I'd never seen before was doing her show for the few men who had nothing better to do before lunchtime.

Liam called it 'doing you classes.' You needed to earn your badges to get night shifts, where you could get a lot more tips.

"You know it had nothing to do with thinking I'm better than this place." I focused on the girl's clumsy moves. I frowned; she looked barely out of school. "You can't blame me for trying to get a better life."

"What's so wrong with this one? Was I treating you unfairly?" He stared at my profile intently.

I threw him a side look. "You know you didn't. I just didn't see myself being a barmaid in a strip joint until the day I died."

"You wouldn't have to."

Knowing full well what he was implying, I took a small step to the side, creating a little distance between us. I could be promoted from barmaid to live-in girlfriend if I wanted to, just like my mother and his father had many years ago.

She wanted something different for me, but the problem was, I wasn't sure it was possible.

"You know there's no getting out for people like us, not really," he added as if he could read my thoughts.

"Can you blame me for trying?"

He pursed his lips, and I knew he could. He took it much more personally than if it had been any other member of staff leaving. I knew he always assumed that, since I was my mother's daughter, I would end up being his girl one day. My mother had done what she had because of her love for me, because of her sense of duty, but I didn't have the same obligations—I had done everything I could to not make the same mistakes.

"Can I come back or not?" I asked when he remained silent, while still feeling his eyes burning into the side of my face.

"Six months, Violet, that's how long you've been gone. Ingrid took over and she's doing a fine job."

I arched an eyebrow and took a few steps to the left, both to create even more distance between us and get a better look at the bar.

Ingrid was there, her breast half on the bar, flirting with one of the customers while completely ignoring another one.

I turned toward him. "I can see that she's doing a banging job. How many drinks can she serve in an hour?"

He frowned, crossing his arms on his chest. "What can I say, she has other attributes that please the customers."

"So, what are you saying?" My heart dropped, but I managed to keep my face smooth. He didn't need to know how desperate I was.

"I'm saying this job has been filled for a while, but there's still the pos-"

"No," I cut him off, shaking my head. "Absolutely not!"

My mother had been their biggest star, with flaming red curly hair, creamy skin, shiny blue eyes, and curves for days—they'd called her *The Irish Pride*. I looked a lot like her, except for the long black hair I'd inherited from the sperm donor who impregnated her when she was only seventeen.

Liam had it in his head to restore the 'Irish Pride' by making me replace her, since I'd been old enough for it to be legal. He'd even come up with a name for me, 'Snow White.' While it was not very innovative, he knew as well as I did that the idea of purity would have attracted the richest perverts around. Men ready to throw money at me in the hope to steal an innocence they never could have dreamed of.

I'd sworn to my mother on her deathbed, when the lack of money and desperation had me considering this path, that I would never become a stripper, no matter how bad things got. I would honor that promise, no matter what it cost me.

"Fine." I turned before he could see the tears of dejection in my eyes. "I think there's nothing left to say here. Have a nice life, Liam."

"Wait! Fuck it, V, wait!" he called as I was reaching for the door. "God! Yes, you can get your job back."

I turned back around; the wave of relief so powerful, I almost sobbed.

His scowl deepened; he was reluctant to give in, that much I knew, but I was also sure that Ingrid sucked like no one else at this job.

"Don't make me regret it. Don't make me question your loyalty again. Because, Violet, if you leave again," he shook his head, "you're *not* coming back."

I nodded. That seemed fair.

He sighed, running a hand over his face before walking back to his desk. "Tomorrow, afternoon shift."

"I'll be there, thank you."

He nodded, taking his seat behind his desk again. "That's what family does; just don't forget it."

The phone vibrated yet again when I exited his office, and I decided to face the music.

The four texts were not from Jake as I had expected, but from Sandra. Did he finally get the message and backed off?

OMG he got fired!

My steps faltered as I read the message.

Reynolds and his bitch niece, GONE!

I stopped walking and leaned against the wall of the narrow corridor, continuing to read her texts.

Got escorted out by security this morning, kicking and screaming. Knew the fucker was shady!

Told you karma was a bitch! Let's go for a drink this weekend?

I chucked, putting the phone back in my pocket. *I'll message her later.* Maybe a drink was a good idea. She was a little over the top, but she was nice and funny, and I needed a friend who wouldn't stab me in the back.

As if on cue, the door from the changing rooms opened to reveal Serena, dressed in her day clothes.

She had the decency to take a step back and looked down with shame. It didn't make things better, but at least she felt something negative after bursting my bubble.

"V—" she started, gripping her bag a little tighter.

"Don't," I warned coldly.

Her eyes flew to mine, filled with surprise. She was used to the nice Violet, the gullible Violet... This would be a nice change.

"Don't *V* me," I clarified. "You're not my friend, nor a person I respect. You've lost any right to call me anything other than Murphy the day you fucked my boyfriend."

She chewed on her bottom lip, sending an uncomfortable look around her. She was right to be worried, there was a certain ethic and code of conduct between the dancers, which extended to all females, really. You didn't cheat, and you certainly didn't go after another woman's man.

"This is not what—" She stopped and sighed. "I did it for you."

"You did it for..." I shook my head, feeling even more insulted than before. How stupid did she really think I was?

"V— Murphy, listen I..."

I raised my hand to stop her. "No, you listen. I've wasted enough time with you and Jake. I'm done now. We have to work at the same place, but you stay out of my way and I'll stay out of yours, understand?"

She opened her mouth, but I shot her a warning look that was enough to make her close it quickly.

"You are dead to me and so is he. Do me a favor, will you? Tell him to stop calling me or try to see me, there's nothing left to say."

"He won't listen to me," she said as I started to walk toward the exit. "He loves you, and he wants you back."

I couldn't help the little laugh, that sounded a lot like a demented squeal, from escaping my mouth. "I'm sure you can keep him distracted long enough for this to pass. I've witnessed the extent of your skills. Do this and the girls here won't know what a hateful, treacherous bitch you really are."

I opened the door without giving her a chance to add anything, knowing she would now do everything she could to keep him away from me.

"I'll see you tomorrow," I shouted to Connor, who was standing by the dumpster, smoking a cigarette.

I gave him a quick wave and hurried to the bus stop

I didn't want to wait and chat anymore—I've done enough of that for one day. The only thing I wanted now was to go home and watch my shows now that I had regained my Wi-Fi privileges.

Despite my run-in with Serena, the bus ride home was actually peaceful. I had my job back, the mistakes I had made were not irreversible, and that included my one-year relationship with Jake. I had invested time into this relationship, but at least I hadn't given myself fully to him. I was still young as everyone loved to remind me. Jake might have wasted a year of my life, but that was done now.

I had just entered my apartment and put my phone on the counter when it started to ring. *Sun Valley* flashed on my screen.

I frowned. "Hello?"

"Ms. Murphy?"

"Yes?" Why were they calling me after the way they treated me?

"This is Mrs. Taylor from *Sun Valley* HR department. Am I catching you at a bad time?"

My lungs squeezed with anxiety. "Are you calling about the Uber ride? It was authorized. I never would—"

"Oh no, no." She let out a little uncomfortable laugh, sparking my curiosity.

I'd met the woman a few times during the evaluation process, and she was the image of a perfect, cool corporate lady. This laugh was not fitting the image I had of her.

Did she think Mr. Reynolds did something to me? Was it why he had been fired?

I leaned against the counter. Were the sexual harassment rumors true after all? "Is it about Mr. Reynolds?"

"Well..." She cleared her throat, probably surprised I had approached the subject so casually, but really, what could she do? Fire me?

"He never did anything inappropriate to me," I added, ready to end the call. I was not meddling in any of this mess.

"No, I—" She let out another uncomfortable laugh. "I'm glad to hear that nothing inappropriate happened, but that is not the reason for my call."

She paused and I waited for her to continue.

"Ms. Murphy, I'm calling today because there seems to have been confusion with respect to your employment. It should not have been terminated. We committed to full-time employment, and we would like to apologize for this termination."

"I see..." I twisted my mouth to the side, not really buying her words. Mr. Reynolds had been a lazy bastard; he would not have organized his niece's employment by himself, so HR had to be involved. I might have been a little naive, but I was not stupid.

However, no matter how badly they treated me, I just had to move on. Holding on to the injustice and unfairness of things would not do me any good.

"It's fine, I'm not going to do—"

"So, are you available to come back to work tomorrow? Let's say nine? No, wait, nine-thirty may be best. I will arrange a meeting so we can go over all your employment documentation."

I pulled the phone from my ear and looked at the screen as if it would show me that it was a joke. "You want me to come back?"

"Well, yes, of course!" She chuckled. "Your evaluation was nothing short of exceptional, and your colleagues speak very highly of you. Here, at *Sun Valley*, we pride ourselves to hire the best of the best, and we believe you are truly company material."

"I don't know what to say..."

I walked to my single bed in the corner of the room and sat on it, suddenly feeling lightheaded.

"You don't have to say anything. We're the ones who made the mistake, Ms. Murphy, and frankly, I'm not sure how this one got past me. I feel personally responsible for all of this." She let out a sigh. "However, I have more good news. In light of the situation and the inconvenience and upset this has certainly caused you, management decided to increase your base yearly salary from forty-five thousand to fifty-five thousand, and added two days of paid holiday to your allowance. So, what do you say, Violet? Will I see you tomorrow?" she asked with a smile in her voice.

I wanted to say yes, of course I did, but what happened had left a bad taste in my mouth.

All the chances, all the leaps of faith I'd taken had always ended up being mistakes. Opening up to Jake and giving him access to my heart, trying to leave the life I'd been assigned to.

If you leave again, you're not coming back. Liam's words played so clearly in my head. If I said yes to this woman, it was done. My safety net would be permanently removed.

I could not take the same risk twice. The first time had been brave, but doing it again would be foolish.

I shook my head silently. The situation at Sunset Strip was not stellar, but they had a loyalty—Irish blood to Irish blood—an unspoken bond that gave me a certain security I did not dare test again.

"Violet? Does tomorrow at nine-thirty work for you?" she asked again, though her voice sounded uncertain.

"No." My heart plummeted as tears formed in my eyes. I felt like I was letting my mother down. I felt like, in a way, I was letting *myself* down, but that fear, that uncertainty, did not allow me to give any other answer.

Would I be proud of my decision tomorrow?

"Oh! Okay, you are busy I presume. Is there a better time for you?"

"No, I—" I blinked a few times under the sting of the tears, and they started to roll softly down my cheeks. "I'm going to have to refuse your offer."

"Ex- excuse me?" She sounded baffled, but how could she not?

"I'm not interested in this position anymore. Thank you for your interest, but you will need to find someone else." I looked heavenward, or rather to my yellow-stained ceiling, willing the tears to subside. It would not be long before she would be able to hear them in my voice. I had to end this conversion now.

"I-I don't understand."

"Goodbye, Mrs. Taylor," I added quickly before ending the call.

I threw the phone onto the bed and slid my back against the wall, pulling my knees to my chest and rested my head on top of it, letting the tears take over.

I would give myself the day to mourn yet another broken dream. But when would my luck truly turn?

CHAPTER 5

Hoka

I leaned back on my seat, bored with this day already. I had to do it. I was the boss, but on days like today, I felt much more like a stern father than a mafia boss.

More like a judge and jury, really.

My computer beeped with a new email, and I just had the time to see it came from *Sun Valley* before Jiro opened the door to let in a trembling, sweating man, who knew it was never good to be called in the boss' office.

Fuck it, I could have used two minutes respite, I thought with irritation, fixing my gaze on the man who inadvertently delayed any news on Violet.

"*Oyabun*," he said reverently, though a little breathlessly, bowing at the waist.

Fear would do that to you.

I kept my face impassive as I jerked my head toward the chair in front of my desk. I was getting seriously bored with the threats today. Well, they weren't threats, not in our world; they were promises as we always followed through.

"Do you know why you're here today?"

He fidgeted in his seat as Jiro came to stand behind him, my ever-present executioner. "I... n-no. I'm not sure."

I sighed. So this was how he wanted to play it? What a waste of my time.

I opened the file on my desk and tapped my forefinger on the sheet of paper detailing his accounts of the past six months.

"The earnings have been constantly down for the past six months, despite the monthly loan amounts being quite steady." I rested my hand on the paper. "Why is that?"

"It's hard for people these d—"

"You know what I think?" I cut him off. Usually, it made me laugh to see them try to come up with a stupid excuse, and I enjoyed the mental torture, but mostly, I enjoyed reminding them who they worked for and the code of conduct—our *bushido* he was bound to uphold. But now I wanted a quick end; I wanted to read that email and move on with the day. "I think that either you are loaning the money to people without strong enough incentives to force payment or you are not assertive enough in demanding our money back." I shrugged. "Either way, loan office 159 is your responsibility. The others are managing, and you should, too."

Jiro threw me a knowing half smile. We both knew a couple were not managing, and one of them was permanently gone now.

He paled and I continued, "Do I need to ask Jiro to come and show you how to do your job?"

The man shook his head vehemently. "No, no please. That is not necessary."

Having Jiro looking into your business often meant death, or at least a *Yubitsume*. Jiro and I had done so many of those in our early days that we now knew how to cut fingers off with minimum blood spurts. It was always so difficult to clean.

"I want these accounts cleared and the profit back up before the end of the year. Do you understand me? *Don't* make me call you back into this office." I stared at him, ensuring he understood fully the meaning of my words. *'Because you would not come out of this building alive'* was very much implied. I looked up at Jiro and nodded.

Jiro tapped the man's shoulder, who jumped out of his chair—clearly overly relieved to be allowed to leave with all his limbs.

He bowed. "Thank you, Oyabun." He took a step back to the door, bowing once more. "Thank you for your generosity." Another step back, another bow. "I will bring the accounts back up." Another step and an even lower bow.

I had to stop myself from rolling my eyes. These lower members were laying it way too thick lately.

"You won't regret giving me a chance," he added with a final bow as his back connected with the door behind him.

"I hope so. Your life depends on it," I reminded him as he opened the door and exited the room as if he were running from the Devil.

But he is though, isn't he? I am the devil.

I sighed. "Follow him and make sure he doesn't piss on the carpet on his way out."

Jiro chuckled. "Akira is here."

I frowned. My uncle usually avoided me; he was not overly fond of giving me updates on how he was handling his side of the business. "Why?"

He shrugged. "Your guess is as good as mine."

I shook my head. It really was turning out to be the day that never ended. "Stall him for a few. I've got a few things to do."

Jiro's eyes tightened in the corners as he studied my desk. He knew I was hiding something, but despite our close relationship, he would not cross this line.

I turned toward the computer as soon as he closed the door and opened the email.

I read it once, shook my head, and read it again. I must have misread; it was the only logical explanation.

No. I let out a groan of frustration as I leaned back in my chair. That silly woman said no to the offer?

I clenched my jaws at the thought of her working at a strip joint. I'd felt such a wave of possessiveness and anger when I read in the private investigator's report that she'd been working at a strip club. The only thing that had stopped me from going there and setting it on fire was because she'd only been bartending, and also because it was in Buenaventura. At least it was one of the best areas of the city.

But why would she refuse? She'd told me how much *Sun Valley* had meant to her, how she wanted her life to be different. I made sure the offer was even better this time around, so why would—

My thoughts were interrupted by a sharp knock on the door, which meant my uncle had waited long enough.

He opened the door and had his usual unhappy glare on his face.

"Oji, what can I do for you?"

He sat uninvited and shook his head. "I've waited almost an hour."

I quickly glanced over his shoulder and Jiro rolled his eyes before closing the door behind him, leaving me alone with my uncle. *Traitor*!

"I had some situations to address. You know what it's like to be in charge. We can't always do what we want."

His lips, which were previously tightened in a fine line, relaxed as I knew they would. My uncle thought he was a mystery, the symbol of yakuza pride, but to me he was only an aging man stuck in his obsolete ways with an overinflated ego. This ego would always be his biggest weakness and feeding it was the best way to defuse a tense situation.

He nodded, bringing his hand up and resting his forefinger on his mouth, showing the tattoo on the back of his hand *'893,'* the symbol of the yakuza. We all had this tattoo in one form or another, but only the older generations wore it for everyone to see. I was proud of who I was, of the mission given to me, but it helped tremendously in life—both in my legitimate and illegitimate side of the business—not to scream my affiliation. Where my uncle saw it as lack of pride or cowardice, I saw it as intelligence.

"The Chinese said you refused to help," he finally said, looking around my office as if he was trying to find something. What? I wasn't sure.

"I did."

"Well," he snorted, "they said your *Nuhi* refused."

I sighed, I was not going to have this conversation again. It irritated me that he dared call Jiro a 'Nuhi,' which was nothing more than a slave—the lowest class possible from centuries ago. I knew my uncle wished this was still in place.

"Jiro is my *wakagashira*, he has always been. He only told them what I would have said myself."

My uncle snorted, apparently still not over the fact that I'd picked my best friend as my right hand, my first lieutenant, instead of his incapable son who was way more interested in snorting coke and getting sucked by anything with a mouth, gender be damned, than to deal with the syndicate.

It's been three years, Uncle, time to get over it.

"We have an agreement with the Triad."

"We do." I nodded, getting more annoyed by having to justify my actions to him. Well, I didn't, not really, but my uncle was one of the oldest members of the yakuza in this country and he carried a certain power which, to my greatest annoyance, I could not ignore. "With respect to business split and areas of operations, just like we do with the Koreans. We never agreed to fight their battles. Just like they tapped out themselves when it was needed, in case you don't remember."

"Don't give me a history lesson. I know full well what happened with the Triads. I was in the middle of it while you were still in diapers."

I rested both hands on my desk and leaned forward, my cool mask forgotten as I threw him a cautious glare. "I highly recommend you remember *who* you are talking to, Oji."

My uncle's nostrils flared and his jaws tensed in anger.

I held his eyes in challenge until he bowed his head, breaking eye contact.

"*Moushiwake gozaimasen*," he muttered, and I knew how much it cost him to apologize to me. The impure blood, the man-child who he thought was unfit for the throne.

"We have enough things to deal with in our own business. We're not here to fight other mafia wars. While the Mexicans are not our allies, I don't want to add them to our enemy list, either." I waved my hand dismissively. "My father thought the same," I added, hoping that would hold enough weight for him to move on.

"The Triads owing us a debt could have been useful, and we can't say your father was the symbol of perfect decision making. He made quite a few *questionable* choices in his time."

I tightened my hand into a fist on my desk. I knew very well what he meant. He never got over my father choosing my mother instead of the perfect Japanese bride that had been picked out for him. That woman had been raised and trained to be his bride, yet when he traveled to meet her, he'd fallen in love with another woman from the village—a *Hafu*, half Japanese, half American woman. It was something my grandfather and uncle always held against my father. My uncle's rancor had run so deep, especially since he had been forced to marry the woman originally promised to my father. A woman who was full of rancor and bitterness at being married to the second son.

Aunt Yua had been a horrible woman, and as sad as it sounded, nobody truly mourned her when she passed away two years ago.

"I will not get involved in their wars. This is the end of it." I cocked my head to the side, cracking my neck. "Well, if that was all you—"

"I have been informed you went to dinner with Ayia Sato."

"I did." That was the worst evening I had in a long time and I had honestly wanted to pull my nails out one by one by the end of it.

"She's the perfect bride for you. Botan Sato is a strong, powerful member of our organization. She has perfect manners and a pure lineage."

"And without any moral compass. As long as I buy her diamonds and designer clothes, she would turn a blind eye to the blood, murders, and occasional side women," I added, unable to hold the bitterness in my voice.

My uncle laughed with a small nod. "Exactly! Isn't she perfect? A true gift from our ancestors!" he agreed, misunderstanding my criticism for compliments. "I see you're making wiser choices than your father."

"Be careful, Oji... The woman you are so easily demeaning is my *mother*."

"That was not my intention; your mother is a fine woman who deserves respect." I knew he meant that because, despite his opposition to their union, it was impossible to dislike my mother. "She was just not right for this life and her position."

"That's your opinion." I tapped my fingers on my desk. "I have work to do."

He nodded and stood, finally giving up. "I do, too. I need to go to Buenaventura."

That caught my attention. "Buenaventura? Why?"

"They don't seem very receptive to Nishimura Holding's newest addition."

"The new office towers? What's their problem? It will bring business to them."

"Some think it will denature the area. They only have small shops, and they don't want that to change."

"All businesses have an issue with that?" *Please say yes. Please give me a reason to see her again.*

He shrugged. "Pretty much yes, except for the lady at the flower shop. Even the strip club is against it." He shook his head. "You would have thought he would be eager to get all the perverts with fat wallets. But don't worry, I'll make them reconsider."

Fate. It had to be fate. "I'll go talk to them." I stated, standing up and adjusting my jacket.

My uncle took a step back, arching an eyebrow in surprise. "You? You always refused to do this part of the job."

"And today I want to. Let me go to the strip club."

My uncle laughed. "I didn't know you were the type. They're all gaijins there."

I shook my head with a dismissive scoff as I leaned down, pretending to take something from my drawer, just in case he could read something in my face I didn't want him to see.

"I've got some standards, Uncle. I won't touch any of the girls." It was not a complete lie. Most of these women did that job out of desperation, and I was not one to feed off this type of desperation. I wanted a woman to join me in bed without fear or obligation. I wanted her to give herself to me because she craved me.

Do you crave me, Violet Murphy? Are you thinking of me the way I'm thinking of you?

I looked up and let my uncle's questioning eyes search mine. Had he said something?

I blinked a couple of times. "What?"

"I said leave them to me. I've been dealing with this side of the business for years."

"And you've been excelling at it," I said in an attempt to pacify him. "But you know who the ultimate owner of this club is, and you know that my presence may carry a little more weight. There's no point starting to torture everyone and anger another syndicate. Don't you agree?"

He shrugged and I let out a little laugh.

"I just wonder why now?" he asked. I really didn't need for him to go look into it too closely and find Violet. She would never be part of this world; I would never do that to her. I'll keep her at bay, just close enough to touch her skin and get rid of this obsession, but also far enough for her to never know who I really was and the danger I represented.

"I wonder why you're so opposed to my visit? Is there something, or *someone,* you're trying to hide?" *Here, let's turn the focus back on you and see how you like it.*

My uncle raised his hands in surrender. "Do as you please, I've got nothing to hide. Let me know if you don't get anywhere. I'll take over."

I had to do my best not to laugh. Who did he think he was?

"Goodbye, Uncle."

He bowed to me. "Oyabun," he said before turning and exiting the room.

I smiled as I secured the gun in my holster.

See you soon, Violet.

I was ushered in as soon as I announced myself at the back door, followed closely by three of my men. This was the kind of visit where I was expected to take a few men to assert my position, despite the fact that I could probably take all the men in this club without even getting my gun out.

I was taken to an office I presumed had not been refurbished since the seventies with an ugly orange carpet and green walls.

I cleared my throat as the scent of old tobacco and stale alcohol hit my nose.

The man behind the desk matched the decor to the T, with his big collared open shirt, overly unkempt red chest hair, and thick gold chain.

It looked like I'd just stepped into one of the bad pornos from that time. I couldn't believe Violet worked for this clown, a man who seemed to be living in an era he was not even born in.

He grinned, his eyes sparkling with a kind of pleasure I couldn't really understand.

People usually didn't like seeing me in their space.

"Hoka Nishimura..." His grin widened. "To what do I owe the honor of your presence? Are you coming here to sway my vote?"

I understood his excitement now. This man was not only a clown, he was stupid too. He had to be if he thought he was worth my visit.

"Please take a seat."

"I'd rather not."

"Are you coming to discuss the new tower?" he asked, leaning back in his chair like a king in his kingdom. "Want me to sway the pressure group?"

"I don't think there's much to discuss or anyone to *sway*. It's just a courtesy visit to remind you who this part of town belongs to. I *will* have my way, but I would recommend that you strongly consider which side you want to be on when this is all finished."

"Do you know who this club belongs to?"

"*Partially*. And yes, I do. But Boston is a long way away from here, and this club is here as a favor to the Irish, not the other way around." I scoffed. "I believe Killian Doyle has other things in his head than potentially avenging the sad fate of a second-rate Irish strip club... things like finding his wayward brother. So please, think long and hard before claiming Doyle's protection."

"I never said I was *against* the project," he interjected, losing some of his bravado.

I threw him a knowing look and walked to the tinted window, hoping to catch a glimpse of Violet—just to make sure she was okay.

"Fine, I'll see what I can do."

I shook my head, slipping my hands in my pocket. "I don't need you to do anything. I was not bluffing; I have things under control. I just need you to stay out of my way."

I heard his chair squeak as he stood to come beside me.

"Can I interest you in a private dance on the house?" he asked, probably mistaking my interest for the scene below. "Serena should be here soon. She's our star."

I frowned. Wasn't Serena the woman who betrayed Violet?

"I don't associate with people like her," I replied dismissively, my eyes still searching for Violet. I was about to give up and ask where she was when she finally appeared from a door behind the bar, holding a couple of bottles of liquor, knocking the air out of me.

I was not ready to feel the way I did, seeing her again.

I looked at her moving fluidly as she placed the two bottles on the shelves behind her. Was she still suffering from her injury?

My frown deepened as a man leaned across the bar, throwing her a flirty smile as he spoke to her.

She smiled back as she reached for a high shelf, allowing her crop top to ride up and reveal her toned stomach and smooth, creamy skin—something I was not okay with other men seeing.

She is not mine. She can never be mine.

"Ah, sorry, but some women are off limits."

I threw him a sideways look. "Are they?" He was not as clueless as I thought as he so obviously noticed my interest.

"She's a barmaid, not a stripper... even though I've tried to get her on stage so many times. She's spoken for anyway."

Just the thought of her naked for other men's pleasure filled me with a homicidal rage I'd never experienced before. I wanted to shoot him right then and there, consequences be damned.

"Spoken for by whom? *You?*" I asked, not able to keep the derision out of my voice. My Violet didn't want him

He glared. "So what? She's mine."

"Does she know that?"

"What?"

I turned a little to the side to look at him straight on. "Violet. Does she know she's yours?"

"She ne—" His eyes widened in surprise. "How do you know her name?"

"And tell me, does your main investor back in Boston know that you're selling your girls for sex?" I asked, ignoring his question.

"Doyle owns a few brothels; he couldn't care less."

"About the prostitution? Probably not. But does he know that you're not giving him his thirty percent on this side of the business like you're supposed to? How long has it been going on? Four years? Since daddy dearest died? I can only imagine what Doyle would do to you." I grimaced. "We both know his stance on loyalty."

Liam paled. We both knew that if I said a word, he was dead. "What do you want?"

"I want you to stay away from her, and I want you to allow her to leave. She got a job offer that she refused, and it was a stupid decision. Make her reconsider, take away this job. I don't care what you do."

He looked at me and squinted. "She's a good person. She's not made for the likes of you."

I arched my eyebrows, not quite sure what he meant by 'the likes of you.' Though, I was hoping, for his sake, that he was not talking about my ethnicity.

"M-mafia," he added quickly. "She's not cut out for this."

"Says the man who wants to exploit her body."

"Violet is as innocent as they come, and innocence is lucrative, but I would have never let another man touch her - especially when no man has ever been allowed to."

I turned my head sharply to look back at her. Was he saying what I thought he was saying? The flame that was gently burning for this girl turned into a fucking inferno. She didn't just transpire innocence, she *was* innocent—and I wanted it all for myself.

I'd come here with the idea of only watching her from afar, to feed the monster who was obsessed with her, and make sure she would leave this place. But now, that seemed impossible.

I had to speak with her, stare into her blue eyes, and feed from her innocence, from her light, from her goodness.

This man inadvertently shot the bullet and it got me right in the heart, stirring up all the things I had barely managed to reign in until now.

"I'm going down now." I turned briskly and opened the door. "Go wait for me in the car, I'll be out soon," I told my men, not even taking a minute to stop.

My lungs were in a vice, and it was like I had to see her close now, hear her voice or I might just stop breathing.

"How do you know Violet?" the Irish asshole huffed breathlessly as he struggled to follow me down the metal stairs to the main part of the club.

"I know her because she *is mine*." I stopped suddenly at the bottom of the stairs as the truth of the words hit me in a way that was both liberating and terrifying.

"Does she know about..." he trailed off, smart enough not to say out loud what wasn't public knowledge.

I turned my head to the side; he was two steps behind me and at eye level.

"She doesn't need to know." I adjusted my jacket, keeping my eyes on him. "However, I would not give much thought of your club and your life if she were to find out. Clear?"

"Crystal," he replied before pursing his lips.

I smiled. "Good."

I walked the length of the room, keeping my eyes on her as she had her back to me, unaware of the predator approaching her as she carefully sliced limes into a container.

Her thick black hair was up in a messy bun, revealing her graceful neck. I licked my lips, imagining it was her neck I was licking and kissing. How I would brand her with my teeth, leaving my mark on her skin like the wild animal I was just discovering I could be. This was unsettling in so many ways, but the image of me possessing her was so vivid that I could taste the softness of her skin on my lips, her sweetness on my tongue.

I stopped at the other end of the bar, a little breathless from my consuming thoughts.

She straightened as if she could feel me, and maybe she could. Maybe she felt the *Kanji*... Maybe the legend of the red string was more than a legend.

She turned slowly, and her small polite smile bloomed into a full one reaching her eyes, making my heart skip a beat.

I couldn't help but smile back, probably giving the short Irish ginger a heart attack. I was not a man known for my smiles.

"Are you following me?" I asked teasingly as she walked toward me, her limes forgotten on the counter.

"You're the one who is in my place of work. Are *you* following me?"

You don't know the extent of my involvement in your life, sweet girl.

"I'm here to discuss the tower my company is planning to build down the road but," I winked, "what if I was following you? That sounds way more fun."

She blushed lightly, but it was so obvious on a skin as pale as hers, even under the dim lighting.

"I would say you must be bored to death."

"I don't think I would be." I sighed, detaching my eyes from hers with great difficulty, if only to see who was around and if I had to do any damage control at so openly showing interest in someone who was not officially under clan protection.

"Can I buy you a drink?" she asked and the apple of her cheeks reddened even more at her words. "I mean, to thank you for saving my life, sparing me humiliation, and taking me to the doctor."

I nodded. I'd do it all over again and so much more just to see her look at me the way she was looking at me now. Like I was her hero.

"It's unnecessary." I brought my hand up to rub at my neck and curse internally. It was something I did when I was nervous, but something I had not done since I was a teen.

"I insist."

"You really want to thank me?"

"Yes!"

Then kiss me. "Have dinner with me tonight." *What in the actual f—* The words had escaped before I could even realize how much of a bad idea it was. Taking her out in public was probably the worst idea I had ever had, and the best way to get Jiro on my back. Yet when her smile brightened and she stood a little bit straighter with glee, I knew I wouldn't come to regret my decision.

"I... yes, of course! Dinner seems—" She nodded. "Yes, I'd like that. I... um, I finish at six tonight."

I nodded. "I'll pick you up at your place. Eight o'clock?"

She nodded again. "It's a date." She widened her adorable blue eyes, her sensuous lips parting with her surprised gasp.

I moved from my position at the bar, much too tempted to lean a little closer to grab her face and pull her to me for a kiss so deep, it would alter both of our beings.

"Yes, yes, it is." I replied playfully, then exited the club while I still had the upper hand.

CHAPTER 6

Violet

After Hoka's departure, I had been surprised that Liam didn't bitch or make me stay later to mess with my date.

I've known him for years, and despite things that were mostly unspoken, I also knew he believed to have a claim on me just because of our parents' history. But instead of messing with me, he had been so much better than I had ever expected him to be.

He'd waited for Hoka to leave and turned toward one of the waitresses to replace me for a few minutes, then took me to his office.

I had been ready to fight him, but he just sat there and looked at me silently for a few minutes before shaking his head.

"You know what I said yesterday? I didn't mean it, Violet. I was angry, but it was not fair of me to threaten you."

I just stood there, much too shocked by his apology. Liam always thought he'd been too good for apologies.

"We're a family, Violet, and the way I acted wasn't like family." He'd looked away as if the next words were costing him something far greater. "You deserve something better than what you do, and I should encourage you to get it, not prevent you."

"Okay...?"

"What I'm saying is, no matter what, you'll always have a job here, so take all the opportunities coming your way. If it fails, we'll still be here."

I narrowed my eyes, feeling unsettled. It was so unlike him. Liam was not selfless or understanding. "Why?"

His head jerked back in surprise, and he scoffed, "Why? I expected a *'Thank you, Liam.'*"

"I've known you most of my life, Liam. Why are you doing this?"

He shook his head. "Because it was what your mother wanted, and my father loved her. He would have wanted that for you, too. Take it as me honoring his memory."

Liam honored nothing other than himself, but it didn't matter... This was the safety net I needed.

I nodded. "Thank you."

He waved dismissively before looking at his watch. "Just go now, you only have thirty minutes left on your shift. You need to get ready for your date," he added, the cold edge in his voice unmistakable, but I was not about to question him further. I'd just take what he gave me and be grateful for it, even if there had to be ulterior motives.

Doomed if I do, doomed if I don't. Well then, don't mind if I do.

I grabbed all my things quickly and rushed out to the bus stop before that version of Liam disappeared and he'd come find me just to say that he had changed his mind.

I had only reached the stop when my bus appeared from the corner. Ah, today was really a decent day.

I smiled as I stepped onto the bus. I'd never expected to see Hoka again.

It's a date. I grimaced as a wave of embarrassment hit me square in the chest as I took my seat on the bus.

I touched my flaming cheeks with a shake of my head, hoping the mortification would subside before I saw him tonight, or I would be a walking, talking tomato during the whole dinner.

I hardly believed he'd ask me out for dinner, and then when I said it was a date, he agreed.

I had done a google search on him when I had the Wi-Fi back, and despite not finding much, I had discovered that Hoka Nishimura was the CEO of a big conglomerate worth billions.

What could a rich, hot man want from little old me? Well, I knew what he could want—I wasn't *that* naïve—but it would be a lot of effort for someone like me, I was quite ordinary.

I was anxious at the thought of this evening. What if he found me boring? What if I embarrassed him?

I was startled at the thought as the bus stopped across my building.

Would I embarrass him? No, He *had* to know I was not a person from his world. I tried to reassure myself as I walked up the path to my decrepit building.

I stopped in front of the rusty door leading inside the corridor and detailed the peeling paint and the less than savory graffiti on the walls.

He'd seen where I worked and where I lived... He couldn't be expecting much, could he?

Why wouldn't you be enough? A little voice that sounded just like my mother's resonated in my head as I turned the key into the main lock while shaking the door as hard as my body weight allowed it in order to dislodge the faulty lock.

I was doing that often—imagining what Mother would have said in some situations.

I'd lost her much too young, just a few days after my sixteenth birthday, but she'd been fading away, losing her battle to cancer for almost a year before that.

My mother fought her cancer like a warrior, showing me an amount of strength, dignity, and courage, I was not sure I could ever reach, but could only aspire to.

My heart sank in my chest as I took the sticky stairs up to my apartment, the echo of the pain I'd felt when she died still very much there, reminding me that no matter the amount of healing time was supposed to give, some cuts would never fully heal.

I'd lost her too young... Well, I presume it is always too early to lose that one person who loves you so unconditionally. I'd lost her before I knew what it was to be me, before I knew what being a woman really meant.

I walked into my studio apartment and sat heavily on my single bed, closing my eyes and imagining her helping me with the stress of my upcoming date.

I imagined her sitting beside me on the bed, and I could almost smell her faint freesia perfume.

She would have smiled at how nervous I was, telling me that it was normal.

I would have asked her why a man like Hoka would want to spend time with a woman like me.

"Because he's clearly a smart man, Vi. He saw what a gem you are without any artifice or theatrics. That man sees a true treasure without the need of the shine. Not everything that shines is gold, sweet girl, and that man clearly knows it."

I kept my eyes closed. I was not ready to let go of the perfect image of her sitting beside me on the bed, her blue eyes, so similar to mine, full of love and goodness, despite life showing her nothing but its hard edges. I leaned back against the cool wall, letting the few tears of sorrow run down my cheeks.

Imagining her was always a conundrum, making me feel better and worse at the same time.

I moved my hand to rest on the spot beside me, her image so vivid I almost expected my hand to connect with her soft, warm skin instead of the overused, over-washed bedspread.

I opened my eyes once my hand landed on the scratchy fabric, the illusion gone.

I took a deep breath. "I miss you so much, Mom."

I stood and shook my head, willing the sorrow to subside and go back in its box for now.

I opened my one door, multifunction wardrobe/kitchen cabinet to realize what I already knew. My whole wardrobe consisted of three pairs of jeans, one pair of dress pants, and the dress Hoka had already seen me wear.

I closed the door and leaned against it. This was a bad idea, all of it. I took the phone out of my back pocket and swirled it around in my palm.

Maybe I should just cancel, I didn't have to give him an excuse. I could just tell him that I couldn't make it.

But I want to go, don't I?

I caught my bottom lip between my teeth. Why did I even want to go? It was not like it could go anywhere. In what universe would a hot, thirty-something billionaire build a life with a dirt-poor, uneducated twenty-one-year-old orphan? That only happened in books and Hallmark movies.

Yet I want to give it a try, don't I?

I rolled my eyes at my personal debate. If I took it a step further, I'd develop a split personality.

"*Regrets are mainly born from missed opportunities.*' My mom had always said and no matter how many times she'd fallen, she always stood up again.

Now was the time to walk in her footsteps and show the world that I was ready to take another risk.

I looked at the silver handle that was peeking from under my bed and pulled out the pigeon-blue hardshell suitcase I'd used to pack my most precious possessions in the world.

I leaned back on my haunches and reached for the towel that was drying on the metal footpost on my bed to wipe the thin layer of dust that had accumulated on the case.

I rarely opened in anymore—it had been over two years since I dared look inside. Opening it, whilst sometimes soothing, often brought a fresh wave of pain, loss, and sorrow.

The suitcase held the essence of who my mother had been. I hadn't kept much, I couldn't. If it had been possible, I would have kept everything she ever touched, everything she ever owned, as if it kept her closer to me somehow.

But unfortunately, the week after she'd died, the landlord came asking for a rent I obviously didn't have. I had no other choice than to leave the place to move somewhere so much cheaper, under the radar of social services until I turned eighteen.

The only thing I could do was pack the few belongings I knew she loved the most in this ugly, old, banged-up suitcase. The couple of paperbacks that were so well-read that the pages were barely glued together. A few dresses I knew were her favorites—most of them presents from Liam's father. I also kept a pearl necklace and earring set I wasn't sure was worth much. I never really asked much about them because I saw the way she handled them with care, that no matter how much they actually cost, to her, they were priceless. We had been in lots of financial troubles throughout the years, but despite selling almost everything she owned—everything that had some value, everything that was pretty—she never convinced herself to sell this necklace. I didn't know who gave it to her, and the sadness in her eyes when she wore them prevented me from ever asking. I suspected it had been a present from my sperm donor. I could not call that man a father, not when he banished my mother for carrying me and refusing to abort.

Oftentimes I felt guilty to have forced her into this life of misery. She always got upset when I said that, though. She said she never regretted having me, that I was the best present a person could have dreamt of. And I tried... I tried so hard to be the child she deserved, I tried to help her by not causing any trouble and not asking for anything. Somehow, I wanted to atone for sins I didn't even commit.

I thought she didn't notice all the sacrifices I had been making, and I didn't think that she was hurting so much to see me do all the things I was doing. But, as she realized she was close to death, she cracked open this big nut of pain. She made me promise to start living, not to be scared, not to drown in my sorrow and misplaced guilt. And I promised her that. To be honest, I would have promised her anything in the world just to ease the worry that was piling on top of her disease.

I let my hand trail over the soft blue fabric of the dress I was going to wear tonight. I had always loved this dress, and my mom wore it seldomly, even though I knew it was one of her favorites. I suspected she kept it in good condition because she always had in mind that I would wear it one day. She was joking about it before she got sick, when we thought I still had a bright future ahead of me. She said she could almost picture me wearing it to my high school graduation. *High school graduation...* Something that seemed so clear in my future, almost written in the stars, but had slipped right through my fingers when we got my mother's diagnosis.

I sighed as I picked up the dress and gently unfolded it on the bed. I sometimes wondered if she could see me from where she was and if she was disappointed with how my life turned out. I didn't get pregnant when I was seventeen as she had, but it was hard to miss all the similarities in our lives. I sometimes regretted dropping out of high school. I had lied to myself, saying it was only for a few months, just to make a little more money to help just a bit more with the hospital bills that were mounting so quickly. There was no paying that back, even if I worked a lifetime. And then she just died, despite all the fight she'd put into it. Despite the most burning desire to stay here with me, she left. Part of me had been grateful, if only for her sake, because seeing the woman she used to be—full of light, life, and laughter—become a shadow of herself was too hard to bear and I could not imagine how hard it must have been for her.

I shook my head again. Maybe opening the suitcase was not the best idea, walking down this memory lane so close to my date with Hoka was crazy. I couldn't allow myself to go down this road because if I did, I wasn't sure when I would see the light again.

I concentrated on the dress, and I was relieved to see those years of being folded in a suitcase did not damage it. I tried it the first time when my mom brought it home. I had been fifteen then, and my body had been more of a child than the one of the woman I was today. I had developed a lot of feminine curves since then, and I wondered if I would even fit in it.

I looked at the time and realized that Hoka would be here in less than forty minutes.

How time flies when you lose yourself in your sorrow.

I rushed to my bathroom, and took the quickest shower in history, shampooing my hair roughly, hoping I would be able to put some order in it. I usually borrowed a hairdryer or a hair straightener from my neighbor across the hall, but she was working tonight so I had to do the best with what I had.

Once I was freshly showered, I walked back into the room in my best pink cotton panties. I picked up the dress from my bed, sliding down the side zipper, and carefully stepped into the silky material. I pulled it up and almost stopped breathing as it felt a bit tight around my hips.

No, please God, don't do this to me, I thought or rather begged a God I wasn't sure even existed.

I held my breath as I pulled a little harder and let out a sigh of relief when the material passed my hips without ripping.

I walked barefoot to the floor-length mirror glued to my entrance door and looked at myself as I slid my arms into the sleeves and pulled the dress up.

I held my breath as I zipped it up. This was the moment of truth. I couldn't help but smile when the zipper cooperated, and I looked back into the mirror. I was the spitting image of my mother, everybody said so. However, today I realized that despite my Ramen noodle diet, I had developed more curves than she had.

The dress made me look beautiful, distinguished, and womanly—all the things I wasn't.

I ran my hand down my sides as it followed the lines of my body like a second skin, stopping just above my knee. The scooped neckline was quite conservative in the front, but when I turned around and craned my neck to look at the back, I saw it opened into a very deep V that ended at the base of my spine.

I nodded in approval. This dress had been the right choice, and I hoped Hoka would agree.

I was actually glad that I didn't give myself too much time to get ready—it prevented me from overthinking everything. He would be here in a few minutes, and if I didn't want to show myself barefoot and without makeup, I couldn't contemplate my choice of outfit any longer.

I brushed my wet hair and pulled it into a bun. I had limited abilities and it was really the only thing I could do. I settled for just a little mascara and some pink lip gloss—again my choices on the matter were rather limited as my makeup case was a plastic soap box containing four discounted items.

Despite my short stature, I settled for a pair of black flats because I was not fully confident with my ankle just yet, and because the heels took away any confidence I had in the simple act of walking.

I looked down at the open suitcase and the burgundy velvet case containing my mother's pearls.

I trailed my fingers over my bare neck, contemplating wearing them. It would add a touch of femininity to this beautiful outfit.

I opened the box and ran my fingers over the smooth, cold, shiny pearls.

Would she want me to wear them? Of course, she would have. She'd want me to have the best of everything.

My phone beeped, and I glanced at the screen to see that Hoka was waiting for me downstairs.

The hesitation was replaced by urgency, and I took the necklace, securing it around my neck, not even taking the time to look at myself in the mirror in case it made me reconsider it all once more.

I had to rush now. I was grateful that he hadn't tried to come up and get me.

I'd been so adamant in my refusal for him to help me up after the accident, way too ashamed to show him where I lived, that he probably remembered. And that made me like him even more somehow, but I was not sure he'd wait much longer.

I texted back quickly as I grabbed the synthetic black shawl, which I'd retrieved from the suitcase to set it on my shoulders, hiding the scandalous dip of the back. Was it a mistake? Was I showing too much? Would he think less of me?

I knew this shawl did not match this dress—it was not nearly as nice or new looking, but it had been either that or my denim jacket.

I stopped at the bottom of the stairs to look at Hoka as I was still hidden from view.

I took a sharp breath at the mere sight of him. How was that possible? How could a man I barely knew caused so many emotions in me?

He was leaning nonchalantly against the passenger side of his car, his hands buried into the pockets of his perfectly tailored black suit, and despite wearing the best outfit I owned, I still felt so out of place, so out of my league.

He was looking up at the building, his eyebrows furrowed, looking so much more like a fierce warrior than a businessman, and I couldn't help but feel like this man could fight the world if he wanted to. Just the look of him both relaxed and fierce made me feel both in danger and safe at the same time. How was that possible?

I took a step closer to the door as my heart skipped a beat, anticipating the moment when his eyes would finally turn toward me.

I pushed the handle down and his head immediately moved to my direction, showing that, even if he seemed lost in thought, he was clearly very aware of his surroundings.

As soon as his eyes met mine, his gaze softened, and a small smile grazed the side of his lips as he took me in before walking toward me with unhurried strides.

My stomach twisted with a wave of eagerness at seeing him. His eyes grew darker and more intense the longer he looked at me, and I couldn't help but blush, knowing that I probably looked like an infatuated schoolgirl.

He stopped just in front of me, much closer than he should have been for being just an acquaintance.

The point of his polished shoes touched the tip of my flats, and he leaned over me, looking down. Between his body heat and the faint dark, smokey and leather scent of his aftershave, I felt like I was being wrapped in his masculine presence like a protective blanket. I didn't feel any fear or apprehension as I craned my neck to look up into his eerie amber eyes.

"Hi," I let out in a raspy whisper and winced internally. Could a simple word carry the extent of your attraction for a person? It seemed that it could.

His grin widened and I had to tighten my shawl as I felt the force of it pierce the center of my chest.

"Violet Murphy..." His deep voice sounded even deeper, more gravelly. "You are absolutely breathtaking," he added before taking a step back, allowing me to breathe again. He extended his arm to me. "Shall we?"

I nodded and rested my hand on his arm as we walked to his luxury SUV, feeling like I'd just walked into one of these regency novels.

"Where are we going?" I asked after he helped me to my seat and he took his place in the driver's seat.

"There's a lovely little restaurant about five minutes from here, actually. Unassuming but the food is to die for." He glanced my way as he started the car. "Is that okay?"

"More than okay," I replied truthfully, feeling a little more relaxed. He was not taking me to a fancy restaurant with five forks and knives I had no idea how to use.

There was nothing fancy around here; at least, not something fancy enough to make a fool out of me.

He had not lied, and almost as soon as we exited my building, he took a narrow one-way street and parked in front of a dimly lit, unassuming restaurant called *Roma*.

"I know it doesn't look like much, but I can assure you, the food is out of this world."

"I'm not worried. Not everything that shines is gold. The contrary is also true."

He stopped as he opened his car door and looked at me as if he was seeing me for the first time. "Yes, I always thought the same."

He came around the car to help me out, and it felt so nice to be treated like I was special. Jake had never done anything like that before. He'd taken me for granted from day one, and I just accepted it.

Hoka rested his hand on the small of my back, and despite the shawl creating a barrier between his skin and mine, I could still feel the trail of fire it left on my skin.

"Mr. Nishimura!" the older man with a heavy Italian accent exclaimed from behind the small wooden bar.

Hoka smiled at him, bowing slightly. "Mr. Beldoni."

"It has been years since you came," the portly man added, rounding the corner and coming to stand in front of us, his cheeks a little ruddy with excitement.

"I know, I'm sorry." He pulled me a little closer to him. "I needed to share this little Italian gem with my friend."

The man turned toward me, his smile widening. "You're the one with the gem, my friend."

Hoka looked at me and the look of dark intimacy in his eyes sent a shiver down my spine. "Yes... indeed, I am."

"Come, come." The man gestured us forward before he started to walk around the tables. "You're lucky to have called. I keep your mother's table. It's the most priced one," he added as he stopped by a booth in the back corner. "How is she doing?"

Hoka nodded as he helped me to my seat, and I felt his fingers run softly down my spine after he helped me remove my shawl, causing my pulse to beat so much harder in both my stomach and between my thighs.

"She's good. She's still home, but she's planning to visit soon," he replied as if he had not touched me at all.

Did I imagine it?

I took a deep, calming breath and looked around the restaurant as the man kept on chatting with Hoka.

The room wasn't big, there were only about fifteen tables, with only a couple occupied. Maybe it was because it was fairly late for dinner.

The ambiance was really soothing, and it felt like I had stepped into an old Italian movie with the dim lights, the checkered tablecloths, and the candles on every table.

"So, what do you think?"

"I like it, it's lovely. No wonder your mother enjoys it."

"Yes, my mother is half-Japanese, half-Italo-American. I think it's part of her heritage."

"Ah yes, it's understandable." Lord knew there was a part of my heritage I was very much trying to kill. "So," I opened the menu, "what do you suggest?"

"Honestly, you're pretty safe with anything on the menu, the food is amazing."

"How come you don't come more often if it's that good?" I looked down blushing, mortified by my forwardness.

He chuckled as I kept my eyes trained on the menu, scanning the choices without really looking.

"I *should* come more often, but I work a lot, too much, really. Most nights I end up getting some takeaway or heating up something my housekeeper cooked before hitting the bed."

I looked up at him again. "It seems very stressful and very lonely."

He gave me a smile that didn't reach his eyes; he looked so sad. "Yes - yes, it is."

We ordered our food—penne arrabiata for me and beef braciello for him, plus a nice bottle of red wine.

"So, anything new with you?" he asked as he poured me a glass of wine.

"Do you mean after the trainwreck you witnessed?" I asked with an amused tone, even if deep down, I was still embarrassed that he met me at my lowest.

"We all have bad days, Violet. I try not to judge anyone during one of theirs."

I gave him a grateful smile as a sort of peace settled between us.

"They called me back, *Sun Valley*."

"Oh." He leaned back on his seat. "When are you going back there?"

I shook my head before taking a sip of wine. I was not an expert, but the fruity taste of this wine was beyond delicious.

"I'm not. It's just..." I sighed. "They just discarded me without a second thought. I can't trust them again."

"But you liked the job, didn't you?"

I nodded warily, unsure where he was going with this. "I did. It definitely beats serving drinks in a strip club where men are quite often under the wrong assumption of what your duties really are."

His nostrils flared and his eyes flashed with something possessive. Was it jealousy?

"What if you came to work for me, then?" he asked with a small shrug.

I let out a startled laugh, not expecting that, but also very sure it had to be a joke. "You don't even know if I'm good at my job, or even what I was doing!"

He shrugged again. "I'm sure you were good at it. I'm a good judge of character and I can see you're very reliable."

Reliable... yep, that would be me.

"And I'm sure you know who I am," he continued, but his voice seemed to contain a certain caution.

I nodded because lying would be stupid. "Yes. I looked you up on Google."

His lips quivered at the corner as I squirmed in my seat. "And what did it say?"

"You're the CEO of a company worth millions."

"Billions," he corrected, humor still floating in his eyes.

"But that's not why I'm here," I rushed. "I don't want you to think I'm having dinner with you because of that. I wanted to see you again, even before I knew who you were. I wanted to see you again as soon as the door to my apartment closed behind me. You're very good-looking and—" I stopped talking, mortified at how much I rambled and all the things I said that I should not have admitted out loud.

I winced and looked at the swing doors leading to the kitchen—willing them, or rather, begging them to open with our food. I needed a distraction like now.

"I'm glad you think I'm attractive. It is reciprocated, in case you couldn't tell."

I started to play with the pearl necklace, not really knowing how to reply. He was just so different from the boyfriends I'd ever had. They were all quite young and immature, most of them just as poor as I was. But Hoka was a full-grown man, sexy and rich.

"That's a lovely necklace," he said gently.

I threw him a grateful look, knowing he only changed the subject for my benefit.

"Ah, yes, thank you." I rubbed it gently, the cool surface appeasing somehow. "It was my mother's, just like this dress actually."

"You were close to your mother?"

The waiter came with our plates, and I was happy to have a few seconds of respite to think about my reply.

"We were. We only had each other in this world you know." I let out a small smile. "It was her and me against the world. She, she passed away when I was sixteen, from cancer, and despite knowing it would happen, despite seeing her fade away, losing her has not been easier."

"No, I don't presume it is. I lost my father three years ago to a heart attack. He was as healthy as an ox and none of us saw it coming. I didn't think I was ready to take over everything, but I was thrown into all of it without warning. Some days I still wonder if I'm able to run his business."

"Yes, I understand. I was with her and then, suddenly, I was alone. I was lucky to have Liam and the club, really. My mom worked there as a dancer, but she'd not been able to for the last year of her life. Liam and his father helped with the bills, and once she was gone, Liam gave me a job. Liam and the girls from the club helped support me. One of them even let me stay at her place for almost a year until I was safe enough from social services to get my own place. I owe him."

Hoka ate a few bites silently. "He's not supportive of your desire for something else?"

I frowned, thinking back to our conversation, which was still not making sense. "Surprisingly, he is."

"Okay, then I don't see the problem."

"I..." I cocked my head to the side. "I want to get to know you, but not as a boss, a rich man, or anything like that. I want to know the man inside, and I think that working for you would prevent me from doing that."

"You really mean that?" he asked with awe. "Okay." He nodded. "What if I helped you get a job somewhere else, but I promise not to get involved and you'll keep it or lose it based on your merits alone. What do you say?"

I wanted something more in life than just being a barmaid but not to the price of our burgeoning relationship. "That would be amazing but I don't like you for what you represent."

He let out a little laugh. "Believe me, I know that. As unbelievable as it is, I believe you and if I'm completely honest, if you agree to the job, it will be much more for my benefit than yours—not to mention for my sanity, too."

I held my fork halfway to my mouth. "Your sanity?"

He grimaced, wrinkling his nose with discomfort, and I found it unbelievably cute. "Yes, I... ah—" He shook his head as if he was trying to find the right words. "I was not exactly happy to see you working at Liam's club, and I was particularly annoyed seeing that man look at you the way he was."

Despite everything, I couldn't help but grin as warmth settled in my chest. I had not been crazy before, he was jealous. I *mattered* to him.

"You're enjoying my dilemma, aren't you?" He narrowed his eyes in a glare, but the playfulness of his voice showed me it was all pretend.

"Maybe a little," I admitted.

"Will you help me, then? Help me not be consumed by jealousy, and save me from having to quit my CEO job to sit at that stupid bar on every shift you do?"

I laughed, getting rid of the last of the tension I felt. The attraction and weird attachment I had felt were definitely reciprocated.

"Oh, I wouldn't want you to lose your job and your sanity because of me. Okay, fine, I'll consider a job, but it needs to be for another company."

"Thank you!" He rested his hand on his chest in mock relief.

I smiled. "Don't mention it."

And we stayed like that for a couple of minutes, just looking at each other with playful smiles on our faces.

This man was already under my skin, and I liked him far too much, too fast. He would soon have all the power; he would so easily become my heaven or my hell. I just had to pray it would be the former.

The rest of the dinner was quite relaxed as we stayed on more neutral subjects, and I asked hundreds of questions about Japan and life there.

We left soon after as Hoka made a promise to the owner that we would return soon, and my stomach flipped with happiness at the mention of 'us.'

We drove back in companionable silence, and I couldn't help but sigh as we stopped in front of the building, and he rounded the car to help me out.

He slowly walked me to my door, as if he too didn't want the evening to end.

I sighed as we reached our destination before turning toward him, knowing that despite my reluctance, it was time to say goodbye.

Hoka stood so close to me, but I was not sure if it was me who closed the distance or if it was him. All I knew was that he felt like a magnet to me.

I startled as he brought his hand up, cradling my jaw as his thumb rubbed my cheekbone softly. "I am trying to be good, but when you look at me like that, with that smile. It's dangerous." he trailed off, leaning down.

He was just too much. Too beautiful, too tall, too large, too close... too dangerous for my heart.

I should have pushed him. I'd just ended a relationship, and I knew this man in front of me could break me in ways Jake never could.

"What is so dangerous? What is there to fear?"

"Me," he replied as his hand slid from my jaw to my neck as his mouth descended on mine.

I stiffened with surprise as his warm lips brushed against mine, once, twice, before pressing more insistently, catching my bottom lip in between his.

He wrapped his free arm around my waist, flushing my body against his hard one. His lips turned more insistent as his hands roamed down my back to grab my hip.

I let out a little gasp as he pulled me closer, and he took that opportunity to deepen the kiss. Sensation exploded in the pit of my stomach as his tongue touched mine.

I couldn't think, couldn't control anything; my lungs expanded unsteadily as his mouth explored mine.

I brought my arms up, wrapped them around Hoka's neck, burying my fingers in his soft hair still secured in a bun.

He let out a growl against my lips before he broke the kiss, letting his lips run softly along the column of my neck as he whispered words in a language I didn't understand.

"Hoka," I moaned as his lips stopped at the most sensitive place in the crook of my neck and he trailed his teeth gently over my tender flesh, licking the most vulnerable spot on my neck.

I was completely drowning in my lust and desire for this man, and for a minute, I forgot that we stood under the unflattering, flickering light of my building entrance. All I wanted was for him to ease the ache I felt low in my belly and between my trembling legs.

He licked back up and stopped as his lips reached the small crevice behind my ear. I felt his smile as he kissed the spot, making me shiver once more.

"God help me, I never intended to corrupt you, but I'm unable to resist you," he whispered, his voice deep with desire. "I have to have you." He caught my earlobe in his mouth, sucking it in.

Have me, then, I thought in a moment of insanity. I was about to say so when the loud metal sound of the main door slamming brought me back to reality.

"There's children in this building," a woman muttered.

"No," I whispered breathlessly, pushing at his chest.

He let go at once and took a couple steps back, his chest rising and falling in a rhythm as erratic as mine, his confused and dazed expression also matching mine.

He had not intended to get carried away like we had. He let his gaze trail to my sore, swollen lips and took a step toward me, his eyes entranced.

He stopped and shook his head as if he was trying to shake away the spell that seemed to have fallen upon us both.

"You should say goodnight and go upstairs now, Violet," he said, his voice tight with unspent desire. "You need to do that now, both for my sanity and your virtue."

"I—"

"Say, 'Goodnight, Hoka,' and turn away now."

He adjusted his position with a wince, and just a glance south showed me that he was just as aroused as I was, but he was offering me an out and I had to take it.

It was much too soon.

"Goodnight, Hoka," I replied and turned quickly, inserting the key into the door, shaking it like a madwoman to open it.

"I'll text you tomorrow," he said, but I didn't risk turning around. I simply nodded and rushed down the corridor.

"Goodnight, *Sourumeito*." Was the last thing I heard before the door slammed shut behind me.

Hoka Nishimura had branded me with that kiss, and I was both elated and terrified to discover what would come next for us.

CHAPTER 7

Violet

Hoka had kept his word, and I had woken up the next day with a text giving me an address and the name of a person who would be waiting the next day at nine a.m. to interview me.

I might have been reading too much into it, but the text had been very clinical, distant—not something I would have expected from someone who kissed me in a way I'd never been kissed before, someone who admitted a certain level of attraction and jealousy.

Maybe I had read too much into everything, because no matter all the shit I'd experienced in my life, I was still quite new at the relationship aspect of things and my track record was far from impressive.

I went through the day wishing for another text from Hoka, but none came, and the later it got, the more deflated I became about our evening together.

Perhaps that kiss had not been as groundbreaking for him as it had been for me. It was possible he didn't think the date went that well, or maybe I had done something that displeased him.

I rested my fingers on my lips. Was I a bad kisser? I had not kissed that many men in my life before him, but I never heard a complaint.

Except for your ex cheating on you... the little voice taunted.

Well, maybe it was for the best. I wouldn't even know how to handle a man like him. He was too mature, too big, too... He made me feel too much, and feelings were dangerous. My mother had made so many mistakes in the name of love when she was young—mistakes that probably never bothered the man who broke her, but mistakes that had followed her in all aspects of her life up to her last breath.

"Yes, it's for the best," I repeated to myself and decided to put the whole issue behind me.

Despite my flimsy resolve that not getting involved with Hoka was for the best, I couldn't help the elation I felt when I opened my door the next morning to leave for the interview and found a gigantic bunch of red camellias in front of my door.

I couldn't stop the wide grin from spreading on my face as I picked up the flowers and set them on my counter.

I grabbed the golden card attached to it and read it, warmth flooding my chest as I read the sweet words I never expected him to write.

Time is priceless, and tomorrow is not guaranteed. I wish so many tomorrows with you. May my wish be granted. H

I flushed with pleasure as I rested the card against the beautiful vase and took a photo, somehow feeling as if I was allowed to text him now.

Thank you for the flowers and lovely note. It means a lot. I hope to see you soon. V

My mood remained at an all-time high, and my silly grin didn't leave my face during the two bus rides it took to the offices of *Mercury Pharma* in the heart of downtown.

Once I got there, things kept on going well when I was brought into a glass meeting room to meet the company marketing director, Ms. Michaela Chase, who turned out to be a young woman full of enthusiasm and ideas—such a contrast with Mr. Reynolds.

She opened her file and looked at the first page before looking back at me. "I hope you don't mind, but Pam from *Sun Valley* said you left their company, but she really thought you would be a great addition for us."

I smiled and nodded, more than grateful to Hoka to have managed to pull something like that with *Sun Valley*. I didn't want that woman to know I'd obtained this interview because of a favor. She was the self-made type, and even if we'd just met, I didn't want her to have a prejudiced opinion about me.

"I won't ask you why you left," she added, "but I presume it was because of Mr. Reynolds." She winced. "Unfortunately, we know what old pervy Reynolds is all about."

I didn't comment, but simply shrugged. I was not here to talk about what had transpired in my previous work environment.

"I just don't think that real estate was for me." I forced a relaxed smile. "I just thought it would be best to try something else."

She let out a little laugh. "How diplomatic of you! Fine, fine, we won't continue on the subject," she added with a little shake of her head, her knowing smile still on her face.

"So anyway," she looked back at the file in front of her, "I can see from the evaluation reports that you have been nothing but excellent during your six months training. I know Pam and the marketing team at *Sun Valley* very well, and they are not the type to give such stellar reviews for anyone less than excellent." She closed the file and rested her hands on top of it. "Which tells me that you can definitely do the job, but now I need to know if you want the job? What are your aspirations?"

"Want the job? Yes, of course!" I didn't have to fake my enthusiasm, as I was sure I would learn so much working with her. "Due to personal circumstances, I had to leave school early, but it's something that always felt wrong. I am eager to learn, and I believe that you would be the perfect mentor for me. I looked at some of the campaigns you did for the company last night, and I was quite impressed. So yes, I want the job, I want to learn. And as for my aspirations?" I shrugged. "Maybe I could become like you one day."

"Oh." She laughed. "I've never been seen as a role model before. It's nice, but it does make me feel like I'm fifty-five."

I looked down at my hands folded on my lap. Maybe I'd said too much.

"I like that though", she added, probably seeing my discomfort. "I believe you have a lot to bring to the company. The degree only gets you so far; we need fresh ideas and fresh minds. We need the point of view of people that are a bit different from the mass already here. Not everyone can be a Harvard graduate, am I right?"

"I'm not even a high school graduate," I said that with derisive humor, although it felt like a true weakness for me.

She shook her head. "A lot of successful people made themselves. Believe it or not, a third of our senior executives didn't go to college. We believe that life education is just as important as college."

I looked at her, trying to find any sign of deceit. Was she for real? Did people really think like that?

She reached for the folded piece of paper beside my file and slid it toward me. "This is our offer. I believe it is quite generous, but based on the evaluations in your file, I think it's justified."

I unfolded the page and read the contractual terms, trying to keep my face smooth despite the shock at seeing the numbers in front of me. They were offering me sixty thousand dollars per year, with two full weeks of paid holiday. I was going to be able to leave my crappy apartment and rent something here downtown. My life was truly about to change, however I couldn't help but think that Hoka had something to do with it. Did he play a part in that offer? I knew it shouldn't matter. I knew I should just take it and thank her, but I had to know. I would have to ask him, no matter the consequences.

But for now, all I could do was nod, as I was too speechless to say anything.

She clapped her hands. "Does that mean you accept?"

I rested my hand on the piece of paper, almost afraid that she would take it back, saying it was a mistake despite my name being printed on it. "Yes, of course! I don't know how to thank you."

"Excellent! You don't have to thank me. Your work will be thanks enough." She looked at her watch. "I have another meeting starting in fifteen minutes, and I know it's very short notice, but I was wondering if you could start tomorrow? Would nine a.m. work?"

I nodded eagerly. "Yes, nine is perfect! Thank you, thank you again, for everything."

She stood. "It's a pleasure, really. Tomorrow morning, we'll go through your contract and all the tedious HR paperwork. But for now, just go home, relax, have a glass of wine, and be ready to start this exciting journey, which I think will be very beneficial for both of us." She looked behind me and gestured to someone.

I turned my head just in time to see an older redhead woman stand from behind her desk and rush toward the meeting room.

"Alice," Ms. Chase said when the woman opened the glass door. "Let me introduce you to our new recruit, Violet." She turned toward me with a smile. "Violet, this is my secretary and one of the admin assistants for the marketing department, Alice." She turned back to Alice and winked at her. "We are all very grateful to have Alice on our team. She is a gem."

Alice rolled her eyes, but I could tell the praise touched her. "You're just saying that because I manage to get all the best office supplies as soon as they arrive."

Ms. Chase laughed.

Alice turned toward me. "It is really nice to meet you, Violet. Welcome to the team."

"I wanted you to organize a taxi home for Violet. I think she deserves it after such a great interview."

Her phone vibrated on the table, and she looked at it with exasperation. "Ah, I'm really sorry, but I have to go now. I'll see you tomorrow, Violet."

I followed Alice to the main reception downstairs as I listened to her give me some tips about the best toilets to use and the best sandwiches to order from the delivery cart. She seemed like a lovely lady, and so far everything seemed right. Maybe a little *too* right.

Don't start. For once in your life, just enjoy the good without thinking that something bad is going to hit you.

I took the taxi home and honestly felt grateful for this little gift. A ride that should have taken me over fifty minutes took only twenty.

I was pondering if I should text Hoka as I climbed the stairs to my apartment, wondering if I should tell him how the interview went. Or maybe he already knew? Would I look needy if I texted him?

I let out a little sigh of frustration. I was really out of my depth with this man.

However, I didn't have to wonder for too long as he was standing beside my door, seemingly as surprised to see me as I was to see him.

I arched an eyebrow. Why would he be surprised to see me? He was in front of *my* apartment. Clearly, I could not read him.

"Violet," he whispered.

I took a tentative step toward him but stopped when a man appeared beside his left shoulder, like a mirage. *Where did he come from?*

Hoka glanced at his side and smiled.

I didn't know him well yet, but I knew this smile was as fake as they came.

"What are you doing here? Who's your friend?" I asked, trying to sound more chilled than I felt as I played with the keys in my hand.

He shrugged. "I just came to see how the interview went and ask you out to dinner again. What do you say? Saturday night? Same place?"

I nodded absentmindedly, keeping my eyes on the man standing beside him. He was not as tall as Hoka, but to be honest, who was? He was also leaner than him, but the look on his face showed me he was lethal. He was also dressed differently than Hoka, who I had only seen in perfectly tailored suits that oozed money and luxury. This man was dressed in a pair of jeans with a black thermal shirt pulled up on his arms, revealing two full sleeves of colorful tattoos. And where Hoka had his hair up in a tight bun, this man's hair flowed to his shoulders. I couldn't help but wonder if Hoka's hair was just as long.

Hoka gestured to the man beside him. "Ah, yes, the introductions. Violet, this is Jiro, my head of security. I was on my way to the airport, but I asked him to make a quick stop here just to see how everything went." Hoka rolled his eyes. "However, he was not too keen on letting me come up alone. I guess he's not a fan of the area."

"Nobody is," Jiro mumbled dismissively, throwing a reproachful look at Hoka.

I was a little taken aback by the cold edge in his voice. It almost felt like I had to apologize for something I had obviously not done. I'd just met the man.

Was I offending him just by being me?

I snorted. "Understatement of the year!" I joked, but I realized I failed miserably when his face remained a cool mask of contempt. *Okay, then, he had a personal problem.*

Finally, Hoka's full sentence computed in my brain. "Airport? You're leaving?" I wasn't sure why I felt this disappointment. I'd barely seen the man, yet knowing he would be away bothered me.

His face softened and he gave me a half smile, probably reading my disappointment. How aggravating was it that the man could read me so well, while I couldn't see anything on him.

"It's just for a couple of days. I have some business to attend to in Seattle. I'll be back before our date on Saturday."

Date. I had to use all my self-control not to squeal like a silly teenager.

"I... Yeah..." Did my face look as red as it felt? Based on Hoka's full grin and Jiro's scowl, I was pretty sure it was.

"So, how did it go? The interview?" Jiro asked, his tone somewhat mocking. "That's why we're here, isn't it?"

Here it was again, the little bite of sarcasm that was meant to offend. I just wasn't sure if it was directed at me or Hoka.

I frowned again, both confused and unnerved by his obvious dislike. I wasn't sure what this man had against me, but it was not pleasant.

I decided to ignore him; it wasn't like I was going to see him again, anyway. I concentrated on Hoka instead. "It went really well. I really liked Michaela Chase. It's looking very positive. I'm starting tomorrow. Thanks again for your help."

He waved his hand dismissively. "Don't mention it, I didn't have to do much. Your file was stellar, it was just a question of time."

Jiro cleared his throat, showing he was done with the conversation.

I didn't know much about being head of security, but I thought that man took a lot of liberties with his boss.

"I better go now. I'm sure you have a lot to do to get ready for tomorrow. And I can't really miss my plane, can I?"

I shook my head. "No, I don't think you can. The plane will wait for no one."

Hoka smiled in a way that seemed to say that what I just said was funny. "I'll see you on Saturday, sweet Violet."

As he passed me, his hand gently brushed against mine too slowly and too precisely to be accidental. That simple, innocent touch affected me so deeply, much more than anything I had ever experienced—except for our kiss, which altered the very essence of me.

Jiro gave me a sharp nod before following Hoka down the stairs.

I turned to my door before turning toward the stairs again. His visit was unsettling and so random. How did he even know I would be coming home now? How did he even get in the building?

I sighed, sliding my key in the lock, and walking back inside my shoebox of an apartment.

The home here wouldn't be mine for much longer. I had so many things to think about before tomorrow, and I had to call Liam, hoping he still meant what he'd told me in his office.

Whatever question I had about Hoka and his visit would have to wait. I could ask him on Saturday night during our date.

Our date... and here I was again, grinning like an idiot.

God help me.

I knew things couldn't stay perfect forever.

I was proven right the next day when I found Jake leaning against his car as I exited the bus after my first day of work.

What the hell was he doing here? Everything had happened almost ten days ago. Why was he coming now? I had thought, much to my relief, that he had given up, and I wouldn't have to face this awkward confrontation.

I looked down, pretending I hadn't seen him, trying to hurry. Maybe if I was lucky—

"Violet!" he shouted as I passed him.

Yeah, I was not *that* lucky. "I've got nothing to say to you, Jake," I said sternly as I kept on walking.

"Just give me five goddamned minutes, Violet. You owe me that much!"

That stopped me right in my tracks. I turned around slowly, looking at him with uncertainty. "I *owe* you? I? Me? The... the cheat*ee*?" Was it even a word? I didn't care enough to figure that one out.

"Your boyfriend made my life a living hell." He snorted, showing me that the passenger side door of his car was of a different color from the rest of it. "I wanted to come before but my car got smashed, then somebody broke into my house and leaked all my projects online, basically ruining over six months of work."

"I've got nothing to do with this!" I replied defensively. "You know I know nothing about computers. Who mocked me because of it?" *Flaming asshole*!

"Maybe not you, but your boyfriend?" He scowled, baring his teeth with anger. "He is on his little personal vendetta."

I waved my hand dismissively. "I don't care what you say, what you think, or even what you want. I have nothing to do with anything, and I don't have a clue what you're talking about." I took a step back, putting my hand in my pocket and unclipping the top of my pepper spray. "You can go to the police and give them my name. I have nothing to fear! You probably have wronged so many people. You're barking up the wrong tree, Jake. You're not worth the effort." I took another step back. "But I can pretend to be sorry for you if you want. Anything as long as you stay away from me, that's all that matters. Have a nice life, Jake." I turned around, ready to leave him behind where he belonged.

"You know what's funny?" he asked as I reached the door, his voice so close that I knew he had followed me down the path.

I sighed in frustration, praying for anything, even a good earthquake, to happen. Anything to distract him and allow me to get in and get rid of him. "If I ask you what's funny? Will you leave me be?"

"The funny thing is that you never thought I was good enough for you," he replied, ignoring my question.

"*I* never thought you were good enough for *me*? *You* were the one always telling me how amazing you were!

How lucky I was that you wanted to be with me. Making it *oh* so clear that *I* was beneath *you*." I pointed at him, not able to rein the outrage I felt at his accusation. He had such a way of spinning the whole situation to make himself the victim.

Shit, how could I have been so blind?

I took a deep breath, trying to calm myself. I would not give him the satisfaction of making me lose control. "But you know what? You *weren't* good enough for me, because only a small man cheats on his woman."

"I cheated for *you*! Not to pressure you into sex!"

I laughed, part in amusement, part in disbelief. "Are you saying you cheated on me for... *me*?" This was now taking the most ridiculous turn, and I had to see it through. "Ah, well, that changes everything! Thank you so much for riding and orgasming into my colleague for me." I rested my hand on my chest. "It means *so* much to me."

He threw me a dark look, pursing his lips in disdain. "I thought you didn't spread your legs because you had some values, and I respected you for that. But I realized that you just held on to your virginity for a man who could pay for it, no matter the amount of blood he has on his hands."

Hoka's face flashed in my mind, but I shook it off.

"You're crazy; you're inventing things."

"Please." He snorted. "You've been seen at the club, you know. I didn't think you would stoop so low for money." He shook his head. "Getting involved with the mafia, Violet, really?"

I laughed. Now I was sure he was making stuff up. "Mafia?" I nodded. "Sure, right..."

"Don't pretend you don't know. I'm not that stupid. Nobody goes on a date with a yakuza boss without knowing it. And a man like *him* won't romance a woman like *you* without getting something in return. You were so quick to give him what you denied me for so long."

I tensed. There was no sign of deception, no sign of doubt. He truly believed that.

"Who said that to you?"

"So, you don't deny it?"

"I want to know who lied to you."

He laughed, shaking his head like I was ridiculous. "When the head of the yakuza goes to a club, people see and people talk... And when one asks my girlfriend—"

"Ex-girlfriend," I corrected him.

Jake glowered darky at me as if I was the one in the wrong. "When my *girlfriend* accepts to go out with another man, I'm informed."

"If only people showed the same loyalty to me and informed me that my *ex*-boyfriend was cheating on me."

I flickered my hand toward his car. "I don't care what people think they know or not about my life or who I'm affiliated with. I'm not committed to you anymore, and lord knows you've never been committed to me." I raised my hand to stop him from denying it, since it wouldn't change a thing. "I'm allowed to see whoever I want. *Mafia* or not." That sounded so ridiculous.

"You're not who I thought you were. How can you even allow him" his mouth tipped don't in disgust, "to *touch* you with all the horrible things he committed?"

"I am clearly not bothered, am I?" I asked, playing along and crossing my arms on my chest, eyeing him challengingly. I was ready to admit anything right now just for him to turn around and disappear from my life forever. "And if you know all about the new man in my life, I would strongly advise you to stay away, understood?"

This time he was the one taking a step back, and that made me happier than it should have.

"Spreading your legs for a murderer..." He shook his head. "You're nothing but a slut!" he spat with so much hate it was hard for me not to take another step back.

"Maybe, but I'm *his* slut," I taunted him. "Now go." I grabbed my phone from my jacket pocket and extended it in front of me like a weapon, hoping he would not notice the trembling of my hand. "Go, or I'll call him right now, and you'll have to deal with the consequences."

Jake's eyes narrowed into slits, obviously wondering if I was bluffing or not.

I was not sure what I would actually do if he challenged me, but suddenly, I saw his shoulders sag and I knew he was giving up.

He threw his hand up in surrender. "You're not worth it. He'll break you anyway, and then I'll be the one laughing. Good luck with him."

I didn't wait any longer outside in case he changed his mind and came back for round two. I opened the main door as fast as I could before taking the stairs two at the time and only took a breath once I was locked inside my apartment.

I rested my back against the door, waiting for my heart to calm and my breathing to turn regular as I replayed his words in my mind.

Now that I didn't have to play a part and pretend, I could really think about what he said. As much as I hated it, it made sense. Liam's reaction to him, the people at the doctor's office bending over backward for him. When I thought about it, it was not only deference I saw on their faces, there was a little fear, too.

"Oh god!" I moaned, sliding down the door to sit on the floor. What if it was true? What if Hoka was a criminal? I couldn't do that! I couldn't... They said that history had a way of repeating itself, but that would be eerie.

I couldn't go on like before; now there was a possibility, now the doubt was there, but I was too scared to ask.

I was scared to find out it was true, but even more scared that it wouldn't make a difference in how I felt.

Could I still be me if it was true? Should I still want to be with him? I needed time.

I grabbed my phone. **Sorry Saturday won't work, maybe some other time.**

Yes, Violet Murphy, you're a coward.

CHAPTER 8

Hoka

How is the job?
Dots appear and disappear a few times. I frowned, not liking what it meant. She saw my message, and her hesitation to reply after she canceled our dinner on Saturday? It didn't predict anything good.

I rubbed my forefinger against my lips, remembering our kiss. Maybe I should not have kissed her, maybe I misread her, but she kissed me back with an eagerness I'd never experienced before. I'd not planned to kiss her, and then I thought that just one quick kiss would be enough to satisfy the roaring beast inside me.

I had not been ready for the effect touching her lips would have on me. What had started as a chaste kiss turned into an inferno of passion and lust. All I had wanted was to put her on my shoulder, take her back home and make love to her for days.

Walking away from her that night had been the hardest thing I could have done, but I had walked away, as much for my sake as hers. She had unsettled me so deeply. I never thought that a kiss could alter you in such a way, yet it did.

I had to keep my distance, at least for a while. Just to make sure it was not just pure lust and desire. I needed to make sure it was what I had suspected from the start...

Violet was my *ikigai*.

Then the flowers came; the flowers were not mine, and it had changed everything. My resolution to stay away vanished when she sent me that photo. They were not just any flowers, but red camellias. She thought they were beautiful, but I knew the hidden message behind them.

Camellias meant noble death within the yakuza community. Even the card, which looked like a sweet message— a little *too* sweet—was a threat. They were trying to tell me my days with her were numbered.

I had no choice then, no matter how much I wanted to keep her my secret. It was out now, someone knew. Someone obviously understood better than I did what she could mean to me. I came to the only decision I could make; I had to involve Jiro, no matter the amount of shit he would give me for this.

I did something I wasn't proud of. I had Jiro break into her apartment—or what she called an apartment—and had him put cameras there.

I had not expected her to come back so early, but fortunately, Jiro was good at what he did. He snuck out of her apartment without her noticing, despite only being a few feet away.

I didn't have to invite her for dinner, and truthfully, I shouldn't have. But my heart, my head, and even my dick had minds of their own where she was concerned. I asked her out before I could even convince myself it was a stupid idea. And when she agreed, it made me far happier than it should have. I felt like a teenager all over again.

Now here I was, in a gloomy meeting room, in rainy Seattle, and even in the heart of difficult negotiations, she was in the back of my mind. I had thought—no, thought wasn't the right word—I had *hoped* it was the same for her, but I wasn't so sure anymore. It felt like she was running away, and it caused a weight very akin to anxiety to form in my stomach. Anxiety was also quite an unfamiliar emotion—at least, since I reached adulthood. I had no time to be anxious, and I never cared much about other people's opinion of me, but again, Violet Murphy had changed that. I couldn't help but imagine a plethora of scenarios as to why she was now ignoring me. They ranged from the simple, she was scared of her feelings, which I could deal with, to the worst end of the scale - she knew who I really was.

I sighed, running my hands over my face. If I had been a good man, I would have left it that way, but I wasn't a good man, and I had only one thing in my mind...

Chase her.

I could lie to myself, pretend it was for her safety because the flowers she received were a clear threat—a message directed at me. But she didn't know that, only Jiro and I did, and this was unforgivable. Nobody was allowed to touch her, nobody other than *me*.

"We need to leave," I told Jiro as soon as he walked into the room with two cups of coffee.

He looked around the empty meeting room, visibly taken aback by my request. "What do you mean, we *need* to leave? The meeting has not even started yet." He looked down at his watch. "The investors will be here in fifteen minutes."

I looked back at my phone on the shiny black conference table—and the screen that remained stubbornly empty of new texts—and tapped my fingers rhythmically beside it.

Jiro sighed, understanding where my mind was. "She's fine," he said coldly. "You made me do everything I'm against, just to make sure she's safe."

I snorted with a shake of my head. "You've done much worse."

He put my cup at the end of the table and slid it toward me.

"I did," he agreed before taking a sip of his drink. "But to people who deserved it, people who knew what they were stepping into. That girl has no clue who she's getting involved with."

"She's not answering," I replied lamely.

"As she should. One of you has to be smart. Somehow, I expected it to be you."

He raised his hands when I threw him my darkest glare, the one that usually screamed murder.

"You can't seriously be considering a relationship with that woman."

"Why not?" I challenged, turning my chair toward him to give him my full attention. "You seem to forget sometimes that I'm a thirty-three-year-old man who's at the top of the food chain. No one has the authority or power to stop me from doing what I fucking want. *No one.*" I pressed leaning forward, leaving my last thought unspoken. *'Especially not you.'*

He gave me his annoying 'know-it-all' look as if he was not a former classmate and an upperclassman, just like I was. He was acting like one of these stupid *Sōhei*. Maybe I needed to remind him he was not a monk but a killer, just like I was.

"You lied to me. You said she was nothing. You've never lied to me before."

He said it in an even tone, but the rigidity of his posture and the tensed line around his eyes showed that it ran deeper than that. Jiro and I had been friends since childhood; we had our own honor code on top of the yakuza code, and one was to never lie to each other.

"This was not a lie I meant for you, it was—" I shook my head, grabbing the cup and taking a sip of the bitter coffee. How could I make him understand when I didn't really understand myself? It was all based on my mother's bedtime stories.

"What happened to Aiya?"

Aiya's name got me out of my thoughts. "What about her?"

"You wanted to marry her not so long ago. She's perfect for you, she'd be a perfect queen."

And that was the problem, wasn't it? She was perfect for the role I played, perfect for the man I had to become, but Violet... Violet was perfect for the essence of me; she was the echo of my soul.

"Aiya's the least of my concerns."

"She will not be when her and her father find out about your little gaijin."

I had no doubt that would be a problem. I just needed to figure out if I wanted to face them all, but seeing how unsettled Jiro became just by the lack of a response, I wasn't sure I had the choice.

"I didn't take you for a snob, Jiro. I remember when it was you going after a *gaijin*."

I saw the fury and sorrow flash on his face, and I knew it was a cheap shot to bring up Anna—especially since I never did before. I regretted it almost immediately.

"Violet Murphy is fine," he replied, his tone much colder than before. "I checked the cameras this morning, as well as her office surveillance. If she's not replying to you, it's not under duress."

I glowered down at the phone. He didn't understand that knowing she was safe was not enough to ease my concern.

The phone in the middle of the conference room beeped and the nasal voice of the receptionist announced the arrival of the investors. Despite my desire to leave, I was grateful to end this conversation because no matter what Jiro would say, my decision was already made.

I pressed the com button. "You can show them in, I'm ready." I turned to Jiro. "I'm leaving Seattle after this meeting. Arrange the plane or don't, I don't care, but I'm not staying."

"You still have two other meetings."

I shrugged. "Deal with that too, or don't for all I care. I'm leaving and that's that."

"Hoka—"

I raised my head and jutted my chin toward him in challenge. "This is an order, wakagashira," I replied coldly, treating him like I treated the other lieutenants instead of treating him like the trusted best friend and advisor he was.

His nostrils flared with anger, but he bowed slightly. "Very well, Oyabun, this will be done," he added before exiting the room stiffly.

It was the first time I acted so irrational, and it made sense that it was concerning him. Hell, it was concerning *me,* but all I could think about was Violet and the potential reasons for her silence.

"I'm sorry, I shouldn't have talked about Anna," I told Jiro as we both sat on my private jet, ready to go home.

I was more rational now, knowing that in less than two hours I was going to be in the same city as Violet and be able to fix whatever had caused her silence. But because of this, I also realized all the mistakes I'd made with Jiro.

"No, you shouldn't have." He confirmed and looked out his window as if the wet Seattle tarmac was the most interesting view in the world.

I sighed. His voice was still as frosty as it has been when I mentioned her. I deserved it, and I knew that if I wanted to thaw him, even a little, I had to open up—even if it showed the extent of my weakness.

"I don't want to *like* her, Jiro. I don't want to *desire* her. It's complicating my life in so many ways." I leaned my head against the seat, but kept my head turned in his direction. "My life is already complicated, I know that. But it feels like I was just going through the motions. I was not living, Ji, not at all. I was rushing that day; I was late for the Chinese, I'd just spent yet another few hours fixing what my uncle was too stubborn to fix, and then she appeared out of nowhere. I exited the car so exasperated, I wanted to tell her off—I had all the words ready, and let me tell you, none were complimentary." I let out a humorless laugh. "I crouched and then she opened her eyes, and I felt it." I closed my eyes, just for a second, as the plane sped up. I could feel it, as if it was happening all over again—the band that tightened around my heart as her deep blue eyes looked at me. "I was wearing dark sunglasses, so I knew she couldn't see anything, yet I felt like she was turning me inside out and saw deep into my soul." I opened my eyes again as the plane took off and saw that Jiro had turned toward me, looking at me from across the aisle, his eyes and face not revealing a thing. "It felt like a vice tightening my lungs and the warmth that spread right there." I tapped at the center of my chest. "It was almost uncomfortable. It's destiny."

He shook his head slightly, but some of his anger had faded. "You're stronger than this. Destiny is not immutable. She's your destiny? Fine. But are you hers? Does she deserve this life?"

It was my turn to be silent. What could I tell him? I had no answer to his questions. All I knew was that I was acting on feelings and impulses. I had no idea how any of this would turn out.

"You mentioned Anna." His voice faltered on her name and despite everything happening almost fifteen years ago, there was still deep pain on his face just by speaking her name. "Learn from my mistakes."

How could I *not* think about her when considering a relationship with Violet? This story had been a huge tragedy.

"It's different this time, Ji. We're older; we know better."

The look he gave me showed just how much he doubted that.

"My father married for love, and he never regretted choosing my mother, despite all the issues it caused him." I insisted.

"Your mother was half-Japanese, raised in Japan, and she knew all about us and our history. This is not the same, and you know it." He sighed. "And you are not your father, Hoka."

It was my turn to turn my head and look out the window. I knew I was not my father, who was never questioned, or doubted.

"I'm not here to tell you what to do or not to do. It's not my place, which you've cleary reminded me of."

I winced, pleased he could not see my face. I'd been an ass.

"But you're not fair to her," he added.

I turned my head sharply, ready to give him a piece of my mind. Who was he to talk about what was fair or not when he didn't even know her and disliked her on sight?

The look on his face stopped me from saying anything. There was no judgment or disapproval there, only huge concerns.

"If you want to have anything with her, no matter how stupid it is in my opinion, you need to tell her everything. She needs to get involved with all the cards in hand. She's about to step into the hornets' nest, and she needs to know exactly what she's risking."

I ran my hands over my face warily. I knew he was right, but that certainly complicated things, especially if she refused me. I wasn't sure I could let her go, because once she knew everything, she would become a liability.

"If I tell her, it changes everything."

"If she's the one then it won't matter, now will it?"

Was he baiting me? Trying my resolve?

I looked away again, my lack of argument was quite troublesome and uncommon.

I spent the rest of the flight going over all the possibilities in my head. Jiro had, infuriatingly, shook my confidence. It was all so insane, something right out of my mother's folklore stories, something you told a little girl to allow her to dream that life won't be as awful as it would be.

But this wasn't folklore anymore, not for me, and that was just shitty because, despite the fact I knew what she meant to me, there was no way to know what I meant to her.

The passion was there—I felt it in her kiss—but it might have been nothing more than pure attraction.

When the plane landed, I almost thought it was too early. I was undecided now. At first, I had planned to just take the car and go to the office she was working at and wait until she finished her day to talk to her. I planned to see what was wrong and how I could fix it, but now I wasn't sure if I should.

As much as I hated it, Jiro was right. She was still free, and if I kept on going, I would steal some of her freedom without her consent.

"So, where to?" Jiro asked as the hostess opened the door and I knew what he meant. *What have you decided?*

I stood, adjusting my jacket, about to tell him that we'd go home, buying Violet a reprieve, but my phone beeped with a message.

I glanced at the screen and frowned at the video link. I clicked the link and my pace to the door faltered. My breath caught in my throat as a cold sweat formed on the back of my neck.

It was Violet from behind, walking to an elevator, oblivious to the person filming her. Based on the angle of the screen, that person was tall and hiding behind one of the concrete pillars.

Think she'll exit this way too? I'll be waiting. Tick Tock... Tick Tock...

I looked at my watch before glancing back at Jiro, who already seemed on high alert—probably seeing the look of panic on my face.

The choice had been made for me. I had to get to her now and keep her safe, even if it meant taking her into my world.

CHAPTER 9

Violet

I looked down at the photos on the conference table, trying to select the three I would shortlist for Ms. Chase's final pick.

I chewed on my bottom lip as I saw the screen of my phone light up on my desk from the other side of the glass wall.

I was an absolute coward, and after everything Hoka did for me, it felt especially wrong to take a step back.

I was confused about everything—how he made me feel, who he could potentially be, and how, as terrifying as it may be, I may not care that much.

Could you really get involved with a criminal? A murderer? A few weeks ago, I would have laughed and said no chance in hell. But now? I just wasn't sure anymore.

"Ms. Murphy?"

I blinked a few times and looked dumbfounded at Michaela Chase, somehow surprised that she was calling me by my last name instead of Violet as usual.

Fortunately, she was not looking at me, but at the phone on the conference table.

"Yes?"

"Could you please come down to HR? It seems you've been given the wrong forms for healthcare, and we need you to update them."

I looked up at Ms. Chase, who nodded her approval.

"Please take your bag, too," the HR person added. "It seems we don't have a copy of your ID and social security card."

I frowned. I'd given them all that the day I started.

The phone beeped, announcing the end of the call.

Ms. Chase rolled her eyes. "I swear, HR..." she muttered. "It really takes a special kind of person to do that job." Her mouth tipped down, showing she didn't mean that as a compliment.

"I won't be long," I said as I stood.

She sighed. "Oh, how sweet and naive of you to believe that. You'll be *forever*. Once you're down there, there's no telling when you'll find someone efficient." She looked down at the table and at the photos I had picked. "You did everything I needed from you anyway, the rest was just for experience. Don't stress yourself up."

I nodded and walked to my desk, annoyed at missing something new. However, this annoyance quickly gave way to guilt when I noticed five missed calls from Hoka, and the text sent twenty minutes ago, *'Please answer, it's urgent.'* I had not meant to ghost him—I had only meant to put some distance between us for a few days to try and let the attraction fade so I could think more clearly and assess all the red flags.

I grabbed my bag and decided to call him as I took the stairs down to HR. It was two floors down, and it would give me the perfect excuse to end the call before I said something stupid and come back on my decision to cancel for Saturday.

I dialed his number as soon as I passed the metal door to the back staircase.

"Violet," he muttered with a relieved huff.

Once again, the guilt gnawed at me. I didn't like the idea of having caused him, or anyone, any worry.

"I'm sorry," I said quickly as I hurried down the stairs. "I was busy, and I missed your calls." As far as excuses went, it was not the worst. I stopped in the corridor between the two floors and paced. "You seem worried. What's happening?"

"I'm not sure," I could hear some women's voices in the background.

I frowned, not liking the idea of him with other women. I was not being fair; I knew Hoka hadn't made any promises. Hell, I was the one who took a few steps back, yet the irrational jealousy was eating me up inside.

"Where are you?" I asked, resuming my walk down the stairs. "What's so urgent?" I now doubted that the urgency had been legitimate. If he had really been worried about something, he would have told me straight away.

"I," he sighed. "I didn't expect you to call me back," he said with a bite of defensiveness in his voice that I could not understand.

I rested my hand on the cool metal door handle leading to the HR office. It was time to end this conversation. "I'm not sure I understand. You wanted to speak to me. You shouldn't be that surprised."

It was my turn to sigh. HR was expecting me and this trip down already took much longer than it should have in any circumstances.

"Listen, I'm at work. I'll call you back later when I get out, and we can talk then."

"Violet, listen—"

I was already in the process of ending the call, and I didn't hear the rest of his sentence. I opened the door and came face to face with the man himself.

I took a quick step back in surprise. How was he here? He was supposed to be in Seattle until tomorrow. I shook my head. Did I conjure him? Was that even a thing?

He extended a hand toward me. "I can explain," he said quickly. "You were not picking up, and I was worried."

Once the initial shock passed, I slid around him toward the HR office. Jiro, his security guy, was standing in the middle of the room, his stoic face well in place. The staff was going on with their jobs like nothing was happening, like these two scary tattooed men were not here.

I looked to my right and saw the woman who called me speaking with a candidate in her office, going through paperwork like she did with me on my first day. She was obviously in the middle of an interview and didn't want to talk to me.

I looked back at Hoka, my eyes narrowing with both suspicion and annoyance. "You did that!" I pointed at him accusingly. "You can't do that!" I added, not even caring I was causing a scene.

Hoka threw a quick look at Jiro, who raised an eyebrow with a half-smile that seemed to say 'I told you.'

"I understand," he replied with a pacifying tone that annoyed me even more. "I would not have done that if it was not urgent."

I stomped my sandal-clad foot on the ugly green carpet like a tempestuous child, my annoyance and anger getting the best of me.

"I don't see what could be urgent enough to mess up my chance of a fantastic career."

His jaw muscles jumped as he was growing irritated as well. "Your life," he spat before showing me his phone and a video of me somebody must have taken this morning without me noticing. The words at the top made my heart stop and my lungs constrict painfully in my chest.

I looked up at his face with wide eyes, not only irritated but terrified. "Why? Why threaten me? I haven't done anything."

He sighed, running a weary hand over his face. "That one's on me," he admitted. "Somebody noticed I cared, and that's worth the money."

I was too worried and scared about the barely veiled threat to really comprehend what he'd just said, what he'd just admitted. I shook my head. "They want me for ransom? Because you are a billionaire?"

Jiro snorted but didn't say anything else.

Hoka shrugged. "It's not impossible, but I need you to come with me now."

I instinctively took a step back, but Hoka was faster, catching my wrist gently as if he was afraid I'd run. Would I have? Maybe. This was just all too crazy!

"Where are we going? I just—" I looked around helplessly, knowing full well that no one would step in to help. "I can't just leave. I'll get fired."

"No, you won't," Jiro piped in as he finally moved from his spot to call an elevator.

I was about to ask him how we knew that when he continued.

"You can't get fired when you bang the boss." He stepped into the elevator and held it open with one arm. "Come on, let's go."

Hoka growled at him, pulling me gently toward the elevators and I followed, way too confused about everything. My mind was much too preoccupied trying to make sense of everything, to tell my body to stop moving.

"Not helping," Hoka muttered as we stepped in, not letting go of my wrist.

"Wasn't trying to." Jiro pressed the button for the underground parking.

I was trying to process his comment. I was certainly not banging Ms. Chase or Mr. Greenall. I was not gay, and Mr. Greenall was probably close to seventy, so that was gross.

I was about to tell him off when the light came on, and I tried to pull my wrist from Hoka's hold, but he only tightened his strong fingers around it.

"You own the company?!" I shouted, anger once again taking the front seat of my plethora of emotions. "I told you I didn't want that!"

He sighed as if I was a petulant child having a fit. "Which is why I didn't tell you," he replied as if it all made sense.

"Oh, you didn't tell her? Oops, my bad." Jiro replied, obviously not bothered at all.

Hoka threw him a withering look, but despite everything, I liked the man. He was an ass who disliked me, but at least he was honest.

As the doors opened and Jiro exited first, I tensed, refusing to exit.

"Violet..." Hoka said my name as a supplication, as if he was just too tired to fight any more. "Let's not do this now. We both know I could move you if I wanted to."

Of course, I knew that the man—who was a flipping giant and at least twice my weight—could move me like I was nothing, but I was not going to make things easy for him.

He must have seen the look of determination on my face because he muttered something in Japanese under his breath, and I didn't need to speak the language to know he was swearing.

"Why are you doing this to me?" I asked, staring at the black car parked in front of the elevators.

I was not a dramatic person; I'd been through way too much shit to be overly dramatic, and I didn't know why exactly, but I knew that, once I stepped into this car, my life would change forever.

His face softened, his earlier fierceness replaced with worry and a certain weariness I didn't expect.

"I'm not—" He looked upward as if asking God for some guidance. "I didn't know I was putting you at risk. I thought that, for once, I could be selfish and have something just for me."

His words were cryptic and didn't mean much, but his honesty and the pleading look in his eyes made me give in, though reluctantly.

"Don't make me regret trusting you," I whispered, knowing that I didn't really trust him, but it was as much as I could muster right now.

He let out a sigh of relief. "I'll try." He rested his hand on the small of my back and guided me to the car.

I threw him a quick look before stepping into the back and settling against the luxurious leather seat, much too worried to actually enjoy the comfort of the vehicle. 'I'll try' was not really the comfort I was going for, but at least it was honest. And at the moment, that was all I could really ask for.

"Where are we going?" I asked after Hoka closed the car door and sat closer to me than required, his woodsy, warm cologne wrapping around me like a blanket.

"My house," he replied, resting his strong hands on his knees.

My heart started to beat furiously, like the rhythm of a hummingbird's wings. I took a few shallow breaths, trying and failing to calm myself down at the idea of entering Hoka's home.

"For how long?" I asked faintly, letting my eyes trail down to his hands on his knees, detailing his long strong fingers, clean short nails, his golden skin. There was no cut or bruising on them as you would expect a thug to have, and I could only notice some faint white scars here and there, but nothing out of the ordinary. These were not the hands of a killer. It was all a mistake, right? A misunderstanding, a rumor without any foundation, just something Jake had said out of spite and jealousy.

I sighed, relaxing in the seat. Yes, it had to be a lie, yet I was not clueless enough not to notice he was hiding a lot from me.

"I can't go to your house, Hoka," I added when he didn't reply to my question and met Jiro's accusing eyes in the rearview mirror.

"Violet, it's just for a few days. I need to figure out if it is an empty threat, and I won't be able to do that efficiently if I have to worry about you at the same time. You'll be all that's on my mind."

Once again, he admitted some of his feelings for me, but yet again, it was not the right time.

"I need the truth, Hoka, no matter what. You can't just bounce me around like I'm just a toy."

He nodded. "I know," He turned toward me, his eyes so intense, as if it was the last time he was seeing me. "I promise, once you're safe at my house, I will."

Jiro muttered something that I didn't understand, but the way Hoka pursed his lips showed it was not nice.

"Can we stop by my place please? I need some things."

Hoka looked at his watch and nodded. "Sure, let's go. Jiro?"

The man didn't reply but took the next turn to my neighborhood.

"Go up with Jiro," Hoka said as Jiro stopped the car in front of my building. "I've got quite a few calls to make. Be quick."

We got out of the car, and Hoka looked up to Jiro, his open expression switching to one of warning, his eyes colder than ice.

"Keep her safe."

Jiro rolled his eyes. "I'm sure I can handle the foot fetish pervert from across the hall," he grunted, grabbing the keys from my hand and walking to the rusty door.

This revelation made me falter, and I almost missed the small step in front of the door.

"How do you know?" I asked Jiro as I followed him up the stairs.

"Know what?" he asked coldly, not even bothering to turn around.

"About my neighbor. About his... *tendencies*," I added breathlessly as we reached my floor. I had a hard time keeping up with him.

He shrugged, giving me back my keys as we reached my front door. "Ask Hoka, he's the man with all the answers."

It was impossible to miss the bite of sarcasm and barely veiled judgment in his voice.

"I'm asking you," I insisted as I opened the door and gestured him in.

He let out a humorless laugh. "Then you're going to be sorely disappointed waiting for an answer." He snapped his fingers. "Come on, move. We're losing daylight."

I glared at him, flipping him off a thousand times in my mind. This man was the biggest asshole on the planet.

I grabbed the small sport bag from under my sink and started to pack a few essentials to last two or three days. I would not give Hoka more than that; this was my life after all.

"Not taking this?" I heard Jiro call from the main room as I took my things in the bathroom.

I walked back into the room and blushed in embarrassment as he held an oversized grey sleeping shirt in front of him, a mocking smirk on his stupid face.

His face was not stupid. He was really handsome and I knew it, but I still glared at him.

It was a sleeping shirt for me, but on him? It looked like a normal shirt.

"That's - No," I replied as I looked at the koala on a branch, chewing on some eucalyptus with 'Spend some Koala-tea time' written on the front.

His mean smirk faded, replaced by something close to concern. He twisted his mouth to the side and threw the T-shirt back onto the bed.

He shook his head. "You're just a child." I would have argued with him if his voice hadn't sounded so sad.

When he looked back up at me, his expression had lost some hostility, but the tilt of his eyebrows and the expression of his eyes looked a lot like pity, and I realized that I preferred hostility to pity. He looked like he was taking me to the scaffold instead of safety.

"I'm ready," I announced as I pulled the bag up my shoulder. I pointed to the blue suitcase that was peeking from under the bed. I knew I was only going to be away for a few days, but I was too scared to leave my mother's things—they mattered too much. "Could you take that for me please?"

He frowned, probably wondering why bother with a banged-up suitcase hidden under a bed for a few nights away, though he took it without question. "Let's go."

I nodded and followed him down, finding Hoka finishing a call, his nostrils flaring with anger, his jaw muscles so tense, they were visible.

Jiro threw him a questioning glance, but Hoka shook his head slightly.

"Ready?" Hoka turned toward me while trying very hard to smooth his features for my benefit, though the signs of his irritation were still noticeable in the tensed lines on the corner of his eyes, the flat line of his mouth, and the cold edge of his voice that I knew was not meant for me.

"Yes."

Was I though?

He reached for my sports bag and gave it to Jiro, who had just opened the trunk. "Everything is going to be fine," he said as he opened the back door, helping me in, and this time I was not sure he was really talking to me or to himself.

We drove for what seemed like forever but couldn't have been more than fifteen minutes. I kept opening and closing my mouth to ask questions, but so many were fighting in my mind that I didn't know which one I should ask first and ended up asking nothing at all.

However, all the questions I might have had flew to the back burner when iron gates opened, revealing a stunning mansion that reminded me of the Spanish revival-type homes I'd seen on a few Netflix shows.

I kept my face glued to the window as we approached the house from the side. It was absolutely stunning, of course, with white exterior walls, red terracotta tiles on the roof, and wooden support beams. I had expected something much more modern from Hoka, something all glass, metal and clean lines. This looked much more like a family home. Just looking at the pretty arched windows and the heavy wooden door filled me with warmth.

"My mother chose it," Hoka said softly, answering my unspoken question, which was impressive in itself as he could not see my face. "Most of the designs both inside and outside are hers, too. She went back to Japan three years ago, but I didn't feel like changing anything."

I nodded, as if I could understand how he felt. I guess I could, in a way, the blue suitcase in the trunk could testify to this.

"I love it. It feels like a home," I replied quickly, as if my opinion mattered. When I turned toward him and saw his pleased smile, it seemed like it did.

Jiro stopped the car in front of the arched double doors and Hoka stepped out before leaning down and extending his hand to help me out.

He was always so attentive, so caring. Acting this way out of instinct, and despite all the warning signs surrounding him, that helped me feel safer.

"Leave the bags for now, they'll take them up for you."

"Who?" I asked, looking around and not noticing anyone, but somehow feeling as if I was being watched. I noticed quite a few cameras and felt concern creep back up. Who needed that much security? Criminals and rich people.

Was Hoka just one or both?

I glanced his way as he settled his hand on the small of my back, and we took the three steps to the main door, which opened just as we reached it.

I looked at the man standing at the door, my mouth slightly agape. He was a bona fide butler! Dressed in his black suit, his back ramrod straight, even his face looked like a stereotypical British employee.

"Sir." He bowed his head slightly. "Miss Murphy" He bowed his head to me. "The room is ready, as you directed, sir."

Nailed it! I cheered internally, smiling at the man's British accent.

At the same moment, a very short, older Asian woman came from a door on the left, wearing a bright blue apron and her look of disapproval was locked on Hoka.

Hmm, it seems Jiro isn't the only one who doesn't like me.

Hoka tensed beside me. I could feel his fingers dip on my back as the woman stood beside the stairs, looking much more like a mother about to chastise her wayward child than an employee.

"Obāsan," he started as we reached the stairs, "this is Violet Murphy; she will be staying with us for a while." The gentleness in his voice was startling.

She threw me a dismissive glance and started to argue with Hoka in Japanese, pointing a finger to him, then at me, and then up the stairs, shaking her head.

Suddenly, Hoka straightened up and his gentle expression turned to steel. He replied to her in Japanese, in an even, calm voice that held a sharp frostiness that made me shiver.

She opened mouth to start again.

"I said now," he said in English, and those three words were enough to terrify me. I could now see the potential mafia boss in him. He looked down at me, his face still guarded. "You go with Himari. She'll show you to your room."

"What?" He wanted to leave me with the harpy? I could totally picture her beating me with a wooden spoon. "You promised to tell me everything."

"And I will, but I'm late for a meeting and I need to get going. Later, I promise. You're safe now."

I opened my mouth and closed it again, looking at him helplessly as he walked out the house at the same time as a young man entered with my bag and suitcase.

Hoka leaned to the side to say something, and the man nodded before passing me up the stairs with my belongings, not even acknowledging my presence.

I sighed as I looked around, now alone with the British butler, the mean cook, and the other man. I almost wished Jiro the asshole was still around!

The hall was exactly what I expected it to be, with its domed ceiling and decorative tiles on the wall. I rested my hand on the wrought iron banister and looked at the woman, ready to face the music.

I forced a smile that I hoped looked genuine despite the apprehension of being in an unfamiliar place, surrounded by strangers who seemed to dislike me on sight. "Hello, my name is Violet. It's really nice to meet you, Himari."

She kept her face completely impassive as she stared right back at me. I twisted my mouth to the side. Did she even understand English? Maybe she spoke Japanese, not to make me feel bad but because she couldn't communicate otherwise. But despite all of that, I continued in English, hoping she would understand some of it.

"I'm truly sorry for barging into your life like this. I know I must be an added burden that you don't need, but I will do my very best to be the least disturbance possible. Also, please put me to work, anything I can do to help." I added, gripping the banister a little tighter.

She looked at me with her cool facade for a couple more heartbeat before letting out a sigh, relaxing her tensed shoulders.

"I'm not angry with you," she said in perfect English, with only a hint of an accent. "You're no trouble, and you're welcome here." She shook her head. "Come, let me show you to your room."

We took the curved staircase up two floors and down a wide corridor until she stopped in front of a dark arched wooden door so similar to every other door in this house.

She opened it, and I couldn't help but look at the room in awe as I stepped in after her. I looked around at what had to be the most stunning room in the world! I wasn't sure why, but I expected to find something with the style of the house—a guest room matching the Spanish style, but this looked personal, like it had been designed with someone in mind. And if I didn't know any better, I would almost think it was designed for me.

The walls were two colors - white at the top, which gradually transformed into a beautiful gradation between white and red that reminded me of cherry blossoms in full bloom. The walls harmonized perfectly with the white-washed wooden flooring.

Himari interrupted my inspection by clearing her throat. "I need to finish dinner. You can contact the staff by pressing the red button on the phone." She pointed at the small white phone on one of the nightstands.

"Oh, okay thank y—" I didn't have the time to finish my sentence that she was already gone. "Charming," I muttered, picking my sport bag off the floor and putting it on the little bench at the end of the bed.

The whole bedroom was white and this same very specific shade of pink. The king-sized bed was white with little pink cushions, and it looked like heaven. The vanity on the opposite wall was white as well, though the chair cushion was pink. However, the place that seemed to appeal to me the most was the soft pink reading chair, strategically placed by the balcony French doors, which gave a view on an Olympic-sized swimming pool and a garden so big, I could barely see the back wall. I could picture myself sitting there in the evening, reading a book with the doors open, enjoying the cool Californian breeze.

I sighed, opening the window and walking onto the balcony, leaning against it and looking at the darkening garden, trying to make out everything that I would be able to explore in my few days here. Everything was a gigantic clusterfuck right now, that much was true, but this house was stunning and the room was something right out of a dream.

I closed my eyes and inhaled deeply, getting a whiff of the salty but fresh scent of the ocean as the breeze turned.

I turned slightly in that direction, where the sun was setting. I stood on my toes, leaning against the wrought and wooden banister, and as I squinted I could make out the ocean as the sun seemed to be undulating on its surface as it swallowed it for the night.

A lot of questions needed to be answered, a lot of issues weren't resolved, but for tonight I decided to just stop thinking, stop worrying, and enjoy this beautiful dream, just for an evening.

CHAPTER 10

Hoka

"She's leaving."

I looked up from the contract I was reading to find Jiro leaning against the door of my office. I didn't need to ask who he meant, especially since he seemed to be gloating a little.

"How can she leave?" I asked as calmly as I could, despite the fact that my stomach dropped to my shoes when he said the words I hadn't realized I dreaded to hear.

"She asked Charles to get her an Uber." He sighed. "Can you blame her? You made promises, and you didn't give her any answers. She was even more patient than I thought she would."

I stood, straightening my jacket. "She can't leave now. I'm not any closer to finding out who's threatening her." I grabbed my phone on the desk and slid it into my pocket. "Where's she?"

"In the kitchen. Himari is teaching her to make gyoza."

I arched an eyebrow. "Himari?"

Jiro's lips quivered as he fought a smile. "Yea."

"Teaching something? To a gaijin?"

Jiro smirked. "She likes her."

"But Himari doesn't like anybody." Though it was true that Violet was impossible not to like. I took a deep breath. "I have no choice, I need to tell her the truth."

Jiro moved from his spot to block my path. "No, you don't have to," he said with a certain urgency that made me stop to listen. "You can just send her away, far from the danger. You can allow her to start a new life anywhere in the world."

I frowned at his unsolicited advice.

"You're a billionaire; you're Hoka Nishimura! You could... I don't know." He looked around as if he was trying to find inspiration. His eyes landed on the black-and-white picture of the Eiffel Tower on my wall. "Send her to work for *Nishimura Corp* in Paris. What woman wouldn't want to live there? Let her go, Hoka. Let her fall in love with a French man and eat croissants. Let her live her life. Don't burden her with your secrets."

"What is it to you?" I asked with a cold edge. "You seem to take it much further than warranted with her."

"You know why. Don't make the same mistakes I did. You still have a chance to free her."

"It's different from your situation. I'm not a fresh nineteen-year-old who believed that love could conquer everything. I'm a man; I've seen enough to know better, and I'm not just anyone, I'm the head of the 893. I'm powerful enough to keep her safe."

"You're taking her choices away, Hoka. She doesn't know what you, answering her questions, could lead to."

I knew he was right; of course he was, but it was too late, and I was not a good man—at least not good enough to let her go.

"Concerns noted." I gestured for him to move. "I'll handle it my way."

Jiro sighed with a shake of his head but moved from his spot.

I went down the corridor to the kitchen and my anxiety increased with each step, still having no clue how much to tell her. I just had to tell her enough to make her stay but not too much so she'd reject me.

I stopped on my tracks when I heard a laugh—*her* laugh—and fuck, it went straight through me and pierced my soul.

I rested my hand on the wall at the melodious sound. I couldn't remember the last time there was such laughter in this house. It was probably sometime before my father's death, when the house was free of guests, and my mother could let go of her controlled personna to let her real carefree character come out.

I remembered when I was much younger, my mother had laughed like that after my father did or said something silly. My father usually let go of his stern exterior and became a carefree man in those moments, and he was grinning as if he was a superhero when he made her laugh like that. I had not understood then what was so special about that, especially since I'd made people laugh all the time, but now, hearing her laugh like that, I understood. I understood everything.

I would have bled for this laugh to be mine, and I knew that if she decided to stay, I would do everything in my power to stop the darkness from reaching her and for this laughter to be a common occurrence despite it all.

She laughed again as Himari's voice raised a little, chastising her nicely that she was putting more flour on her face than in the bowl.

"It's all the fun of cooking, Himari. You're supposed to make a mess."

I couldn't help but smile when I walked into the kitchen, but my good humor quickly plummeted when her smile dimmed and her shoulders tensed. She was frustrated and irritated with me.

She would have to get used to it because even if I'd tried my best to be the man she deserved, I knew it would not always be possible. She deserved the best, and I wasn't him—though I was going to try and keep her anyway.

"Himari." I straightened the lapel of my jacket, trying to give myself something to do under the scrutinizing eyes of both women. "Violet." I glanced at her bag and suitcase resting against the kitchen wall. "I see you decided to leave us."

"What did you expect? She's a scared young woman who has no idea what world she just stepped into, and you became a ghost, leaving her in the care of an irritable old woman. I'm surprised she stayed this long," Himari shouted at me in Japanese.

I couldn't help but wince despite my wish to just take it like a man. Himari's criticisms were rare but touched me a lot more than anyone else's.

"I had things to do, Himari. Things to protect her. I had decisions to make." I replied calmly in the same language.

Violet eyes narrowed, her gaze going from Himari to me and back again. Her frown deepened and her face took on a lovely red hue, but it was not induced by lust and other romantically-inclined feelings, she was getting more and more frustrated.

It was rude, I knew that, but it was not a discussion I could have in English before we had our own talk.

"What decision?" Himari continued, throwing a dumpling into the boiling water in frustration. "Whatever decision you needed to make was made for you when you walked her through these doors and gave her that room. They all know she's here, and they all know what it means. Don't delude yourself."

"I don't need you to be her champion, Himari!" I raised my voice, despite all the love and respect I had for the old woman, who I considered like a grandmother. She was crossing the line and saying things I hated to hear.

Because they're all true, a little voice taunted in my head.

But Himari didn't bow down, and I should have known better. Her glare just deepened as she reached for a wooden spoon. I was not certain she didn't intend to use it on my shins like she did when I was younger. "Why not? Someone has to be, and it's clearly not you, my boy. I'm disappointed."

That made me recoil, forcing me to take a step back as if her words were a physical blow. I was done arguing with her.

"Fine," I said in English before turning to Violet, who was removing her apron. "Violet—"

"I'm going now," she interrupted me, and I hated how uncertain and small her voice sounded. "Could you please have someone drive me home."

I took a step toward her but stopped when she sent me a warning glare, taking a step back. Was she worried? I frowned, hating that rejection coming from her. It hurt like a motherfucker, and that was not something I could accept.

"Just give me a few minutes, please. There's a long-overdue explanation, and I apologize for not coming to you earlier."

Himari muttered some unsavory expletives under her breath as she turned to concentrate on the pot of boiling water.

How did Violet manage to become the woman's favorite in less than forty-eight hours was nothing short of a miracle. Himari hated strangers and it usually took her years to even be civil toward someone.

"I think we're past that," Violet replied, wiping at her face to remove some of the flour. She missed a spot on her lower jaw, and I could picture myself leaning down and licking that spot clean.

My body reacted at once, and the zing of desire at the base of my spine made my dick twitch. *No, not now!*

I cleared my throat, forcing myself to think of everything that was a mood killer, and my uncle's judging face flashed in my head, instantaneously killing any desire I felt.

"Ten minutes, Violet, please." My voice sounded much rougher than it usually was.

I didn't miss the surprised look that Himari threw my way. I was not the type of man to say 'please' and mean it—nor was I used to sounding like a begging idiot.

She let out a little sigh as she nodded, and I felt like I'd just won a clan war.

I gestured for her to follow me, and we silently walked side by side. Despite the lack of words, the tension between us was so palpable, it made it hard to breathe.

I took her to my main office downstairs, the one I usually used to conduct business. It was the one that had been fully designed by my father and looked very Western. He had said that it made businesspeople more comfortable, and I understood what he meant. Katanas displayed in a mafia boss office tended to make people nervous.

"Please have a seat," I offered, gesturing toward the comfortable brown leather chairs by the fireplace.

She shook her head. "I'd rather stand, thanks," she replied, and I hated the edge of wariness in her voice, the tension in her body. It looked like she was bracing for a fight or flight situation, and it was a way I never wanted her to feel in my presence.

"Very well," I replied, taking a seat, hoping that, after a few minutes, she would follow my lead. "So," I extended my legs and crossed them at my ankles, resting both arms on the comfortable armrest of my usual chair. "Where do you want me to start?"

"Are you mafia?" she blurted as she rested her back against the wall by the door.

I couldn't contain my surprise at the question. I arched my eyebrows so high, I was pretty sure it reached my hairline as my mouth hung open.

"What?"

"Are you in the mafia?" she repeated, and I could see the side of her neck pulse in sync with her heartbeat.

The woman was completely terrified, yet she still asked the questions. She was bravery personified.

I took a deep breath as my heart hammered with apprehension. "No, Suītohāto, I'm not *in* the mafia."

Her eyes narrowed slightly, showing her doubts.

"I *am* the mafia."

She took a deep intake of breath, flattening her back against the wall. She might have suspected it, she might have even been told about it, but hearing the confirmation coming from me made all the difference.

I didn't move a muscle, worried that one move would scare her and make her flee. I just stared at her, as if I was made of stone, trying to decipher all the emotions going through her at once.

She furrowed and smoothed her eyebrows, cocked her head to the side as if she was having some internal debate. She opened and closed her mouth a few times, and I just waited as patiently as I could, trying to keep my face as emotionless as possible, despite the vice of apprehension squeezing my heart and stomach to the point of physical pain.

She was trying to make sense of everything, trying to decide if she wanted to know more or walk away.

I let my eyes trail down to her chest, watching rise and fall in quick successions with her short intakes of breath. Then my gaze trailed down to her lovely small fingers that she twisted together so hard they were red. I wanted to stand up, take those lovely hands in mine to stop her from hurting herself. I wanted to kiss them, kiss every lovely finger, trace my tongue along the lines of her palms, promising her that if she gave us a chance, she would never regret it.

But I can't make that commitment; this life is too dangerous to promise that. And yet I was ready to.

"Ar-are you going to kill me?" she whimpered.

"Of course not. I'd rather cut off my own hand than ever hurt you," I told her with the solemn tone of certainty. It was evidence, like a written rule. She was my Ikigai. I could never hurt my Ikigai.

She looked at me, her blue eyes shining with unspent tears, uncertain of what to do with my words.

"How long have you known?" I asked her, wondering who I'd have to punish for this since it has been my secret to tell. I had planned to tell her a certain way and this spoiled everything.

Suddenly, it dawned on me. "Did you know when you canceled our dinner date?"

She chewed on her bottom lip, a tell of her anxiety. Yes, she knew.

She nodded, and I was grateful for her constant honesty. I was truly worried now. I didn't think she would not accept me. I didn't think she could possibly walk away, but it was because I assumed her feelings for me were just as intense and overwhelming as mine, but if it was not the case? What then? It changed everything. Jiro told me I needed to give her the freedom to have a simple and safe life. I'd disagreed because I thought that her need to be with me would be a match of my need to be with her. But if it wasn't the case, then I had to grant her this freedom.

"You don't have to be afraid," I offered as gently as I could. I was not used to trying to soothe people, I was much more versed in terrifying and threatening them. "This is not the end of it, Violet. I know someone threatened you to get to me. It was clear with the flowers and the video but—"

"The flowers weren't yours?" she asked, and the chagrin and embarrassment in her eyes made me regret even more not being the one sending her flowers. She should get flowers every day for the rest of our lives.

I shook my head.

"Oh my god." She covered her face with her hands, and I hated losing access to the window of her feelings. Her eyes were an open book and I needed to see them. "I'm so embarrassed. Oh god... The message I sent you then..." She kept her hands on her face.

"I wished I sent you these flowers, I wanted to... If I'd listened to myself, I would have bought every red rose in town and have them delivered to your door, but I didn't want to scare you with the intensity of my feelings. Though, I guess I managed that anyway." Seriously, did my tone sound as sad and pathetic as it did to my own ears?

She removed her hands from her face, her cheekbones and nose a lovely shade of pink. Her eyes lost some of the fear and weariness, and she looked more curious and conflicted now. Maybe showing her my vulnerability was the key to her heart.

"You don't have to be afraid," I repeated. "The flowers and videos are concerning, yes, but it's nothing that can't be dealt with. You don't have to stay here with me or even date me to be safe." I took a deep breath. Those words hurt me a lot more than I expected. "As you know, I've got companies everywhere in the world. Pick a location and I'll set you up there. You can start your new life on the right foot."

"Do you want me to go?"

Fuck no! I want you in my life, in my bed... I want you everywhere, wrapped around me as you already are wrapped around my heart, my brain, already running wild through my bloodstream, like an obsession that took over.

"It would be the safest, most reasonable option for you." I replied evasively, the words hurting in ways that almost brought me to my knees.

"But do *you* want me to?"

"No, of course not." *I want you here with me forever.*

"I canceled because I didn't know how I felt about all that, mostly because it didn't bother me as much as it should have."

I leaned forward in my chair, resting my elbows on my knees as hope bloomed in my chest, slightly releasing the vice of worry.

She looked at the two-seater sofa across my chair and moved to sit on it. I almost hooted in victory as she visibly relaxed.

"I—" She stopped and looked around my office, as if she was trying to make sense of her feelings, trying to explain them.

Good luck with that, sweetheart. These feelings we shared were straight out of an old women folklore storybook.

"I see myself as a good person, and I'm not sure what it says about me to want to be with someone who is - " She stopped and made a little comical grimace as she looked at me.

"Not so good?" I finished with a half-smile.

"Yea..."

"It's fair. I won't be trying to justify who I am and what I do. I was born and raised in this life and for this position. I'm not a monster and I never hurt the innocent. I've got a moral code, and while it may differ greatly from yours, it's there."

"Why was Himari so angry with you the other day?" she asked. I was a little confused about her change of subject but assumed she needed time to process.

"She didn't tell you?"

She shook her head. "No, she told me to ask you."

"She was opposed to the room I gave you." I hoped it would be enough of an answer, but I should have known better as she looked at me expectantly, waiting for more.

I sighed. *Here goes nothing.* "I gave you the *Tsuma*'s room, the wife's room," I translated quickly. "She didn't think it was proper in this situation." I completely disagreed.

"Oh." The color came back to her cheeks and my heart bloomed once again with hope. Was she pleased with that? "The... um, wife. She—" She squirmed on her seat and it intrigued me.

I pulled myself to the edge of my seat, still leaning forward, trying to close the distance between us without actually moving from my seat.

I was close enough to smell her faint floral perfume and saw her pupils dilate in reaction to my nearness. I couldn't stop the cocky smile from spreading on my lips. She may not have been emotionally as deep and intoxicated as I was, but she was showing all the signs of deep attraction and lust—and that was something I could work with.

"Yes?" I encouraged her with a smooth tone, and my smile widened when she shivered.

"The wives, they... they don't share a room with their husbands?" she asked, the lovely shade of pink on her cheek deepening to a bright red.

"Ah, I see."

She looked down at her hands on her lap, and all I wanted to do was jump from my spot and sit beside her to kiss all her worries and concerns away. I wanted to kiss her until she forgot how to breathe, until she understood that, if she was mine, I would do anything in my power to spend every night beside her.

"A lot of marriages are arranged, so having two rooms helps. When it's a union created by love, like my parents were," *And like ours would be,* "the couple keeps two rooms in name only. It's good to have your own space sometimes... You know, if your husband is in the doghouse, at least then he doesn't have to sleep on the sofa." I chuckled.

She looked up to me with a small smile. "And so, I shouldn't have slept there?"

"It gave a certain view of our relationship, and it wasn't fair for me to do that without giving you all the information." I cocked my head to the side. I had to approach the more sensitive part of this discussion—the part I thought might still make her reconsider a relationship—and I hoped that, if it was the case, I'd be honorable enough to let her leave.

I let out a deep breath, somehow regretting not serving myself a deep glass of hard liquor before starting this conversation. I leaned back in my chair, breaking the intimacy in order to give myself a little more clarity in what I had to explain now.

"Being with me won't be easy." *Understatement of the year.* "A lot of people around me are - " I thought for a second, cocking my head to the side, trying to find the words to express what I wanted to say without worrying her more than necessary, "*old-fashioned* and won't look very kindly at us being together."

"Because I'm not Japanese?"

I nodded. "It's part of it, yes, but also because you're an outsider and as you can understand, we don't usually take very kindly to outsiders. I'll shield you as much as I can, but unfortunately, the darkness surrounding my life will affect you." I rested my chin in my hand. "You need to decide if you want to give this a try or if you want to go."

"What does it mean for my job?"

I had to admit that it hurt like a bitch. I wasn't sure what I had expected, but part of me had hoped she would just say yes and be mine no matter the cost. The answer to that question was one I knew she wouldn't enjoy but no matter how I wanted to sway her, I couldn't lie to her.

"This one might be difficult whether you stay or go. I'm... I'm a man of few weaknesses, and I live in a world of sharks. If they see an opening, they'll go for the kill." *Way to sell yourself, idiot. You'll be lucky if she doesn't run away before the day is out.*

"And I'm this opening."

"You are."

She took a deep breath and averted her eyes, looking at the black-and-white picture of the Eiffel Tower that Jiro was looking at before. "I didn't know."

Guilt reared its ugly head again. It was becoming such a recurring feeling, which was quite ironic since it was something I barely ever felt before. She was right though, and I knew that. From the moment I rescued her, I knew I was making mistake after mistake, condemning her to unknowingly become a target. I had known I was not fair, yet I kept going down this path.

"No, you didn't. I made sure of that," I admitted, showing her a glimpse of my ruthlessness. "Stay or go, this job is dead now. You can go to Paris if you want, and I'll set you up nicely. You'll be far from any danger."

"I'll be far from you," she murmured, keeping her eyes on the photo.

I held my breath. Was it reluctance I heard in her voice? Was I reading too much into it? Was I hearing what I wanted to hear?

"That's the idea. If you're far, you won't be seen as a weakness anymore. If you stay though, I'll keep you safe, but in order to do that we'll," *Don't lie to her, Hoka.* "You'll have to make sacrifices and give up some of your freedom."

"I see," she replied evasively, turning toward me again and sucking her plump bottom lip between her teeth.

You really don't. "You'll be able to work still, of course, but for me this time. You'd be here to help me with the other side of my business, the legit one. It's a lot to ask either way. It was not a choice I should have sprung on you like this." It's not a choice she should have had to make at all, and if I'd been stronger, she wouldn't have to.

She nodded again. "It's a lot to take in. I - I need time," she replied with a small smile.

The hope I'd felt before deflated. I'd hoped she would just accept everything and maybe declare her undying love for me in the same damn breath.

"Of course." I stood up. I needed to leave this room now before I did something I would regret, like shamelessly begging her to stay. "I've got a meeting to go to but—" I cleared my throat, the lump of disappointment and hurt lodged right there, making it hard to swallow. "You're staying, right? I can't protect you out there. Just promise you'll stay until you decide what you want to do."

She nodded, following me with her eyes as I walked to the door. Could she see my anguish at her hesitation?

I looked at my watch as I reached the door. "I'm late, sorry." Late for nothing and with nowhere to go. I could go to the casino, I suppose. Breaking a few bad payers' fingers always cheered me up and helped taking some of the edge off. "I'll see you later."

I didn't give her the time to agree and left the room briskly, running away from my own office and house.

I didn't know what she was going to do but I knew what I wanted her to do. I wanted her to choose *me,* choose *our* future.

I wanted her to see me as worthy; that despite all the darkness, blood, and danger a life with me would entail, I was enough to make it all worth it.

How conceited did that make me? How selfish? I'd said it before, and I would say it again. I was not a good man, but for her? I was ready to try.

CHAPTER 11

VIOLET

I was not sure what to do or what to say. I had wanted answers—all of them—yet now I wasn't sure it was such a good idea.

He was the criminal I was told he was. He was not only in the mafia, he was the head of the mafia, and the worst part of it all was that it didn't bother me as much as it should have. What did it say about me? I never really understood how my mother had been involved with my sperm donor—how she'd let herself fall for a man like him—yet here I was, in a very similar situation with a man just as dangerous and now, for the first time, I started to understand.

I'd avoided him last night and the entirety of today. I felt guilty doing that after he opened up to me, showed me glimpses of his vulnerabilities, and the depth of his feelings for me.

None of it made sense—not our connection nor our overwhelming attraction. The way it physically hurt me just at the thought of walking away from him.

I took a quick cold shower to calm my burning skin, but I didn't think that any amount of water could soothe this heat. It was not due to the Californian summer; no, it was due to the man who I knew was in the room only a few steps away from me.

I changed into my blue shorts and tank top pajamas and stood in front of the mirror of the bathroom. I look the same; I still look like the same little Violet, the girl who was scared of everything, scared to open her heart more than necessary. Determined, to the point of paranoia, of not committing the same mistake as her mother had made. Mistakes that seemed to be repeating, no matter how hard I tried not to but maybe this relationship would be different. Maybe I could break the curse. Hoka wasn't married, and I was not his dirty little secret. He cared for me, truly.

I rested my hands on the cool white Italian marble counter and leaned forward, detailing every line on my face. The thing was, I knew what I *should* do and what I was *going* to do and they were two very different things. I was not sure my brain had been ready to accept this choice, especially not when I knew that once I picked a path, there would be no turning back.

The choice was completely mine, without any pressure—even though I knew he probably wanted me to stay as much as I wanted to stay.

That sacrifice alone was enough to comfort me in my decision. I padded barefoot to the reading chair, ready to immerse myself into one of the novels I'd borrowed from the library, anything to keep me from thinking about him.

I heard a noise, and I looked out the window just in time to see him fasten a robe around himself. He had just been for a swim, and I cursed myself for taking too long pleasuring myself in the shower, trying and failing miserably to take some of the edge off.

Seeing his almost naked body, swimming, would have given me much more material for my nightly self-pleasuring sessions which were featuring no other man.

He looked up as if he could feel my eyes on him, and I froze as his tawny eyes connected with mine.

Even from that far away, I could see the wariness and sadness floating in them, a sadness that was only reinforced by the attempt of a smile he gave me.

He thinks I'm going to leave him, that I don't care for him enough to stay.

Today, once I had been certain Hoka had left the premises, I went down to the kitchen and Himari told me as I helped her with lunch that Hoka was a very solitary man, both due to circumstances and then choice.

I understood what she wasn't saying as well. Hoka needed someone to fight for him. Someone who only cared about him, not the power he conveyed or the fear he could induce. Hoka needed to be seen for the man he was, not the role he represented.

And I was seeing him, the man, the weary, beautiful man. I rubbed at my chest where my unsettled heartbeat caused some discomfort.

How could I feel so intensely about him? How could I be so deep so soon? It was not only unsettling, it was terrifying! If I voiced how I felt, I would open all the doors, let all the walls down, and I'd be completely vulnerable—giving him all the weapons to utterly destroy me.

I leaned back on the reading chair and closed my eyes, conjuring my mother's memory. I needed her help, her wise advice. I needed her love and unwavering optimism, even if it was only in my head.

I could imagine her sitting at the foot of the chair, putting my feet into her lap and tapping on my toes one by one.

"Should I give him the power to destroy me?" I whispered.

The image in my head smiled, and I could almost feel the heat of her palm against the arch of my foot, the pressure of her squeeze. *"Wouldn't the opposite be even worse?"* she would have asked wisely. *"Not exploring something that is already so incredibly passionate? Always wondering what could have been? Could you live with the regret of walking away without being sure to ever feel anything even remotely close? Give it a try, baby, you owe it to yourself to take the plunge. It's terrifying, exhilarating, and overwhelming all at once, but once you dive you will feel a freedom like nothing else—an inner peace with no equal at having made the choice. Be brave."*

"Be brave," I repeated, opening my eyes and looking at the empty spot she'd been occupying in my thoughts. "Be brave!" I stood, ready to share my decision with Hoka. Despite the late hour, it couldn't wait. I couldn't give myself a chance to reconsider, or to be scared again.

I knew what I wanted to do. I'd known from the very moment his lips had touched mine, and now I had the strength to admit it.

I exited my room and walked to Hoka's with determined steps.

"Be brave," I muttered as I stood in front of his door and opened it without being invited.

Hoka chose that moment to exit the bathroom, a towel low around his waist, his hair wet from the shower he just took, flowing freely down his shoulders and back. I knew for a fact now that his hair was much longer than Jiro.

He stopped when he saw me, tightening his hand around the knot of the towel.

"Violet? Are you okay?" He arched his eyebrows in surprise.

"I'm being brave," I replied as I pushed the door close behind me, resting my back against it.

He took a step toward me. "You're already brave."

"I'm being braver, then," I replied, taking a couple of steps toward him, my eyes locked on his chest and arms. There was almost no skin showing at all under the beautiful integrated designs, full of colors, red flowers, and Koi. I kept my eyes on them, trying to decipher the smaller pieces as I walked closer, hypnotized by his body.

He remained where he stood as I came closer, finally close enough to see every little detail of his tattoos and smell the herbal scent of his body wash.

I kept my eyes on the drop of water that formed at the end of a strand of hair, and followed as it fell, running down his pec, his rock-hard abs, to the dipping V before getting absorbed by the thick fabric of his white towel.

I swallowed hard as my heart hammered in my chest. I could feel my desire everywhere—in my head, in my belly, between my legs.

I raised my hand, wanting to trace the snakelike pattern in the middle of his chest but stopped midway up.

He raised his hand as well, slowly resting it on the back of mine and pulled it against his chest, over his heart, which seemed to be beating just as fast as mine.

I flattened my hand on his skin, loving the warmth and softness of it. He inhaled sharply as he let go of my hand and instead of removing my hand, I let my fingers trail down his skin.

"Violet?" His voice was deep and breathless, like he was fighting to keep his control, but I wasn't sure I wanted him to.

I stopped as my fingers reached the hem of the towel, and I looked back up. His amber eyes looked black now, his pupils dilated to the maximum. I was no expert, but I knew without a shadow of a doubt, that he wanted me as much as I wanted him.

"I know leaving would be the best decision. It would be the simplest choice, the healthiest one," I started, my voice shaky, my breathing rapid, "but the problem is that it means being away from you, saying goodbye, and never being with you and that seems so much harder than anything else." I let my fingers slide just under the edge of the towel, and he took a step closer, looming over me, his strength surrounding me. "I can't walk away from these feelings. I don't want to wake up one day wondering what could have been. I might not be an expert, but I've seen enough in life to know that the connection we have is rare, and I can't bear the thought of turning my back to it. I want to be with you."

He raised his hand and brushed his knuckles against my cheek. "It is rare," he agreed, his voice a flirty whisper, making my lower belly clench and creating the moisture of desire between my legs. "It's so rare in fact, that my people made it part of our folklore."

I leaned closer and kissed his skin, making him shiver. Despite my apprehension at taking the plunge, I couldn't help but feel gratified at the reaction I had on this big, experienced man.

He rested his hand on the back of my head and hissed as I licked his nipple.

"Violet, sweetheart, I'm not known for my restraint. If you don't stop now, I don't think you'll leave this room with your virginity intact."

I looked up and met his eyes to show him I had no doubt at all—at least, not about giving myself to him completely.

"I don't want to leave this room at all."

He pulled me toward him, flushing my body against his so tightly that I could feel every ridge, including the hardness of his erection against my belly.

He crushed his lips on mine as he grabbed my ass, squeezing it and making me gasp, allowing him to deepen the kiss and invade my mouth, dominating me in this kiss as he dominated everything in his life.

He tasted like fresh mint, and I never thought that toothpaste could be arousing, yet that kiss alone made me burn from the inside out, my panties soaked and my body yearning for an intrusion it's never known before.

How could my body yearn for something it had yet to experience? One of his hands let go of my ass and trailed up my back, stopping at the sliver of bare skin, tracing my burning skin to the point of combustion.

I gripped the towel tighter and pulled on it, letting it fall to the floor.

Hoka growled against my lips, his strong fingers cupping around my jaw and neck, turning my face slightly upward to deepen the kiss even more, possessing me completely. His hands tightened as he pulled me to the side until I felt the softness of his bedspread on the back of my thigh and never breaking the kiss, he pushed me down onto the bed.

He finally broke the kiss, letting his soft lips trail gently on my jawline and down the side of my neck, sucking on my pulse point gently.

It was mesmerizing how a man so big, so full of virile brute force could be so gentle, treating me like I was made of glass.

"Hoka," I whispered, sliding my fingers through his hair, closing my eyes to concentrate purely on the feel of his lips on my skin, his weight on me.

His leg slipped between mine, his thigh pressing against where I ached so desperately.

His lips kept going down my throat, exploring every little corner as if my skin was a treasure map, leading him to the most precious gift.

He nibbled the tendon connecting my shoulder to my neck, and my hips raised unconsciously, rubbing my core against his powerful thigh, giving me both instant pleasure and a second of relief.

I raised my hips again, once, twice, rubbing faster, trying to get my release any way I could.

He licked the outer shell of my ear and hissed, "You're so wet for me, beautiful. I feel it through your shorts."

In any other circumstances, I would have been horrified to know that my arousal was that evident, but I was too far gone to care—the desire and lust robbing me of the last part of my self-consciousness. All that mattered now was that we satisfied the ache that was spreading through my body.

I moaned his name, rocking my hip higher and more forcefully as his thigh gave the right amount of pressure on my overly sensitive bundle of nerves at the top of my slit.

He moved his leg, and I whined as I lost the delicious friction. I opened my eyes and frowned in frustration at having been cut off from my impending orgasm.

"Patience, sweetheart. We have all night," he whispered as his lips trailed down my chest to stop at the exposed skin of my navel. "It would be a shame for you to come just yet." He looked up, his chin resting on my belly as he locked eyes with me.

His drying hair was a mess because of my roaming fingers, and his lips were red and puffy from our passionate kissing. The man was hot before, but now, lord have mercy, he was just so beautiful, it hurt.

He leaned down and I let out a yelp of surprise as he ran his tongue around and in my belly button. "I've got so many plans for us tonight, so many scenarios I fantasized about, over and over again, when I jerked myself with you in my mind. I'm going to make you come so many times tonight that you'll beg me to stop." He trailed his hands up, grabbing the bottom of my tank top. "Tell me, sweetheart, did you touch yourself thinking about me, too?"

I caught my bottom lip between my teeth and nodded. There was no point of lying to him.

He growled with satisfaction and pulled my tank top up, out of my arms, and threw it on the floor in one swift movement.

I've never been this far with anyone before. I participated in some heavy make-out sessions, some over-the-clothes exploring and fondling, but never something like that.

I didn't have time to feel exposed as he looked at my breast.

"Stunning," he whispered before he brushed his lips softly over my nipple and lapped at it with long, hard strokes.

I buried my fingers into his silky raven locks, wanting him to stay there and pleasure my breast until I couldn't breathe. He closed his lips, sucking my nipple into his warm mouth, swirling his hot tongue around the hardened tip.

I closed my eyes and moaned loudly, arching my back. *Is it always so good?*

"Oh... Oh god. Hoka, this is—" I let out a small cry as he tugged at the tip, not hard enough to cause any real pain, but just hard enough to induce an electrical current to run down my body and stop at my entrance, creating a new wave of wetness to completely drench my shorts.

He repeated the same ministration on my other nipple before kissing down my body, as his big strong hands stayed on my breast, cupping and kneading them. His lips stopped just at the hem of my shorts.

"Are you sure you want this?" he asked, letting go of my breasts and hooking his fingers into my shorts. "Because once you're mine, sweetheart, you're mine. There won't be any turning back."

I knew he was just as gone as I was, his body probably aching as much as mine, yet he was still concerned about my consent, my desire, and that made him even more precious to me.

"Yes." I rocked my hips slightly to give some emphasis to my words. "I want it all with you."

He pulled down my shorts just a little to kiss my hip bone, almost reverently, before pulling them down completely.

I was naked, in front of a man, for the first time in my life. I squeezed my eyes shut as I tightened my hands on the bedspread, trying to stop myself from covering my body.

I shivered as I felt some of the cool night air that drifted from the open window against my sex.

"Open your eyes, Violet. I need to see your eyes." His voice was gravely, barely recognizable both because of his lust and his effort of restraining himself.

I opened my eyes and looked at the beast of a man standing at the foot of the bed in all his naked glory looking at me with so much burning passion that I felt like a virgin sacrifice on an altar, and he was the wolf about to eat me.

As if he could read my thoughts, he licked his lips and I had to stop my legs from spreading instinctively.

"I don't know what I did to deserve you," he said, letting his eyes slowly roam from my face, to my chest, and down my stomach before stopping at the apex of my thighs and the thankfully neatly trimmed strip of hair. His scrutiny had been so intense that it had felt like a burning caress on my skin.

I let my eyes roam down his body and excitement gave place to fear as I landed on his erection jutting proudly high. It was not difficult to guess that he was well above average and much bigger than what Jake had. I swallowed hard. It was impossible for such a big part of him to fit in me.

He seemed to read my fear and came back on the bed, molding his body against my side, his thickness resting against my hip.

"It will fit, sweetheart. You're made for me, and I'll make sure you're ready." He moved and kissed the swell of my breast. "I don't want to hurt you, and even if some pain is inevitable, I'll make sure that before the night is done, you will be drowning in pleasure."

He started to lick and nuzzle at my throat as his hand trailed down my stomach until it cupped the most intimate part of me in such a possessive gesture that I widened my thighs ever so slightly.

"Hmm, good girl," he purred against my jawline as his fingers rubbed up and down, parting my slit.

"Oh Hoka, Hoka..." I moaned, undulating my hips under his soft caress, his strong calloused fingers having a much stronger effect than mine ever had.

"I don't think I'll even get tired of hearing you moan my name, sweetheart. It's the most enticing sound in the world." He pressed his thumb against my clit before slowly inserting it in me.

I let out a whimper, not sure how to put into words all he was making me feel and what I wanted him to do. I wanted to reach down and push his thumb deeper inside me, anything to ease the insanity of this burning sensation in my core.

"More..."

He kissed me savagely, letting go of any pretense of softness as his dominant side completely took over and his thumb pressed completely inside me, moving in torturously slow circles.

"More..." I begged again. I wanted his full erection in me, no matter how ready I was or how much it would hurt, because I felt like if he kept going like this, keeping me on the edge of pleasure, I'd lose my sanity forever.

He broke the kiss and raise his head, making me whimper in pained pleasure.

He brought his thumb to his mouth and sucked on it, his eyes rolling back in pleasure.

"I want to taste everything," he said before crawling down the bed until he reached the bottom.

I gripped his hard shoulders which were parting my legs wide open, hiding nothing from his view, and just his hot breath so close to my opening made me shiver.

His mouth went down, pressing a couple of closed-mouth kisses between my legs before licking between my lips, opening me and pressing the flat of his tongue on the inner flesh.

I let out a broken gasp as I tightened my hold on his shoulders, my nails biting into his hot skin.

He grabbed my hips to keep me in place as he buried his face fully between my legs, his lips and his tongue playful and demanding, alternating between light biting and soothing licks. His breathing was rapid and it was a certain comfort to know that he was as lost as I was.

I rocked my hips in helpless movement, seeking something that only he could give me. Suddenly as his tongue entered me, an orgasm exploded without a warning, blinding me by its force as I finally fell of the edge, shouting his name.

He raised his head, his lips and chin glistering with my arousal, pride mixed with lust in his eyes.

He kissed his way back up my body as I tried to catch my breath, and he stopped at my mouth, his kisses harder than before. Tasting myself on his tongue and lips made it all even more erotic. I let my hand roam between our bodies, and I rested it against the hard length of his throbbing erection, the coldness of apprehension settling once again in the depth of my stomach, despite my urging physical need to have him deep inside me. I ran my fingers over his length, feeling every ridge, every vein, somehow in awe that such a hard, impressive, masculine feature could be so soft. I hesitantly wrapped my fingers around his hardness, feeling it pulse in my hand and squeezed gently.

Hoka groaned against my mouth, and I removed my hand immediately. Maybe I shouldn't have squeezed like that.

"Did I hurt you?"

He grabbed the hand I just had wrapped around him and kissed my palm. "No, sweetheart, quite the contrary. Your hand on my cock feels so good, it's like heaven, but I can't have you do that now. I want you too much, and I want to come with my cock buried so deep inside you, we wouldn't be able to say where you start and where I end.

I blushed and parted my legs to let him fully between them and drew my knees up to encase his hips in an intimate embrace, his penis pressing against my slit.

"Hoka... Hoka, take me now. I w-want you inside me. I want you more than I want my next breath. I want... I want..." I moved my head from side to side. "I want—"

He didn't let me finish as he interrupted me with another deep kiss, his tongue playing with mine as his left hand grabbed at my breast.

He moved slightly, and I could feel the bulbous head of his shaft against my entrance, pressing gently.

"Mine?" he asked, breaking the kiss and nudging my entrance a little just to slip in the tip.

"Yours," I agreed, letting my hands trail down his back, making him shiver before turning my head to the side to kiss his strong bicep resting just beside my head.

"Say it again," he commended through gritted teeth, slipping just a little more inside, just enough for me to start feeling the stretch of his invasion.

"I'm yours."

On that last word, he moved forward in one long, hard thrust, and I couldn't stop the cry of pain. Hoka threw his head back and let out a sound that was more animalistic than human as he was fully seated inside me, clearly lost in his pleasure.

Seeing how lost he was in me helped to ease some of the burning pain at the forceful invasion. I had known that no matter how wet and ready I was, having something that thick and long inside me was going to hurt.

"I'm sorry," he said with a strangled voice. He moved a little and I winced, making him freeze immediately. "I won't move until you're ready." His voice was jerky, and I knew that it was requiring a superhuman will to stop his body from following its urge to thrust.

He started to kiss me everywhere he could reach in an attempt to soothe the pain. He kissed my throat, my breast, tracing my nipple with his tongue, murmuring words of love and passion I was not certain he truly meant.

He moved a little and my grip around his shaft loosened as the pain slowly faded.

He arched an eyebrow in a silent question, and I nodded. He started to thrust gently, easing in and out of my gripping, tender flesh until the pain was completely gone, leaving a wonderful fullness in its place.

I moved my legs, resting my heels on the dips of his ass, allowing my legs to widen even more.

He let out a guttural moan and started to thrust deeper, harder, faster, filling me until I was stretched tightly around him. Instinctively, my hips started to follow every movement, every deep thrust until the soreness disappeared completely, leaving the exquisite pressure of his length inside of me.

I felt the tension build, higher and higher with each of his powerful thrust.

"Come for me, my love," he whispered darkly in my ear as one of his hands trailed between our bodies and pinched my throbbing clit between his fingers.

Once again, I felt my world implode in heavenly fire, heightening all my senses so I could feel every line of his hardness as my body clamped around him with every orgasmic spasm.

The pressure of my spasms was enough to make him lose control, and after a couple erratic thrusts, he came groaning my name.

He fell heavily on top of me, as breathless as I was, his rapid heartbeat echoing mine. The gentle buzz of pleasure continued even after our breaths went back to normal and I let out a relaxed sigh, enjoying the weight of his body over mine.

He let out a sigh as he rolled to his side, forcing himself to withdraw from me.

"I wouldn't want to smother you," he said, his voice gravelly and drowsy. "Are you okay?" He looked down at me in concern.

I smiled, rolling to my side and snuggling into the crook of his arm before bringing my hand up to cradle his jaw. "I'm more than fine. That was like nothing else in this world. I never thought someone could get so much pleasure." I kissed his lips in a gentle caress before settling once again on his arm, my face buried in his neck.

"It's not usually that good," he replied as he moved his leg to grab the blanket that was folded on the side of the bed and pulled it up over our naked bodies. "I've never known a pleasure like that in my life. When I was inside you, I realized that was the way I wanted to die—buried deep into the tight heaven of your body."

I shivered. "Don't talk about death now. I'm too happy to think of danger." I rested an arm on his chest and lifted my leg to stay between his, feeling his now soft dick against my leg as I snuggled closer to him.

I closed my eyes and traced idle patterns on his chest as I started to drift into an exhausted slumber.

I felt his lips brush against my forehead. "You sleep, my love. Your dragon will be watching over you."

And I fell asleep, feeling safe, happy, wanted, and loved for the first time in my life.

CHAPTER 12

Violet

One night turned into two, then three, and four. I had not slept in my room since that first night, and a few of my things were creeping into Hoka's room, including my toothbrush beside his in the bathroom, or my shower gel and shampoo sitting in his gigantic Italian shower.

It was all too new to make much sense, but it felt like we were settling into a sort of comfortable cocoon which I was reluctant to step out of one day. Right now, we were in his home, surrounded by very few people, and I'd seen a glaring Jiro only from afar.

Hoka was away for a good part of the day, and I was left alone to explore, learn how to cook with Himari and immerse myself in all the Japanese Folklore and culture books, translated in English I could get my hands on.

I wanted to feel close to Hoka the best I could, and it seemed that learning about his origins was the best way.

I rested the book on the brief history of the Samurai on my knees as there was a soft knock on my door.

"Come in," I called, and I was surprised to see Hoka. "Home already?"

"I missed you," he replied with a dismissive shrug.

I laughed it off and moved from the reading chair, allowing him to sit.

"I've been looking for you for a while," he said, sitting down.

"And coming to check my bedroom didn't cross your mind?" I replied with a grin, nudging him playfully with my foot.

He caught it in his hand and brought it up, kissing the top of it before resting it on his lap, running his hand up and down my shin.

"Are you hiding?"

I rolled my eyes, but he was not far from the truth. I knew Jiro was in the main house today, instead of the guest house he usually occupied, and I quite hated meeting his eyes full of disappointment.

"I just think you'd be better in my room, you know."

"It's just different when you're not there. It's your space. I feel like I'm intruding when I'm in there without you."

It was the truth. Hoka's room was so perfectly him, so masculine and organized, with his priceless katanas on display and his private office at the side. God only knew what kind of scary secrets this room held.

He frowned, stopping his gentle caress and squeezed my foot. "I don't like that. I want you to feel at ease there. Do you want us to redecorate?"

My heart hammered in my chest as I sat straighter, but his neutral expression showed that he didn't think anything special of it.

"Your room is beautiful, it would be a shame to change a thing." I pressed my foot against his groin in a not so subtle invitation.

"You're killing me," he groaned as he stood. "I wish I had the time, I would have you naked and bent over this bed faster than you could stand, but I've got to go."

I felt arousal coat my slit at the images of him bending me over and taking me from behind. He'd done that last night, after a supposedly quick shower that made us both very late for dinner, and I'd loved it—the dominance of the position, the deep penetration, his warm breath against my neck... I could almost come just at the thought of it.

His nostrils flared as his golden eyes turned almost black as his pupils dilated with desire.

"Stop it woman," he ordered, his words only carrying heat.

I shrugged and extended my hand for him to help me up since I wasn't sure my legs would be strong enough. "You only have yourself to blame here. If you didn't use your *katana* so well, I wouldn't be craving it all the time."

He threw his head back and laughed uproariously. I loved this complete abandonment of pretenses when he was just Hoka—my man, my lover—an not Hoka 'the boss' I saw when we were in the presence of his staff.

"My katana?" he asked, dabbing at the corner of his eyes to dry his tears.

I gave him a coy smile. "It did *slay* me."

He shook his head, kissing my forehead, my nose, my mouth, and then my chin. He did that every day before he left, and it was in these particular moments that I could feel him steal more pieces of my heart. I loved him, there were no two ways about it.

"Ah, Violet, *anata no soba ga, watashi no okiniiri no basho desu.*"

I cocked my head to the side, loving it when he spoke Japanese but hating that I didn't understand. I would soon, though—I was taking online classes to surprise him.

"Together with you is my favorite place to be," he repeated in English. "Ah, somehow, it's easier for me to say all that in Japanese." He rubbed at his neck subconsciously.

I opened my mouth. I was ready to say the words now, but he stopped me as he reached into his suit jacket and got out a long flat box.

"I won't be home this evening, but this is for you. I hope you like it."

"Of course, I will. It's from you," I replied sincerely, and his face softened as if these types of interactions were rare in his life.

"I'm not used to this softness in my world. You feel everything so deeply it's so—"

"Is it a bad thing?" I asked, stopping myself from opening the box.

"No, but it must be exhausting."

"Not really, being with you makes it worth it." I opened the box and inhaled sharply at the stunning necklace. I trailed my fingers over the beautifully crafted dragon that was the exact copy of the one that covered Hoka's back. There were some very small stones mimicking the red camellias that were around his dragon tattoo and it held something that looked suspiciously like a diamond between his front claws.

"It is a platinum dragon with ruby and diamond," he said as I kept looking down, my eyes burning with tears at the overwhelming emotions.

"You shouldn't have, Hoka. It's so beautiful." I looked up, giving him a watery smile.

He reached up and cupped my cheeks gently before running his thumbs under my eyes to dry my tears.

"So you'll always remember that your dragon is your champion; he will always be there for you, protecting you." He reached for the necklace. "Turn around."

I silently complied and let him slide the chain around my neck, the cool metal of the dragon doing wonders on my hot skin.

He rested his hand on my shoulders and kissed where the necklace closed.

I turned around, resting my hand on top of it and took a deep breath, hoping not to butcher the sentence I've learned and repeated to myself to make sure it was perfect.

"*Suki da yo.*" *I love you.*

He froze. "What?"

"Oh..." I blushed, wanting the floor to swallow me completely. I failed at the most important thing I wanted to say. "I'm sorry, I didn't say it right. I m—."

He leaned down and gave me a hard, bruising kiss. "No, no it was perfect, absolutely perfect. I just want to hear you say it again. Please, say it again."

"*Suki da yo.*"

"Again."

"*Suki da yo.*"

"Again." His voice was getting breathless, his hand on the side of my neck shaking a little.

"*Suki da yo.*"

His eyes shone slightly and his hand on my neck tightened. He was overwhelmed by what I said, and I wasn't sure if it was a good thing or not.

I was about to tell him he didn't have to reciprocate when he grabbed my face between his hands, and I once again marveled at how such big strong hands could handle me with so much softness.

He started to pepper my face with kisses. "*Suki da yo.*" He kissed my cheek. "*Dai suki da yo. I love you so much.*" He kissed my other cheek. "*Anata wa watashi no sekai desu. You're my world.*" He then crashed his mouth on mine, running his tongue on the seam of my lips, asking for entrance, I opened my mouth, and he invaded, kissing me with shallow laps of his tongue, starting an erotic dance we both knew we could not finish.

He growled, taking a step back, "I'll see you later."

I nodded, resting my fingers on my lips. Would kissing him ever lose its novelty?

He walked to my bedroom door, and opened it, but stopped just before reaching the threshold and turned his head to the side. "Say it again."

I laughed. "*Suki da yo.*"

He rested his hand on his chest. "I love you, sweet angel."

I sat on the bed, looking at the closed door before letting my hand trail to the necklace. I did it; I told him that I loved him and as unbelievable as it was, he loved me, too.

I let out a little squeal, letting myself fall back onto my bed. I was loved, *really* loved!

I looked at the ceiling for a couple of minutes, letting my emotions settle before roaming to the library to pick another book as I was going to spend my evening alone.

I was going through the shelves when the door opened behind me. I turned around with a small smile, thinking it was Hoka coming back for another kiss, but my smile froze on my lips when my eyes connected with Jiro's judgmental gaze.

I let out an inward sigh. "Jiro," I offered as amicably as I could.

He opened his mouth and closed it again before shaking his head a little. "He gave you the choice, and you chose wrong."

I turned around to face him fully, done with false pretenses. "Why do you hate me?"

"Hate you?" He sighed with another slight shake of his head. "I don't hate you. Quite the contrary, actually... I'm quite fond of you."

I frowned, crossing my arms on my chest. Was it some kind of rivalry to steal me away from Hoka? Had I missed the signs completely? I opened my mouth to tell him he was wasting his time and energy.

He chuckled and raised his hand to stop me from humiliating myself. "No, I just realized how it must have come across, but I don't mean it like that." He took a couple of steps toward me. "I know you're a good person, and I know without a doubt that you truly care for Hoka."

I didn't just care, I loved him deeply, but I was not about to argue with Jiro. "Is that so wrong?"

He nodded. "Yes, it is, because you clearly don't think straight, and I think he likes seeing himself through your eyes."

It stung, mostly because it was a fear of mine, too. Not that he was vain enough to want me just because I saw him like he was my personal hero, but that he wanted me mostly because of the novelty it all was.

"We shouldn't mix." He raised his hand. "It's not racist, it's a fact. Go ahead and marry any Japanese man on the street, that's not a problem. The problem is marrying one of *us*." He pulled his shirt out of his pants to show me the tattoo on his flank, the one matching Hoka's. "This mark is an ancient tradition. We've been raised a certain way; we have a wide culture that is so different from yours. Hoka," he sighed with weariness, "is too blind to see that you will never be accepted as one of our own. You can't be one of the clan because you've not been born into it."

"I can learn," I whispered as the veracity of his words wrapped its cold hands around my heart, squeezing it to the point of pain.

"No, you can't. You can try, sure, but it's not just a few rules and customs. It's an entire culture—thousands of years of stories, legends, and rules—that has been passed to us from the first Samurai. And Hoka's not just anyone, he's our leader, the vessel of all these traditions. How can he compel people to follow the rules when his own partner can't?"

"But I... people like me," I offered rather lamely.

"They do, just like I do." I sat down with confusion as Jiro explained, "They do, but only because they think you're a phase, the whim of a bored king. They accept you because they're convinced you're just a harmless, temporary distraction."

That cut even deeper than it was probably intended because this also played into my insecurities.

"But you don't think I am?"

"I do, but I think he'll realize it too late, once the damage is done to both of you. But I know he knows. Deep down, he does. He *ought* to."

I should have ignored it; I never should have opened the door to doubt, yet I couldn't help it. "What do you mean?"

"Do you know where he is going tonight?"

"Somewhere you're not either," I replied childishly.

He gave me a half smile. "I'm going there. I just needed to retrieve a bottle of special *shochu* that Hoka forgot to take when he left. Hoka is at a family wedding where everyone is taking their partners—wives and girlfriends—yet here you are, in your yoga pants whilst he is parading there, single. Why do you think he took you to that Italian restaurant he never goes to?" He walked to the dark cabinet on the corner and retrieved a bottle from the lower shelf. "I have no pleasure saying any of this."

I let out a humorless laugh, the pain of his words stinging so deeply, but I knew he meant that. "Sure, you don't."

He turned around. "I don't," he repeated with conviction. "Do you think I enjoy crushing your hope? Dimming the light in your eyes? I don't. It's like crushing a baby bird."

"Why are you telling me that?"

"Because I keep telling him to let you go, to free you, not to make the same mistakes I made, but he's not listening. I think he's convinced that he can be the man you think he is. But he's not, no matter how much he tries." Jiro shook his head. "A leopard never changes its spots, no matter how much he wants to. One day, Hoka will wake up and realize he can't change, and you will see the real him, the ruthless man I know he is." He let out a weary breath. "And you *will* be collateral damage."

"Is your own experience clouding your mind? We're all different. It's not because you hurt her, and she left you that it would be the same for us."

Anger and pain flashed in his eyes, and I regretted my words immediately. He took a step toward me and despite my fear, I stood my ground. "Being with you makes his life so much harder than it needs to be, and one day when the passion, lust, or whatever you both think it is, will have faded, he will wonder if it was all worth it."

"I am not making his life more difficult."

"Don't tell me you're *that* naive. You think because he's the king he can do whatever he pleases?" He rolled his eyes and snorted. "Of course, you are an added problem, and deep down, you know it. If you are honest with yourself, you have to see it. His late nights in his office, his secret phone calls. His choices are being questioned."

"I make him happy," I replied stubbornly, much more to convince myself than him.

"For now," he agreed with a nod. "He is just so wrapped up in the lust, passion and the novelty of it. Being seen as the hero is exhilarating... I know, I've been there, but trust me, one day or another the truth hits you right in the face."

"He told me all there is to say about himself."

Jiro scoffed, "No, he didn't, because if he did, you wouldn't be standing. You'd be six feet under."

"Hoka wouldn't kill me," I replied as discomfort settled in my stomach. I was alone with this man, who despite saying he was fond of me, gave me all the sign of a murderer ready to strike. *Is he? Are you an expert now? Netflix gave you a PhD in murder?* the voice taunted me as I took a step back. The back of my legs hit the cool soft leather of Hoka's armchair. I fell heavily into it, both exhausted and scared.

"No, he wouldn't but I would. If I had no other choice, I would." He cocked his head to the side, detailing me. "Did Hoka tell you about my role?"

I shook my head mutedly, not wanting to give him a reason to do whatever he wanted to do.

"He told you I was his head of security, and it was not a complete lie. I'm his second in command, but above all, I'm his executioner." He kept his dark orbs locked with mine, trying to make me understand the implication of his words, and I understood them only too well.

Executioner. A shiver of fright ran down my spine.

"I get my hands dirty when his need to stay clean, and I take the hard decisions when he's unable to make them."

"What do you want me to do?" I asked, hating how my voice broke with fear. "Leave him or you'll kill me?"

He sighed with frustration as if I was missing the whole point. "No, leave or stay is irrelevant. I said my piece. If you were a traitor, on the other hand..."

"I won't betray him."

"Then you've got nothing to fear from me. It's all the rest you should worry about." He looked at his watch and walked toward the door.

I should have let him leave; he had said way more than enough to make me think about everything Hoka and I were or who I thought we could be, yet I could not stop myself. "What do you want me to do then? Why tell me all that?"

He shrugged. "Because part of me feels guilty to see you getting submerged without knowing anything. It's like a lobster in water—when it's hot they fight, but when we put them into cold water and progressively heat it up, they don't notice until it's much too late. Now you have all the information, now you can make a truly informed decision, and now I can wash my hands of whatever happens."

"Ah, clean conscience," I snorted, raising my chin challengingly.

He laughed but it lacked humor. "Ah, it's much too late for that. Call it..." He looked behind me, but I refused to turn and see what he was staring at. "Call it my repayments to the universe, to karma or whatever you want to call it." He looked back at me. "But just know that, one way or another, I have nothing to gain here. Leave or stay, it won't impact my fall, but it will cause yours without a shadow of a doubt. Good night, baby bird," he added mockingly.

Once the door clicked shut behind him, I lost my bravado and let the bite of Jiro's words and doubts completely submerge me.

Everything he said had added brick after brick back on the wall that used to protect my heart and added a fresh coat of self-doubt as mortar.

The necklace that had felt like a protection, a show of love, felt heavy around my neck. It felt like a gift of guilt—a mistress gift.

I sometimes forget you could be the mistress even if the man was single—it was easy to be nothing more than a shameful little secret.

I turned to leave and met my reflection in the glass doors for one of Hoka's display cases holding the Samurai armor.

My smile was gone, my face was tight; at that moment I looked a little too much like my mother for my liking.

I went through the motions, wondering how to approach the subject with Hoka, but also wondering if it was true that I was making his life harder. It had not been my intention.

Himari ate dinner with me, asking me a few times if I was feeling ill. It was true that I was not my usual self, and I didn't feel like talking, especially to someone who was part of Hoka's life, not mine.

If I truly thought about it, my life revolved around Hoka. I was in his house, surrounded by his people. What did I have for me? The only certainty I had was that I would still have an apartment when I decided to go back home, as Hoka paid six months' rent in advance, despite my numerous protests.

What did I have that was not revolving around him? Nothing, and that also gave me a vague echo of my mother's life—of the stories I'd inadvertently been a witness to when I was a child.

I was to the point of missing the club, the girls, and even Sandra from *Sun Valley*. I couldn't say that I'd been best friends with any of them, but it would be nice to have a woman to talk to, to confide in without having the whole mafia factor.

Maybe I should call Sandra and take her up on her offer for a drink, just to get out of this house and my head.

I yawned as I finished my plate, the recent long nights I've had as Hoka made love to me and all overthinking from this afternoon really drained the little energy I had left.

Himari refused my help for cleaning up as I usually did and ordered me to bed. I looked at the kitchen clock as I stood, it was only eight p.m., and I couldn't help but imagine what Hoka was doing now at that party. Would he be dancing with a woman? Someone fit enough to be seen with him in public? A woman who would make him forget his problems, instead of piling them on him? A woman *worthy* of him?

I made my way upstairs and passed my room to go to his, but I stopped before reaching the door and turned back toward mine.

He'd been right; having my own space was priceless, and I needed one night away from him.

I awakened with a jerk, looking around the dark room as if someone was there, spying at me in the darkness.

I sighed and turned to my side, my back wet with perspiration—the wooden ceiling fan not really helping me on this clammy night.

I looked at the alarm and sighed. It was only two-thirty a.m., and I felt too restless and hot to go back to sleep.

I walked to the window and pulled open the heavy blackout curtain, letting in the bright light of the full moon.

I opened the window, welcoming the light breeze, despite the fresh soil smell and clamminess that followed the recent rainfall.

I tiptoed barefoot on the wet tiles of the balcony and looked around the dark grounds as my skin slowly cooled down.

I leaned precariously against the railing, trying to have a peek at the corner and see if I could make out any light in Hoka's room.

Was he home now?

I shook my head, leaning back and brought my hands up, tightening my hair into a bun on top of my head, letting my neck enjoy some of the coolness as well.

I was not tired anymore, but I couldn't just stay on the balcony like this, either. Maybe a cool shower and a book would help put me back in a sleeping mood.

I walked back in and stopped as my eyes landed on the chest of drawers by the door. The full moon was so bright, it lit the room completely, especially the bunch of roses that had not been there when I went to bed.

I closed the patio doors behind me and walked to the flowers. I was not crazy, someone had been in my room, and I knew who it was.

My heart accelerated at the thought of Hoka watching me sleep, somehow trying to ignore the fact that the door had been locked when I went to bed. I turned on the lights and looked at the most beautiful, brightest red roses I'd ever seen.

My hand trailed on the card with my name scribbled on it. I now knew Hoka's handwriting and wouldn't mistake it with anyone else's ever again.

I opened it and a little string of red thread fell by my feet. I picked it up and looked at it and the two hoops on each end.

Violet,

This is the thread of destiny. It is customary for the newlyweds to give one to every male guest, then in turn, he is supposed to hook one side to his finger and the other one to the finger of the person he loves. It is a sign of good luck and a long, meaningful relationship. Unfortunately, the person holding my heart wasn't there with me.

Love, always

Hoka

I sighed, resting the card and thread against my chest. This couldn't be fake. I took a step toward the door and stopped again.

I had another choice to make now—either stay here, hold my ground and have a chat with him in the morning, or go to him now, slip into his bed, and forget it all.

I couldn't deny that Jiro's words had rung true on so many levels, and I couldn't ignore all the past experiences and how my upbringing shaped me, but at the same time, actions spoke louder than words, and if we disregarded that wedding, Hoka had not done anything worthy of my doubts.

I set the card and thread back on the dresser and left the room, going to Hoka's room as silently as possible and cracked the door open.

I frowned as I peeked inside, his bed was still perfectly made, and he was nowhere in sight. I took a few steps in and noticed that the door of his private office was cracked open, light coming from it.

I walked to the door, ready to knock when Jiro's words played in my head. Why was he working so late? Was it true that I made his life difficult? Maybe spending his nights making love to me prevented him from concentrating on work.

I was not from his world, I couldn't understand. Maybe it was something other women would understand better, encourage him to do his things and not be wrapped around him the way I have been.

"Violet?"

His deep voice made me jump, and I pushed the door open to find him sitting behind his desk. He had discarded his hairband, his tie, and jacket. His shirt had a few buttons open, and his sleeves were rolled up to his elbows, revealing his sexy tattoos.

"How did you know I was there?" I asked, standing on the threshold, leaning my shoulder against the frame.

He gave me a smile that looked wearier than I think he wanted it to look. "I'm quite aware of you. Your smell, your breathing. I just knew." He leaned back in his chair. "How are you?" he asked, and it seemed like such a generic question at that time of night.

"I received your present, it's lovely, thank you."

"Is that why you came? To thank me?" he asked, resting his hand on top of the papers on his desk, just beside the tumbler of liquor, and turned his seat a little toward me.

Now that I could see him face on, I noticed the deep purple shadows under his eyes, even more striking under his unflattering desk light.

Is he having issues? Is there anything I could help with?

I let my eyes trail to the papers on his desk before looking at him again.

"You should be asleep, you look tired. You need to look after yourself."

He let out a little laugh. "How nice of you to care about my wellbeing," he said it as a joke, but the warmth in his eyes showed how much it touched him.

Were people not concerned about him?

He let out a little sigh. "Somehow the idea of sleeping without you beside me was not very appealing."

My heart filled with so much love right then, and my shoulders relaxed, letting go of some of my worries.

"We're not sleeping much when we're in your bed." I reminded him with a raised eyebrow.

"True, but we could. When I fall asleep with you in my arms, it makes my night so much more restful." He cocked his head to the side. "What happened, Violet?"

I wouldn't insult him by pretending I didn't know what he was talking about. He expected me to be in his bed, which I hadn't been, and he wanted to know why. "My friends call me V," I replied without thinking. I was not sure how to formulate the answer to his question. So many things had happened, but I didn't want to get Jiro more involved in our story than he already was.

"That's nice. But I'm not your friend, Violet." He pronounced my name slowly, making it feel like one of his erotic caress that made me instinctively press my thighs together. "I don't want to be your friend. I want to be so, *so* much more."His eyes trailed down my cotton shirt and stopped mid thigh at the hem. "So much more," he said again, his eyes no longer golden but much darker. He stared at me, running his forefinger along his bottom lip.

You are so much more, and it's terrifying.

"Tell me why you pulled away?" he repeated, and the softness of his voice didn't match the urgency I could see in his eyes.

"Are you ashamed of me?"

He recoiled on his seat, his eyebrows arched high. "What?"

"Are you ashamed of me?"

"Wh... I just—" He shook his head as if my words made no sense. "Ashamed of you? Why on earth would I ever be ashamed of you?"

I shrugged and looked down at my feet, feeling way more exposed than I wanted to.

"Use your words, sweetheart, I won't be able to guess because it makes no sense."

"You didn't go out for work tonight, did you?"

He shook his head slowly as if he still couldn't really understand where I was going with that.

"Why didn't you take me with you? Are you hiding me from them? I-I would be careful, you know. I wouldn't embarrass you in front of your friends."

HIs eyes widened with understanding, and he pulled his seat back, turning it fully toward me. He gestured me forward and despite all my uncertainties, I was way too eager to be close to him.

I stopped at the edge of his desk, but he reached forward, grabbed me by the hips, and pulled me forward until I was standing between his legs.

"Ashamed of you?" He pulled me even closer to kiss my stomach, the feel of his lips even though the T-shirt burned my skin. "I would never be ashamed of you or hide you." He circled my waist and looked up to me. "I'm so proud you chose to be with me, sweet, gentle, and caring Violet. You have a softness that is soothing my soul in ways I can't explain because I can barely make sense of it. I'm not hiding you; I'm hiding *them*. I..." he sighed, "I'm scared that at any given moment, something will just be too much, and you will run away, kicking and screaming."

"Oh, so I *am* making your life a little harder."

"What? No!" His brows furrowed and his eyes shone with an intensity that made me shiver. "I'm not sure how you could think that. Violet. You're making everything so easy! You're so accepting, so accommodating. You're giving me so much! It's crazy how easily we can get used to things. I've never shared this bed with anyone before you, yet when I came home tonight and found it empty, I had no desire to get in because I knew I would not sleep well without you by my side. I'm already used to having my body wrapped around yours, like perfectly fitting puzzle pieces. I'm used to your soft silky hair smelling faintly like flowers, brushing against my nose, the soft breaths that are lulling me in a peaceful sleep. You're not making my life harder, you're making it *worth* it."

My heart leaped in my chest at his words; it was so much more than I could have dreamed of. I buried my hands in his long hair, scrapping my short nails on his scalp, making him sigh with content.

"I will not run away, Hoka. I may seem gentle and soft, but I've had my share of losses in my life, my share of pain."

"And I want to spare you from feeling this pain ever again."

"But you can't, and I wouldn't want you to kill yourself trying." I trailed my hand from the back of his head to cup his cheek. "You have to give me more credit, I will stand by you if you want me."

"Forever?"

I chuckled. "If that's what you want. I love you Hoka Nishimura."

His face relaxed as his eyes lit up with happiness. "I love you, too."

I wanted to help him relax. I wanted him to feel better and show him that I was there not only for the good time but also for him to lean on me, to share his worries with me. I heard the girls talking at the club about how men loved blowjobs, how it relaxed them. I heard them compare notes about what men liked best and part of me was glad I remembered.

I sank on my knees between his legs, running my hands up and down his legs.

His cock twitched as comprehension filled his face.

"Sweetheart, no... you don't have to." He rested his forefinger under my chin to keep eye contact.

"I know that, but I want to. I want to make you feel good. It will be my first time, but you can guide me, show me what you like. Show me how to make you lose control." I could see his dick starting to strain against the zipper of his pants, and I knew he was losing his own battle.

"I won't be able to reciprocate after that. Blowjobs are my weakness; I'm going to want nothing more than sleep after that."

I started to unbuckle his belt, pleased that my hands were not shaking despite my nervousness. "You're always taking care of me, always making sure I come first. Let me take care of you for once, let me show you that this is a partnership. You don't always have to pleasure me. Let me pleasure you, let me love you."

He removed his finger from under my chin as a silent surrender. He leaned back on his seat, resting his head against the leather and looked down at me.

I unbuttoned his pants and slid the zipper down, freeing him. He was rock-hard and once again, I felt a wave of tenderness knowing that, despite his obvious desire and want for this attention, he still wanted to make sure I was happy and not doing anything I didn't really want.

I circled him and ran my hand up and down his length as a gentle caress. I leaned down and licked the drop of precum on top of his bulbous circumcised head, making him hiss.

I looked up. "Is it okay? I don't know—"

He nodded, caressing my hair. "Yes," he breathed. "Yes, it's more than fine. Much more than fine."

"Teach me."

He gripped my hair in a tight fist and tightened his lips. I could see him fight his beastly side—the side of him he was starting to show in bed, the sweet brutality I enjoyed more than I would admit.

He inhaled deeply through his nose before loosening his hand. "I'll teach you," he replied with a voice so deep and gravely, it sounded nothing like him. I licked at his head again, rolling my tongue around it before sucking the tip into my mouth like a popsicle.

I lightly cupped his balls in my hand, enjoying the noise of rapture he made as I started to fondle them.

I traced my tongue along the underside of his length and it jerked under my attention. I did it again before sweeping my tongue over the head and tasted the fluid that had oozed out of the slit. I looked him in the eye and swiped my tongue over my lips.

His nostrils flared as his eyes darkened, and his hand twitched by his side. He was fighting with himself and his urge to take control.

I opened my mouth to cover just the tip, and I slipped my tongue across the head and circled the crown.

Hoka's chest raised unevenly as his breathing came out in gasps, and his control slipped as he thrust his hips upward, trying to make me take more of him into my mouth.

I took a few inches in, working my jaw open as wide as possible and pressed my tongue on the underside of his shaft. I sucked him shallowly and hearing him groan with pleasure was incredibly arousing and sexy, and the most rewarding sound in the world. I wanted to please him more than anything.

He entwined his fingers in my hair and gently pushed my head down, taking control, and I was more than happy to give it to him. I let him thrust his cock into my mouth deeper, even if he never pushed far enough to hit the back of my throat. His hand fisted my hair again, hard enough to make my scalp burn, but somehow this pain, this dominance, aroused me so much more.

After a couple minutes, Hoka raised his hips at the same time as he pushed a little deeper, just reaching the back of my throat as his breath became more ragged, and I felt the vein along the underside of his cock pulse harder on my tongue.

"Violet!" he roared as he locked me in place, his shaft deep into my mouth and he came, flooding my mouth with his cum. I swallowed happily, surprised that I didn't dislike his warm, salty taste.

I kept him in my mouth for a few seconds as he went limp on his chair.

I finally pulled it out and wiped the sides of my mouth before looking up at him.

He was looking down at me through hooded eyes, and despite the relaxed, sleepy set of his gaze, I could read all the adoration in his face.

"Violet, that was..." He was breathless as he put himself back in his pants.

I started to stand up, but he grabbed my face between his hands and pulled me to him. I fell on top of him, and he wrapped his arms around my waist, flushing my body against his as he kissed me lazily.

I moved my legs to sit on his lap, uncaring that he could feel the extent of my arousal through his pants.

"Did you like it?" I asked, breaking the kiss.

"Like it?" He shook his head tiredly. "Saying I liked it would be an insult. I'd happily go and follow death after the pleasure you just gave me. It would be worth it."

""Oh no, no death please." I kissed the bridge of his straight nose. "I would miss you too much."

He gave me a lopsided smile that made him look almost boyish. "It's good to know." He pecked my lips. "Was it okay for you?" he asked and the concern and uncertainty in his voice made him even more endearing. "I- I didn't want to lose control, especially for your first time but your mouth and tongue..." His hands drifted down to grab my ass. "I lost it completely and let the beast out."

I snuggled close to him, burying my face in his neck as I was about to admit the truth to him. "I like him, your beast. I enjoy it when you dominate me, when you make me yours."

He growled against my temple and pushed my ass forward. "If I was not that tired, I'd fuck you on this desk, showing you the full extent of my beast."

I kissed his neck, where I could feel his pulse. "Next time."

"Tomorrow," he promised, standing with me in his arms. "Now we sleep."

I squealed, wrapping my legs around his trim waist as he walked us back to his bedroom, only stopping to remove the cover and lay me down.

He kissed my forehead. "Remove everything," he ordered before rounding the bed, discarding his clothes on the floor and stepping in the bed as naked as I was.

He spooned me and wrapped his arm around my waist. "I'm taking you to Japan."

I froze and turned in his arms, but his eyes were closed, his face fully relaxed and at peace. "What?"

"Japan." He opened an eye. "I want you to meet my mother. Don't you want to go there?"

"Of course, I do! Japan is at the top of the travel list in my dream book."

He opened his other eye, "Now I'm intrigued, dream book? Can I look at it? Maybe I can help you fulfill some of them."

I blushed a little. "Oh, I don't know, it's quite intimate."

"Sweetheart, I've been inside of you, and you just had my cock in your mouth. I don't think it can get more intimate than this."

I turned my head again, feeling my cheek redden. "Fine, maybe. I'll think about it."

He let out a little laugh, pulling me a little closer to his body before letting his hand trail between my thighs. "Just let me give you a little orgasm," he said sleepily against my ear. "It will help you sleep better."

I was already so aroused at seeing him, a powerful man come undone with just my mouth and tongue that it only took a couple of gentle strokes over my clit to make me scream his name.

As I fell asleep at the sound of his deep breathing, my worries eased completely

But for how long?

CHAPTER 13

Hoka

I left Violet deep asleep in my bed. She didn't ever stir when I got up, when I took a shower, or when I placed a kiss on her lips.

I smiled as I looked at her, sprawled in my bed, her shiny black hair spread on my pillow, the sheets revealing her slender back and the small red marks I'd left when I had woken up in the early hours in the morning. I gave her all the pleasure I had been too tired to give her earlier that night.

Despite the seriousness of the situation and what I was going to face once I left this room, I couldn't help but feel my proud male ego swell, knowing I exhausted her to this point of deep slumber.

I took a last look at her before exiting the room and walked toward Jiro's guest house—the earlier tenderness I'd felt watching Violet sleep replaced by anger with every step I took.

I knocked, and as soon as he opened the door, instead of telling him all I wanted to say, my clenched fist connected full force with the side of his jaw.

He fell to the floor, looking at me with surprise as he cradled the side of his face. I knew that if it had not been for me taking him by surprise, this punch would not have landed. Jiro had been trained just like I was, and he would have deflected it easily, but it had to be the first time I hit him with the burning wish to do it over and over again.

"What the fuck was that for?"

I took a step in and kicked the door shut—I didn't need any of the men touring the perimeter to suspect there was some bad blood between me and my second in command. It would start rumors, which would not only hurt me, but also Violet, and it was the only reason that made me rethink it all.

I pointed an accusing finger at him. "Stay out of her head!"

He leaned on his forearm and grabbed his lower jaw, moving it from side to side.

"What did she tell you?"

I threw him a death glare. "She didn't tell me anything. She showed you a loyalty you don't deserve, but you're the only one who would dare."

He sighed, standing swiftly but staying at arm's length. Smart man. I wasn't sure I would not throw another punch, and this one would most likely break something, like his nose or teeth.

"I would not be the only one daring,'" he corrected, rearranging his shirt. "I'm the only one who has access to her. You're hiding her so well." He shrugged, crossing his arms on his chest. "Can you deny it?"

"Deny what?" I asked carefully.

"That you're hiding her. I only told her the truth."

"*Your* truth, not mine."

"The truth is the truth, Hoka. It's universal and immutable, that's the beauty of it."

I pursed my lips. It was true I was hiding her, but not for the reasons he led her to believe—and not even for the reasons I told her last night. I was hiding her because she was my precious treasure, a woman I knew I could be vulnerable with. Violet was a woman I could show a side of Hoka Nishimura that no one has ever seen before, and it was a side of me I would not be able to show her if we were in public, in the middle of my people, and I was not certain she would be receptive to all the other sides of me.

He shook his head, grabbing the bottle of water on the counter, and I realized he had been in the middle of training. "Your silence is an answer enough."

"I'm not ashamed of her, and you made her believe I was."

"I just told her the truth. How she saw it and interpreted it—"

"Is entirely your fault!" I spat. "She accepts me for *me*! She knows what I do, yet she still wants me. Is it so hard for you to accept that someone so gentle could be with me? Is that too good to be true?"

"Yes, it is!" He threw his hands up in exasperation. "Either she's delusional or she has a hidden agenda."

I frowned. I was certain there was no hidden agenda, but *delusional* wasn't far from the truth. Even if I refused to admit it, Jiro had a point; I was hiding a lot of things from her - too much.

"I'm done hiding her," I announced, more to myself than to him. "I'll organize a party for *Showa* the weekend after next and—"

Jiro's brows furrow with concern. "Hoka, you should think about it. Hearing rumors of a gaijin being involved with you is one thing but flaunting it and making it official is another."

I knew it was a risk—of course, I did. I was surrounded by vipers and vindictive women who would try to eat her alive to take her place in my life and in my bed.

I waved my hand dismissively. "You will stand by us, showing your unwavering support."

"I support you. I do!" he insisted, seeing the incredulous look I was sending him. "I don't approve—that much is true for the both of you—but I will not turn my back on you."

My face softened and some of my anger faded because, despite my annoyance, Jiro and I had been friends since before we could even walk, and we had each other's back throughout our whole life. I was there for him when everything happened with Anna, and he'd saved me from some serious beatings from my rigid father when I rebelled against the institution.

I sighed, relaxing my stance, and leaned against the wall.

"I took the official oath three years ago when you stepped up to take your father's seat, but we both know my commitment to you is much older than that. My disapproval is only something I express in private. My loyalty is yours and always will be."

I nodded. "This party will happen."

"Fine." He took a sip of water.

I walked to the door. "I'll call Sakura and have her organize it."

"It will create havoc."

"Possibly, but I think I deserve to have something for myself for once." I grabbed the handle and turned. "And Jiro?"

"Hmm?"

"I say this in all sincerity... Try to sabotage my relationship again and you are gone, understand?"

"Clearly. If it is to choose between the woman you just met and the friend who had your back for thirty years, it will be her."

"No. I will choose the person who is not betraying me. Loyalty is everything to me and by doing this, you would be betraying me."

He looked at me and nodded sharply.

I nodded as well and left in silence, hoping that I was not making one of the biggest mistakes of my life.

I was not sure organizing this party had actually been a good idea, especially since I had initiated it out of frustration and fear. Fear of losing her, fear of her thinking she was not good enough. And frustration because, despite everything, Jiro was right on so many levels. I just hoped I would not pay as dearly for my selfishness as he did for his. At the same time, I knew that my time hiding her was coming to an end. Jiro had been right—rumors had been flying about the unknown outsider I kept hidden in my estate. The rumors were getting crazier and crazier, and after a month of having her under my roof, the delay of an official introduction was close to expiration.

I'd done what I needed to do. I'd introduce her to my world on my own terms, under my own roof, where I could keep it controlled and keep her *safe*.

I adjusted my suit for the fifth time, pulling a little on the high collar as if it was choking me. It had been a while since I wore one of our traditional suits. I always preferred the Western cut, but this was an important event, and I chose this cut, which was usually only worn during weddings, to send a message.

I glanced at my bedroom door, wishing for her to come here so I could appease her doubts and apprehension in officially stepping into my world. She had been so worried when I told her about the party, and I didn't think she fully bought my confidence when I tried to reassure her. This woman could see through me, but it was because I was not trying to hide from her. I was doing it most of the time, and it was exhausting to always be on my guard, to always show the ruthless warrior the yakuza wanted and needed to see to not step out of the ranks. It was peaceful to be with her, to not have to hide, and to allow my weaknesses, flaws and uncertainties to roam freely while this beautiful angel soothed and loved them just as much as she did my strengths.

I smiled, rubbing the spot over my heart—my love for her so overwhelming that it expanded my heart to the point of pain. I was terrified of how much I loved her, terrified of the power it gave her over me, terrified of what losing her could mean.

I took a shaky breath at the horrible feeling that mere thought caused and shook my head.

No, not tonight! Tonight, I'll show the world that Hoka Nishimura can get what he wants.

I looked at the door again. Violet was getting ready in her room with the makeup artist and hairdresser that Sakura had picked for us. I saw the two women come in, carrying a black dressing bag, and I wondered if it had not been a big mistake not to ask her to show me the dress first.

I trusted Sakura more than any other woman for many reasons—mainly because I was the keeper of her best-kept secret. Sakura didn't like men, and when we were teenagers trying to figure out who we were, I had protected her from a scandal that would have ruined her in the eyes of her traditional family and would have changed the regards my father had for her and her family. We created a bond then and despite being the boss now, I couldn't help her any further until she was ready to step into the light. I was still protecting her as much as I could, providing her with a safe haven and ensuring that she and her *employee*—who was in fact her long-term girlfriend—could live their love in relative peace.

I trusted Sakura to show me the same regard and help me thrive in my relationship with Violet, even if she displayed the same level of wariness Jiro had when I had informed her of my decision to make things with Violet official.

Now was the time to see if I had been right to trust my instincts, which I usually was.

I walked to the side window and saw all the expensive cars coming down the long driveway where some cars were already parked. I wouldn't be able to delay our arrival much longer, and I wondered if Violet felt the same amount of apprehension as I did. I'd half expected her to run away with fear. I'd been waiting for her to come and tell me she'd changed her mind and didn't want to be part of my word after all—that she'd rather call it quits now and go to Paris, London, or New York...

If she did that, would you let her go? the voice of my conscience asked tauntingly. I should have been able to say yes with certainty because it was the right thing to do, but there was that dark, possessive, and obsessive part of me that was lurking just below the surface. That part of me was all darkness, and I feared that, should she decide to leave me, this part would keep her near—against her will if need be.

I sighed once more and met my uncle's challenging eyes after his chauffeur opened his door. I held his eyes impassively until he broke eye contact, glancing at someone talking to him.

I turned and walked briskly to the door. It was now or never.

I stopped by her door and leaned close, not hearing any voices. I frowned. I had not seen the women go, but they probably were gone by now. What if Violet left with them?

I knocked at the door, my heart racing in my chest, but I let out a breath of relief when I heard the clicking of heels as someone approached the door.

When she opened the door, anything I had planned to say vanished into thin air and all the blood that used to irrigate my brain went straight to my cock.

That dress... Fuck, I had no word for that dress. It was elegant and obviously expensive, but at the limit of decency. This evening would not only be a trial for our relationship, but also for my self-control. I would have to fight my desire to murder people just for resting their eyes on my temptress, my goddess, the very miracle of my existence.

Sakura was so clearly a lover of the woman's body as she chose a dress that enhanced Violet's every curve. The dress was in blood-red silk and black lace, with thin straps and revealed deep cleavage. The material molded around her luscious breasts, wrapping around her flat stomach, wider hips, and round bottom like second skin, before flaring down with an overlay of black lace to the floor, but with a slit so high, it stopped at the top of her leg. This dress showed the span of her alabaster, flawless, smooth skin, from her shapely calf to her toned thigh. So much skin... the skin I loved to lick, kiss, stroke.

Her hand trailed to her neck as she played with her dragon, a sign of her nervousness. I knew I had been silent for much too long, but I was too overwhelmed by her beauty to say anything.

I let my eyes roam back up her body, once again stopping at her chest before trailing up her slender neck to her full lips painted in a red as vibrant as her dress, her make-up a reminder of a vixen from the old movies. The smokiness around her eyes made them even bluer, and her hair had been left down, flowing to the middle of her back in silky waves.

My hand twitched with the desire to wrap in her hair and pull her into a kiss so heated, it would not stop until her dress was on her floor and I was buried so deep inside her I could feel her heartbeat all the way down my cock.

"Is it too much?" she asked, running her pink tongue over her lips. She threw a self-conscious look in the mirror. "I... I told them the dress wouldn't work. It's just too m—"

"It's perfect." Fuck, did my voice really sound that needy?

She gave me an uncertain look.

I extended my hand to her. "You're so beautiful tonight, I want to fall on my knees and weep. Then I want to move that scandalous slit to the right and bury my face between your legs until you scream my name."

She blushed, giving the skin on her chest a soft pink glow that drove me to the border of insanity.

"You could damn all the saints in heaven with the way you look tonight." I nudged my hand in her direction. "Come on, goddess, let me show you off."

She took my hand and as I intertwined our fingers, I could feel nothing more than the unwavering certainty that we were meant to be.

I kissed the back of her hand and looked into her eyes, feeding off all the emotions I saw there—her love, her trust, her innocence—and I prayed to all the gods willing to listen that it would still be there, intact, at the end of the night.

We walked hand in hand until we reached the end of the corridor, and I pulled her toward me, wrapping my arm around her. I saw her look of uncertainty as she assessed the stairs.

"I'm not used to heels so high," she explained, and I glanced down, finally noticing the black stiletto heels that, despite the added height, only made her grace my shoulder.

"I won't let you fall, ever," I replied and with the way she looked up at me, she understood it was not a statement only for now. I was making a commitment to her.

We went down the stairs and as we reached the last step and faced the main entrance, the few chatters of the late arrivals died in an instant. I noticed the obvious shock on their faces.

I winced internally, knowing it was just a snippet of what we would face when entering the reception room.

As expected, as soon as we walked in, the conversations died simultaneously and all eyes turned toward us—some curious, some shocked, others disapproving and some point-blank hostile. But my girl stood tall, her face a perfect mask of cool confidence, even if I could feel her shake slightly against my side.

I looked around the room, throwing warning glares at the most hostile of them, giving particular attention to Aiya and my uncle.

"Thank you for coming," I finally said in English. "Please enjoy this party celebrating Showa Day."

The guests bowed slightly—a sign of respect for my station—and I could see that a certain number of them, especially the older generations, had a hard time doing so as I was holding a gaijin against me.

"It could have been worse," Violet whispered softly as we walked to where Jiro was standing. Conversations picked back up, even though I knew, if only by the quick looks thrown our way, that Violet was in everyone's lips.

Jiro bowed his head to me before he dipped even lower in front of Violet, showing her great respect and consequently, giving to the audience an impression of approval he was far from feeling.

He met her eyes with a small smile, and despite her surprise, she smiled back as if she understood how crucial the appearances were tonight—and maybe she did.

Jiro looked behind her and jerked his head. "I think your uncle wants to speak with you."

I turned my head to the side, meeting my uncle's murderous glare. He looked stoic, like he always did. The extent of his fury was visible only in the flat line of his mouth and the redness of his ears. It was also clear what made him angry by Aiya's father leaning toward him, whispering into his ear. I was sure my uncle made a deal with him, probably promising the man a union between me and his daughter. I wondered what my uncle got out of it.

I wanted to ignore him, but I also knew there was a risk of him coming to me and forcing me to be quite unpleasant in front of Violet, which was something I was still very much inclined to avoid.

I sighed. "Do you mind?" I asked Violet, squeezing her hip tenderly. "I will be quick."

She shook her head with a smile, and even if I could see the worry in her eyes, she was trying to look brave to stop me from worrying.

"No, do what you have to do. I'll stay right here."

I looked at Jiro. "Stay with her and keep her away from the snakes," I ordered in Japanese before reluctantly letting go of her hip and going through the crowd to my uncle. The trip that should have taken a few seconds, took minutes. I was stopped every two steps by one of the men, eagerly reporting their recent success, trying to shine and win points without realizing that my level of annoyance kept rising with each interruption until I reached my uncle with nothing other than annoyance and frustration left.

"Who peed in your tea?" I asked as a way of greeting. I was not a twelve-year-old boy he could chastised with a dark look and some stupid life lesson. He was working for me, not the other way around—even if he seemed to forget it most of the time. Our blood relationship, his age, and the high respect of the troop for him gave him significant leeway during my father's reign—something that kept going during mine, especially at the start when I felt out of my depth, but it was not the case anymore. I only had a little patience left for the man.

He hissed through his teeth at the insult, and his eyes narrowed into angry slits. "Was this the reason you wanted to honor our emperor? To insult your name, your blood, your legacy, and above all, our emperor by using this opportunity to show off your whore?"

I took a step back with surprise. Had he just called Violet a whore?

I recovered quickly and leaned over him. "Have you just called my woman *a whore*?" I demanded coldly, ready to take his life right in the middle of the crowded room.

He saw he was walking a fine line and toned down his aggression. "Look at the way she's dressed! There's nothing left to the imagination."

I shrugged. "I picked the dress. She's stunning, so why hide it?"

"This is a sacred night, son. An ode to our emperor! It's not a night to have a teenage rebellion to show your defiance to authority."

I let out a startled laugh. "Is that what you think it is? A demonstration of defiance?" I cocked my head to the side. "To whom exactly? I *am* the authority."

"Then act like it!" he spat, his face plum red now. "Keep your perverted kink hidden; there's no need for your people to know your preference against nature."

I rolled my eyes. For him, loving a non-Asian woman was probably as messed up as being gay. That man was not a traditionalist; he was an idiot.

"What about my Aiya? H-how c-can you disrespect her like that?"

I slowly turned toward Botan Sato standing beside my uncle, and he lost all his bravado and previous sense of self-righteousness as I looked at him silently.

"And how, pray tell, am I disrespecting your daughter?" I asked coldly, keeping my eyes on him, making him squirm like a worm.

"You said you wanted to marry her."

"Years ago, and she refused." I shrugged. "I moved on." A true blessing really, something I would probably thank the ancestors for until my last breath.

"She reassessed. You asked her out for dinner. She is ready to take her rightful place."

I arched an eyebrow at this man's confidence. "*Rightful*? What makes it hers?"

Botan threw a look full of uncertainty to his right. "Akita said—"

Ah, there it is. My uncle was making commitments in my name. "I'm not sure what my uncle has said to you, but he doesn't speak on my name." I turned to my uncle. "Have you spoken in my name, *Oji*?" The lightness of my tone and the relaxed stance didn't hide the underlying threat in my question or the warning in my eyes. This would be a betrayal, and I was past the point of forgiveness.

"I said to Botan that you still wanted to marry Aiya, and after the romantic dinner at *Le Trésor,* the speculations all went that way."

"I see..." I nodded. That was utter bullshit. "Is that right, Botan?"

The man nodded quickly. "Yes. Aiya is overwhelmed with joy at the thought of becoming your wife. She's even been looking at wedding dresses and started to plan it."

"If your daughter imagined things that are not there, it's her problem, not mine... and certainly not Violet's. When I considered marrying your daughter, it had been in a moment of ill-placed grief. The dinner last month has been nothing more than a misunderstanding. A dinner I attended to avoid her any shame. Should I have known the consequences, I would not have attended. Should Violet not be in my life, the outcome would be the same. Aiya is *not* the right woman for me."

My uncle opened his mouth, but I stopped him with a gesture of my hand.

"I would recommend that you think well before talking. Should your next word be about my personal life, there will be consequences... for both of you." I was done with these two for the evening. I'd already left Violet much longer than I should have, and for no good reason.

My uncle closed his mouth and swallowed, scrunching his face as if he had just swallowed something sour.

I bowed my head at them. "I wish you gentlemen a lovely evening and advise you to try the shrimps; they are to die for."

I walked back, eager to stand beside Violet, to let her presence calm me and let mine deter anyone from talking to her.

I stopped mid-step, finding Jiro in the middle of a conversation with one of our investors.

"Where's Violet?" I asked, not concerned about interrupting them, suddenly forgetting all the conventions.

Jiro turned to me, confused for a second.

"Violet," I repeated slowly, trying to rein in my nerves. "Where is she?"

"Oh, she needed to use the restroom. She refused my help."

I turned, my jaw grinding so tight I felt like my teeth were about to turn to dust. I was towering over the room, but she was so short. How could I find her like that?

I took the direction of the toilet close to the office downstairs, assuming that she was too insecure on her heels to attempt going to one of the higher floors.

As the door of the reception room closed behind me, I enjoyed the coolness and relative quietness of the hall, finally realizing how noisy and hot it was in that room.

I had just rounded the staircases when I heard Aiya's high-pitched nasal voice. Violet's smoother, lower tone followed Aiya's aggressive words.

I balled my hands into fists, about to take a step to my left and reveal myself, ready to defend Violet and any ludicrous claim Aiya was making.

"Don't." Jiro pulled at my arm. I turned around as if he was crazy. Aiya was a snake, and she was going to destroy Violet. Jiro rested his forefinger on his lips. "She needs to be able to defend herself if she's to live in our world, you know that," he whispered, pulling me deeper into the dark crook of the staircase. "Give her a chance, at least."

I pursed my lips but stopped fighting him. Damn it, he was right. I would not be able to protect Violet twenty-four-seven. I could maybe ensure her physical safety, but it would be impossible for me to stop the venomous snake strikes with their lies and hurtful comments. She had to be able to avoid those herself.

"Are you slow?" Aiya asked with a haughtiness that only she could muster. She was acting like a queen when she was barely more than the daughter of a prosperous fish importer.

"I don't think I am," Violet replied gently. "Though to be fair, would I know it if I was?"

A half-smile formed on my lips as pride filled my heart. I rested my hand on the coolness of the wall, relaxing a little, even though Jiro was still holding my arm.

"Why don't you repeat that, just to make sure I understand?"

"Hoka Nishimura is *mine*. You're not one of us; you're just a white popper thinking she can come and steal our men."

"Oh no, I don't want your men. Just this one; you can keep the others."

I felt Jiro shake with silent laughter, and I knew it cost him to show any positive feeling toward Violet.

"This one is not available!" Aiya screeched. Violet was obviously getting on her nerves.

"And does he know he's taken? I'm just asking because he doesn't seem to be that concerned when he fucks me three times a day."

My dick stirred when I heard that word come out of her mouth. I closed my eyes for a second and took a deep breath, trying to calm my body. It was not a lie; I had a hard time not being inside her. However, we rarely fucked; I was mostly making love to her, revering her body, but there would be some fucking later, that much was sure.

Aiya hissed, "You're just a warm hole to him, an outlet for his frustration and frivolous dream of normality. He proposed to me." Her tone had lost some of her bravado as she realized she was losing this battle.

Violet sighed. "So you said. I'm not saying he didn't, but you said it yourself, it was three years ago, and you refused him."

"And you don't care?"

"Of course, I care!" Violet exclaimed, and it sobered some of my amusement. "I'm angry! No, actually, I'm furious."

Fuck. I pursed my lips. I should have intervened, not let Jiro stop me. I pulled on Jiro's hold, needing to intervene, but his hold tightened.

"Why on earth would you refuse him? That makes me so angry!"

I stopped fighting him, my whole body going slack in surprise. She didn't stop surprising me.

"But I'm glad you did," Violet continued. "Now I have him and his cock, as you so nicely put it, and I'll be going to Japan with him in two weeks. He can't wait for me to meet his mother. A bit of a crazy move for someone you called a 'temporary craving' but hey, free holidays, am I right?

I loved her, I knew that. I just never realized I could love her even more, yet here we were.

"You're just a money-grabbing, power-hungry whore," Aiya spat, but her words transpired only desperation at having lost to Violet. I didn't think it was something that happened very often.

"Takes one to know one," Sakura interrupted, and for that I was grateful. "Your father is looking for you, Aiya. He seems to be ready to leave. Violet, isn't it? Good, come with me. Himari wants your advice on something."

I rested my forehead against the wall, relaxing as relief overtook me. I'd made the right choice in letting her immerse herself in my world. My woman knew how to fight and defend herself.

"She passed the test?" I asked Jiro once the noises of heels clicking against the tiles had completely vanished.

"She did," he replied reluctantly. "It seems I underestimated her."

I wasn't sure of the underlying caution in his eyes, but I was much too relieved to care.

"She's strong, my girl," I replied, puffing my chest. "The ancestors would not have given me an ikigai who is too fragile to handle this world."

Jiro's head jerked up. "Is it what you think she is? Your ikigai?"

I shrugged as if it wasn't a big deal.

"Hoka," He sighed. "Ikigai is just a fairytale for little girls. It's not real."

I stepped back into the corridor. "I thought so too, until I met her. I didn't believe it and then I looked into her eyes and—" I shook my head, burying my hands in my pockets. He would not understand; I didn't think anyone could until they felt it for themselves. "I wish you to feel it one day. I truly do."

Jiro stepped into the corridor. "Don't curse me with this disease, Hoka. I don't want to have any of that," he replied.

I could do nothing other than raise my eyebrows at the coldness of his tone.

"Go back to your party; your woman is waiting." He turned around, taking the opposite direction from the party and disappeared into the office library at the end of the hall.

I walked back to the party to find Sakura and her *colleague*, Sara—secretly known as her wife—talking and keeping Violet company.

I threw Sakura a grateful look as I stopped beside Violet, kissing the top of her head.

She looked up at me and grinned, her love for me still very much the same as it always was, and I was once again thankful to the ancestors for giving me such a perfect woman.

Violet concentrated on Sara again, discussing what was the best variation of ice cream and the best mix.

"They've been at it for much longer than ice cream flavors deserve," Sakura muttered, coming to stand on my other side.

I smiled down at her, uncaring what the subject of discussion was, only enjoying the passion Violet was expressing.

I let my eyes trail down Violet's naked back. "I didn't thank you for the dress. It was a real trial for my libido."

"You're welcome. Your woman is a miniature work of art, a pocket-sized goddess. We needed to show that off."

I let out a startled laugh. *'Pocket-sized goddess'* fit her so perfectly.

"I like her. She has fire, passion, and a strong sense of loyalty," she added softly enough to make sure no one other than me could hear. "I think she's good for you."

"You seem to be the only one," I admitted reluctantly, keeping my eyes on Violet.

She shrugged. "And I'm usually always right, so who cares?"

I chuckled; she was infuriatingly correct.

"Give them time. It's all new and some will never accept it because they don't understand what it means to want to be happy and just grab it." She rolled her eyes. "Most of them would not recognize happiness even if it hit them in the face."

"It hit me in the face. I didn't expect it. I was not looking for it, but fuck, I grabbed it."

"It's usually the way it is. True love is not supposed to be easy; it's not supposed to be convenient, but it's so powerful and overwhelming that it makes all the rest insignificant."

"You're wise, my friend."

She winked at me. "So I've been told."

I spent the rest of the evening with Violet, and despite my apprehension, some of the younger members of the family seemed to warm up to her. I should not have been that surprised; it was almost impossible not to like Violet, you had to be actively trying to push her away for you not to like her.

I reluctantly let her into the care of Himari as I said goodbye to some of the highest and wealthier members of the organization.

When I came back to the house, Himari informed me that Violet went upstairs, and I was free to join her in her room whenever I was done.

I took the stairs two at the time and didn't even bother to knock on the door. I walked in to see her heels discarded by the door and she was standing on the balcony, still in her tempting dress, her hands on the banister, letting the breeze play in her hair.

She turned her head a little to the side and smiled. "It was too hot, and my shoes were killing me." She let out a sigh, turning forward again. "The breeze is wonderful."

I discarded my jacket on her bed and walked to the balcony, resting my hands on either side of hers. I pressed my body against hers, letting her feel my hardening cock against her back.

"This dress had been a trial to my self-control all night, sweetheart." I leaned down and licked the shell of her ear. "I feel like I should punish you."

"Punish me?" She tried to sound shocked, but the shiver of desire that went through her body showed me she enjoyed the thought of a punishment.

"Uh huh..." I let my lips trail down to her shoulder and ran my teeth against it, biting gently. "Showing what is mine to all these men. Men I spent a great part of the evening wanting to murder for looking at you with lust."

"They didn't."

"Oh, I can assure you they did." I crouched down behind her and ran my tongue slowly up her spine, tasting her sweet skin as I stood back up.

She let out a moan as I pushed her hair to the side and bit her neck. I pressed against her again. I was fully erect now, and I growled into her ear as she swayed against me, enjoying the feel of me.

I wrapped my arm around her waist and trailed my left hand up her side, sliding underneath her dress and kneading her breast, pulling on her hard nipple, making her moan.

"I only had you once today," I told her with amusement, letting go of her breast and reaching between us to unbuckle my belt and open my pants. I pulled them down a little, just enough to free my aching cock.

"Hoka. Not here! You can't," she said as I reached for the slit of the dress, pulling it back to reveal a black thong that drove me crazy.

I ran my fingers between her legs, the flimsy fabric already soaking wet. She wanted me right now as badly I wanted her.

"But we must. You wouldn't want to be a liar, do you? You told Aiya I was fucking you at least three times a day," I chastised her playfully as I moved the fabric to the side and lined up at her entrance, pushing inside slowly.

"You heard," she gasped as I pushed a little more inside of her.

"Yes." I kissed her temple. "And sweetheart, I'm so proud of you," I growled as I thrusted hard, filling her completely.

Leaning her head back against me, she moaned loudly.

"Hoka," she called as I thrusted again. "They will hear." She let out on another moan as I thrusted harder.

"Let," thrust, "them," thrust, "hear," thrust.

She stood on her toes as I took her hard and fast, fucking her with the masculine domination that I knew drove her crazy.

"You're mine, your body is mine." I wrapped my free hand around her throat. "Let them hear your pleasure; let them know who you belong to," I ordered with one punishing thrust, and she came, screaming my name into the night. As she squeezed me so tightly inside her, I followed her over the edge with my next thrust.

"I am yours," she agreed breathlessly as she leaned against me.

I wrapped my other arm around her, supporting her weight as her legs shook. I had my answer; it was clear now. If she had run away, I would have followed.

Violet Murphy was not my queen; she was my fucking kingdom.

CHAPTER 14

VIOLET

"Do you need anything else?" Hoka asked when he stopped his car in front of the café where I was supposed to meet Sandra in ten minutes.

I shook my head. "No, you already gave me too much," I replied. I felt really self-conscious about the amount of money I now had in my wallet.

"It wouldn't be such a problem if you just accepted the card," he replied, extending the credit card toward me again.

"Hoka, please." I sighed. All this money talk was making me overly self-conscious of my leech status, and Aiya's words, *'money-grabbing whore'* kept playing in my head. I would hate for anyone to believe that was true, that I was with Hoka for anything other than himself.

He could repeat a hundred times that it was a fair salary for all the work I've been doing as his assistant at home, but he just handed me five hundred dollars for just classifying the company marketing campaigns of the last three years. We couldn't say it was especially taxing work.

"Is your friend coming with you to buy what you need?"

I shrugged. "I think so, but I haven't asked her yet."

I saw his mouth tighten and his eyebrows furrowed with worry. I reached for his hand and squeezed. "I'll be okay even on my own. I've been on my own for years, and I've been doing pretty well."

"Yes, but that was before you were mine," he replied, bringing my hand to his lips and kissing the back of it.

I laughed despite the emotions warming my heart. Except for my mother, nobody had ever been so concerned about me, and it felt so good to feel cared for, to know that should you disappear, at least one person's world would be altered. It was nice to know that I mattered.

"I just have a few things to get for our trip, and it's just here." I pointed at the red neon sign of the small shopping mall on the corner of the next street.

He looked at it pensively for a few seconds before his phone beeped, reminding him of his upcoming meeting.

"You're going to be late."

"Yes," he replied, though he didn't let go of my hand.

"Hoka." I laughed after a few more seconds.

"Fine, fine." He pulled me toward me and kissed my lips soundly. "Have fun, but be good, okay? If anything feels off—"

"I'll go stand by a security guard and call you immediately."

He looked at me, rubbing his jaw, indecision written all over his face. He let out a weary sigh, finally letting go of my hand. "And text when you're almost done. I'll send a car if I can't come myself."

I shook my head. "Don't be silly, I can take a Ub—"

"Non-negotiable, sweetheart. Either you agree or I get out of the car now and go with you, the hell with my meetings."

I rolled my eyes, but I didn't doubt he meant it. "Fine, I promise." I leaned down to brush my lips against his. "I love you."

"I love you, too."

I exited the car and waited for him to merge back into the heavy morning traffic before I walked into the busy coffee shop.

I looked around, but I couldn't see Sandra. I frowned and pulled my phone out. Despite all her flaws, she was not the type to be late.

I started to type her a message when a woman in a green apron approached me.

"Your booth is ready," she offered with a bright smile, pointing to a booth at the back of the room, quite secluded from everything. It was a great spot for privacy, not that

Sandra and I were sharing any groundbreaking information.

"Oh okay! I didn't know we could book here." Sandra impressed me there.

I looked down at my phone and texted her that I was sitting at our booth and that it was a good call to book something since the café was almost full.

I sat on the comfortable red bench and took the wooden menu she extended toward me. I was at hipster central, that much was certain.

"Have a look at our drink selection. The latte of the day is cinnamon, pear, and carrots, with honey from the Canadian mountains."

I smiled politely with a nod. "Thank you," I replied, raising the menu in front of my face, hoping she would not see my disgusted look.

"Cinnamon, pear, and carrots? That sounds horrific," a deep voice spoke my thoughts.

I chuckled and pushed the menu down. "My thoughts exa—" I froze in shock as I felt my heart drop like a lead balloon to the bottom of my stomach.

This was not real; it was a dream. I looked around the café before looking at the man sitting across from me, an easy smile on his face, his arms crossed on the table.

"It seems that based on your expression, you know who I am." He cocked his head to the side, a glint of humor in his onyx eyes. "You're lucky I'm not taking offense easily, because that reaction could hurt any man."

I opened my mouth and closed it again a couple of times like a dying fish out of the water. I didn't just look like a fish, I felt like one too as I was gasping for air and my vision blurred a little. I was having a panic attack.

"Breathe," he said gently, uncrossing his arms to rest his warm hand on top of my arm.

I looked down at it, at his olive skin on top of my creamy one. How his hand was so gigantic that he could probably circle my forearm with it.

His touch was burning me, as if he was trying to brand my skin like cattle.

I removed my arm briskly. "Do not touch me!" I spat, glaring at him with all the hate I could muster.

I didn't need to have ever spoken to the man to know who he was. Alessandro Benetti; Playboy millionaire and head of the Chicago outfit in his spare time. I'd dreamed so many nights for him to come save me from my misery after Mom died. I'd even written him a letter, asking if I could come to Chicago. I'd been desperate and borderline homeless, but of course, no one came to my rescue. I was not sure why I'd expected anything else after what his father had done to my mother.

He cocked his head to the side, detailing my face. "Who would have thought that an Irish and Italian mix would turn into something so beautiful?"

"I've got nothing to say to you. My friend will be here any minute."

"No, she won't. She had car issues, but don't worry, she's getting help right now. And nothing to say to me?" He rested his hand on his chest. "Sister, you wound me."

"I am *not* your sister!" I recoiled with anger and disgust at being associated with him. "I'm just the daughter of a poor, underaged girl who has been abused by a much older, unscrupulous man."

"I'll give you that. Your mother was only five years older than me."

"And your father was a forty-six-year-old man who seduced a seventeen-year-old girl, then threatened her life when she became pregnant."

He shrugged. "Not denying that—the man was a pig. But that doesn't change the fact that you and I share DNA."

"DNA doesn't make you family."

"That's *literally* what it means."

I shook my head. "It makes you *related*, not family, and I want you gone."

"My father is gone now. I'm in charge."

He was saying that as if it made a difference. He was a grown man and his father had been gone for over a year. He could have come to me before; he could have helped me.

"I know he died. I wished I had the money to come to the funeral."

"To pay your respect?" he asked with a mocking smile.

"To spit on his grave."

Alessandro laughed, his booming laughter attracting some looks. "You'll have to take a number, *sorella*; there's probably a daily line for that. I even join it every once in a while."

I was surprised by him voicing his dislike of his father so openly, but I suspected it was a trick to mollify me for whatever he wanted.

The waitress came and set a tiny cup in front of him and a tall glass in front of me.

"Double espresso and hazelnut latte."

I pushed the drink away when she left. "I don't want it."

He pushed it back toward me. "Of course, you do. It's your favorite. Just have the latte, Violet."

I got a whiff of the drink as he moved it and it did smell delicious.

"What do you want?" I asked, wrapping my hands around the cup.

"I am offering you a place in our family. Come back to Chicago with me, leave this whole mess behind you and be my sister, officially. Hell, I'll even drive you to his grave on the way home and we can spit on it together. I know you want that."

I used to, so many years ago. I dreamed of my brother coming to save me. I never had any hope for my genitor, who was a hateful man. I knew he only saw me as a liability, and I think that was also why my mother decided to go on the other side of the country and work for the Irish to gain some flimsy protection.

"What do you want? You're not offering this from the goodness of your heart, especially since I'm not certain you even have one."

"Ouch, that hurts." The laughter in his eyes denied his words completely.

I kept my eyes locked on him silently, refusing to engage until he explained what he wanted.

He sighed, finally understanding that I would not indulge him. "I want you to tell me everything you know about Hoka Nishimura."

I raised my eyebrows in surprise, leaning back against my seat. He had to be joking, right? I couldn't hold the fit of laughter at the seriousness of his face, and my laughter increased when his face morphed into a scowl of annoyance.

"You want me to betray my - my boyfriend for a place in a family I don't even want?" I asked. It sounded even stupider out loud.

"I'm blood."

"Blood I rejected; blood I would actually suffer to have bled out of me." I leaned forward in what must have looked like a moment of connivance for outsiders. "What did you expect me to say, huh? Oh, my brother, I love you so much. My loyalty is to you and always will be. No one would ever change that. Tell me what you want to know about Hoka; I'll tell you everything." I let out a derisive snort. "I want you to listen, listen very well, and I need you to trust me when I say that, with all due respect, I despise everything to do with you, your name, your heritage, and even your city. I will never betray Hoka, no matter the offer, but for you? I wouldn't even betray my worst enemy."

"He will rip your heart out one day and leave you to bleed out without remorse. Mafia men are a different breed. Some think they can love, but they're wrong."

"Talking from experience?" I asked sarcastically.

"Yes."

I looked away, trying to hide my surprise at his straight answer. I had not expected that.

"After all the effort it took me to get you into the house and the life of the most solitary and suspicious Mafia boss, you're going to hang me to dry?"

I frowned. I knew I shouldn't take the bait, yet I couldn't stop the question that escapes my mouth in a whisper. "What do you mean?"

"The flowers? The threatening texts? The video." He beamed. "All me!"

My mind was reeling. He did all this! I was not even in real danger? I shook my head. He was lying.

"How would you have even known?"

"Ah, you think because you're two thousand miles away that I'm not keeping tabs on you?" He shook his head. "You're blood, and even if it means nothing to you, it means something to me. Imagine my surprise when I was told you attracted the interest of the head of the Yakuza. It was too good to be true."

"So, you used me as bait?"

"You were always safe."

I pushed back my untouched, now cold latte, and grabbed my bag. "It was wasted effort; I'd never have any loyalty to you or what you represent. I much rather bleed out on the pavement, as you so poetically put it, than make any kind of deal with you. Stay out of my life, now and forever." I stood. "I'd like to say it was a pleasure, but we both know it would be a lie."

I left the café, my back straight, acting much more confident than I felt at all the revelation he had given me.

My phone beeped just as I exited the café, and I almost expected Alessandro to be messing with my head some more, but it was Sandra informing me that someone just helped her fix her car issues, which I was sure my brother had also created and that she would be with me soon.

I replied telling her that the café was getting too crowded, and she could meet me at the mall where we would be able to grab a drink.

I was feeling uneasy during the five-minute walk that it took for me to get there, and I couldn't help but look behind me at any shop I stopped at. I also concentrated on the reflections of the stores' windows to see if someone, anyone, was just standing there spying on me.

I shook my head and finally entered a small store that sold all things beach-related. Hoka said the family house was in the middle of the mountains, but that there was a huge lake bordering his property that we could go swim in.

Hoka. My heart contracted with a feeling of guilt, and even if misplaced, it was quite powerful. Should I tell him what Alessandro told me? Should I tell him that the man who got my mother pregnant was not just an unknown sperm donor who didn't want anything to do with me and my mother, but the former boss of the Chicago Italian mafia?

I had the opportunity to tell him that my blood was tainted, too. I had wanted to tell him, but I decided against it. I had feared that it might influence his opinion of me or impact our relationship.

I was not a Benetti, not even a little. I was hundred percent Murphy, and I refused for this horrible mistake to create even more issues in my life.

What would Hoka think if I told him the truth now? I picked a couple of random swimsuits to try, not really in the frame of mind of doing any shopping anymore.

I knew I should tell him about Benetti being the source of the threats—that they were not real—but then what would it bring?

"I love this one!"

I jerked in surprise and turned around to see Sandra beaming at me.

"What?" I asked as she pulled me into an awkward hug. I was not very touchy-feely usually, but I was so grateful for her presence to help me get out of my head that I returned it.

She laughed and pointed at the hanger I was holding. "The bathing suit."

"Oh yes." I looked down at the royal-blue two-piece suit that seemed to belong in one of Marilyn Monroe's movies. "There will be some lake swimming."

She grabbed a couple of other swimsuits and extended them to me. "Oh, try these, too!" She made a shooing motion toward the dressing rooms. "Come on, chop, chop. Go try those, then we can go grab a coffee and a croissant. I'm fading away."

I shook my head as I took the direction she indicated. "You're always hungry."

"I'm not joking. I feel like my stomach is going concave! It's probably eating itself as we speak."

"Drama queen," I muttered as I walked into the dressing room and pulled the mustard-colored curtain closed.

"I heard that!" she huffed as I heard the squeak of the leather chair she probably threw herself onto.

"You were meant to!" I looked at my reflection as I pulled up my green summer dress.

I didn't look that worried now; Sandra was a godsend. I could get a couple of hours of fun, and maybe then I would have figured out what to tell Hoka. I just needed a little time to get over the shock of speaking to Benetti for the first, and hopefully, the last time.

I tried on the first suit over my underwear and turned around in front of the mirrors. That blue looked really nice on my skin, and it also seemed to enhance my curves.

"Show me!" Sandra called loudly from the other side of the curtain.

I blushed. "I don't think—"

"Come on, it's only you and me and the weird saleswoman. No offense."

I chuckled and rolled my eyes. How could anyone not take offense at being called 'weird' by a stranger?

I sighed and pulled the curtain open. I stayed in the cubicle, but I gave some stereotypical model poses while grimacing.

Sandra whistled. "Damn, girl! Who knew you had a body like that when you worked at *Sun Valley*?" She cocked her head to the side. "Maybe it's a good thing because with the old perv you were working for..." She made grabbing gestures with her hands.

I made a gagging sound as a shiver of disgust ran down my back at the thought of Mr. Reynold sweaty hands. "I didn't have that body then; it's what a diet of normal food instead of expired ramen will do to you," I replied, closing the curtain. I removed the swimsuit to try the neon pink one she had picked.

"Do ramen even expire?" she asked seriously. Leave it to her to pick the most random part of the conversation to focus on. "Those things are so full of chemicals, I'm pretty sure they'd be edible until the end of days."

"True," I replied, opening the curtain and modeling again.

She shook her head. "Nah, the first one is better. Well, whatever you're eating, it's working for you. You're like my sister when she was pregnant. I was jealous of her until she passed the 'sexy curves' stage to the 'I can't see my feet' stage." She continued to ramble once I had closed the curtain to try the last one. "You may still want to grab that one though, but in a different color. The bottom is wide enough that you could wear a tampon if your period is due."

"No, I—" I stopped, one leg up, about to step into the third bathing suit. *Period!* I let the bottom of the suit fall to the floor and grabbed my bag, unlocked my phone, and opened my period tracker.

Nine days late! I kept my eyes on the screen, resting my back against the plastic wall of the changing room. *Nine days!* I was never late, not even one day. Could I be...? I saw the flat coral plastic shell-shaped box peeking out of my bag. I was on the pill; I had been for about six months when I had started to consider taking the leap with Jake. I could not...

"Are you okay?" Sandra's voice brought me back to reality.

I'd forgotten for a few seconds where I was and what I was doing.

"Y-yeah, I'm fine. This one doesn't fit."

"Want me to get it in another size?"

I shook my head pointlessly and faced the mirror, resting a shaky hand on my lower belly. "No, I'm good." *Am I?* "I'll get the blue one. Give me a sec."

Was I pregnant? If I was, it would only complicate things even more. I told Hoka we were safe after our first time, and he took me bare every time after that, thinking it was the truth.

It was messy, complicated, terrifying, and despite all that, I couldn't help the little feeling of joyful trepidation to slip into my heart at the idea of having a little Hoka growing in me.

I rubbed my belly gently a couple of times. Nothing was certain right now, nothing to do until I was sure.

Next stop, the pharmacy, to confirm if, on top of being the girlfriend of a mafia boss, I was also about to become the mother of his child.

What an utter mess....

CHAPTER 15

Hoka

Something was different with Violet—an edge, a certain caution that was not there before, and it was driving me crazy.

I sat at my desk in my bedroom's office and couldn't manage to concentrate on the financial reports for the loan side of the business.

I was distracted by the soft running of water in the bathroom as Violet showered, getting ready for the day. Violet, soaping her naked skin... My dick stirred in my pants, and

I swirled my seat around. I could go in this bathroom right now, and she would welcome me with open arms and, depending on the mood I was in, let me make love to her or fuck her hard. I gazed through my open office door to the rumpled bed.

No, sex was not the problem—she was still craving my touch—but even during the moments of deep passion, when she was on the edge of orgasm, she was not completely letting herself go, as if there was an invisible barrier between us. Not enough for anyone else to notice, but enough to frustrate me.

I was frustrated, but mostly scared. Scared of losing her, scared that she finally decided that this life was just too much for her and wanted out. Just the thought of letting her go made me nauseated.

I ran my hands over my face. I'd asked her a couple of times, but she didn't give me a straight answer and that was also unlike her. I was the head of the Yakuza so, when I wanted to know or have something I just demanded. Either people complied nicely, or I took it by force, ultimately, the choice was theirs.

But I couldn't do that to Violet. I couldn't just sit her on a chair and keep her there until she told me what I wanted to hear so I would know how to fix things. My Violet was all softness and heart, and I couldn't use the brute force I usually displayed.

I looked at the calendar on my desk and the date circle in red. *Three days...* In three days, we would take my private plane and leave all the worry of our lives behind. It will be ten full days of us being *us*. She would meet my mother, who I had no doubt would adore her. And then, through patience and love, she'd end up telling me what was wrong, and everything would be right again.

I smiled at the thought of the two women I loved the most in the world finally meeting.

I unlocked the first drawer and took out the little black box I had there and ran my thumb over the soft surface. I would take her to the lake not too far from the house—the one I spent all my summers as a boy swimming and fishing in. I would sit her down, facing the stunning view of Mount Fuji, and I would remind her how much I loved her. I would remind her how, despite all the darkness and danger surrounding my life, she brought hope and a light so bright that it not only kept the darkness at bay, but made it completely disappear when she was smiling at me.

I opened the box and looked at the platinum, four-carat diamond ring, surrounded by a row of sapphires that reminded me of her eyes.

I'll go down on one knee right there, surrounded by the cherry blossoms, and ask her to become my wife, the mother of my children. I'll ask her to be my savior, to stay by my side to stop me from drowning in the life I'd been born to lead.

I closed my hand around the ring box, holding it tightly. "Three days, Hoka... Just three days," I muttered to myself.

"Hoka?"

I jerked my head up in surprise and threw the box into the drawer before slamming it shut. I'd been so lost in my proposal plan that I didn't even hear her approach.

She frowned at my reaction, her eyes bouncing from my hand to the drawer a couple of times.

Way to look suspicious, idiot.

"Is everything okay?" I asked as my phone vibrated on my desk. I rejected the call when I saw it was Jiro. He could deal with whatever it was.

"I... Yes, I'm fine. I just want to talk to you about something but..." She caught her bottom lip between her teeth. My girl was nervous.

The phone started vibrating again, and I rejected the call without looking.

"But? What is it, sweetheart?" I encouraged her, trying not to sound as desperate as I felt to hear whatever was causing the trench between us.

She opened her mouth to answer but she stopped as the phone vibrated on the desk again.

Jiro was going to die—it was a fact. Once I got my hands around his neck, he was dead.

"You're busy," she replied, sounding somewhat relieved by the interruption, as if she wasn't sure she wanted to talk to me or how.

"No, sweetheart. I'm never too busy for you. Whatev—" I stopped when my eyes landed on the screen and texts from Jiro started to appear.

DEFCON ONE! Come now! Urgent.
Hoka. Traitor uncovered. Come now.

Jiro was not a drama queen, so whatever this was couldn't be less than mass homicide.

I looked back at her, and the expression on my face seemed to tell her everything I could not say right now.

"You do what you have to do; we'll talk when you come back," she said gently, wrapping her arms around herself.

I hated how understanding she sounded, how *resigned*. It was like she expected to always come second, as she had for all her life. Despite the appearance I was giving right now, she was my priority. If I left her in this moment of uncertainty, it was because Jiro had uncovered the traitor who was threatening *her* life, *her* safety, *our* happiness.

By leaving now, I was choosing her, and while she didn't know that, I would explain when I came back.

"It's very important," I stated apologetically, standing and grabbing my suit jacket from the back of my chair. "But I promise as soon as I come back, we're locking ourselves in here and I will not step out until you've said everything you want to tell me. Deal?" I gave her a bright smile.

"Deal." She smiled back. It was sincere—at least, it seemed to be, but there was a wariness in her eyes despite the brightness of her smile that was not there before.

I walked to the door and as she moved to let me go through, I wrapped my arm around her waist and pulled her against me. I loved how her small body molded to mine; how, despite her apparent fragility, she could take and more importantly, enjoyed all the roughness and strength I couldn't always contain.

It's because she's made for you, my heart whispered as I leaned down to give her a soft kiss. "I'll be back as soon as I can."

"I know you will," she replied, running her hands over the lapel of my jacket.

I made it to my unofficial office–the headquarters on the less legal side of the business—in record time. By the time I opened the door of the private area on the second floor, I was ready to rip both Jiro's and the traitor's head off.

I stopped in my tracks when the only person in the room was Jiro, leaning against my desk with a thick brown envelope in his hands.

"Where the fuck is the traitor?" I barked, stalking toward him, my hands balled into shaking fists at my sides. "I swear, if it's one of your ploys to—"

"Sit down," Jiro said gently, pointing at the chair behind my desk.

"The fuck I'll sit down!" I shouted in his face, and to his credit, he didn't even flinch at the sudden uproar.

"Sit down!" he repeated more forcefully, and the only reason I actually complied was the grim look on his face.

"You have five minutes, and it better be good because the shit you just pulled on—" I stopped dead as Jiro threw a stack of photos on my desk.

I looked at them incredulously, my body suddenly feeling cold as if ice had replaced the blood in my veins.

I reached for them slowly, like they were going to strike me, and I pulled them closer to have a better look.

Violet and Alessandro Benetti were sitting across from each other in a discreet booth at a downtown coffee shop. In the second photo, he had his hand resting on top of hers in an intimate gesture.

He was going to die a slow, painful death for touching what was mine, I thought darkly as I tapped my forefinger on the photo, where his filthy hand had touched her.

He was laughing in the third photo, and in the fourth—for me, the worst of the lot—my Violet had her head back, laughing as I've never seen her laugh before.

"Did you take these photos yourself?" I asked, barely recognizing my own voice. The pain was building little by little—scrapping the layers of happiness and trust I'd been feeling so strongly recently.

Jiro shook his head.

"It doesn't mean anything. These could be fake photos. It wouldn't be the first time people tried to mess with my head." My voice cracked. Truly, I didn't believe my own words as I said them.

Jiro pushed his hand into the envelope and retrieved a USB drive.

"Plug it in and listen," he said morosely. "It's safe."

"Did you listen to it?" I asked, grabbing it from his hand.

"Yes."

I didn't ask when he got it or how, since those were questions for later.

I turned on my laptop, my mind numbed, already bracing for the worst.

My hand shook as I tried to plug the USB in—the only external mark of the storm brewing inside me.

Jiro noticed but didn't say a word as he sat in the chair across my desk.

At first, I only heard the background noise of people talking and cups clattering.

"Come back with me to Chicago. Leave all this mess behind you and be my sister, officially."

I tensed at Alessandro Benetti's voice and paused the recording.

I was not really familiar with him, but I'd met him on a couple occasions a few years back when my father had tried to make a pointless deal with the Italians, which had blown up at the first hurdle. Mafia were not meant to create alliances. We already had so much trouble getting along internally—within our own clans—trying to create an alliance with another mafia family altogether was nothing short of stupid.

His voice though, I remembered it well, and it was unmistakably him.

Sister... I met Jiro's eyes questioningly, and he nodded slowly. I thought they were lovers when I saw the photos, but his sister? I was not sure if it was better or worse.

I took a deep breath, preparing for the blow as I pressed 'play'.

"*I'm not certain.*"

That voice. My heart squeezed painfully at the low tone and gentle lull of her voice. There was no mistaking it; it was my Violet talking, her voice was so unique, like an old-time female singer who had smoked a little too much. I knew her voice by heart.

"*After all the effort it took me to get you into the house, and the life of the most recluse and suspicious mafia boss.*"

I stared at the screen feeling a fury and pain I'd never felt before. It was so intense that I felt trapped, unmoving, paralyzed by the overflow of emotions. All I could do was stare at the modulating line on the screen, my hands balled into fists on my desk.

The killing blow came a mere second later.

"*Oh, my brother, I love you so much, my loyalty is with you and always will be. No one would ever change that. Tell me what you want to know about, Hoka. I'll tell you everything.*"

Nausea rushed up my throat, and I half expected to vomit my breakfast on the laptop.

She played me! She made me believe that— I shook my head and flung my arm, sending the laptop flying and crashing against the wall. It was not possible. I couldn't be *that* gullible! She couldn't be *that* good.

I was breathing heavily, my chest rising and falling quickly as my rage overtook the pain of betrayal, at least for now.

I looked up at Jiro, my eyes hard. "Are we sure this is true?" I didn't recognize my voice under the harshness of my tone.

Jiro sighed. "We are."

"Don't pretend to be saddened at the thought" I spat. "Don't pretend you don't enjoy my fall after warning me that it might just be too good to be true. Don't pretend—"

"I'm not pretending. She fooled me, too."

I threw him a scathing look, and I was sure that if looks could kill, he would be lying on the floor right now. It was not the same, not at all, and he knew it.

"Talk," I ordered, not ready to indulge in his false platitudes.

"We received this envelope yesterday morning by an anonymous benefactor, or so it said on the front. I looked at the photos and listened to the recording."

"Why didn't you tell me immediately?" I shouted, jumping from my chair and leaning forward over my desk threateningly. I had to blame someone right now, and Jiro was the perfect victim.

He remained seated, his calm appearance infuriating me even more in light of my own turmoil. "I needed to make sure it was real before opening this door. I was informed that Benetti came to California five days ago. I did a little digging, and a few things about Violet's mother conveniently disappeared—I believe only powerful men could manage something like that. I called a couple of contacts to look into it. Tomo came back this morning and told me there was an old rumor about Benetti Senior. Apparently, he enjoyed high school girls and caused a bit of drama about twenty years ago. His wife even left for the old country for six months after that. It fits."

Of course, it did. Of course, she was his sister! I paced the length of my office, trying to get a hold of the ragging feelings. I needed to think rationally, and right now I was just too unhinged. I didn't know if I wanted to go there and put a bullet through her skull or fuck her roughly, painfully, for days as repayment of all the hurt she had caused.

"How did she get past...?" *Past, what? Security? Jiro's vigilance? My own paranoia?*

"I think the car accident was really an accident; I don't think all of it was premeditated. I think it just became an opportunity along the way."

Not *all* premeditated. That was just as bad. I'd been fooled, and I was to become the laughingstock of our syndicate.

I suddenly stopped walking and swirled toward Jiro. "Who knows?" I asked as dread piled on top of my anger and pain. If anyone knew what she did, it would be out of my hands.

Jiro shrugged. "Your guess is as good as mine. However, I think it's someone who's on your side because anyone else," he tapped the envelope resting on his lap, "would have used this at one of the family meetings."

I winced. That would have been a complete disaster, for me as much as for her. "That's betrayal," I said slowly, burying my hands in my pants pocket.

"I know."

I walked to the window, looking down at the empty casino. It was much too early for players to be there.

Despite the anger I felt toward her, I also felt defeated. Defeated because, no matter the unforgivable things she'd done, I didn't think I could do what was required of me.

"You know what the code says about betrayal of any kind..." I added as if Jiro hadn't known what I'd meant before.

"Betrayal is death."

I nodded and closed my eyes as weariness filled me completely. No matter what, I couldn't do it.

"I can't do it," I admitted, hating myself for this weakness.

"I know." There was no judgment in his voice, only resigned sadness.

I turned my head and held eye contact. "And you can't, either. I don't think I could ever forgive you for that." It made no sense, I knew it didn't, but it was true, nonetheless. Despite her despicable nature, part of me would probably always love the person she was pretending to be, and I didn't think I could ever forgive the person giving her the killing blow—no matter how much she deserved it.

"I know."

I frowned. Was that all he was going to say? That he knew everything?

"You don't have to have her killed," Jiro said. "The person who sent the evidence is giving you a chance to rectify the situation." He waved his hand in the air. "Send her away, humiliate her publicly. Show everyone you didn't care for her at all, and if things ever come to light, she'd be far away in Chicago under her brother's protection."

I gritted my teeth, my neck muscles painful under the pressure. I hated her with every fiber of my being. I hated her for making me love her, hated her for making me believe I deserved the light. I hated her for making me weak to the point that I could not do what I was supposed to do—what I had been raised to do. I hated her for breaking me. And most of all, I hated her because part of me was still in love with her.

I let out a broken cry of frustration. I wanted to rewind time, nine weeks back when I almost hit her with my car. I should have left her there and kept going. I rested my forehead against the cold glass. No, in reality, I only wanted to rewind the last twenty-four hours. I wanted to go back to last night, knowing it would be the last time I would kiss her and make love to her. I would have taken the time to kiss every ridge, every dip, every freckle. I would have satisfied that craving I knew would keep on burning long after she was gone.

"I'm sorry, Hoka."

I whirled around, throwing him a hard glare. "No, you're not. Keep your fake solicitude for someone who wants it. I've dealt with enough false pretenses for a lifetime. You were right, I was wrong. You were the clever one, I was the fool. Is that what you wanted to hear?"

He opened his mouth to reply but I raised my hand. "I don't care about any answer you could possibly give me. I need to call Sakura, I have a traitor to chase away."

CHAPTER 16

VIOLET

"I'm pregnant!" I shook my head looking at my reflection in the mirror. *No, that was too blunt.*

I had to be gentler. I took three pregnancy tests in the mall bathroom before I even started to believe it and that was three days ago, but it all seemed so surreal.

I cleared my throat. "Hoka, I know we've not been together that long, but I believe in us, in our feelings for each other. Things are changing, and it isn't a bad thing. It is exciting actually... You're going to be a dad." I smiled, resting my hand on my stomach. *Yes, that was the way to say it.*

I was being silly, anyway. Hoka loved me and he would love our child, no matter how I announced it to him.

Once that was said, I would have to have yet another awkward conversation—the one about my genetic heritage, the undesired part of me. Now that Alessandro Benetti had appeared in my life, I had to tell Hoka.

I heard a beep coming from his office, announcing the gates opening. I walked to the window just in time to see his car speed down the driveway.

My heart jumped in excitement, and I checked I was presentable before rushing down the corridor.

I was going to tell him straight away; just rip the Band-Aid off and close the gap between us. The longer I waited, the worst it was getting and the more on edge I felt. He could feel it, and I couldn't wait any longer.

I rushed down the stairs, ready to throw myself into his arms, but my steps faltered as I saw him enter the house hand in hand with one of the women from the party.

They were both laughing, and I missed the last step, sprawling on the cold hard tiles of the main hall when he pulled her toward him and kissed her as passionately as he had kissed me.

Pain shot all over my body as I landed on my hip.

It's a nightmare. Violet, wake up. Wake up! I begged, shutting my eyes tightly to avoid looking at the horror unfolding in front of my eyes.

"Stand up."

I opened my eyes, hardly believing the cold, hard voice I was hearing was Hoka's and that he was addressing me.

He was looming over me, straight and proud, his face a mask of contempt.

"Hok—"

"Stand up!" he demanded, his tone similar to a whip against my skin.

I scrambled to my feet, standing up despite the burning sensation going down from my right hip to my foot.

"I don't un—"

He waved his hand dismissively. "Listen, Violet, you're a nice girl, and I'm sorry it's happening like this." His face was not apologetic, but instead, full of annoyance as if I were nothing more than a tedious task, a lead weight he had to discard.

I threw a curious look behind him at the stunning woman from the party, who at least had the decency to look away.

"The thing is, I've always wanted to be with Sakura."

Sakura, yes, that was her name.

I looked away from her and concentrated on Hoka again, too stunned to utter a word.

"She didn't want me, and at first, I thought bringing someone new home would help. I thought it would make her realize that she was going to lose me and make her come to her senses."

I frowned, looking down at my bare feet. It made no sense, not after everything he told me, not after the way he touched me. No, it was not possible!

"But you said you loved me."

He let out a bitter laugh that carried so much darkness that it added another lead balloon to my heavy stomach.

"Love you?" He shook his head, rolling his eyes as if I were a stupid child he was humoring. "Sweetheart, please be realistic for a minute, will you? I'm a thirty-four-year-old billionaire with responsibilities and obligations you could never even start to comprehend." He tipped his mouth in a disgusted pout. "And you're an uneducated, poor girl barely out of childhood. What could I possibly love in you? You know we only marry our kind; Jiro told you."

I took a step back, the blow going right through any defense I may have had, stabbing my heart with a killing blow.

What could I even argue? It was true. I had been so beneath him on so many levels, but for some reason, I had hoped that my heart would have been enough for him.

A wave of nausea hit me, and I rested my hand on my mouth to keep it down as blood heated in my lower belly as if the baby was trying to remind me that he was there.

"What about Japan?" I whispered, uncertain.

"It was the only way for her to realize she had lost me. Meeting my mother is the ultimate commitment, which is why I told her about it at the party."

I looked back at the woman, but she was still looking away. I couldn't deny when I looked at her that they made sense. Both were absolutely stunning, with the same origin and culture. She was the wife he needed, but I loved him. I loved him more than life and I had our baby in me.

He would kill you and your baby, the voice of self-preservation screamed in my head. *Just like your father wanted to.*

"You're free to go now. I'm done with you"

Nausea won and I vomited on the floor, some drops spattering on his shiny black shoes.

He let out a grunt of disgust before muttering something in Japanese that sounded anything but complementary.

"I want you gone. *Now.*"

I opened my mouth and closed it again.

Go where? I have nothing.

"But I need to talk to you"

He rolled his eyes again. "Nothing you can say matters anymore. I've got Sakura now. You were a sweet distraction—just different enough to make sure Sakura knew that she could lose me and come back. What did you think?" he snorted.

"Hoka," I tried again, my eyes filling with tears. "I... I love you."

Doubt flickered in his expression, but it died so fast that it seemed I had imagined it.

I never would have thought that those three words could infuriate someone but based on how his face transformed from cool indifference to absolute outrage, I wanted to swallow back the words.

He reached inside his jacket and pulled out his gun. He pressed the barrel against my forehead, the feel of the killing machine much softer and cool than I could have ever imagined.

His eyes were locked on mine as I heard the unmistakable click of him cocking the gun, and the pain I felt at that moment was almost unbearable. I was sure it was just as powerful as if he'd actually pulled the trigger.

"You will leave now before causing a scene and before you make Sakura doubt her choice of being with me. I want to shoot, I really do. Don't make me do it." he seethed, his eyes spelling death as his nostrils flared with an anger he had trouble reining in. "You have two minutes to leave, or I swear, Violet, I'll pull the trigger."

The overwhelming terror I felt at that moment made me lose all control of myself.

"Hoka, look," The soft voice behind him made me want to die.

Hoka looked down to see my jeans turning dark at my crotch. "You *peed* yourself?" He laughed, and in that moment, I died—trigger pulled or not.

"Fuck, you're so pathetic. Get out of my house now!"

I threw a helpless look upstairs. "My things..."

He pointed at the door. "The car is waiting. Your things will follow." He turned to Sakura. "I need the room now anyway for the legitimate occupier."

I walked to the door, feeling so numb that I didn't even care that I had no shoes on.

"Violet?"

I grabbed my bag on the counter and turned to look at him, too defeated now to feel anything at all.

"Pray I don't see you around," he warned, and part of me wished he would just end my misery now. I wished he would just raise the gun at his side and shoot me.

He raised his hand toward Sakura and pulled her to him. I turned around just as he leaned down to kiss her, not wanting to see that ever again.

She said something to him in Japanese, her voice unsure, and he snapped a response as the heavy door closed behind me.

I stepped into the car, and the driver threw me a sorry look as he slid into the driver seat. I could not see my face, but if I looked only half as bad as I felt, I understood his concern.

I let the tears fall as we reached the gate, the numbing fear now receding and leaving the overwhelming sorrow of betrayal and broken promises in its wake.

He will rip your heart out one day and leave you to bleed out without remorse. Alessandro had told me this would happen, and I'd not wanted to believe how right he had been.

What should I do now? I rested a shaky hand on my stomach. *How will I raise this baby?*

Here I was heartbroken, destitute, scared, and pregnant. My mother's past, her curse, had fallen upon me. How eerie was destiny? Despite doing everything I could not to repeat the past, it had happened anyway.

No one could escape their destiny as no one could escape death. Hoka Nishimura had been my *Appointment in Samarra*.

Four days.

That was how long it took me to realize that Hoka was not coming back. I stayed in my apartment, grateful that he had paid six months' rent when I freaked out about the job when he first took me to his home.

I should have realized it when an austere man had appeared at my door the day after my dismissal with my mother's suitcase and all my clothes—including everything I had bought with the money he had given me and everything he had bought me himself.

But for four days I had hoped, prayed, and cried staring at my phone, eating the leftover boxes of ramen I had in the cupboard and takeaway orders I made using what I had left of Hoka's money.

Every night I fell asleep, wrapped around myself, hoping that when I'd wake up in the morning, I'd be back in his king-sized bed, snuggled against his warm body.

On the fourth day, I woke up feeling a presence in my room and found Alessandro Benetti leaning against the counter, staring at me.

I jumped out of bed, my heart hammering in my chest.

"What are you doing here?" I asked, wrapping my arms around myself—well aware I was only wearing a pair of underwear and an old, worn-out T-shirt.

"I came to ask you to reconsider." His voice was so serious that I took a step closer, scrutinizing his face, barely visible in the dim, early morning light.

His face had lost the playfulness and the hint of mischievous banter it had at the café, it was now just as serious as his voice. If I didn't know better, I would have said he even seemed concerned about my wellbeing, but I knew better. I knew it all.

I looked at the plastic clock on the wall, it was not even five a.m. yet.

"How long have you been here?" I asked, ignoring his question.

He shrugged, looking around. "How long have you *lived* here?"

It seemed that dodging questions was a family trait.

"Since my mother died. This is what happens to bastard children unwanted by their family."

He sighed, straightening up. "I didn't know how it was."

I shook my head. "I don't care. I meant what I said at the café. I would never betray Hoka. I never want to be a part of your family, and I never want to see you again."

He frowned, pursing his lips in annoyance. "He broke your heart, just like I predicted he would."

"How do you even know?"

Alessandro waved his hand dismissively. "How I know doesn't matter. What he did to you matters. He kicked you to the curb, crying and defeated."

I gave him a bitter smile. "Thank you, but I was there. I know how it ended." It took three showers before I felt clean again, somehow still smelling the urine on my skin.

"You are picking his side, even after everything he did?" he asked.

And everything you didn't do.

"I'm not picking anyone. I'm staying out of everything. I told you at the café that I wanted you to stay out of my life."

"Come home with me, please. I won't ask you to betray him again."

"Of course you will, and when you'll see that I won't, you'll kick me out in the streets of Chicago or sell me to someone."

"*Madre de dio*, you've got the Benetti stubborn streak. I will *not* sell you or betray you. You are my sister, and I want you to leave this hellhole and come home where you always belonged." He looked down at his expensive watch. "My plane is ready on the tarmac. We'll be leaving in an hour. I will respect your loyalty to him as long as you give me the same."

"No." I was done with mafia men, and I would never give any of them the ability to reach me or hurt me again. "You can leave now and please, if you have any decency, just forget I ever existed."

He narrowed his eyes. "You're throwing away the potential of a family and a life of luxury for this?" He gestured to my poor excuse of an apartment. "I swear to you, I will forget you ever shared the bed of a Yakuza."

I shook my head again. "No." I pointed at the door behind him. "You're years too late. You need to leave now, and never come back."

He sighed and reached inside his jacket, and I couldn't help but recoil when he got his hand out. If the man I thought would love me forever put a gun to my head, I half-expected my estranged brother to actually do what Hoka didn't.

His expression turned grim, showing he didn't miss my reaction and was offended by it.

He set a white business card on my counter and tapped it. "This has my cell number and email on it. Call me day or night, whenever you are ready to say goodbye to this dump of a life, and I'll buy you a plane ticket home."

"Your home, not mine."

"It could be yours if you gave it a chance."

"Goodbye, Mr. Benetti," I replied, looking pointedly at the door.

He looked at me for a couple of seconds as if he was trying to figure out an alternative plan before shaking his head and whirling around, leaving the apartment silently.

I took the card and closed it into my fist before throwing the ball of paper into the trash can.

A couple of things were clear now, in the harsh morning light. Hoka was not coming back to me, he would not make amends, and Alessandro Benetti would not give in.

I had to leave, disappear, and start fresh somewhere else, far from the memories and as far away as possible from the mafia, any mafia.

I touched the dragon still around my neck and thought of the luxury items that Hoka had bought me and the few that belonged to my mother. If I sold them all, I could maybe start a new life far from here, offering a real chance to the baby growing inside me.

I rested my hand on my stomach and rubbed gently as the new plan took some of my sorrow and morphed it into determination.

I was going to leave California today.

CHAPTER 17

HOKA

Eight weeks later...
I was standing by the library window, my gaze fixed on the garden, unseeing. Work was piling on my desk that I wasn't able to complete, no matter how hard I tried.

I knew sending her away would be difficult, that I would miss her and the way she looked at me. The terror in her eyes when I put that gun to her head had almost brought me to my knees despite all the way she *hurt* me, despite the way she *betrayed* me.

I felt myself caving under her earnest eyes, almost believing that, despite all the staggering evidence, she was innocent. I needed her gone and used the only thing that would do the trick. I showed her the extent of my dark side and as she stared back at it, she lost herself into a fear so deep, something had broken within her. I saw it and I felt it inside me. I thought her lies and betrayal had broken me completely, but her look at that moment had managed to finish the job.

"What you've done will never be repaired," Sakura had told me as Violet rushed to the door.

"She's leaving with her life which is much more than she deserved." I'd snapped before pulling her in for one more kiss neither of us wanted.

There had been a millisecond as I set the gun on her head that I had wanted to pull the trigger, the pain taking me to the edge of madness, but I'd known then as I knew now that if I'd taken her life that day, I would have died along with her.

I had so many things to concentrate on, so much unfinished business, and the sword of Damocles was still very much over my head. Who had known she'd been a traitor? Who held this against me? Who had the advantage on me? The cards proved my lack of judgment and the evidence that I was not the unfailingly leader they all expected me to be.

I still went through my routine the next few days after sending her away, despite the agony I felt—and feeling Jiro's knowing eyes on me with every step. I warily waited for everything to come to light, but nothing came of it, and as the days passed, I stopped anticipating, I stopped caring, and I let the full extent of my dark feelings swallow me whole as I holed up in my home.

The worst part was that I had not been able to let her go, and even though she wasn't dead, I felt her essence everywhere I was. She was the worst kind of person—she was a traitor, a liar, a master manipulator, and the sister of the Italian scum I've always despised. Yet there was still that little unshakable certainty deep inside me that was convinced she was my one and only.

I shook my head, turned more fully toward the window, and fixated on the wooden bench under the shadow of the palm tree. I could almost see her there, sitting in one of her summer dresses just looking at the pond.

I was demented—there was no other explanation for this longing. I'd kept her nightshirt that had been hanging behind my bathroom door when I sent all her things away. I kept it because it smelled like her, though I knew that, by now, it probably smelled more like me than it did her, but part of me still believed it was there.

Even for a few days afterward, I'd hoped that she would call me, admit the truth, and tell me that she'd fallen in love with me, regardless of the circumstances and wanted to be with me.

And I'd known that, if she'd called and apologized, I would have been pathetic enough to forgive her and bring her back into my life. I let out a humorless laugh. What kind of fool did that make me? I used to sneer at couples forgiving each other, thinking that betrayal deserved a second chance, yet I'd been ready to forgive the worst of them all.

I would never again be that callous.

But of course, she never called. Why would she? She had a life that was not centered around me.

I licked my lips and looked at the well-stocked bar. It was too early to start drinking, yet for the past few weeks, I found myself drinking more and more, earlier and earlier.

I gave up and walked to the bar, helping myself to a triple dose of bourbon.

"It's nine a.m., Hoka."

I glanced at the door and saw Jiro all suited up. I took a long sip of my drink and shrugged. "It's one a.m. in Fujinoyama, it's still party time."

He pursed his lips and detailed my clothes with disapproval. It was true that for the past few weeks I'd not been showing the most composed, boss-like attire. Like now, I was wearing a rumpled black T-shirt I'd slept in for the past three days and a pair of dress pants just as wrinkled and stained with both food and a variety of liquor.

"We're going to be late."

I took another sip. "Where?"

He sighed, taking a step into the room. "The quarterly review."

I waved my hand dismissively. I couldn't imagine anything worse right now than being in a room with all the *kyodai* going on for hours about all the *giri* and *shobadai* they collected, the *kuchidomeryou* they paid out to ensure that the business was running smoothly, and guarantee the authorities looked away.

It was something that could have been done just as efficiently as a paper exercise, but it was a competition between them—who would please the boss more? It was basically a game of who had the bigger dick for that quarter, and I was there, listening and congratulating, like a father praising his children—except that today, I was not in the mood for that.

When are you in the mood for anything anymore? my father's voice chastised me from the grave.

Usually, the fear of not honoring the role he raised me to occupy was enough to make me do the right thing, but today not even that seemed to motivate me.

"You do it," I told him, turning toward the window again, my glass still in hand.

"I do it?" He snorted. "Have you lost your damn mind?"

I cocked my head to the side, pondering the question seriously. "It's quite possible." I replied, not even bothering to turn around.

"Hoka, I can't do it, even if I *wanted* to. I'm your wakagashira, yes, but I'm not blood. I have no authority. I've already stood for you at the last two monthly meetings. Hoka, people are starting to talk."

"Then have my uncle do it. He's blood, and he craves the attention."

"Hoka." He let out a weary sigh. I knew I was making his job so much harder, having him fight me at every corner, but I was just too tired to care. "You'll be giving him one more opportunity to take over. You know it's what he wants, what he always wanted."

Let him have it, I thought bitterly. "I've always done what I was supposed to do, and what do I have to show for it, huh?" I asked rhetorically. "Is it all worth it?"

He was silent for a few seconds, and I relaxed, thinking he had finally left.

"All that because of her?"

I frowned and turned around, disliking the edge in his voice.

"She is none of your concern. And she's not being questioned here. It's what she represented, the chance of being the man and not the boss. It was the chance of experimenting what the others take for granted. I know a part of you understands, you've experienced something relatively similar."

He shook his head, narrowing his eyes a little. "You can't still be wanting her! You can't still be missing her."

I'll never stop wanting her. I'll never not miss her. Despite everything, she still was my *ikigai.* "I can't accept that none of it was real. I can't accept being so wrong."

"The gaijin changed you."

I finished my glass silently and walked to the bar, ready to pour another one.

"You'll never recover, will you?" he asked and there was a finality in his tone that made me pause. It was not a question, not really.

I looked back at him, bottle half tipped down, about to pour.

He was frowning down at the iPad in his hands, resignation settling over his features. "What if you haven't made a mistake?"

I put the bottle back on the bar and turned to him, now sporting the same expression as he did.

He looked up at me, and I saw something under his weariness and resignation. I saw a hint of guilt that sparked some life back into me.

"What are you saying?"

He looked heavenward, as if he was asking for some guidance before looking back at me. "What if you've been led to believe things that were not true?"

I took a step toward him, my hands shaking slightly with apprehension.

"What do you know? Talk now!" I commanded through gritted teeth, taking another step toward him.

He could probably see the murderous intent on my face, yet he kept his face as stoic as ever.

"I have nothing to do with the envelope we received, but I've suspected who sent it for a while. It was someone who wanted you to hurt her because he couldn't reach her. This is also why nothing else came out of it."

I shook my head, the lack of sleep and alcohol abuse making me slower than usual. "What do you mean?"

"You asked me to disconnect all the security at her place, but I didn't listen. I wanted to see what she was going to do after. I wanted to be ready to act and do what you couldn't do."

Cold sweat ran down my spine at the implication of his words. He wanted to see if he needed to kill her or not.

"Continue." I took another step closer. I would smash his head against a wall to make him talk faster if I had to.

He sighed again and turned on his iPad, tapped on a few things, then extended it to me.

I sucked in a loud breath as my heart squeezed painfully in my chest. Here she was, lying on her bed in a fetal position.

I zoomed on the screen to look at her face. I was both grateful and resentful at seeing her in high def. I'd missed her face so much, but I could see the swollen eyes and blotchy skin. She had been crying because of me.

My hands tensed on the edge as she startled awake and looked at Alessandro Benetti standing in her room.

I listened to the conversation, hardly believing everything I was hearing as a fresh layer of pain and betrayal coated my heart. However, the main difference now was that the pain and betrayal were not mine, but hers.

I betrayed *her*.

I hurt *her*.

I—

I looked up, horrified. I'd broken her. "Jiro," I said slowly, having a hard time catching my breath, "how long have you had this video?"

"I thought it was for the best... She didn't belong in our world, and you had already done the hard part, Hoka. I kn—"

I gripped his throat and pushed him against the wall with all my strength and his skull connected with a loud, satisfying *thud*. I tightened my fingers around his neck, pressing on his jugular hard enough to stop the blood flow.

"How long?"

"Since the start," he gasped.

I let out a roar of pain and frustration as I pulled him from the wall and slammed him against it again.

"You stole her from me! You make me—" I let him go and he fell heavily on the floor, bringing his hand to the back of his head. When he removed it, I saw his fingers covered with blood.

Good!

"I did not. You made your—"

"You lied to me! I—" I glanced at the katana on display behind me, my hand itching to reach for it and end his life right now. I closed my eyes and let out another roar of frustration, knowing that I could not kill him, I had no ground. What he did was not against our *jingi*—our moral code—no matter how much I wanted it to be.

"Where are you going?" he shouted as I exited the room. "She's gone!"

I stopped in the hall, ironically enough, right where she'd vomited that day. I turned around and looked at him walking toward me, swaying a little from side to side, obviously unsteady after the two hard hits to his head.

"Gone? Gone where?" I asked, trying to keep my voice down. Being in the hall, we were much more likely to be heard now.

"I don't know."

I pinched the bridge of my nose in frustration. I was going to snap again and this time, I was going to get my gun and blow his brains out.

He jerked his head to the side and winced with pain. "Come with me."

I followed him stiffly, seething inside at whatever drama mystery he was playing now. I wanted him dead on the floor, and I didn't believe it would ever change.

We walked into the summer house he occupied, and we went to the spare bedroom. I was about to ask him what game he was playing when he pulled the wardrobe door open, revealing the dress she was wearing during the party—a dress I remember packing with all her things.

"What is this?"

"The jeweler called me about seven weeks ago; he said you were not picking up the phone. He'd been trying to call you for days and—"

I made a rolling gesture with my hand. "Straight to the point. I don't care about the details."

He leaned against the wall. "He received a call from a pawn shop on the south bank about a necklace. There was a serial number on the diamonds, and the pawn shop wanted to know if anyone would be interested in buying it back." He grabbed a black box and gave it to me.

I opened it and my stomach dropped at the dragon necklace I had custom made for Violet.

She sold her protector.

But why wouldn't she? Her protector had become her abuser. She had no need for that.

I looked back up at him in a silent invitation to continue.

"I went to the pawn shop and asked him to show me everything the girl brought in, and I bought it all."

"What did she bring?"

My heart sank even deeper when I saw what I was scared to see in the lot. Her mother's pearls, her most prized possession, was in the lot. How desperate she must have been to sell them because, even in her darkest time, even when she had nothing to eat, she'd never resigned herself to part from it.

I ran my fingers on the pearls as Jiro showed me all the dresses she sold—it was all her mother's and the few luxury items she had allowed me to buy for her.

"How much did he give her for all that?" I asked with a choking voice I could barely recognize myself. The lump of guilt and sorrow of what I had put her through stopped me from breathing right.

"Thirteen thousand."

I snorted, "That's not even the price of the dragon! The dress alone cost eight grand!" That man was feeding off people's desperation. *Not unlike you!* my stupid, nagging conscience added.

"I have everything here."

"I want everything moved to her room now."

"Her room? Hoka, she's gone. I know, I checked. Go there if you don't believe me."

"I don't believe you," I said, snapping the box with the dragon closed. "I don't think I'll ever believe a word you say again, but that's irrelevant. Here or anywhere, I will find her. There's not a place in this world she can hide from me. It may take days, weeks, months, or even years, but I'll find her, and I'll bring her home, where she belongs." I took the direction of the door and turned around. "Also, so we're clear, as you mentioned it so clearly before, my position here has been compromised, so I can't do what I want just now. But know that, once she's home and has become my wife, once my position is secured again, you will leave your position by my side. You will take a plane and go far away from me, and you will know that, until the last breath leaves your body, I will hate you more than I've ever hated anyone."

"You're my brother, my best friend, Hoka... I just did what—"

"I wished I had not saved your life that day. I wish I'd let you die with your Anna."

Jiro looked away. "I wished that for many years..."

"I should have granted you that wish," I added bitterly, leaving him behind for the last time.

I was a man on a mission, looking for his soulmate.

Violet Murphy, my love, my heart... where are you hiding?

CHAPTER 18

VIOLET

Four weeks later...
"Thank you for coming on such short notice," Tracy huffed with relief as she threw me a green apron.

"Come on, it's not like I was doing anything exciting, and I owe you that much."

Her expression turned serious as she turned toward me. "No, you don't. Listen to me," she rested her hands on my shoulders, "I mean it when I say that you don't owe me anything."

I nodded, even though I disagreed. I forced a small smile despite the tears that were burning the back of my eyes.

Tracy was nothing less than a savior for me. She had been there for me on the worst day of my life, and I was not sure if I could ever repay her. I'd once thought that the day my mother passed away in the charity-owned hospice had been the worst. Then, it had been the day Hoka broke my heart, but I'd been wrong... I'd been so, *so* wrong.

The worst day of my life happened six weeks ago, and the physical and mental scars were still throbbing. I never thought they would heal, despite what everyone else was saying.

Carol, the waitress I was going to cover for, came out of the changing room, muttering under her breath.

"Thank you so much, V. I swear that boy will be the death of me."

I chuckled. "What did he do this time?"

She rolled her eyes before looking in her huge bag to find her keys. "He thought it would be funny to scare his grandmother and hide in the apple tree."

I winced.

"Now I have to pick him up from the hospital with a broken leg."

"Ouch." That little boy really was a trial for his mother. "You know boys will be boys," I said in an attempt to cheer her up.

"Take him if you want. Oh!" She rested her hand on her mouth, her face completely decomposing as Tracy and the cook, Mario, stiffened, eyeing me warily. "Violet, I'm so sorry. I didn't mean—"

I waved my hand dismissively, letting out a little laugh that I wanted to be light, but it quivered with the underlying loss. "Don't be ridiculous, it's nothing. After all you told me about the little scoundrel, I think I'll settle for a litter of German shepherds before taking your son."

"And it will be a lot less work," she replied with discomfort. She then turned to Tracy before moving to walk away. "See you tomorrow, boss!"

"I swear, there's not a limb that kid didn't break at least twice, and he's still so young," Mario muttered with his heavy Spanish accent. "You'll see, he's going to grow up all crooked." I laughed earnestly. I loved this man.

He winked at me with a small smile before flipping a burger.

"Are you sure you're okay with working now? You had two long shifts."

"I'm fine. Besides, it's only for a few hours until you close." I wrapped the apron around my waist and reached to tighten my hair into a bun once again—the action more in memory than anything when there was nothing to twist.

I'd acted on impulse before leaving California and cut my hair short. Where it used to stop in the middle of my back, now it stopped just at the base of my neck, only allowing me to do a tiny basic ponytail.

She looked at me, then looked out the round window on the swinging kitchen doors. "I could have done it, actually; the accounting could have waited a couple more hours, and it's quite dead."

"Honestly, you're doing me a favor. Bobby is driving me crazy with the noise."

"He's still not done with his stupid project?"

I shook my head. "Nope."

"I swear... husbands." She sighed. "Fine, you go, but let me know if you want to leave. No problem, okay?"

I pulled her into a hug and said nothing. This woman has been a saving grace.

When I left California with just a sports bag and a bus ticket to Great Falls, Montana, I had no idea what to expect.

What I had not expected was meeting an angel along the way, a ray of light that allowed me to believe that my mother, high above, was probably looking out for me, after all.

The bus broke down about thirty miles out of Great Falls, and as we waited for it to be fixed, I wandered around the small town and stopped in front of *Tracy's Kitchen*, a lovely little restaurant with a blackboard on the sidewalk that said, *'Carb and Dairy may not fill the void in your life, but it's worth the try.'*

I laughed and after days of not even smiling, it felt like a breath of fresh air. I'd walked in, despite the sign still reading closed, and it was then that I'd met Tracy. She was a middle-aged woman with such warmth radiating from her that despite only smiling at me, I felt safe, as if I had a mother figure right there.

She took a single look at me and made me sit at the counter. She went in the kitchen and came back five minutes later with the most luscious chocolate milkshake I ever had.

She asked me why I looked like the world had just swallowed me whole, and I just opened the floodgates and told her as much as I could—ranging from my dead mother, absentee father, cheating boyfriend, horrible breakup, and the unplanned pregnancy. Though, of course, I left out all the dangerous parts.

I'd not gotten back on the bus that day, or any day after that. I rented the little studio apartment above her garage that her son had vacated when he moved out after college and started to waitress for the restaurant.

I'd started to build my life back up, not going back to the woman I once was—that woman was dead, but working to become a better version... a stronger, wiser version of herself. I worked hard to become a woman who would be a good mother... until that stopped being a motivator during the most horrible night of my life—the night Tracy once again saved my life.

The chime at the door announcing customers got me out of my dark thoughts, and I pushed the door while looking out of the kitchen window in habit. I froze as a wave of nausea hit me.

I took a few rapid steps back, praying that they hadn't seen me. The first may have, but I'd never seen him before, and when his eyes turned toward the kitchen, they didn't spark with recognition. I only saw the profile of the second one for less than a second, but it was enough for my body and heart to react with both fear and pain...

Hoka Nishimura just walked into *Tracy's Kitchen*.

I looked around the kitchen and my eyes connected with Mario, who frowned at the look on my face. *"Que passa?"*

I shook my head, reaching behind me with shaky hands to undo my apron. "I'm not feeling very well. I think Tracy will need to finish the shift."

His frown deepened as he walked to the serving hatch and looked out.

"You know them?"

"No." But my wobbling voice was enough to unveil my lie.

"Want me to go talk to them?" he asked, already moving in the direction of the door.

I grabbed his arm. "No, please don't. I beg you... just stay here. Mario, please."

He sighed and nodded. "Okay, *Pequena*." He jerked his head toward the office. "Tell Tracy to come and go home. It's okay."

I walked into Tracy's office, knowing I probably looked as pale as a ghost, and told her I had to leave now.

She immediately took over, her maternal instinct always applying to me as much as her own son, and she sent me home.

I walked as slowly as I could, and as soon as I reached the outside and saw Hoka's luxury SUV parked there, I started to run. I ran as if my life depended on it, as if there was a monster chasing me.

And even if it was a metaphor, it was also very true. There was a monster chasing me. A monster who had no reason to be in a small forgotten town in Montana; a monster who was probably here to finish what he started and kill me.

Maybe it wouldn't be such a terrible thing. Maybe you'd finally be able to sleep and be at peace, the dark voice suggested. A voice that had appeared only three months ago but kept on getting louder and louder.

I made it to my little studio flat, breathless and shaking. For once, I was thankful to hear Bobby's noises in the garage just below me. It was comforting to know I was not alone.

I double- and triple-checked to make sure that all the doors and windows were locked, before turning off all the lights and sliding into a warm bath, trying to calm my nerves.

Maybe it was a coincidence, a way for life to show me I needed to stay on my guard. A way to show me that life was clearly not finished with me.

I slid under the water and stayed in the protective cocoon of the warm, lavender-scented water, looking at the ceiling until my lungs started to burn and scream for air.

If I stayed under just a minute more, just one, I would probably just pass out and take away the option of him hurting me. I could just go on my own terms, not the way he intended me to go.

But then my mom's face flashed in my mind, and I shot up with a loud gasp as air filled my abused lungs. She wouldn't want me to give up, to just lay down and die. She'd fight like a lioness, she'd fight even when her body had given up, and I couldn't disgrace her memory like that.

I changed into a pair of flannel pajamas and sat on the bed as I brushed my short hair. I looked at my gaunt face in the mirror, tracing the deep purple circles under my eyes, letting my finger trail down my sunken cheek. No wonder Tracy had been more concerned than usual today. I looked like the walking dead.

I had two bad nights filled with nightmares and woke up, almost certain I could feel the wetness of blood between my legs.

I closed my eyes and shook my head. "You have to stop, V. What happened, happened," I told myself before pulling open the drawer and taking out the small yellow tube of sleeping pills the doctor had prescribed me to help.

I was reluctant to take them, fearing the dark impulse that sometimes made me stare at that bottle for much too long, but I couldn't allow myself a third night of sleep deprivation. I needed to be sharp and rested before I decided what my next move should be, and if I needed to disappear once more.

I opened my hand and dropped a pill in it. I looked at the small red and white caplet. It was only seven p.m., but I hoped it would do the trick and knock me out for at least twelve hours.

I took the pill with a glass of water before sliding into the softness of the bed. I closed my eyes and after a few minutes, the exhaustion and meds took me away.

I woke up in the middle of the night from a dream of Hoka so vivid, I could smell his cologne in my room. I felt movement on the bed beside me as someone slid closer to me.

I screamed, but a big hand immediately covered my mouth.

"Shh, sweetheart, it's me," Hoka whispered in my ear.

I let out a sob. "Don't kill me, please." I tried to beg from under his hand.

He leaned over me and as my eyes adjusted to the darkness and with the faint light coming from across the street; I saw his face soften. "We need to talk. I need to apologize. Sweetheart, I'm so sorry."

I shook my head as he kept his hand on my mouth, and he quickly explained how he'd thought I betrayed him. How he found out I was a Benetti, and he assumed the worst.

I kept crying silently. His words did nothing to ease my mind.

"I'll remove my hand now, okay? I want to hear your voice." He removed his hand slowly and brushed his fingers against my cheek.

I moved my head briskly, wanting to avoid his touch. "There's no turning back."

He loomed over me, his eyes so intense that even in the dim light, his amber orbs seemed to be on fire.

He cocked his head to the side, cupping my cheek despite my previous rejection. "At least tell me what you had wanted to tell me that day. What was it? Was it about Benetti? I've been obsessing over it ever since you left."

I looked away, keeping my eyes on the window. "You don't want to know... trust me."

He leaned down a little and skimmed his nose on my hair. "Humor me."

"If I tell you, you'll leave me alone?" I asked, my voice breaking.

He brought his hand up and caught my chin between his fingers, turning my face toward him. He looked into my eyes, as if he could read me. How amber and beautiful his eyes were. He ran his fingers over my lips as a strand of black hair which had escaped his bun brushed my cheek.

"Watashi ga anata o miru toki, me no mae ni watashi no nokori no jinsē ga miemasu."

I shook my head. He always turned me into a puddle whenever he talked to me in Japanese– whenever he looked at me like I was his world.

"Yes or no?" I insisted, not letting myself be sidetracked by his lies.

He sighed. "Tell me. You know who I am, so you know I'll find out anyway."

"I thought I did..."

He recoiled slightly at the jab, but I didn't feel guilty—it was nothing compared to the pain he put me through, nothing compared to how I continued to suffer.

"I wanted to tell you I was pregnant," I said coldly.

He froze as he looked down at me, his hand stopped mid-air. I used these few seconds of surprise to force all my weight to turn to the side.

"But it doesn't matter anymore," I added as I turned my head, because looking at him hurt me much worse than I expected it would.

He settled behind me and slid his hand up my hip, resting it on my flat stomach, and I felt the echo of the pain I felt six weeks ago when I lost our baby.

"Akachan?" His voice trembled ever so slightly.

I knew that word. I'd learned it when I stupidly tried to learn Japanese for him, when I tried to be good for him, worthy.

I shook my head. "Not anymore."

"Did you—" He stopped. "You lost it." The sadness in his voice almost reverberated mine when I'd woken up in pain, bleeding and alone in the middle of the night.

At least he didn't assume the worst of me this time. He knew I would not have aborted our child; I never could have done it.

"I did. I think the universe knew that child was not meant to be, despite how much I loved him." I took a shaky breath.

His hand tightened on my stomach, his fingers dipping in my flesh.

"Aishitemasu," he whispered in my ear, and the pain cracked my chest in two.

These were unfair words, empty words. You trusted people you loved; you didn't hurt them; you were not cruel. He'd sent me away, treating me worse than a rabid dog, not even letting me explain that I was not really a Benetti.

"Leave me now, please."

He spooned me from behind. "I wish I could, but it won't work. I've been looking for you for weeks like a madman. How do you expect me to walk away now that I finally have you back in my arms?"

I turned my head to the side, looking at his eyes full of determination.

"Because there's no saving us... there never was anything to build or anything to save. There was never an us. I am not the same woman I was. This woman knows better, and she wants you gone."

"No, you *will* forgive me, and you *will* take me back. We can make it work. You'll forgive me, and you'll marry me. We'll have plenty of beautiful red-cheeked babies. I will make you so happy that with time, you will start forgetting how badly I hurt you until you only remember the happiness we have together. It's not broken you and I, even if you think we are. We're *kintsukuroi*."

I let out a humorless laugh. "I'm not a century old pottery; I'm a person who's been hurt more than she should have... more than she deserved."

He trailed his lips on my cheek, keeping his arm around me. *"Shitte iru. Gomen'nasai."*

"Then if you know and you're sorry, let me go," I demanded, trying to push his arm away.

His arm tightened around me as his head shot up. "You speak Japanese."

I shook my head, stopping my struggle. I could not force him to free me from his hold unless he allowed me to—this man was a killing machine.

"I tried to learn when I thought I was in love with you. I remember a few words here and there."

"You still love me." There was no doubt in his voice. "A love like ours can't just vanish in a few months."

"Depends on how much hurt we pile on top." I blinked back tears. "I've got a life outside of you now, Hoka. I'm done with you."

"But I'm not done with you."

"You owe me that much," I insisted.

"I agree."

"So, you're going to let me go?" I asked with hope, even though my already fractured heart broke in my chest.

I felt his fingers trail up my neck. "*Īe,*" he replied, and I felt his finger press against the base of my neck before everything went black.

CHAPTER 19

Violet

I turned around in bed and opened my eyes, looking at the katanas on the nightstand.

I blinked a couple of times and let out a sigh of contentment as I raised my arms above my head and arched my back in a morning stretch.

As the sleep-induced brain fog started to fade, I stiffened as reality came crashing down on me.

I sat up in bed, finding Hoka sitting on the armchair in the corner, his elbow on the armrest and his hand under his chin, looking at me intently.

"Don't panic," he said, not moving a muscle.

"Don't panic?" I pulled the comforter tightly against me. "Don't panic? You kidnapped me! I—" I shook my head. "What did you do to me?" I asked, remembering the pinch on my neck and nothing else. "How did you get me here?"

"I have a plane, so the logistics don't matter. We need to talk."

"The logis— Do you even hear yourself?" I pulled the covers off me and stood, somehow grateful to still be wearing the flannel pajamas I had when I went to bed, whenever that was. "You didn't need to kidnap me and take me a thousand miles from my home to *talk*."

He moved his hand from his mouth but stayed seated. "Kidnapped is such a strong word," he said with light chastisement in his tone. "I just brought you back to where you belong. Parish Fall, Montana, is *not* your home. *This* is your home." He gestured to his bedroom. "This is *your* room, *your* bed."

I let out a humorless laugh. "No, apparently this is my jail! You could have said whatever you needed to say there." I started to pace the room and looked at the door, though I knew it was pointless. I saw the grounds; even if I passed this door, there was no chance I'd even reach the end of the corridor before he caught me.

"No." He moved to lean forward on his chair, and I recoiled quickly, my heart jumping in my chest with fear.

His eyes flashed with frustration and sadness as he rested his forearms on his thighs. "You've got nothing to fear. I won't hurt you, Violet."

I would have laughed if I was not so shaken. He hurt me more than anyone in my life ever had! Being with him cost me almost everything.

"Yeah, okay." I had no plan to argue with him. "Tracy's going to worry. She'll call the cops, and somehow I don't think you own those ones."

"You'd be surprised who I own, and don't worry about Tracy... I handled her."

I stopped pacing and faced him, looking at him fully for the first time since I woke up. He looked just as stunningly beautiful as he had always been, maybe just a little less neat, with more pronounced signs of worry and sleep deprivation visible in the tighter lines around his eyes and the deeper coloring under them.

He gave me a look full of incredulity before shaking his head with a weary sigh. "What opinion must you have of me?"

That you're a cruel, heartless, ruthless, cold-blooded criminal, I thought with pursed lips but simply stood there, waiting for him to tell me exactly what he did to her.

"For the love of the ancestors," he muttered, his nostrils flaring with frustration.

He was trying to keep control of himself and whatever was boiling just under the surface. I almost wished he would explode and let go of the fake veneer, showing me the monster lurking underneath once again.

"I have not hurt her or anyone else. I don't hurt innocents."

Agree to disagree. I looked down. I didn't need him to try to convince me of the contrary since it would be wasted time and effort.

"I spoke to her at the restaurant and told her you needed to spend time with your family."

"My family's dead."

"I'm your family," he replied stubbornly.

"No." I crossed my arms over my chest. "I want to leave."

"No." He crossed his arms over his chest, mirroring my position. "Tell me what happened."

"You know what happened. You threatened me and kicked me to the curb, sick and covered in my own urine," I replied coldly, and felt a little twinge of victory when he winced.

"You know that's not what I meant." His voice was sharp, but his eyes were soft, the pool of liquid gold I loved when he used to look at me warmly. "What happened?"

"If I tell you, will you let me go?"

He shook his head. "No, we have too many things to work out, too many things to discuss."

"What would Sakura say? Knowing I'm here." No matter how over it I pretended I was, I still felt the pinch of pain and jealousy at the thought of that woman in his life. "Has she changed her mind again? Is that why you came for me? Did she make the right choice?" The one I was too stupid to make when I was blinded by love? I hated myself for not walking away when I had the opportunity.

"Sakura has nothing to do with you and me," he replied with a tone that didn't leave any room for discussion. "She's my best friend, nothing more. She doesn't love men, never did. Do you want to hear it from her mouth?"

I shook my head. "No need." I wanted to tell him that it was pointless, that there was not a thing that he or the woman could say or do that would change my mind, but Hoka was the most stubborn man on the planet. He just needed a couple of days to see that, and then he'd grow tired of me.

"Can you at least give me my own room back? Just the idea of sharing your bed..." A shiver raced down my back, though it was not one of desire. Just the idea of his hands on me...

He stiffened, the indignation so flagrant on his face as he tightened his hands into tight fists resting on his thighs. "Fine, you can have the room back."

I sat on the foot of the bed, as far from him as possible, knowing it was the best he would give right now.

"I was scared, alone, and pregnant." I looked down at my hands, at my nails that I chewed down almost to the point of blood. "I felt like I was drowning, but I realized that I had to leave and I found my saving grace in Parrish Fall. Tracy threw me the lifeline I desperately needed, and I started to build myself back up. It was shaky grounds, of course, because it's hard to build back foundations when they'd been reduced to dust, but I tried. Then I went to the doctor and," I smiled despite the incapacitating pain that overflowed my heart, "I heard my baby's heartbeat, and it was the most beautiful sound I'd ever heard. It was magical, strong and steady." I felt the familiar warmth and wetness of tears running down my cheeks. "I knew I had to fight for my baby. I needed to be the mother this baby deserved, and it worked until—" I stopped as the sorrow of loss took my lungs into its vice, squeezing too hard for me to breathe. I closed my eyes for a few seconds, taking some labored breaths, forcing my body to cooperate—to override all the pain, if only for a moment. I let out a small sob, and I was grateful that he didn't come to comfort me. I didn't think I could have handled his touch. "But then I woke up in the middle of the night, with a pain so intense I thought someone was cutting me inside out. I pulled the covers off and the blood… I've never seen so much blood, and then the pain came again. I screamed, and I passed out." I could still see the images in my head. "When I woke up two days later, I was in the hospital. My baby was dead, but they announced that they'd managed to save my uterus." I rested my hand low on my stomach, where the small incision was on my bikini line. "I didn't care about my uterus or ovaries or whatever. All that mattered was that I'd lost my baby. A baby I'd seen on the screen. I'd heard his life, I'd seen him. I loved him so much and he was just… gone. Someone else who I'd love was gone." I looked at him from under my eyelashes.

He was frozen in time, his forehead wrinkled in a painful expression, his eyes shining with tears. His pain, his apparent expression of loss, took some of my grief away and replaced it with resentment and indignation similar anger. How dare he pretend he felt anything at all? Why did he think he had the right to grieve?

I raised my head and looked at him with as much disdain as I could muster. I faced his expression, faced the loss he was experiencing but didn't deserve.

"The funny thing is that I was a virgin for so long because my mom always said that sex was important and you shouldn't share it with just anyone. I was so convinced of that my whole life growing up. I was convinced that once I found the one I wanted to give myself to, it would be the right one, the man I would end up spending the rest of my life with." I let out a humorless laugh. "She had me way too young. She had me with the shameless criminal she gave her virginity to. She'd been too young, too naïve, and she had believed all his big words and promises of tomorrow." I took a deep breath. "It's ironic, almost poetic in a William Blake or Robert Frost kind of dark way. I made the exact same mistakes she'd made while trying so hard not to. But maybe life had been more charitable to me or the child I was condemning to a life akin of mine. Maybe they took my baby away as a merciful gesture, not as a punishment." This was what I'd repeated to myself for the past few weeks, and the more I said it, the more I believed it.

"No, you didn't make your mother's mistakes," he said vehemently, standing from his chair and coming to stand in front of me.

"Why?" I asked and looked up. The determination on his face almost knocked me down.

I gasped as he fell on his knees in front of me, grabbing my hands that were resting on my thighs. I had not realized how cold mine were until I felt his burning skin on mine.

"Because I *love* you," he started, leaning closer, fanning my face with his warm breath. "Because I chose *you,* always *you.*" He brought my hand to his chest, resting it right in the center, over his heart, which was beating faster than usual. "Because you own me completely, body, heart, and soul. Because there's not a thing I wouldn't do to make it right to you, to take some of the pain away."

I tried to pull my hand away from his chest, but his hold tightened. I opened my mouth to tell him –that I wanted him to let me go.

"Ask me to repent, to atone for my sins. Ask me to bleed, to beg, to crawl, and I'll do it… but don't ask me to let you go, Violet. I can't do that, not now, not ever."

He pulled my hand from over his heart and kissed my palm, but once again, the touch that used to soothe and initiate desire only caused more pain and discomfort.

"I love you, my soulmate, my heart. You'll forgive me, there's no other way." Despite the certainty of his words, his voice was pleading.

He leaned in and I turned my face just before his lips touched mine.

"Please stop touching me. It makes my skin crawl," I said honestly.

He jerked back and released my hand as if I'd just slapped him. He moved from his kneeling position to sitting on his haunches in one graceful movement.

HIs eyes searched my face speculatively, and I met his eyes. I was not sure what he was looking for, but I was way too broken for him to find whatever encouragement he seemed to be looking for.

I saw the light of hope dim in his eyes as he stood. "Fine, let me take you to your room."

I let out a sigh of relief to finally be free of his presence. "There's no need; I know where it is."

He turned toward the door. "Please."

I followed him silently to my room, wondering if he had actually taken the time to pack my things or if I would have to live in my flannel pajamas for the foreseeable future, which was bound to be uncomfortable in the Californian heat.

He opened the door and gestured me in silently.

All my questions were answered as soon as I walked in. Along with the bag I had in Montana, I also found all the clothes I'd sold before leaving—and all of my mother's belongings I'd been heartbroken to sell.

I let out a tearless sob when I saw the pearl necklace on the chest of drawers and quickly reached for it, clutching it against my chest.

"I thought I'd never see it again!"

"Everything you sold is here," he replied from his spot on the threshold.

I nodded, grateful that he didn't step into the room. "I don't care about most of it... only my mother's things."

"Your dragon necklace is in the box there," he said, pointing at the vanity.

I shrugged. "You can keep that. It's worthless to me." I didn't even say that with any ill intent, it was just the truth. The dragon had made me feel safe; it was like I was carrying a piece of my ruthless warrior with me, my shield against the world. But that shield didn't protect me from him.

"It's yours. It was made for *you*."

I sighed. "Just don't be surprised if it's sold as soon as I get out of here."

He pursed his lips, standing a little straighter, bracing for a fight I was not going to give him. I just wanted peace.

"I have to go now. Go as you please within the grounds. I will see you for dinner tonight."

"I doubt it."

HIs eyes narrowed slightly. "There is no way out, Violet, you know that. "

"I do. Are you done?"

He gave me a sharp nod. "For now."

I turned my back to him and started to unpack my sports bag, very aware of Hoka's eyes on me, though I ignored him and kept methodically removing my clothes from the bag until I heard the faint click of the door closing.

I let out a breath of relief and turned to look at the closed door. I was finally alone, free to think without interference, and what was the first thing I had to figure out?

How to get the hell out of here.

CHAPTER 20

Violet

It has been five days since Hoka had taken me back to his home—five days during which I'd not been any closer to find a way out, and despite my cold, dismissive behavior, he didn't seem closer to letting me go than he'd been on the first day.

I'd made avoiding him a sport, but he always found me wherever I was hiding. He'd sit there, wherever I was, in complete silence as he ate the plate of food he was carrying.

I might have found that endearing—his determination to have his dinners with me no matter what I did or where I was—but not now, not after everything we'd been through.

He didn't get discouraged. He kept leaving presents in front of my door that I simply picked up and left unopened in the corner of the room.

The only highlight in this house was Himari and her obsession with feeding me as she kept muttering about how thin I was and how I needed to return to the young woman full of sunshine I'd been.

I ate her food; well, not all she put on my plate but most of it. She was right; I was too thin, and if I wanted to escape this place, then I needed to get my strength back.

The most awkward moment had been yesterday when Sakura came to talk to me. I listened to her for a few minutes as she gave me the same well-versed excuse Hoka had given me. When I couldn't take the lies anymore, I'd stopped her and explained in clear terms that whatever she said, true or not, wouldn't have any impact on my life going forward. I told her it would be much better for her to save her breath and my time by turning around and to never talk to me again.

She'd agreed and left me alone until Hoka came into the kitchen, sitting at the counter like a miserable puppy while I finished eating my lunch, washed my plate, and walked out as if he'd not been there at all.

I'd been walking around the house and grounds a lot more than I did before—mostly to see if I could find a weak spot, but also to find the one person I'd not seen yet. The one person I used to avoid before, but who I now saw as my saving grace... Jiro.

I'd almost given up on finding him, suspecting he might not have been here anymore, when he walked into the library in the early afternoon as I was nestled in the leather chair under a thin blanket, reading a book. I often got cold these days. Himari said it was because I had no fat left, and I thought maybe she had a point, after all.

"Oh!" His eyes widened when he saw me and he took a step back, looking around uncomfortably. "I didn't expect you to be here."

"I'd rather be anywhere else than here. But my room is becoming a cage, and I always liked this room. It's rather nice to be here when he's gone."

"I'm not supposed to—" He stopped. "I just need to pick up a few things for a meeting. It's... I'll only be a minute."

I closed the book and sat a little straighter. "No, it's fine. I have been looking for you, actually. I need to talk to you."

"To me?" he asked, pointing at his chest, giving me a side look full of incredulity.

I nodded.

"We shouldn't be talking. Hoka wouldn't approve."

I snorted. "Like I give a frig about what Hoka approves of or not."

Jiro's eyebrows shot up in surprise, but he didn't say a word.

"I want you to help me..." I started, going straight to the point. I was always worried to hear his car come down the drive, forcing me to retreat into my room. Lord knew when I'd be able to talk to Jiro again.

"Help you do what?"

"Leave." I pointed to the window of the library that I knew for a fact was locked. "You don't want me here; *I* don't want to be here. Just tell me how to escape, because I'm sure you know."

His dark eyes studied me for a few seconds before he shook his head. "No."

"Why not?" I all but whined.

"Because I—" He shook his head again. "I was wrong."

Any other time I might have gloated, the almighty Jiro admitting he was wrong. I almost expected him to choke on the word.

"No, you weren't. You were actually right from the very first moment, but I didn't see it. You opened my eyes, and for that, thank you."

He narrowed his eyes suspiciously. "I didn't do anything."

I snorted and waved my hand dismissively. Either he thought I was completely stupid or clueless, but either way, it was far from being a compliment.

"You showed Hoka the pictures of me and Alessandro Benetti; you researched my bloodline. You planted the seed of doubt in his head, knowing very well I was not a traitor."

He closed the door behind him and rested his back against it. "How would I know that?"

"Because if you really thought I was a traitor, I'd be dead."

He pursed his lips but remained silent, giving me all the confirmation I needed.

I moved my legs from under me and sat more properly on my seat. "You told me one day that you were Hoka's executioner. That you were the one doing all the things that Hoka couldn't or shouldn't do. You said you acted when he had to keep his hands clean."

"I know what I said," he snapped, apparently not pleased to have been called on his own words. "I'm in my thirties; I'm not senile."

I nodded. "Hoka should have killed me that day; he never should have cast me away."

"Yes, he should have. Traitors are immediately killed. He spared you because he loves you."

I snorted again. "I wouldn't have pegged you for a romantic, Jiro. How disappointing."

His nostrils flared, the only sign that my jab landed. "And I wouldn't have pegged you as a cynical bitch, yet here we are."

I shrugged with a genuine smile. "That's what almost a year in your world did to me. The light didn't survive the darkness, and only a fool could have thought otherwise. You should give yourself a little pat on the back, though. Thanks to you, I am much wiser." I waved my hand at the reply I knew he was about to give me. "Feelings are irrelevant here, anyway. I know you would have done what he couldn't do. If you'd suspected, even for a minute, that I was a traitor, then I would have been dead before sunrise."

He let out a hissing sound as he ran his hand over his face, leaning even more against the door. He looked back at me and despite how much he was trying to hide it, I saw how impressed he was by my deduction.

He shrugged. "What if I did or didn't? I don't see what it has to do with this situation."

"You don't?" I arched an eyebrow. "Really?"

He pursed his lips and stared at me.

"Fine, let me educate you," I added sarcastically. I no longer cared if I annoyed him or not, if he hated me or not. This detachment was so deliciously freeing.

"The man who I've been sleeping with, the man who I trusted with everything I had to give, albeit not much, believed I was a traitor without a second thought. A few photos, a family tree, and bang, he ended it. However, you," I pointed my finger toward him, "the man who barely knew me and who wasn't a fan knew better. Tell me, Jiro, what does it say about *our love*?" My voice dripped with venom that was now poisoning my whole being.

"I thought getting rid of you would make him stronger, more focused on his role, on his legacy, but instead, it made him weaker. You may not have been who I would have chosen for Hoka, but you are exactly what he needs. That's why I showed him the video of you in your apartment when you stood your ground in front of Benetti. To be fair, I knew he was looking for a way to bring you back. He was not the same man without you, he was barely existing without you. He just needed a way to bring you back home, and I merely gave him the excuse."

"I see." I nodded. "So you won't help me?"

"I don't think you were listening to what I said."

"It doesn't matter what you said. Either you help me, or you don't."

"He made a mistake, like you did when you didn't tell him who you were. Like you did when your brother came to you, and you kept the secret."

I pursed my lips. "I never pretended to be perfect." I looked away. "But I've given too much to this fight, and I've got nothing left to give to this relationship. I lost my baby," I added, turning toward him.

He looked down in shame. "I know... I'm sorry about that, and I'll do anything to make it up to you both."

"You will?"

"Yes."

"Then help me leave. Plead my case to him, Jiro." I pointed at the door. "Tell him that I'm done. Make him understand that whatever plan he had by sending you and Sakura to plead his case is nothing but a wasted effort. There's no cause left to plead."

"You think Hoka sent me?" he asked, arching his eyebrows in surprise. He let out a little laugh. "Hoka specifically ordered me to stay away from you." His mouth twisted in a sad smile. "Believe me when I say that Hoka didn't send me, because he's done with me. I don't think he'd piss on me if I was on fire."

His expression was too sad, too unguarded to be fake. Jiro was all about strength and lack of sentimentality. Showing this side of him must have been nothing less than excruciating.

"I'll pee on you."

"What?"

"If you were on fire, I'd pee on you. I'm very good at peeing myself in public; you should ask Hoka," I added with a wry smile.

He winced at the snappy comment, but other than that, he looked at me like I was missing something.

"You understood what I said before, right? *I'm* the one who caused it all." He pointed to his chest. "I'm the one who withheld information for weeks. *Me*." He tapped his chest. "No one else."

I shrugged.

"You can't be angry at Hoka and not at me. It's not fair."

I laughed. "Oh, Jiro, we both know that isn't how guilt or anger works." I nodded and started to fold the blanket I've been using. "And after what you all put me through, I think it's my prerogative to feel any way I damn please."

"But—"

"You gave him information. You didn't alter the photos or the recording. You presented him with what you had." I shook my head and carefully put the blanket on the back of the chair before turning toward Jiro. "It would have taken Hoka two minutes, *two minutes* of his time, to get everything right. *Two minutes* to prevent all the drama that followed; *two minutes* to spare the amount of suffering I went through. But I was not worth it... After everything I had given him, I wasn't even worth the decency of a real explanation." I picked up the book from the side table and walked to the shelf I'd picked it up from. "If he'd granted me those priceless minutes, he would have known that I'd never seen that man before and never intended to see him again. Well," I tapped my finger against the leather spine of the book I'd just put back, "never intended to see him again on my own free will."

"He came to your place and asked for your allegiance against Hoka."

I nodded. There was no point denying what I knew he saw on the video.

I turned toward him and leaned my shoulder against the shelving unit. "Apparently, a scorned woman is a force to be reckoned with." I let out a tired laugh. "Benetti should have known better, really."

Jiro cocked his head to his side. "But you had to know that by saying no, you were giving your allegiance to Hoka despite the way he'd hurt you."

I shrugged. "Maybe I'm just not big on seeking revenge."

"Yet you're making him suffer more than he ever has. Being here, close enough for him to touch, but also so far and untouchable." Jiro's eyes were so sad. "I don't need him to talk to me to see the agony inside him."

"It's in no way my intention," I replied, walking closer to him, hoping he could see the sincerity in my eyes. "I wish him the best, truly. I want him to be happy, and one day he will. One day, he'll find someone other than me, and he'll thank you for it."

"I highly doubt he'll ever forgive me, and I also can't believe he'll ever be over you."

"I'm not the one for him. I know that now, and one day he'll know that, too. He will find the woman made for him, the one born to be by his side, and he'll forget all about the little gaijin."

"You're not just anyone, you're his—" He stopped and looked away for a few seconds, his eyes fixed on a poster on the wall I knew he was not really looking at. "You know, I know it won't excuse what I did, but once upon a time, I had fallen in love with someone just like you."

"The bastard daughter of an enemy? What were the odds?"

He gave me an irritated look. "She was an outsider, and we loved each other very deeply."

"Ah, but sometimes love is not enough, right?"

He threw me a surprised look. "You said the exact opposite not so long ago."

"And I was wrong, and you proved it to me. Congratulations, you were right."

"For once, I wished I wasn't," he muttered, leaning his head against the door and closing his eyes.

I sighed. "He will let me go soon, you'll see. Once he realizes that we're done, he'll let me go."

He had to let me go because I didn't know how long I could keep my sanity while being close to him.

Hoka Nishimura had once been my heaven, but now he was my hell. I just didn't know how long I could keep on walking through the flames without burning completely in the process.

He had to free me because my heart could not take another blow. I could not lose myself completely. I only had a little light left, and I had to preserve it with all I had.

CHAPTER 21

HOKA

I thought having her back here with me would make things better and help me hurt less, but it was almost worse.

Seeing her every day so stoic, so cold, still the same but so vastly different, and knowing I was the only one to blame was soul-crushing.

She was the most precious thing in the world. She was my everything, and I'd broken her like I'd been warned I would.

She was still beautiful, but the light in her eyes had vanished. Her cheeks didn't turn the lovely shade of pink that used to drive me crazy. Everything I told her was met was a vacant look and a nod.

She was acting too similar to the broken wives from the older generations, the women whose spirit had been broken to become the living *things* their husbands needed.

I'd never wanted that in my life and knowing that my mistrust stole something from Violet killed me.

I knew there would be hurdles. I expected anger—I could deal with her anger; I could come up with a plan—but I didn't expect this nothingness, this complete lack of emotion, other than the automatic disgusted recoil every time I touched her.

Even during the night, when I snuck into her room to watch her sleep, she didn't look at peace. Her eyebrows were etched, her lips pursed. She was worried, even while she slept—almost in pain—and all I wanted to do was lay beside her, kiss her brow, and promise that everything would be alright. But I was not allowed to comfort her when I was the source of her pain.

I looked at the ultrasound image on my desk—the one I found in her nightstand drawer, just under the box of sleeping pills. I ran my fingers over it as the feeling of loss burned in my chest. She went through hell, and I would sell what was left of my soul to take some of her pain away, but despite my desire to do so, I couldn't.

I was grieving, too. I was grieving a baby I loved even in death; a baby I would have wanted so ardently I could barely breathe. A baby with Violet, a piece of *us*. That was a miracle to which I aspire. I wanted to take her in my arms and grieve with her, take some of her pain and carry it. Kiss and cuddle her until she felt a little better, until I saw the light come back into her eyes.

Himari and Sakura told me she needed time. They told me I needed to be there in the shadows and wait until she wanted to reach for me, but it seemed that the more she was there, the less hope I had.

There was a soft knock on my door, and my heart skipped a beat. Not a lot of people would dare enter my bedroom to disturb me in my private office—a space I usually occupied when I needed complete confidentiality or calm. These days I was using it for the privacy it gave me—the certainty that no one would see me cry.

Please be you... I begged, but my face fell when Jiro poked his head through the crack. "You're not welcome in this home or in this office."

"I know, but Himari—"

"You may still be my *wakagashira* in public, but it's for appearance only. I told you before that once this situation is settled, you're gone."

"I know!" he snapped. "Trust me, I'm counting down the days just as much as you are. I'm not really thriving in an environment filled with hate and resentment."

I frowned, understanding all too well. I was living in that environment too, but with the love of my life. "What do you want?"

"Alessandro Benetti is waiting at the front gate."

I turned my head to the side, giving him my ear. I must have misheard him. It was not possible otherwise. "Who?"

"Alessandro Benetti. He's requesting an audience now. He said if his request was refused, he would start a war."

I scoffed, arching my eyebrows, "Oh, did he now?" I almost wanted to call his bluff. I nodded, my issues with Jiro temporarily forgotten. "He threatens to start a war with me in my town?"

"He said you hold a member of his family against her will, which is against the code."

That sobered me up quite fast. If I held a member of the Benetti family against their will, it would be a reason for war.

I sighed and stood. "Let him in and him alone. Don't let him out of your sight until you deliver him to the library."

"I see you're trusting me now?"

I shook my head. "No, absolutely not. I just trust him even less."

Jiro nodded and left the room as I rushed to change my rumpled shirt, straightened my hair, and grabbed a suit jacket.

I exited my bedroom and stopped for a second in front of Violet's room. I rested my hand on the door, seeing the soft light coming from it.

I knew she'd taken my side twice when she was confronted by Alessandro Benetti, but would it be the same now? After I took her home against her will...?

Kidnapping, Hoka. It was a kidnapping. I heard her voice in my head.

I let out a little growl of frustration as I hurried down the stairs. I'd just served myself a glass of liquor when Jiro opened the door to let Benetti into the room.

I glanced at Jiro. "You can wait in the corridor. Mr. Benetti won't be here long."

He nodded, but the slight frown showed how opposed he was to this idea. Normally I would have asked him to stay—it was the wise thing to do—but I could only deal with one snake at a time.

I detailed the man standing in my home, his face hard and accusing, as if I'd wronged him somehow.

I took a sip of my drink, detailing his face with more attention now that I knew Violet shared DNA with him. I was trying to see some similarities. I could see it in the darkness of their hair and maybe in the squareness of their chin, but there wasn't much more there. She was clearly more Irish than Italian.

"I'd offer you a drink, but you will not be here long enough to enjoy it," I told him, not inviting him farther into the room.

"No, I won't." He turned toward the bar and grimaced. "Plus, you clearly wouldn't know good liquor if it hit you in the face."

I'd met Benetti a few years back when neither of us were in charge yet. Back then, we were just trailing along with our respective fathers, both not fully agreeing with their old-fashioned decisions. There was no lost love between the Italians and us, but back then, if only for a few hours, we'd understood each other.

"I'm not sure what you're trying to accomplish showing up at my home unannounced, throwing threats."

"They're not threats; they're promises."

I let out a little laugh. This man was just as much of a hothead as I was, and in any other circumstance, I may have appreciated it, but today was not the day.

"I could have your head for this." And deep down, I was considering it, if only to avenge some of the injustice Violet had suffered.

You will need to chop off your own head, then.

"I'd like to see you try." He gave me a half grin. It was the smile of a man who rarely was denied or challenged, the smile of a man who saw himself as untouchable. I knew that because I was the same type of man... or at least, I used to be.

"No man is an *island*, Benetti. We all have that weakness, no matter how or where we hide it—behind walls or in the middle of the Pacific Ocean. There's always that one person who knows."

He tensed, the corded muscles on his neck pulsing in his attempt to control whatever he was feeling. His challenging gaze quickly turned into a murderous death stare.

I smiled. I knew his deeper secret and now he knew it, too.

I shook my head. "Go back to Chicago while I still have a modicum of patience left."

He nodded. "Of course. I'll be on my way as soon as you hand me back my sister."

That stopped me, my glass halfway to my lips. "Excuse me?"

"Violet."

"I know who she is," I snapped, angry to hear her name coming from his lips. "I know her better than you do."

"Possibly." He shrugged. "But she's been brought here against her will, and that's not something I take lightly."

I narrowed my eyes in suspicion, wondering who the rat was who told him. I half suspected Jiro to be the source, especially since I had not a sliver of trust left in the man.

"And you think threatening me with a war would help? *If*, and that's a big *if*, she was brought here against her will, do you think it would be smart to put her in the crossfire? Allow me to doubt your good intentions."

"What do you want for her?" he asked, as if he was surrendering. "I'll give you Sacramento."

That crumbled all my theories about Benetti's visit. Sacramento had been a source of contention between our two syndicates for as long as I could remember. The Italian mafia in California was weak—only in place for certain key businesses, which were flourishing on their actual East Coast territories. Sacramento was one of the cities they had, and their betting business there was a source of pain for our own gambling and loan extension in Northern California. The head of the Italian mafia in California was Benetti's younger cousin, and he or Gianluca Montanari of the New York Italian mafia could stop this whenever they wanted.

If I said yes now, I'd succeed at something my father failed in doing, despite having tried for years. I'd expand our hold to the whole state.

All my education, all I was born to be, pushed me to say yes. I might even have done it when I'd just first met Violet, but it was not possible, not anymore. Somewhere along the way, Violet had become much more important than my duties, than my role within my own syndicate.

By choosing her now, over this insane offer, I was breaking not only one of the main rules of our *jingi*—our code of conduct—but I was also going against the *bushido*—the old Japanese Samurai code of conduct that was the base of everything we built.

And yes, despite all that, I didn't even have a second of hesitation. Violet was coming first, no matter the offer that was on the table.

I was grateful that the offer had been made behind closed doors and it would be his word against mine because if my refusal was public, .

"Keep Sacramento. I think your sources are mistaken."

"Fine." He crossed his arms over his chest. "Let me talk to her, then. Let me ask her face to face."

I took another sip of my drink, finishing it in one go, trying to hide my apprehension over how this meeting could potentially go.

He cocked his head to the side. "Is there something wrong?"

"No, I'll go get her for you."

"I'd rather see where she's staying, if you don't mind."

I did mind. I fucking minded a lot. I didn't want the Italian bastard roaming my home, not with Jiro, who I wasn't certain was not working with him.

"Fine." I walked to the door and opened it. "I need to ask her if she wants to see you first."

He arched an eyebrow. "Oh, I see. Let me guess, she will not want to, huh? How convenient."

"I don't know, but if she doesn't, then you will leave, war or not." I turned to Jiro. "Take him to the second floor and wait at the end of the corridor. I'll go ask Violet if she wants to see him."

I turned my back to them, and I was finally able to let go of my mask of cool contempt to let the worry finally run its course.

If they spoke and she decided to follow him, there would be nothing I could do. I would have to watch her walk away. My heart ached at the idea of losing her for good.

She might not be mine right now, but her presence helped me to go on. It helped me keep the little hope that one day she'd talk to me willingly, without being pressured; that she would share a meal with me, that she will stop recoiling every time I touched her.

I stopped in front of her door and knocked once.

"Violet, it's me," I said gently, knowing I had an audience.

As expected, she didn't answer, but I walked in just as if she did and thanked all the ancestors that she hadn't locked the door. It would have looked particularly awkward if I'd taken the key out of my pocket to unlock it.

She was seated in the reading chair by the opened French doors, which I suspected was something she did every night. It had pained me to see that she'd stopped reading all the books about Japanese culture and folklore; she'd stopped caring about fitting in my world, and it wounded me a lot more than anyone could imagine. She was still dressed as she'd been all day—in a pair of old sweatpants and a pale-yellow T-shirt that had seen better days. She looked like a homeless person most days, refusing to wear any of the clothes I had bought for her.

"Good evening, Violet," I said as formally as I could, despite her lovely floral scent overwhelming my senses.

I couldn't be intense with her. Whenever I was too much, she retreated into her shell and nothing else could go through.

She closed her book on her lap and looked at me silently; her face a mask of cool indifference.

I looked at the title of the book she was reading, *The Road Not Taken and Other Poems* by Robert Frost. How fitting to the current mood of our relationship.

I took a couple of steps in. "Robert Frost." I pointed at her book. "Some light reading, I see."

"What can I do for you tonight, Hoka?"

Why did her cold tone hurt me so much? At least she was talking, and I should be grateful, but still, I missed her warmth. It was like a part of my lungs had been removed, and I could not breathe quite right with this version of Violet.

"Your brother is here to see you."

Her eyebrows shot up, the only sign of her surprise. At least I knew for certain that she'd not be the one asking him for help. She schooled her features and shook her head.

"I don't want to see him." She waved her hand to the door. "Send him away."

Fuck, I wished I could, but he'd been right. If I dismissed him, he would assume the worst—which, admittedly, wasn't that far from the truth. She had to see him and send him away herself.

"Your brother cares about your situation. He offered me Sacramento in exchange for you."

She pursed her lips, visibly displeased at being treated like a business transaction.

"I refused," I added quickly.

She shrugged, running her hand over the soft green book cover on her lap. "I've no clue what that even means. But I suppose I should thank you for not selling me to the highest bidder."

Frustration reared its ugly head, and I tightened my hands into fists to stop myself from snapping at her. There was nothing I could do that she would consider being right. "He thinks I have you against your will."

"You *are* holding me against my will."

"Not really." *Not really? What kind of fucked-up reply was that?*

"Yes, you are."

I rolled my eyes and tried a different angle. "He thinks I will hurt you."

"You have hurt me," she replied in an even tone so natural that it somehow hurt more than if she had said it with anger.

Fuck, that one really stung. "Unwillingly."

She cocked her head to the side. "Agree to disagree."

"Stop being so difficult and talk to him so he can leave."

"Let me go," she said challengingly, sitting straighter on the chaise lounge.

"No," I replied, and added a glare with good measure.

"Then I won't stop being difficult. Don't worry about my brother; he's more interested in what I can bring to him than anything else. He'll give up soon enough." She sighed and leaned back in her chair, clearly done with this conversation.

Well, fuck it. I was done, too.

"You know what... I'll send him in, and you can tell him yourself. You say whatever you want to say." I waved my hand dismissively. "Start a fucking syndicate war and see how many deaths will be on your head. I just hope you're ready to bear that cross."

"You should know."

"Yes, I do," I hissed through gritted teeth. The guilt was heavy, even on the darkest souls.

I turned around briskly and walked to the door. I opened it and gestured him forward. If she wanted to wreak havoc, she could do it herself.

If she wanted to burn the world, I'd hand her the matches and burn along with it. I would not keep on fighting this; I was too tired.

Alessandro walked briskly, his shoulders squared, and his hands balled into fists by his side.

"Took you long enough," he spat as he reached me, but stopped as I stood in the threshold, blocking his access and view of the room. "What did you threaten her with?"

"I was naked." Her voice came from behind me. "I'm sorry I was not ready for visitors, especially one I specifically demanded never to see again."

I let out a little sigh as some tension left my shoulders. Maybe she would be on my side, after all. It was not a battle of who she loved the most; it was who she hated less and despite all the pain I caused her, I suspected I was still the winner there.

I moved slightly, forcing him to slide between me and the doorframe.

He threw me the darkest look as he squeezed past me, and I smirked. *Let the games begin, asshole.*

I turned around after he was inside and saw his features soften immediately when he looked at Violet's face.

It was surprising, really, and she might have been much too wrapped in her own feelings to see what was right in front of her. Alessandro Benetti cared deeply for his sister.

She gestured at herself. "As you can see, I'm alive and relatively well." She made a shooing gestured to the door. "You can leave now."

His jaw ticked in frustration, and I coughed once, trying to hide the laugh I could not contain. I knew exactly how he felt and somehow, I could empathize for what he was about to go through.

This version of Violet would be a trial for even the most patient man.

"I have to talk to you."

She rolled her eyes. "Let me guess... you won't leave before you do?"

I saw the side of his neck jump with the rapid influx of blood, showing his patience was running thin.

"You're correct," he replied, his voice colder than before. He threw me a sideways look. "Can we have some privacy?"

I nodded and turned to leave when Violet stopped me.

"No, the more the merrier, right?" She turned toward me, trying to soften her eyes to fool her brother, but my Violet was not a very good liar and she wore her heart on her sleeve. "Stay and close the door. Mr. Benetti won't be staying long."

I could have kissed her right then, and if I didn't risk getting my eyes clawed out and my tongue bitten off, I would have, witness or not.

"Speak," she demanded, moving from her spot on the chair and resting her bare feet on the wooden floor, ready to stand.

"I've been informed that you were brought here against your will."

"Okay?"

"Okay?" He frowned. "What do you mean, *okay*?"

She shrugged. "Here, willingly or not, I'm not sure how it has anything to do with you. I assume you want me for some leverage against Hoka. Just tell him what you want right now and be done with it."

"Is that what you think? That you're a commodity?" His voice carried a certain sadness.

"Twenty-one years it took for you to appear, and despite being sent away twice, you've appeared again. So, either you're slow," she said, raising one finger, "which is very much doubtful, or you've got something big riding on me coming with you." She raised a second finger. "Which I honestly think is the case... so just tell us what it is."

He threw me a side look, visibly self-conscious of sharing whatever he was about to share in front of me. It was too bad because I was not going anywhere.

"When you were ten, you wanted a bicycle. It was a big birthday, double digits! You kept saying you were not a little girl anymore." He smiled.

I glanced at Violet, who was completely tense, her face a mix of confusion and sorrow at her childhood memory.

"There was that bike at the secondhand store a couple of doors down from your apartment. A blue and green one. It was a boy's bike, and it was a little banged up, but you kept telling your mother that it was the one you wanted. It was not the case, of course, because you wanted the pretty peach one with the white basket in the front. The shiny new one that you looked at every time your mother walked you to school, but you knew it was too expensive and you didn't want to make your mother sad, so you didn't tell her." He took a few steps toward her and leaned against the foot of her bed.

"How?" She let out in a broken whisper as her eyes filled with tears.

"A mother knows." He took a deep breath. "I wanted you to have that bike; you deserved that bike. I bought you the bike and—" He reached inside his jacket to retrieve his wallet and extended an old, abused picture. You could see by the folding marks that it had been looked at often.

She held the photo with a shaky hand.

"That smile, the missing front teeth made it all worth it."

I turned to look at him and, despite only seeing his back and neck, I realized the truth, which was so abundantly clear in his voice. This was not a ploy, it was not a game, not for him. He genuinely loved his sister.

I looked down at my shoes, fighting with my own moral sense. Now that I knew that, I should have encouraged her to go with him. To be with someone who didn't hurt her the way I had, someone who could offer her the love and care she deserved. A healing love that she rejected from me.

But unfortunately, I was not that man. The idea of letting her go was too painful, too unbearable to even consider. It would tip me right off the edge of insanity.

I looked back up just in time to see her extend the photo back to him.

"I've been in your life as much as I could without raising suspicion. I was still very young, and I was not high enough in the family at the time, but I can assure you that I helped from the shadows whenever I could—even in the end, when your mother needed all this care. The charity didn't cover it all, I did."

She looked down at her hands on her lap as she twisted her fingers together, and my heart sank. She was doing that because she was conflicted, and for the first time, I really thought she was going to choose him.

I closed my eyes for a second. *Don't do this, don't choose him. Don't make me start a war.*

"Why did you leave me all alone when she died? If you kept an eye on me, why did you?"

"Because, believe it or not, with Giovani Benetti still in charge, you were better off poor than home. He would have–" He shook his head. "You were better far away, and I didn't have the power to protect you. Once he was gone, I needed time to ascertain my position and then," he glanced at me, his eyes full of accusation. "Things got complicated." He turned back toward her.

She looked up from him to me, and my heart leaped in my chest as her gaze remained on me a few seconds longer than usual.

"Say the words and I'll walk you out of here and take you home to Chicago with me. What do you say?"

"Will I be free?"

The dread I felt before was now mixed with despair. She was leaving me. I took a shaky breath as my lungs refused to fill, and she threw me a quick side look before looking at Benetti again.

"Free?"

"Yes. Free to come and go and do as I please."

He brought his hand up, rubbing at his jaw. "I suppose you can say that, yes, but I will recognize you as my sister and as a mafia... *princess*." He obviously disliked the word as much as I did. "So, you will have to take some safety measures, but I'll give you as much freedom as I can."

She nodded. "I see." She took a deep breath and looked at me again. "Thank you for the offer, but I think I'll stay here."

I opened my mouth and closed it again. Had I actually heard that, or was my brain playing tricks on me?

"What? After all I told you?" he asked, mirroring my level of shock.

She nodded. "I'm not here against my will, Mr. Benetti."

"Please, call me Sandro. We're family."

She gave him a little smile. "I'm grateful for what you did for me in the past, truly, but I'm not looking for a family. I had one, and she is gone. I wish you the best, Mr. Benetti. I wish you find that family you're craving, but it won't be me."

"You... Please, just—"

"I think you heard her," I said sharply once I recovered from the surprise. I could not believe my luck. Despite all the odds, she picked me, and I didn't want to give her one more minute to reconsider.

I opened the door and gestured him out. "Jiro will walk you back to your car."

Alessandro took a few steps toward the door and turned around. "If you need anything or change your mind... just call me, day or night."

"Will do."

He narrowed his eyes at the dismissiveness of her tone. "Do you still have my details?"

"No, but if it's meant to be, I'll guess them."

He muttered something under his breath in Italian before walking away. He stopped in front of me, extending a white business card. "Could I at least ask you to give her that when she recovers her senses and decides she wants to call me?"

I nodded, taking the card and sliding it into my pocket.

I watched him walk down the corridor and once he reached Jiro, I closed the door and turned toward her. She was already lying back on the chair, a book in hand again.

"You chose me?" I was still so surprised that I couldn't help my voice making it sound like a question. "After everything... you chose me."

"So it seems."

I took a few steps toward her. I wanted to shake her, kiss her, shout at her. I wanted emotions, no matter how destructive. I didn't want this shell of a human, this numb, broken woman she was so infuriatingly trying to be.

I looked at her opening her book again, and something just snapped inside of me—maybe due to the fear I just had at almost losing her.

"Stop it!" I shouted, making her jump. "You can't just pretend to feel nothing at all. This is not you, Violet! You can fake it as much as you want, but you are not this cold, unfeeling robot you've been pretending to be for the past week! Fuck!" I ran my hand in my hair in frustration, untying the knot in the process. "Curse me, shout at me, cry! Do something! Fuck it! Be a fighter!" I took a deep breath. "Be more like your mother."

I saw it as it happened, the switch of anger and indignation, and I knew she was about to blow up and I was going to take it.

She jumped from her seat. "How dare you talk about my mother?" she roared, coming up to me and pushing my chest as hard as she could, but I didn't move. "It's because of her that I'm still here today! I *wanted* to die!"

She threw her hands up in exasperation as my blood turned to ice. I knew she'd suffered, but death? I never thought she contemplated death.

I opened my mouth to speak but she continued.

"I contemplated all the ways I could die. I was so alone; I'd just lost everything! My body was working against me and took the one little being that would have loved me without restriction." Her voice broke as she paced in front of me. "I wanted to die so many times, hoping I'd just fall asleep and never wake up. I'm so tired, so tired of everything. I'm tired of never being the first choice, tired of always being in pain, of things never getting better. I'm tired of fighting for a future that seems to be getting gloomier and gloomier. I'm just tired, Hoka Nishimura." She stopped in front of me, her hands balled into fists at her side. "But I will always remember how she fought to stay alive. How even when everything, including her own body, was beating her down, she fought to keep on breathing and I couldn't do it. I couldn't end my life." She wiped her eyes angrily, drying her tears with the back of her hand. "I couldn't insult and betray the person she was by doing that, so I kept on walking, one step after the other."

My chest cracked open, and my knees buckled under the powerful blow of sorrow and grief her words conveyed. I sat heavily on her bed, completely silent.

I thought I could take it all, but I'd been wrong.

She resumed her pacing. "The only way for me to keep on going was to feel nothing at all. Do you really think it's so easy to get over everything? To get over *you*? Don't you think I wouldn't give anything to let go? Because no matter what now, I lose, Hoka. *I. Lose!*" She tapped her forefinger so hard on her chest, I could see the redness appear on her skin. "I can't forgive you. I need to stop loving you! I need to *nothing* you, and the only way to do that is for you to help me. I need you to let me go, and I know you will once you realize there is no saving us. You will let me go and then, finally, I'll be free. It's a freedom I'll never get if I enter Alessandro's world."

How could I have caused all this pain to the only person I ever loved?

"You betrayed me!" she shouted again. "You betrayed our love, my trust, my loyalty to you! You betrayed everything I believed in. I was all alone when I should have been grieving with you, when you should have helped me carry the burden of the pain of losing our baby. You should have been there! The only other person who could understand that loss because this baby was a part of you too!" She took a gasping breath. The emotions all too much to bear. "Where were you when I needed words of reassurance? When I needed the comfort of your arms? When I needed hope? You left me all alone, and even if it didn't kill me, something inside me died that day."

I rested my hand on my chest, hardly believing that my heart was still inside my chest and not on the floor by her feet. I never thought that words could hurt, yet I would take a thousand stab wounds rather than have a discussion like this again.

I nodded. I needed to try one last time, and then, despite my selfish nature, I'd have to let her go. I had to atone for my sins by making the greatest sacrifice...

I'd lose her.

"A week," I whispered.

"What?"

I looked up and her breathing was labored, her cheeks were red from her outburst, and it was the liveliest I'd seen her since I found her in Montana.

"I promised you Japan once. Let me take you. We'll leave on Sunday. Give me a week there, and then if you still want to leave, I'll let you go." Nausea shot up my throat at the thought.

She narrowed her eyes. "What's the trick?"

I shook my head. "No trick. A week during which you'll be completely mine as you were before, as if the last few months had never happened. We take the trip we were supposed to take, and you let me kiss you, love you, be with you, and then if you still want to leave, I'll help you."

"How do I know you mean it?"

"I give you my word."

"Sorry, but those don't mean much. You swore to never hurt me before…"

I took the blow silently. "What do you have to lose?"

She tensed, her face closing up, and I knew what she was not saying. 'So much.' She pursed her lips before catching her bottom lip between her teeth, and I knew she was considering the idea.

I rested my hands on my thighs, trying to look much more relaxed than I felt.

"You expect sex?" she asked tentatively.

I nodded. "I won't force myself on you, but if you want to keep the end of your bargain, then yes, I expect willing sex. I'll know." I ran my finger over my bottom lip, almost feeling her warm wetness on it, almost tasting her on my tongue.

She looked up to the ceiling before looking back at me again. "Fine," she huffed. "But I have one condition. You will use condoms."

I frowned, not happy at the thought. "I'm clean. I've not been with anyone since you."

She shrugged. "It doesn't matter. When you kidnapped me, it messed with my pill, and I won't make the same mistake as I did before."

I stood, a hit of offense now filtering in the sadness. "You consider our child a mistake."

"Life obviously did." She crossed her arms over her chest, jutting her chin out in defiance. "Condoms. Take it or leave it."

I ground my teeth at the idea of wearing a condom with her, but being able to touch her again was just too much of an allure.

"Deal," I replied, walking backward toward the door. "Pack your bags. In less than forty-eight hours, you'll be all mine."

She turned her back on me, but it was not before I saw a little excitement mix with her fear and apprehension.

You will see that you can forgive me, Violet; that you can give us a chance again, I thought as I walked down the corridor to my room.

I needed to call my mother and arrange everything.

Once we got back, Violet would be wearing my ring. Any other alternative was not acceptable.

Violet Murphy belonged to me. She just needed to remember that.

CHAPTER 22

Violet

I sat in Hoka's private jet as he walked to the front of the plane to talk with the pilot. A few moments later, the flight attendant closed the door and sat on the folding seat by the cockpit door.

I wondered how I'd be able to handle a twelve-hour flight with Hoka so close to me.

I turned toward the window and looked at the thin drizzle coating the tarmac. Rain was extremely rare for this time of the year in California, and I couldn't help but wonder if it was some sort of omen of what was to come.

I'd wanted to accept Alessandro Benetti's offer so much more than I had expected, but I didn't want to let anyone else in.

I was learning from my mistakes, and I was not buying all the *shoulda, coulda, woulda* anymore. If Alessandro had wanted to be part of my life, he would have found a way. All the rest were excuses.

The same could be said about Hoka. Ultimately, he hadn't trusted me enough. He had not loved me enough to give me the benefit of the doubt, and that, in itself, was the issue.

Letting go and lashing out at him the other day had been the right call, and it had lifted some of the heaviness that I'd been carrying around. I was breathing better now, and I also realized that he had broken me deeply enough for me to understand what I was worth—and it was more than his flimsy trust.

I accepted going to Japan for a few reasons. The first was because it was an opportunity of a lifetime. The second was to prove to him that, even without all the obvious walls and distance between us, there was no fixing this. Finally, I wanted to give this relationship a proper goodbye—to have a last kiss, a last orgasm – and knowing it was the last.

My seat shook a little as Hoka took the one beside me.

"You know the other twelve seats are unoccupied, right?" I asked, looking pointedly around us.

"I'm aware, thank you. I like being seated beside you." He jerked his head toward the cockpit door. "The plane will take off in a few seconds, and as soon as the tires leave the ground, you're mine."

The heat in his eyes and the low promise in his voice made me shiver with anticipation and fear. This was a risky gamble, and the more I thought about it, the more I feared to lose.

You can't lose yourself again, Violet. You can't let yourself fall for him again because he will break your heart again, and this time you won't be able to survive it. This would be my mantra for the next seven days. He had to help me move on, and he could only do that by letting me go.

The engines roared to life and the apprehension of flying managed to distract me from Hoka's possessive eyes for a few minutes.

The plane started to move slowly, turning until it was facing the long runway. As it started to go faster, I leaned back in my seat, closed my eyes tightly, and grabbed the armrest with all my strength.

"Are you scared of flying?" Hoka whispered, and I could feel his breath on my face. He was so close, too close, but despite everything, feeling him there made me feel better.

"I don't know. I've never flown before," I replied with my heart in my throat as the plane picked up speed, the engine deafening.

He unwrapped my hand from the armrest and intertwined our fingers, palm to palm, and I squeezed his hand as hard as I could.

"Let me distract you." I felt his lips brush on the outer shell of my ear.

I was about to tell him that nothing could distract me from the flying death machine when I felt his free hand cup my cheek and he turned my face toward him.

I didn't even get a chance to open my eyes before his lips were on mine—soft, warm, and reassuring. He kissed me gently at first, simply brushing his lips against mine. Without even any conscious thought of my own, I ran the tip of my tongue along the seam of his lips, and it had the effect of gasoline on the fire.

He grabbed the back of my head and as I let out a little gasp of surprise, he invaded my mouth with his tongue—tasting me, possessing me, branding me with all the powerful masculinity that made him who he was.

He bit at my bottom lip, and I immediately reciprocated, making him smile against my mouth.

"Here you are, kitten. I missed you," he muttered before deepening the kiss so thoroughly that it felt as if he was trying to turn me inside out.

I moaned and grabbed his bun, pulling him close and letting me dive into the sensations flowing all over my body like hundreds of little electrical currents running through my veins. I drown in the taste of him—strong coffee and something else I couldn't quite identify, but I expected it was just something hundred percent Hoka and absolutely addictive.

When he finally broke the kiss, he rested his forehead against mine as we both tried to catch our breath.

I opened my eyes and blinked a few times, knowing I should move from his embrace but unable to do it just yet.

"So, did it work?" he asked, moving slightly and bringing his hand up to cup my cheek.

"Work?"

He gave me a half-smile full of pride. "The distraction." He brushed his thumbpad against my cheek. "I take it as a yes."

"Oh!" I gasped as I looked out of the window, noticing we were now high in the sky. "I... Yes, I guess it worked," I replied rather stupidly.

"Good." He kept rubbing my cheek gently and pecked my lips, once, twice, before letting go and facing forward, gesturing the hostess forward.

I ordered a glass of white wine, hoping it would calm my nerves because letting him give me all those little acts of tenderness was hurting my soul by how much I love his touch, how good his lips could make me feel, and how easy it would be for me to fall back into our relationship.

"Where do you live in Japan?" I asked once we had our drinks and a plate full of mouth-watering snacks.

He leaned back in his seat, his liquor glass in his hand. He sighed with contentment as if everything was right in his life. As if he'd forgotten that this pretense was only temporary.

"We have a domain in the mountain, away from everything and everyone. It's about an hour from Fujiyoshida and borders Lake Kawaguchi. Just across the lake, you have a stunning view of Mount Fuji."

"Sounds like paradise," I said, trying to picture it in my head.

"It really is. It's been in my family since 1571, and my great-great... many times great-grandfather, a very powerful Samurai, built it for us."

"I hope it has been updated since then."

He chuckled, and despite everything, I enjoyed the glint of humor in his eyes. "I promise it's all state-of-the-art. There will be no bathing in the lake, using a bucket as toilet, or cooking your food on the wood fire. It's more like a Jacuzzi bathtub in all the eight bathrooms, flat screen TVs, speaking fridge, and other ridiculous gadgets! My mother will not live anywhere less."

That sobered me a little more. It was one thing for us to pretend to be together again, to pretend we could fix it, but it was another thing to involve other people and dupe them.

"What have you told your mother about me?"

He took a sip of his drink and turned his head toward me. "Nothing that's not true."

I twisted my lips to the side, not liking the evasiveness of his answer.

"Hoka..."

He rolled his eyes. "I told her I was bringing the love of my life."

"Hoka! You – you can't say things like that to her."

"Why not?"

I shook my head. "Because it's not true!"

He frowned. "Yes, it is. You *are* the love of my life, Violet Murphy, whether you believe it or not. Nothing I told her about you, about *us*, is a lie."

"I—" What could I tell him? He was not willing to listen. I grabbed a smoked salmon canapé and stuffed it into my mouth.

"I want you," he said bluntly, making me choke on my food.

I threw a look toward the hostess, who was fairly good at faking being busy arranging the glasses on the small bar.

"I think it will be difficult doing anything with witnesses around."

He grinned and stood as if he had been expecting me to fall into his trap.

"Don't worry about it." He gestured behind him. "I've got a nice bed waiting for us."

I took his hand and followed him down the aisle to the impressively large bedroom.

My already too confused heart was hammering in my chest. I was not ready for this—to give in to the intimacy I had been addicted to, the intimacy I still craved, making me hate myself.

I pushed him onto the bed and straddled him. I had to keep control because I was sure that, if I lost myself in his arms, I would not find myself again.

He smiled, resting his hands on my hips and lifting his pelvis, rubbing his hard cock against my jeans.

He squeezed my hips. "I missed you, sweetheart. I missed you so much."

I leaned down and kissed his sharp jaw, down his neck, opening the buttons of his shirt, kissing his chest, going down slowly.

I couldn't deny that I missed the smell of his skin, its softness, the heat of his big body, and his beautiful tattoos that described his whole story.

I stopped kissing him when I reached the center of his chest and noticed the new tattoo in the center. I lightly traced it with my fingertips.

He rested his hand on top of mine. "I had this one done a couple of months ago, when I was looking for you." He ran his fingers on the back of my hand. "This is the only tattoo that is not related to my role or my culture. This tattoo is the most precious one I have because it's us, our love." He let go of my hand so I could look at it.

"It's a bunch of violets, surrounded by camellias. You and me, always."

Always... If only it were true, I thought as I kissed the tattoo and resumed my way down his body.

He hissed and raised his hips as I unbuckled his belt and pulled his pants and underwear down, his hard cock springing free, bobbing hard and angry against his stomach.

I wrapped my hand around it, squeezing a little how I knew he liked it.

I swirled my tongue around the tip, and he let out a moan as I licked away the drops of precum. I never would have expected it, but I loved giving him blowjobs; I loved the power that my mouth had on this man. How just my tongue could undo him.

I started to lick him up and down, my hand circling the base of his cock and stroking up toward my mouth, alternating between my tongue and my hand.

"Violet, fuck... I love you," Hoka growled in ecstasy, bucking his hips.

I wrapped my lips around the head of his cock and slowly lowered my mouth on him until he hit the back of my throat. I started bobbing my head up and down with fervor.

He bucked his hips faster, harder, groaning and moaning shamelessly. I started to suck more firmly with every downward stroke.

I couldn't help but moan, enjoying his pleasure so much that I felt the wetness coating my underwear.

I pulled his cock inside my mouth, swallowing as he hit the back of my throat to get him as deep as possible.

He groaned louder as he fisted his hand in my hair, pushing me down on the remaining inch. His cock was completely inside my mouth, his thighs pressed up against my cheeks, my nose on his lap.

His breathing turned erratic as he let go of my hair and called my name, his voice begging for release.

I started to fondle his heavy sack, and he muttered words in Japanese—a sign that his orgasm was imminent.

"Violet, Violet! This is—Oh, fuck! I missed your wicked mouth. Sweetheart, you're killing me!" he cried out, and I increased the pace and intensity with each stroke.

I felt his erection flex, and I focused my mouth and tongue on the head of his dick. He exploded with a roar, and I bobbed my head quickly, swallowing spurt after spurt of hot cum as it shot down my throat.

Completely spent, he sighed, his arms heavy by his side, his eyes half-closed. I slowly removed his soft cock from my mouth and placed it back in his pants.

I was about to stand when he reached for me. He was insanely fast for someone on the edge of sleep.

"Stay with me." His voice was heavy with sleep. "Please," he added as he saw the hesitation on my face.

I sighed and laid beside him, resting my head on his chest as he wrapped his arm around me. "I love you, Violet."

I kissed his chest but remained silent, knowing that if I said the words out loud, I would start bleeding again.

As soon as his breathing deepened, I moved and looked at his relaxed face. I traced the straight line of his nose, the sharp edge of his jawline.

I kissed his lips gently. "I love you, too... God help me, I do. I just don't want to," I whispered before exiting the room and closing the door behind me.

I sat on the seat I was occupying before and looked out the window, seeing nothing more than blue sky.

I accepted the food and drink from the hostess, then reclined the seat to lay there with one of the books I had taken from Hoka's library. How sad was it that a plane seat was so much more comfortable than most of the beds I had slept in?

I read a few pages until my eyes started to grow heavy—the lack of sleep over the past two nights and the emotional turmoil was draining me completely.

Alessandro's visit had been unexpected, and all his words sounded just too good to be true, too well rehearsed, but the things he knew about me and my mom, the photo... it was hard to deny. Then there was Hoka and all his words of love and devotion.

Giving in would be easy, sweet and comforting, but I was not the same woman I'd been, and I didn't see him with the same tainted glasses I had before.

I closed my eyes with a sigh. I needed to sleep. I needed to be ready to face the world and Hoka's other life as soon as the plane landed. I curled on my side, facing the wall, and tried to let go of all the worrisome thoughts as the dull sound of the engines lulled me to sleep.

I was awakened by a hand gently stroking my cheek.

"Hmm?" I kept my eyes closed, nuzzling my face in the warm hand.

I felt lips against my forehead, and I opened my eyes, blinking away the blurriness of sleep.

"Hoka?" My mouth was dry and heavy. I could only imagine the breath of death I had.

He kept leaning over me, sitting in the seat beside me. "Sweetheart," he said, still touching my face with his gentle fingers, removing a strand of hair from my forehead.

He was freshly showered, wearing a crisp, clean suit, his unique scent of verbena soap and woodsy cologne so comforting in my half-awake state. I wanted to just curl up against him and bury my face in his neck.

His face broke into a tender smile as his hand stopped to cup my cheek.

"Morning, beautiful." His voice was deeper than usual as his golden eyes swirled with a mix of emotions, seemingly just as much at war with his feelings as I was with mine.

I turned onto my back, breaking eye contact and my growing desire to kiss him. I rubbed my eyes. "What time is it?"

"It depends where you are located in the world. If you're wondering what time it is at home, it's probably seven p.m., but if you wonder about Fujiyoshida... it's eleven a.m."

I nodded while stretching.

"We'll be landing in a couple of hours. I thought you might want a shower."

I turned back toward him. "Already?"

"Yes." His smile turned wicked. "It seems that giving me that mind-blowing blowjob relaxed you as much as it relaxed me."

I felt the heat of a blush taint my cheeks.

Hoka took a sharp intake of breath. "Oh, how I missed your blush. I missed your life." He leaned down and brushed his lips against the apple of my cheek. "Don't think I don't know why you did that," he murmured against my skin. "If you're not ready for physical intimacy, you don't have to trick me—not that I didn't appreciate it." He chuckled.

I turned my head to look at him silently.

"It's okay if you don't want to have sex, you know. I understand that it must be hard to give yourself to me that way after... after everything."

"But the deal?"

His happy smile turned a little mournful. "The deal is not important. I just wanted you to try as much as you are ready to. I don't want you to give yourself to me unless you really want to."

My heart filled with a wave of gratitude. "I have not done anything I didn't want to do."

Relief washed over his face, and he kissed the tip of my nose before sitting straighter.

"I left clothes and a towel for you on the bed."

I nodded and rushed away to the bathroom. The cubicle was so small; it felt like I stepped into a sci-fi film.

The shower was wonderful, and I quickly dressed in the lovely green dress Hoka had picked for me and pulled my hair back with the matching hairband. I looked at myself in the mirror and felt a certain contentment and peace I had not felt for months.

My cheeks were fuller, my skin was back to its normal milkiness, leaving the grayish tone behind.

My lips were still a little swollen and red from the blowjob I had given Hoka, and the little flush at the memory made me look healthier.

I looked like the girl I'd been before, and if it wasn't for the throbbing scars on my heart, I could almost believe I was.

When I walked back to the main cabin of the plane, Hoka gestured at the hostess, who set a plate of warm food on the table in front of my seat.

"Come, eat and enjoy the view," he said, reaching for my hand.

I took it and once again, just the small contact made my body buzz with awareness as he gently pulled me down the aisle to my seat.

I sat and looked out the window at the shape of the island that was getting clear as we slowly started to descend.

"We're here," I whispered, hardly believing that I was in Japan.

"Welcome to my second home, *Suītohāto*." He pressed a kiss on the back of my neck. "I can't wait to share it with you."

CHAPTER 23

Violet

Hoka's description of his home was not rendering it justice. I stepped out of the plane on the private airfield, and we were ushered by the security team into the black luxury Range Rover. My face had been glued to the window until we reached the security outpost of Hoka's family's estate entrance.

I was so enthralled by the beauty unveiling across my eyes that I was not bothered that Hoka held my hand from the moment we stepped out of the plane. I didn't even get a chance to feel properly nervous at meeting his mother until the car stopped in front of the gigantic red and white Minka, and a stunning older woman with eyes as golden as Hoka's stood on top of the stairs with a smile.

She'd welcomed me with a bear hug and enthusiasm I had not expected. She had even asked me to call her by her first name, Ena.

For some reason, I had expected Hoka's mother to be all about decorum and cold politeness, like a political wife.

I had not expected a joyful, accepting woman who didn't look a day over thirty if it was not for the white streaks in her hair.

She had taken me in her arms and showed me the house with excitement, and I threw a last look at Hoka before rounding the corner. The look he gave us made my stomach flip.

This week was going to be the trial of my life...

"I thought I would have to send a search party."

I turned my head to the side and saw Hoka coming down the dusty path, his hair in a messy bun and wearing a pair of pajama bottoms. I got a delicious full view of his toned chest and defined abs—all of which I loved tracing with my tongue.

I glared at the tempting view and turned my head toward the placid lake that was reflecting Mount Fuji, which stood proudly on the horizon.

He sat beside me under the cherry blossom tree and remained silent, as if just being close to me was enough.

"I didn't realize it was that early," I admitted after a while, bringing my legs up and resting my chin on top of my knee. "The sun was already so bright, and I woke feeling so well rested."

"Yes, the sun rises really early here, and I'm glad you slept well; it's always difficult in a new place."

I turned my head toward him, keeping my position, my temple now resting against my knee. "Did you sleep well?"

"Yes, it could have been better, though, but I can't complain." He ran his hand down the length of my back. I knew what he meant, his mother had put us in connecting rooms, and Hoka had left the door between them open. It was obviously an invitation for me to take the first step, but after everything that had already transpired between us on the plane, I was not reckless enough to take it.

"You looked so peaceful sitting here. I almost didn't want to bother you."

"You're not bothering me." I turned toward the lake again, feeling warm just by his hand resting on my back. "Your mother gave me a tour of the grounds yesterday, and this place is just..." I closed my eyes and took a deep breath, enjoying the faint floral scent the breeze carried. "No wonder she decided to stay here."

"She loves you," he said, running his thumb along the base of my spine.

"She's an amazing woman," I replied, purposely ignoring his comment.

"You fit right in this picture, you know. You'll see it at the party tonight."

Apprehension filled me once more. Hoka's people in America disapproved of me, and I could only imagine how his people here would see me.

I shouldn't have cared about how they saw me. It would actually be for the best if they hated me, giving me one more reason to walk away from Hoka.

"I learned to swim here, but my grandmother told me a story about a dragon living in this lake. I was so terrified, but I didn't want to show my father, so I bravely went in. Then I saw something move in the water—it was probably a small fish, intrigued by the movement in the water—but the story my grandma had told me just popped into my mind." He laughed. "As I ran out of the water, I let out a high-pitched scream so loud, my mother had heard it all the way on the other side of the house."

I laughed, relaxing my legs and turning toward him again. I could see him in my mind so perfectly after his mother showed me pictures of him as a boy last night. I laughed even harder, imagining his stern father trying to calm him down.

Would he tease our son the same way? The thought popped into my head without warning, and my good humor drained in a second.

I felt the emptiness of my belly again, and the echo of the loss slapped me across the face.

Hoka noticed the switch as his smile vanished, and he reached for me.

I rolled to the side to dodge his touch and stood, dusting the back of my yoga pants from the soil I'd been sitting on.

"I better go get ready for the day. Your mother wants to take me around the village, and then I need to get ready for the party tonight."

"Where did you go?" he asked from his spot on the ground, the corner of his eyes tense with worry.

I looked back toward the path. "I just came back to reality. I seemed to have forgotten myself for a minute." I admitted sadly. "That won't happen again." I turned, slowly moving back toward the house, leaving him to digest my words.

"Marry me."

I stumbled on a small stone and spun around.

Hoka had followed me up the path so silently, I thought he'd stayed by the lake a couple hundred yards back.

"What?"

"Marry me," he repeated, standing straight, his face showing the determination of a man going to war.

I looked almost pleadingly at the house. It was so close! I could just take a few steps and hide in the comfort of my room.

"Hoka," I shook my head. "No."

"Don't you see how well you fit in all this? In this house, in my life, in my heart. Don't you see this life is where you belong?"

"Now's not the time to discuss this." *Never* would be best.

"But you see it, right?" He took a tentative step toward me. "You see that you belong with me."

"I see that you believe it." *For now*. I took a deep breath and shook my head. "I've got to get ready. I'll see you later."

"*Watashi wa anata to issho ni iru toki, motto watashi rashiku naru*," he called as I reached the stairs.

I looked up to see his mother in the shadow of the open door, her hands resting over her heart as she looked at me with a compassion that almost brought me to my knees.

I nodded as I passed her, not trusting my voice at the moment.

"I'm much more me when I'm with you," she whispered as I walked past her.

I stopped, keeping my back to her.

"That's what he said. *'I'm much more me when I'm with you.'*" Her voice carried a sadness that I imagined was a mother's grief when faced with her child's turmoil.

I closed my eyes and tried to swallow past the lump of emotions in my throat.

"And I lose myself when I'm with him," I replied just as softly, but with a desperation that I hoped conveyed my own struggle. I resumed my walk, grateful she didn't add anything until I reached the relative safety of my assigned bedroom.

"Is it really okay for me to wear this—" I stopped, not remembering the name.

Ena rested her hands on my shoulders, and I met her eyes in the mirror. "Wafuku, and yes, why wouldn't you?"

"Oh, you know I'm not..." I let a couple of seconds pass by, not certain on how to put things. "Japanese."

She giggled, enjoying my discomfort. "You don't need to be, dear; this is not how it works. Only insufferable, stuck-up people like Hoka's uncle seem to think it is."

I turned, looking at her with my mouth opened in shock.

"What?" She shrugged. "You can't deny it."

It was my turn to laugh, resting my hand on my mouth. "No, I'm not."

Ena was wearing a similar outfit as mine, but hers was more sober, made of brown and deep red fabric. Mine was blood-red with white and yellow flowers.

"Do the colors mean anything?" I asked, peeking at myself in the mirror again, watching how she pinned my hair and did my make up.

"You are so beautiful," she said with a prideful smile that almost made me weep. It was the kind of smile my mother used to give me.

She walked closer and gently ran her finger toward the corner of my eyes to wipe a little of the black kohl that had smudged.

"I've always wanted a daughter. I'll have to thank the ancestors tomorrow for giving me one."

A pinch of guilt added to the already growing pile I felt at deceiving the woman.

"You know, I'm... I'm not sure what Hoka told you, but we're not together, not really, not like that."

"I know." She nodded a couple of times. "But I see how he looks at you and the way you look at him when you think no one is looking."

I looked down and blushed at being so transparent, even to someone I barely knew. "I am not made for this; I'm not made for his life. No one approves of us."

She cupped my cheek and kissed the other. "I do. I approve with my whole heart. I've prayed for someone like you."

"Why?"

She sighed. "Everybody is worried about the power, but I only care about his heart. You love him, deeply."

I glanced at the door. "We'd better go, no?" I was much more inclined to face a room full of disapproving people than to have this heart-to-heart with Hoka's all-seeing mother.

She gave me a half-smile, showing she knew exactly what I was trying to pull. "We need to wait for the call," she replied quickly. "I saw you this afternoon, you know, standing in the shadows of the temple, looking at Hoka in the field."

My cheeks burned with shame. I felt like a peeping Tom looking at him, bare-chested and kneeling, making movements with his katana, his powerful back muscles shifting with each of his precise movements. "It felt private, and I didn't want to interrupt." What a lie! Watching him made me horny as hell, and I knew that one heated look from him would have been enough to get me willingly under him.

"It was penance; his request to the ancestors to grant him his soul, his life-force back," she explained.

I frowned. "He lost it?" He seemed pretty powerful to me.

"Yes," she replied sadly. "When he lost you."

That hurt me on his behalf, and even if I wanted to make him feel better, make him feel whole again, I had to protect myself first. "Too much has happened."

"But you love him."

"Less." There was no point denying that I still loved him. The truth was, I saw him clearly now, which had stopped me from being the way he wanted me to be, the way he *needed* me to be.

"It is not too late to allow yourself to forgive and be happy." She reached down and took my hand in between hers. "There is a duality in my son. The kindness he shows you and the cruelty he shows the world... and sometimes it seeps through."

I opened and closed my mouth, unsure what I could even say when a loud gong made me jump.

"Ah." She gave me a playful look. "You're literally saved by the gong. Come on, *Yome*. Let's go."

When we walked into the reception area, I was relieved to see that there were a lot less people than I had expected. I was also pleased to see that most looks in my direction were curious and speculative, devoid of any objection or disapproval.

I smiled at a few people as Ena introduced me in Japanese, and I used the few words I remember like *hajimemashite*, which meant 'Nice to meet you.' The people here were just thrilled at my efforts, and after a few minutes, I felt relaxed enough to smile a little more naturally.

At least it was the truth, until a door at the back slid open and Hoka walked in, followed by a few men. They were all wearing black kimonos, but Hoka's had a golden band which matched his black and gold katana hanging at his side. He towered over everyone, looking so fierce and powerful.

When I looked at him like that as he searched the room, I almost forgot everything that stopped me from taking the leap again and soaked into the sense of safety his mere presence in the room ingrained in me.

"That's the look I was talking about." his mother whispered in my ear. His eyes connected with mine and the heat that radiated from his gaze made me shiver, but it was not due to cold or fear—it was my body calling out to him.

He strode across the room, keeping his eyes on me, parting the people like a man on a mission.

He stopped right by my side and wrapped; his arm around me, pulling me close to his body.

"Thank you for this gift, Okan. I'll take it from here," he said to his mother, leaning down to kiss her cheek before turning back toward me, looking down at me with so much emotion in his eyes it almost looked like he was about to cry.

"Hoka?" I tried, a little embarrassed at his silent, heated looks. It must have been so awkward for the people around us. I chanced a glance to the side, but noticed that his mother and the two older ladies she'd been talking to were now gone. "Hoka, say something."

He bent down and brushed his nose against mine before looking up again.

"I could have sworn this morning that I couldn't love you more than I already do, yet right now, I just topped that, and I know I will tomorrow as well." His hand tightened against my hip.

"What's the gift?"

He gave me a wicked smile. "She made you dress like a new bride. Seeing you like this only motivates me even more to make it official."

Oh! I looked around and threw an exasperated look at his mother, who only raised an eyebrow with a sly smile. "She's crafty."

"She's the best. Come on, love, let me show you around."

"Hoka, don't," I hissed as he pulled me through the crowd to the group of men he arrived with. "I'm not your bride."

"You are. Maybe not officially, maybe not even for you, but for me... you are. I've made that commitment to you in all the sense that matters and through a blood oath to the ancestors." He looked down at me just before we reached the men. "You may not see yourself as mine, but I'm yours, Violet, and it's all I need to know."

I'm yours too, Hoka Nishimura. I'm just not willing to give you back that power.

CHAPTER 24

Hoka

Seeing Violet dressed as a bride slayed me completely. All I wanted to do was fall on my knees in front of her and beg for another chance. Beg her as I had begged the ancestors for their help in getting her back.

My mother showed her full support by dressing Violet like that and being by her side when they entered the room. I didn't think Violet understood how much weight this evening would hold for us. She met the true elders tonight—the most powerful men in the *yakuza*. The elders were much more powerful than I was, but I led her to believe they were my slightly senile uncles. Her big heart and compassion for the most fragile took over like I knew it would, and she charmed them as easily as she'd charmed me.

I knew that by tomorrow, the news of Nishimura's bride would have reached the US, along with the elders' approval.

If I was lucky enough, Violet would take the leap once more. I knew she was brave enough to give it another try. She didn't think she could, she didn't think she had the strength, but I knew better. I saw it with my own eyes. Violet had the heart of a lioness. She just needed to want to fight just one more time, and I'd make it my life mission to never hurt her again, to never doubt her again, and to make sure she'd never regret giving me one more chance.

I stretched my neck and winced at the soreness. The outfit and katana at my side all evening had not been the most comfortable, and I started to feel the pain.

Violet and my mother had retired over an hour ago, but the elders had wanted to talk a little more about the US business, and I had no choice but to oblige. After all, I'd been delaying my trip for far too long.

I stopped in front of Violet's room and wanted to knock. My cock stirred again at the image of her dressed as my bride. This woman was my addiction.

I took a deep breath and forced myself to take a few steps toward my room. The connecting door was open, so it was her decision.

I entered my room and even if I didn't see her yet, I knew she was there. My body hummed in recognition as it did whenever she was close. My mother assured me it was the *ikigai* bond; she knew it because it was what she shared with my father. She assured me that, no matter how much Violet denied it, she probably felt the same.

I turned toward where her perfume seemed to originate, and I found her looking out of the window with her back to me.

"The moon seems to be so much bigger here," she murmured after I slid the door closed behind me.

I removed my katana and placed it on the floor before taking a few steps and lit the candle on the mantle, too scared to turn on the light and break the charm of whatever moment we were about to share.

"Yes, I noticed that, too." I stopped behind her, not close enough to touch but close enough to see all the signs of her nervousness and apprehension. I could see it in the flutter of the pulse on her slender neck, the shallow breath she was taking, and the way she was wringing her hands together.

"Everything is so much more beautiful here. The colors are more vivid, the food has more flavor, the stars shine brighter. I feel like I'm in a particularly good dream, and I don't want to wake up."

I took a small step closer, and as I pressed my chest against her back, I leaned down to kiss the top of her head. "Why don't you want to wake up, sweetheart?"

"Because I fear that I won't feel what I feel now. Because I don't want to wake up before doing all the things I want to do."

I wrapped my arms around her and pulled her against me, knowing she could feel my hardening cock against her back.

I expected her to move away from the growing bulge, but my heart jumped in my throat as she pressed into it just a little more, a silent invitation at giving her what I wanted.

I growled with satisfaction as I let one of my hands trail up and squeezed one of her breasts as the other trailed down and rubbed her pussy through the heavy material of her *Wafuku*.

She let out a long moan, and it was enough to get me into action.

I whirled her around and took her lips in a passionate kiss, thrusting my hips forward as she opened her mouth and I slid my tongue to meet hers, licking intently as I intended to do to her pussy.

As I kissed her, I reached to the sides and undid the knots that were keeping her outfit together. Once it was done, I broke the kiss and took a step back, pushing the material off her shoulders, making it fall heavily to the floor.

I took a deep, shaky breath as I looked at my goddess standing there, in nothing more than her white, bikini-style underwear, her nipples peaking with desire.

I fell to my knees in front of her, and because of our height difference, my mouth was just in line with her magnificent breasts.

"Good enough to eat," I muttered before sucking one nipple into my mouth, rolling my tongue around it.

She moaned my name, and I felt precum leak at the tip of my cock. I wanted to take my time and enjoy her body;

I wanted to get reacquainted with every dip and curve, but I knew if I waited too long, I'd come in my kimono like a fucking schoolboy.

I released her nipple with a loud *pop* and took care of the other one while massaging the one I just left.

I let my lips trail along her ribcage, and I stopped for a second to look at the small tattoo that had not been there before. It was a small heartbeat tattoo, finishing on a flatline and a date. *That fateful date.* A day I'll regret not being with her for the rest of my life.

I rested my lips on the tattoo, forcing the guilt and shadows away, concentrating on the willing woman in front of me. The woman who owned all of me.

I kept dotting small kisses down her stomach until I reached the edge of her underwear. I pulled it down and as I kissed her bikini line, I noticed the thin red scar that was now there, too. It was only a couple of inches long, but I knew the impact it had on her as well. I kissed the scar and kept pushing her underwear down until it puddled around her ankles.

I carefully lifted one foot and slid the underwear through. I did the same with the other leg, but instead of putting her foot back on the floor, I hooked it over my shoulder and raised it a little until she was open and my mouth was in line with her slick opening.

"I love you more than anything," I told her with a broken voice. She didn't say it back, but I saw it in her eyes, and I knew it would be as much as I could ask right now.

My dick leaked even more precum at the musky smell of her desire for me, and I knew I only had a few minutes to loosen her up and make her come with my tongue before I had to sink my cock where it belonged.

I grabbed her hips tightly and buried my face between her legs, licking, biting and drinking her in a way an animal fed from his prey. I could tell by the way she wrapped her hands in my hair as she bucked her hips, trying to ride my face as she mewled shamelessly, that she enjoyed the savagery and messiness of my mouth and tongue.

She came shouting my name and her knees buckled; the only thing holding her up was my tight grip and my face crushed against her dripping, swollen pussy.

I stood, picking her up in my arms, and I licked my lips as I carried her to bed. I put her on the bed and removed my kimono in record time, ripping some of the stitching along the way. I crawled between her spread thighs and impaled myself in one powerful thrust.

I took her just as violently as I ate her, with rapid, hard thrusts that made the bed hit the wall. I'd wanted to take my time and be gentle; I wanted to worship her, but I'd wanted her like a madman. The weeks without her had been torture, but the recent weeks, when she was close enough to touch, yet so forbidden, had been hell on earth. I had no control over the beast inside me right now; he was asking for his due, her body, his only redemption. The only reassurance was that her hips were meeting me, thrust for thrust, and her cries were of pleasure, not of pain.

I came much too soon, and the only hope I had was that, after a nap, she'd be willing to grant me round two and allow me to show her all she deserved.

I pulled out of her and laid on my side, pulling her against me. She allowed the contact—much too satisfied and exhausted to say or do anything.

Despite my exhaustion, I couldn't stop the cocky smile from spreading on my lips as she nuzzled against me.

"Sleep, my love. The dream doesn't have to stop in the morning. One word from you and it can continue until our dying breaths," I whispered as her breathing returned to normal and deepened as she fell asleep.

I pulled her even closer and rested my hand on her stomach, closing my eyes and falling into a peaceful, dreamless sleep—the first one since I'd sent her away.

I was awakened by a jerking of the bed and opened my eyes just in time to see Violet's naked form rush into her room.

I got out of bed, intrigued by her reaction. I expected a little more cuddling, maybe even more sex, but not a grand escape.

I grabbed my pair of gray sweatpants from the bottom of the bed and stepped into them, tightening the waist as I entered her room.

Violet was wearing a pair of shorts and a tank top, rummaging furiously into her bag.

"Good morning."

She turned around, looking at me with pursed lips. "You didn't wear a condom!"

I took a step back, taken aback by the accusation in her voice.

"Violet—"

"I asked you one thing, Hoka! I had one demand." She pointed at me.

"I'm sorry... I didn't use my head. I was so lost in us, so lost in you." *Just as you were*, I added to myself, but she was much too angry. "Please don't worry, sweetheart. Everything is okay."

"No, it's not, but it will be."

I finally noticed the blue and white box in her hand. "What is that?"

"A solution to a problem. I had to have a Plan B, just in case."

A surge of anger and offense hit me all at once. I was not sure what angered me the most—the lack of trust in me or her complete rejection at having a child with me.

"Would having my child be that terrible?" I asked softly.

"Yes," she replied, opening the box.

I knew the likelihood of her being pregnant was minuscule, but just the thought of her ready to destroy the possibility bothered me.

"Please, Violet, don't do it. Don't take the pill."

She looked down at the box and took a pill out. "Will you stop me?" she asked, holding the capsule between her fingers.

"No, it is your choice... but I'm begging you, don't take the pill."

The look in her eyes was enough to cut me deep.

"I'm sorry," she said, and I walked past her, unable to look at her as she took the pill. I was so angry and hurt, I would probably say something I would regret.

I went to my father's office and my anger increased exponentially. I was angry at him for raising me the way he had, for teaching me that outsiders were dangerous, and for making me think there was always a hidden agenda.

I reached for the vase on the side table and threw it across the room with a howl of pain and anger.

"*Musuko?*"

I turned toward my mother, who looked at me with concern in her eyes.

"She will never get past it… Never!" I pointed toward Violet's room. "She will never forgive me for what I've done. I could bleed!" I shouted, showing her my wrist. "And she would just watch me die. I took so much from her, I know that, but now she's taking *everything*! I know I never should h—"

"No!"

I closed my mouth in surprise. I didn't think I ever heard my mother raise her voice, not even when she was chastising me as a child.

"I love you, you're perfect to me, Hoka. You're my greatest achievement, and when I think of you, I see everything I've done right. Don't." She shook her head. "I suspect that what you have done must have been particularly cruel to hurt this strong woman, but I don't want to know what you did. I can't." She gave me a side smile. "I don't think I could bear looking at you differently, and part of me knows that if you tell me, I will."

My shoulders hunched, hearing that from my mother drained all the anger out of me, leaving only my weariness.

"I am grieving, too. I'm grieving all I have lost because of one decision. I'm grieving what could have been and what should be. But I am not allowed to feel that; I'm not allowed to express that because I am the monster, the villain of the story, and I can't get redemption. The only thing the villain deserves is eternal torment. This is why the ancestors gave her to me again last night, only to take her away again to torment me more, to take me over the edge of insanity." I fell on my knees in exhaustion. How could I be so defeated? "I can't do it anymore, *haha*, I can't. I thought I was strong enough but—" I stopped talking, hanging my head low in front of her, as if she was about to proceed to an honor killing. Right now, with the sorrow I felt all over my body, I would take that blade as an act of mercy.

I saw her feet in my line of vision as she approached silently and she ran her fingers softly through my hair.

I wrapped my arms around her and rested my head on her chest as she caressed my temple like when I was a little boy.

And right now, I felt like one—not able to control my feelings and irrational thoughts, craving comfort like I did my next breath.

"No matter what, the water keeps flowing, Hoka-chan. That woman loves you deeply, but she is wounded, and it takes time for people to heal. You can't force it, just as you can't stop the water from running. It hurts you both so much because it's real and raw. Love is not always healing, you know. Sometimes it hurts, bad." She kissed the top of my head, and I tightened my hold around her.

"There's no perfection in life or in love. There'll always be struggles and anger and pain; you can't avoid that, but it's all about finding the one you want to struggle with."

"She's my everything, Mother. I never thought I could love like that, but I fear I have to let her go." My voice was thick, and I realized I was crying.

"Maybe you have to for now. Maybe you need to stop fighting until she heals, because right now, she is fighting her love for you, fighting so hard to keep you away from her bruised heart that she's not healing. If she loves you as much as I think she does, she will come back."

"What if she doesn't?" I asked with a shaky breath, crying earnestly now.

My mother didn't answer, and I kept on crying, my face buried in her dress to muffle the sounds of my sobs.

How low had I fallen? I went from this all-powerful, cold man to a kneeling, sobbing mess, crying on my mother's skirt and yet I couldn't stop.

I kept on crying for some time—crying for the hurt I had caused Violet, the child we lost, the love she refused to give back, and the future that was escaping me.

After a while, I stood and turned away, gazing at the window and the lake in the distance.

I cleared my throat. "I'll go take a swim. I think the water will do me good."

I opened the side door of my father's office and walked out onto the terrace. The air was still chilly this early in the morning with the sun hiding behind the dark clouds, warning of impending rain.

It seemed that the sky mirrored my gloomy mood.

"Things will work out. Where there's love, there's hope... always."

I nodded. "I wished I shared your conviction."

"You do. You might not feel like it right now, but you do, and this is why you're fighting so hard."

I sighed. "I'll see you later. Thank you."

I walked down the path and discarded my sweatpants before running into the frigid water. I swam to the middle of the lake and went under, the water so cold that it felt like a thousand needles poking at me at the same time. But right now, I relished in the physical pain because it helped ease the pain in my heart.

I stayed under for a while as my body got used to the cold. When I swam back up, I broke the surface with a loud gasp, my lungs screaming for air.

I turned toward the shore and saw her standing there, her feet in the water. Was she even real?

I started to swim back slowly and stopped a few feet away.

"I'm naked," I told her as I stood in water that reached my waist. It was nothing she had not seen before, nothing I was not hugely proud of, but I didn't need to fluster her.

She blushed a little as she turned around.

I walked out and stepped into my sweatpants.

"I didn't take it," she said with her back at me.

I frowned, confused. What was she going on about?

She turned around slowly and let out a little huff of relief. "The pill, I didn't take it."

That made my heart sing. I took a step toward her as hope filled my heart.

She raised her hand to stop me. "I'm forgiving you, but it doesn't change anything."

How could she say that? Her forgiveness was *everything*.

She wrapped her arms around herself and looked at the lake. "Maybe there'd be a chance if I stop being scared of you, but I'm not sure I can."

"You're *scared* of me?" My voice carried the pain her words had caused.

She turned toward me and nodded.

"Violet, my love..." I took a couple of steps toward her and rested my hand over my heart. "I'd rather take my own life than cause you any harm."

She gave me a sad smile. "I know you think that. I know you even *believe* that, and I did too, before everything. I knew what you were. I knew you could be ruthless and cruel. I knew you were surrounded by darkness, but it didn't matter because I was certain that the cruel side of you would never be directed toward me. I knew what you did, but there was a certainty in me that knew you loved me enough to spare me."

"I love you. I always have."

"But then you threatened me with a gun," she continued, as if I hadn't just declared my love to her again. "I could see the conflict in your eyes, Hoka. You wanted to pull that trigger; deep down, you really did. You laughed at me when I—" She took a gasping breath as the agony was almost too much for her to bear. "When I *soiled* myself. You only came for me when you found out I was not a traitor, and even if I sound like a broken record, I have to say it again. You didn't love me enough to trust me."

I stood there silently, taking all her words that were spoken so evenly, without anger or accusation, and that almost made it worse.

"Not taking that pill today *terrified* me because I kept thinking, what if we have a child? Will you take him or her away from me if you're unhappy? Will you ban me? Would you do that? It doesn't matter if you swear up and down, promising that you won't. The doubt is already here." She pointed at her temple. "The fear is here," she added, pointing at her heart.

I felt it then, the surrender to the fight. "I thought that you being angry and rejecting me was the worst that could happen, but I was wrong," I admitted. Her fear of me was so much worse, so much.

My mother was right. I had to stop fighting because I was hurting her even more in the process, and that was unacceptable. "We should go home now," I told her somberly. "I'll go ask for them to set up the plane."

Her eyebrows shot up in surprise, and I saw regret flash in her blue eyes, but she simply nodded.

I'll give you your freedom back, my love... but please, come back to me.

CHAPTER 25

Violet

Things were different between us from the moment we shared at the lake, and I was not sure how I felt about it.

When he told me he was going to organize the return flight—four days before we were supposed to leave—it was a clear message that he was giving up. He was stopping the fight and giving me back my freedom. It has been exactly what I had wanted, what I'd been asking him since the moment I woke in his bedroom. But then why was I feeling so sad?

Why had this feeling of finality been choking me since the moment we stepped on the plane and he didn't sit beside me?

I knew it was the right choice. I survived without him before, even while facing one of the biggest losses a person could ever experience. I could survive without him again.

But is surviving enough? the voice asked as the night of passion we shared continued to make my skin buzz and my body flutter.

Surviving was all I could afford right now, because facing his cruelty, his dismissal almost killed me the first time, and I had the little life inside me pushing me to fight. Now I had no reason left to fight.

My mother always said, *'When people show you who they truly are, believe them the first time.'* It was that doubt that stopped me from trying again.

"What is it?"

I blinked a few times, meeting Hoka's questioning look from across the aisle. I quickly realized I'd been staring at him unseeing while lost in my thoughts.

"I—" I shook my head. "Nothing."

"What if I walked away?"

"From what?"

"This life, this role. What if I gave it to my uncle, and we just moved wherever? What if I could give you the white picket fence life you deserve? The dog and the two-point-five kids? I secretly suspect that point-five might end up being my favorite."

I let out a little laugh, and for a minute, I could picture that life with Hoka. Our babies, our Sunday barbecues in the back garden, but this version of Hoka was not *my* Hoka. He was not the man I loved, and I knew if I made him choose, that he would regret it one day, and he would resent me for it.

"No, you're where you're supposed to be. This is who you were born to become."

"I suppose so... I was born to be a monster." My warrior looked so defeated right now with the way he looked at me. It was like he laid down his weapon and lost his soul in the process.

I wanted to make him feel better, if only for a few hours—to say goodbye the right way. "You know," I pointed at the bedroom at the back, "I'm technically still yours for the next hour."

He looked at the room behind him and smiled, but his eyes remained as sad as they were. "As tempting as the offer sounds, I think I'm going to pass."

"Oh... okay, sure." I turned back in my seat, pretending to look out the window so he could not see how badly his rejection had hurt me.

"Could you leave us, please?" he asked the hostess, and once she was locked in the other room, giving us privacy, he continued, "I want you, Violet. In ways that would scare the most insane men, but I can't keep having only parts of you. I can't have you for just a few minutes. It's not fair to me, and even if I'm an addict always looking for my next fix of you, I know there will be one shot that'll kill me and last night almost did."

I turned my head to look at him. He was turned to the side, his head resting on the headrest, the weariness so intense I could not say anything.

"I can't be satisfied with parts when I know what it's like to have you entirely. So, I'm letting you go, but I am not giving up because I can't. There's no one else for me, Violet, only you. So, I'll wait for you to be ready to take a chance on me again. I'll wait a day, a month, a year, a lifetime for you to come back to me, if that's what it takes. You might not see yourself as mine for now, sweetheart, but I will always be yours."

"Hoka..." I didn't think he knew how much his words affected me.

"I don't expect anything from you, not now or ever. You deserve your freedom, and if we conceived a baby last night, I swear to protect you both and never split you up. I didn't turn out as cruel as my father, because my mother let some of her light affect me. You're all sunshine, love, and compassion, my sweet love, and I want nothing less for our child. I want a break from the past, and I don't want our child to become me. I want him to be happy and not ruin the good things in his life like I have."

"I would be happy for our child to be like you."

He let out a humorless laugh. "That's because you're full of love. I would never want to curse him with that."

It was quite ironic, but actually accepting my choices, by letting me go as gratefully as he had, by letting me know he would be ready to wait for me made me question my choices. For the first time since he brought me back, I started to think I could maybe trust him again.

"So, what now?"

"Now? Well, there'll be a car waiting for you on the tarmac. It will take you to the Marriott downtown, where Lucy, a *Nishimura Corp* employee I trust completely, will be waiting for you with jobs and locations for you to choose from." He winked, seeing the surprise on my face. "I need to make sure you're safe, well-provided for, and happy while I'm waiting for you to come back to me."

I shook my head with a small laugh. "There's no way for me to be mad at you when you put it like that."

"That was the plan." He sobered as the pilot announced we were on our way to landing. "For all it's worth, even if you are coming back to me, I don't think I'll even be able to forgive myself for letting you go through that loss alone. I had to be there, no matter what. You deserved to have support and love at that moment, and even if I'll spend the rest of my life to atone for this, I might never forgive myself."

"It's okay, you didn't know. I can't blame you for something you didn't know." Even if I did. It was anger that had helped me after the loss.

"With the way I loved you, with the way I knew you loved me... it didn't matter. I should not have sent you away. The thing is, I already had such a hard time believing a woman like you could love a man like me, could see past all the flaws and sins and still want to be by my side. It was so much easier to believe you were a traitor; it made much more sense than believing I was good enough for someone like you."

I looked at him with all the incredulity I felt. This man had many flaws, many scars, and a cold ruthlessness that could destroy a person—I'd even experienced it first-hand. But I also knew how selfless, fierce, protective, and loving he could be. This man could be both heaven and hell, but for me, he was my heart.

Everything we just discussed made all my certainty crumble to dust, and the only thing I wanted to do was jump into his arms and beg him to take me home.

I grabbed his hand as the door of the plane opened, and I gently kissed his palm. I would take a few days away, just to make sure it was truly what I wanted to do and not all the emotions that were clouding my judgment.

He kept my hand in his as we walked down the stairs. I looked at the driver taking my suitcase and bag in the other car, waiting for me on the other side of his.

He pulled my hand to his lips and kissed the back.

"Wait for me." I had not meant to say it out loud, but when I saw the light shine in his eyes, I didn't regret it.

"Always," he replied, letting go of my hand.

I walked to the car and turned one last time. He was still standing at the bottom of the steps, his hands buried deep in his pockets, looking at me with a smile of his own.

"I love you, Hoka Nishimura," I whispered and stepped into the car.

I looked up as I closed the door and sitting across from me was the man who had been with Hoka's uncle at the party—the man Hoka told me to stay away from.

"What the—" I reached for the handle, but the doors locked.

"Hoka," I screamed, seeing him walking to his car. "Hoka!" Something was sprayed close to my face and my vision blurred as my throat started to burn.

"Ho—"

I closed my eyes and sank into oblivion.

I crinkle my nose, the smell of fish so strong and pungent, I felt my stomach heave.

My neck hurt, too. I tried to move, but my arms refused to cooperate. I tried to move again, and I felt a burning pain around my wrists.

I opened my eyes and saw a concrete floor. I moved a little and saw my bare feet, red and swollen, as they were bound too tightly to the legs of a chair. I moved my toes, but I could only feel numbness. It shouldn't be a surprise being both on the cold floor and with only limited blood circulation. I moved my head to the side and let out a little gasp of pain at the stiffness in my neck and shoulders. How long had I been tied to this chair? All I remembered was the man in the car, and I was now in what seemed like a warehouse, probably on the docks if I based the location on the smell.

I moved my wrists again, and the rope burned my skin. I let out a muffled cry behind the gag over my mouth. Was this how I was going to die? Bound on a chair and left to starve?

I blinked back the burn of tears that would not come as I tried to scream again, but I had barely any energy left. My tongue was heavy, my throat so dry that every attempt to swallow felt like I was trying to take a mouthful of sand. No wonder the tears didn't come; I was severely dehydrated.

I let out a huff of defeat as I pulled my head back, trying to ease the tension in my neck. The roof was made of glass, and I saw it was daytime, but it was a gray day, which was not the case when we landed in the late afternoon.

"Hoka..." I tried pointlessly. I should have told him that I loved him when I had the chance. Now I was going to die and—

Voices stopped my train of thoughts, and I tried to shout again, using the last of my energy.

A metal door opened, and two men walked in briskly. All hope died when they got closer, and I recognized the man from the car and Hoka's uncle.

I was going to die.

Hoka's uncle was shouting at the other man, pointing at me aggressively. He was not impressed about something, but I doubted it was my kidnapping.

The other man shook his head, sheepishly replying something, but I only caught the words 'ancestors' and 'mission.'

My eyes caught movement above me and I saw a few men, heavily armed, standing on the upper-level bridge, looking out the windows.

Hoka's uncle turned back to me and walked a little closer, but then stopped a few feet away with a sneer on his face, as if getting too close to me would taint him somehow.

"You should be dead already," he spat, as if addressing me was below him. "Not even able to speak Japanese. A real disgrace." He got a gun out of the holster in his jacket and glared at me. "Hoka dug your grave when he took you to Japan to seek the approval of the elders. Once they granted it to him, you were a dead woman walking. I've let my family legacy be tainted once when my brother married his half-breed bitch. I'd rather die than see the day my family marry a full ganji. These children would be more white than Japanese. No, they could not lead the *yakuza*."

All this because of skin color? All this because I didn't fit in his perfect bloodline? This man was demented!

The young security guard from Hoka's house walked in. No wonder his uncle was a step ahead of everyone else; he had a rat in the house.

He walked closer and threw me a quick look, as if he was looking for any fatal injury. Yeah, I was really losing it now.

The older man from the party told him something, and the young man looked at him with so much condescension, it was obvious he was not just a security guard.

"I'm not your minion. I'm not killing people for you," he replied in English, which surprised me.

"I don't care who kills her!" Hoka's uncle growled with frustration. "She was not supposed to get out of the car alive."

Wow, thanks, asshole.

"I want my daughter to marry into the Nishimura family, but not at the price of a life. The ancestors would not approve," the other man said with a thick accent.

"What about the deal? What about the money you promised me! Imagine how your business will flourish if your daughter becomes the Nishimura queen."

The man threw me an uncertain look. I rolled my eyes, wishing I could tell him that my death would not get his daughter the throne.

"She needs to die now. Every minute we keep her is a risk of Hoka finding her."

"It's only been a little over twenty-four hours. We still have time," the young man retorted. "Nishimura is not that special. I spied on him right under his nose for over a year, and he saw nothing."

I had been out for over twenty-four hours? No wonder I was dehydrated.

"I'll take her out, but you will have to get rid of the body. Can you do that at least?" he asked the other man.

My heart started to beat furiously, realizing I was only a few minutes from dying.

"Yes, I'll take her to the fish incinerator in the basement."

I frowned when I noticed the young man take a few steps in my direction, stopping so close I could feel his body heat.

"Two minutes," he muttered under his breath.

"Fine." Hoka's uncle raised his gun, pointing it directly at my head. I saw it then, the glint of murder in his eyes, and I realized, standing at death's door, that Hoka didn't have that in his eyes when he threatened me. He had never intended to shoot.

Everything that followed went both so fast and in slow motion at the same time.

Hoka's uncle pulled the trigger as the young man beside me hooked his foot on the leg of my chair, causing it to fall on the side. Because of that fall, the bullet only grazed the side of my head.

"Now!" he shouted, and all hell broke loose as the doors opened with a loud bang.

I was not sure what was happening, and it was even scarier than before. I could only see shadows as blood trickled from my temple into my eyes.

I felt the coldness of a blade on my cheek and yelped.

"Shh, my name's Oda, and I'm freeing you. I'm on your side," the young man said, removing my gag and my bindings in seconds. "Stay down and play dead."

I wiped at my eyes just in time to see Hoka's uncle raise his gun toward me as everybody was fighting around us.

"No!" I heard a roar, and as I looked to my left, I saw Hoka run toward me at full speed. As his body connected with mine on the floor, I heard the shot, and Hoka's eyes widened as I felt the impact of the bullet hit his body.

"Hoka!" I rolled him onto his back and let out a sob as fresh blood started to spread slowly on the concrete floor. "Somebody help!" I screamed, looking around, but both sides were too busy fighting and avoiding bullets.

"It's okay..." Hoka whispered with a small smile. "I'll be fine." But the paleness of his skin and the blood spreading contradicted his words.

"No. I love you, Hoka, please." I looked up as his uncle walked closer to us, his gun raised.

"Look what you made me do," he said, his face as pale as Hoka's. "You'll die together and share a grave. How poetic."

I leaned over Hoka's body and closed my eyes, bracing for impact.

I heard the shot, but I didn't feel any pain; instead, I saw Hoka's uncle fall to the floor.

I raised my head, keeping my body flush on Hoka's, and saw the bullet hole right in the middle of his uncle's forehead.

I looked around and froze, seeing Alessandro Benetti, his cheek and shirt splattered with blood, standing in a room full of angry *yakuza*, his gun still directed where Hoka's uncle stood.

Jiro came in and paled at the scene. He whispered something to Alessandro, who shook his head.

Jiro jerked his head toward me and extended his hand to Alessandro, who gave him his gun with clear reluctance.

"Save him, please. I'll do anything you want," I sobbed, touching Hoka's pale face.

"You need to move, *Sorella*."

I hesitated for a second, tightening my hold on Hoka's unconscious, defenseless form.

"I will not hurt him, I promise. But you have to let me look."

I moved and sat on the floor beside them as Alessandro took off his jacket and lifted Hoka.

The grim look on his face as he glanced at me was not helping.

"We need help, pronto!"

A couple of men came and spoke to him in Italian as the older of the two set a leather bag on the floor and ripped the back of Hoka's shirt.

Alessandro was still holding him up, and I was grateful at the gentleness of his movements.

As the man worked on Hoka, some of my adrenaline crashed and the side of my head started to pound. I winced as I rested my shirt sleeve on my temple.

Alessandro's eyes zoomed in on me, and he looked at the other man and spoke rapidly to him in Italian. All I understood was 'Sorella' and 'Violetta.'

The man came toward me and crouched beside me before grabbing my arm and wrapping it around his shoulders. He stood and pulled me up with him. Only the arm around his neck and his arm around my waist kept me up.

"Come on, we need to go," he said with a heavy Italian accent.

"No." I tried to jerk again, but I was too weak and dizzy to even nudge him.

"Go with him, Violet," Alessandro sighed with irritation. "I'm not taking you away. You're going to his home, and I have this one to make sure I don't do anything fishy." He pointed in the general direction of Jiro, who was talking to his men, all the others now dead on the floor. "We can't take care of him and you at the same time. Milo is a doctor too, so let him help you."

"I'll be here, too. I'll make sure you get home," Oda, the young guard who saved me, said.

Alessandro told him something in Italian, and Oda smirked. "I'll be good."

"Alessandro, *brother*, please." That word felt so foreign in my mouth. "Don't let him die. I love him... I-I won't survive him."

Alessandro pursed his lips and nodded. "Now go," he repeated before moving a little, hiding Hoka's injury from my sight.

Milo forced me to turn around and walked me to the exit, flanked by Oda on the other side.

"I need to stitch you up before it gets *infetta*... infected," the doctor said, eyeing my scalp critically.

"Is he going to be okay? Hoka?"

The doctor opened his mouth and closed it as he helped me into the back of an SUV.

"Of course he will," Oda replied before closing the back door. "He has you to fight for." He sat in the front seat.

"Drink this," the doctor said, dropping a bottle of water on my lap.

Oda started the car and drove away as I drank.

God, ancestors, or whoever is listening... please, save him. Do that for me and I swear I will not spend another minute away from him.

Before, Hoka may have been the source of a lot of my torment, but he was also the essence of my poor, beating heart.

CHAPTER 26

Hoka

Violet! I sat straight up and gasped at the sharp pain I felt all over my back.

"Violet is perfectly fine. Calm down, you're going to pull your stitches." I felt a cool hand on my shoulder, and I fell back heavily in the middle of the soft pillows.

Jiro leaned over me. "You scared us. We almost lost you for a minute there."

I shook my head. All I could remember was bursting into the warehouse, seeing Violet's face covered in blood, and my uncle about to shoot her.

I also remember the sharp pain of the bullet hitting me, and then I was sure I heard her tell me that she loved me and beg someone to save me.

"How's she?" I asked, my voice raspy with thirst.

Jiro grabbed the glass on the table and gave me a little to drink before helping me down on the bed again.

"She's okay; she's pretty banged up, but terrified to lose you. Despite her ordeal, we didn't manage to make her leave your side until Benetti reminded her that she stank and needed a shower." Jiro chuckled, sitting back on the chair beside my bed. "She took it and fell asleep. She's going to have our head for this. She wanted to be by your side when you woke up."

"I thought she was going to die."

"I know. You both almost did." He ran his hands over his face, obviously as weary as I was. "This is not something I want to experience again."

"Akira?"

"Dead."

I nodded with a sigh of relief. At least it was something I wouldn't have to do myself.

"Who killed him?"

Jiro stayed silent for a few seconds. "I did."

I tried to turn on the bed and hissed, pulling at my stitches.

"Fucking hell, Hoka. Chill the fuck out! The bullet caused some serious damage. You lost your spleen. You *need* to calm down."

"Why did you kill him? You know how bad it will be for you now. You had no authority to; no matter what he wanted to do to Violet, you were only supposed to incapacitate him. Now, now..." I shook my head.

"You have to cast me away." He gave me a sad smile. "This is what you wanted to do anyway."

"Not really." I had been angry and hurt, but Jiro had always been my best friend. The few days in Japan and the selfless decisions that ensued had allowed me to see that all his misguided decisions were driven by his desire to protect and spare me the pain he'd suffered. "I need you."

"No, you don't. You have a lovely woman who's so desperately in love with you she used her body as a shield to protect you, as you did with her. She begged everyone and their dogs to save you, and I even heard her say a prayer to *'Hoka's ancestors I don't know.'*" He let out a little laugh. "She's strong, brave, and so resilient. I was wrong, my friend, this woman is made for you. And now you'll even have an Italian brother-in-law. You'll be able to create the alliance our clan always wanted. This is the answer to all the problems. Nobody will ever look badly at her or try to steal your spot, ever."

I looked at him silently. How he seemed to be trying to justify all the good things in my life, as if he was trying to convince himself of something along the lines.

"You didn't kill him, did you? You wouldn't have, you know better."

"It's better that way. Just let it go, Hoka."

"Nobody working in the family would have killed Akira. They would have wounded him." He cocked his head to the side. "Only an Italian would have done that."

Jiro pursed his lips.

"Why are you covering for him? He helped us save Violet, but—"

"It has nothing to do with that."

I frowned. "Then what is it?"

When I got home and I'd been told that Violet never made it to the hotel, I'd been both angry and scared. I'd contacted Benetti and threatened the life of every Italian in California in exchange for Violet.

His outburst of anger at her disappearance and my 'flagrant inaptitude' at keeping her safe were enough to let me know he had no play in any of this.

He informed me that he'd be getting in his jet and would meet me in five hours. He also made me swear immunity to his mole. I would have sworn anything he wanted, as long as it helped me get my Violet back.

This was how I found out about Oda. I liked the kid, and I had no idea he'd been half-Japanese and Italian when he joined our rank when he was seventeen; he was probably the best spy I'd ever met. He was not only a double agent working for me and Alessandro, but he informed us that he'd been working for my uncle too. Just to make sure things didn't go off track too much.

He swore up and down that he didn't know about Violet's kidnapping, and I was happy to grant him immunity for his help, even if I was still going to send him packing all the way to Chicago. I didn't need a spy in my house.

"He saved your life, Hoka. If you're here today, it's because of him and his doctor. He protected you; he acted so fast and with a precision that chilled me to the bone. He was acting like he'd been a surgeon himself, and he stitched you up and kept his hand pressed on the wound for an hour until we got you to our actual surgeon."

I looked at him with incredulity. "It's ridiculous! Why would he do that for me?"

Jiro rolled his eyes. "He didn't. The man dislike you very much. He did it for *her*. He would do anything for her. She begged him to save you, and he fought for your life as if it was his." He took a deep breath. "She needs him in her life. Admitting he killed Akira would only start a family war that will cause damage on both sides and will hurt Violet the most."

I nodded grimly. No matter how much I hated it, Jiro was the perfect scapegoat. "I'll find a way, I'm the boss. I don't have to send you away."

"You do, and honestly, I want to." He leaned back in his chair. "I need to reassess things, I'm not sure. I – I thought I had accepted Anna's death, but I don't think I did. I need to work on that."

"Where will you go?"

"I don't know yet, but I need to discover the man I am. I know you can understand that."

"I do but, despite my anger, you're the person I trust the most in the world."

"No, not anymore." He smiled. and it had a bittersweet edge to it. "She's the person you trust the most, as it should be. You are her world too, Hoka."

"She's pretty special..." I smiled. "I'll miss you."

Jiro rolled his eyes. "I think the painkillers are making you emotional. I'll be gone, not dead. I'll have a phone." He looked at the clock on the mantle and stood. "I need to tell the doctor and everyone else that you're up."

"And if you see Violet—"

He raised his hands. "Nope, I'm not telling her. She'll throttle me for not calling her as soon as you opened your eyes. She's short, but terrifying."

I chuckled. "She's fierce, my little firecracker."

Jiro opened the door and turned toward me. "I should have said all that a long time ago, but I'm glad you're happy, my friend. Love suits you."

As soon as Jiro left the room, I sat up and turned to the side of the bed pulling my legs over the edge with a painful grunt.

I ground my teeth and closed my eyes tightly as I rested my hand on the nightstand to help myself up.

"Motherfucker." I'd been shot, yet it felt like my whole body had been battered. Fuck. I looked down at my feet on the dark wooden floor. Even my fucking toes hurt. How was that even possible?

I forced my sorry ass to the bathroom, trailing my feet on the floor like a sick old man. I wanted to use the toilet and make myself a little more presentable for Violet. She was obviously worried about me.

I did what I had to do and turned toward the mirror, resting my hands on the counter. There was a bandage around my lower half, but except for that, I didn't look as close to death as I felt.

I washed my face and tightened my hair into a bun before attempting my way back to bed.

My head started to spin as I reached the threshold, and I grabbed the doorframe before I found myself face-first on the floor.

There was a sharp knock on my door, and I swore under my breath. Now was not the time, but I didn't think I could make it back to my bed without help, even if it was from my five-foot-two soulmate.

"Come in," I called, trying to stand straight, and smoothing my features for her not to see the extent of my discomfort.

Alessandro Benetti walked into my room, and I was not sure if it was better or worse than Violet.

He looked at me with his eyebrows raised and glanced behind him before closing the door.

One of the heads of the Italian mafia was standing in my bedroom while I was hurt and weak. What could *possibly* go wrong?

"What are you doing up?" he asked, his voice a mix of irritation and impatience.

"Why? Are you worried about me?" I asked with a cocky smile, but any attempt at bravado vanished when I tried to take a step forward and my knees buckled.

"*Cretino*," he muttered before hurrying toward me. He wrapped his arm high around my back and helped me walk to my bed. "No, I really don't care, but you're going to mess up my impressive work and then Violet will blame me for it."

He let go of me as soon as I sat on the bed and took a few steps back, as if he wanted to put as much distance between us as possible. "You owe me a new suit, by the way. I ruined my custom-made Cucinelli linen jacket to put pressure on your wound and save your sorry ass."

I snorted. "I'll make a bank transfer." I frowned at his clothes. "Are those mine?"

"Yes, it was that or my clothes covered in your blood." He looked down at the crisp white Egyptian shirt. "A bit tight, though... I guess I've got more muscle than you do."

Ah, it was an *'who's the strongest'* moment.

"Um, but a bit too long, I see." I pointed at the hem of the black pants that I knew were mine. "I guess I'm quite taller than you are." I was exaggerating. I only had a couple of inches on the man, but the tightness in his jaw showed I hit him right where I wanted to. "Thank you, though," I said reluctantly. "I know it must have cost you to save an enemy."

"Not saving you would have cost me so much more." He sighed and took a seat uninvited. "You're not my enemy. Well, not *anymore*, at least." He added when he saw the disbelief in my face. "You're never going to be my friend or my ally, but I'll tolerate you, just like I know you'll tolerate me. For Violet."

"There's nothing I wouldn't do for her," I admitted, not worried that it would be used against me as we both shared the same weakness.

"I know, and it's infuriatingly the same for her." He shook his head and rested his forearms on his thighs. "I know you and I will never see eye to eye and it's fine, but Violet matters to me. She may think it's all an act, but it's not. She doesn't understand the circumstances, but you do." He pursed his lips. "You know the little value the older generations of any syndicate put on the lives of women."

"Broodmare and connection," I agreed, hating that but so grateful my father didn't treat my mother that way.

Alessandro nodded. "She doesn't see the full picture, and I won't force her to. But yesterday and today she thawed to me, I think we can build a relationship and if that means having you around..." he shrugged, "then so be it."

"I want Violet to have a family besides me. I'm not immortal, and in our line of work, nothing is certain. I'll be more at peace knowing that should anything happen to me, she'll have you to protect her. I won't interfere in your relationship; I'll even encourage it. Besides, we're going to be family soon."

"*Madre de dio,* you're going to marry her, aren't you?"

I couldn't help but laugh, causing a little twinge of pain on my back. "The first chance I get."

He rolled his eyes and stood, helping me recline in bed before reaching for the plastic pill bottle on the nightstand and pushed it toward me. "Don't play the hero, take the pills. Two every six hours."

"They make me a little drowsy. I want to see Violet first."

"Violet fell asleep while eating her sandwich. She's on the lounge chair, dead to the world. You've got time."

He sighed, looking around my room but not looking for anything in particular.

"What is it?"

"Your friend is taking the blame."

I nodded grimly. "Nobody can afford a war right now."

"I'd do it again, even knowing the consequences."

"And I don't blame you. He deserved that bullet, but it would be best if you forgot you're to blame."

"I'll try. You know secrecy is not common in our line of work," he replied mockingly.

I moved in the bed and groaned.

"Take the damn pills! You want my sister to be more worried than she already is?" He cocked his head to the side. "Do you want her to see you as an invalid?"

That kicked me into action, and I popped two pills at once with a glass of water. I loved that my Violet saw me as her superhero when she didn't see me as her monster, and I wanted to keep it that way.

He nodded and walked to the foot of the bed. "I'm going to leave tonight. Not that I don't enjoy your amazing company, especially when you're passed out, but the secret about Violet is out and I need to manage it."

"Do you need me to do anything?"

"I think you've done enough. Despite my reluctance, you will marry her." He gave me a bitter smile. "It's not like I could stop you, anyway. I may be thousands of miles away, but it will never be far enough if you ever hurt her again. Do you understand?" His face held all the seriousness of a man on a mission, and I was happy it was to protect the love of my life. "If she as little as calls me in tears, I will hunt you down and I won't fear any war."

"I understand, and if I hurt her, I'll give you my katana."

Alessandro tipped his mouth down. "Swords? We're not in medieval times anymore. A gun is the way to go."

I felt the warmth of the pills start to spread over me and the pain started to subside.

"I won't hurt her. Well, not in a way she doesn't enjoy."

Alessandro let out a noise of disgust. "You're getting high now. I'm going."

"I'll give her lots and lots of babies. I love being inside her."

He made a gagging sound, and I heard the door close. My eyes were closed as I continued to explain all the ways I was going to bring her pleasure.

When I woke up, I was not alone in my bed. Violet was lying on her side, her wide blue eyes watching me.

"You know, you were right. Waking up with someone staring at you while you sleep *is* creepy." I gave her a small smile.

"I thought you were going to die," she whispered, not moving from her position on the bed. "I didn't really realize before then what it would mean for me. It was an agony I never want to face again."

"I'm still here, sweetheart; there's no taking me away from you. I'm too stubborn for that." I let my eyes trail to the dressing on the side of her head. "I know how you feel," I replied seriously. "When I walked into that warehouse and saw you lying on the floor, half your face covered in blood—" I shivered at the fresh wave of horror. "If you had died, I wanted to die with you."

She slid closer to me and as she rested her cheek against my shoulder cautiously, I forgot all about my pain and discomfort.

That woman was not only a balm for my soul, but for my body, too. I turned my head to kiss the top of hers.

"When I thought I was going to die, I was not afraid. All I could think about was that I didn't have the chance to tell you that I still loved you, that you were still, and always would be, the only one for me, and that I feared more my reaction to you breaking my heart again than you hurting me." She whispered, her warm breath caressing my neck.

"I want to make it right. I want you to wake up with this certainty every day."

"You almost died for me."

"And I would do it again."

She moved up to kiss my jawline. "I rather you didn't. I need you alive."

I turned my head and pecked her lips. "Likewise. I'd appreciate it if you didn't kill us because, sweetheart, my heart lives in your chest. Take care of it, because if you die, I die."

We stayed silent for a little while, just enjoying each other's presence.

"You're staying, right?" I asked tentatively.

"Of course."

"Forever?" I asked hopefully.

She looked up with a glint of humor in her eyes. "That's the plan."

"Good." I smiled back. "Can I ask you a favor?"

"Of course. What do you need?"

I jerked my head toward my office. "Can you get to the first drawer? The code is 884. Can you get the square wooden box?"

She nodded and rushed to my office. As soon as she was out of view, I pulled myself to a sitting position before she could see the wincing and grunting it caused.

"Here you go."

"So, I'm sorry I'm not doing it the way I planned, but..." I opened the box and retrieved the smaller black one inside.

Violet inhaled sharply and sat on the bed.

"When I proposed to you in Japan, it was not an impulse. I bought this ring before I sent you away. I bought it after we made love for the first time, and I guess when I imagined my proposal, it was in this bed naked, possibly with me still so deep inside you."

She blushed, and I grinned. Sometimes, it was the only reason I did that—just to see the lovely coloring on her skin.

"You're my *ikigai*, Violet Murphy. You know what it means?"

She shook her head, looking at the closed box in my hand.

"*Ikigai* means your purpose in life, but it is also your reason for being or your bliss. It's what inspires you to get out of bed every day. Violet, my purpose in this life is to love you, care for you, to live alongside you. You are who I think of every morning and every night. You are the reason I keep breathing."

"Hoka, I love you." Her voice was thick with emotion.

I cleared my throat, getting just as emotional. "I made a lot of mistakes in my life, committed a lot of sins, but the one thing I did right was give my heart to you. You're so much more incredible than any dream I ever had, and I know the timing is probably not right. It may still be too early, but please, Violet, I beg you." I opened the box, revealing the custom-made ring to her. "Save me and become my wife."

She blinked rapidly and had a cute little sniffle. "Call me old-fashioned, but I'd definitely marry a man who's willing to take a bullet for me."

"Is- is that a yes?" For some reason, despite all the signs of her love for me, I still doubted her answer.

She nodded, sniffling again.

"I need to hear the words, sweetheart."

"Yes, I'll marry you, darkness and all. I think we love each other enough to keep it at bay from our love, and I can't see myself anywhere other than by your side—it's my favorite place to be."

I put the ring on her trembling finger and kissed her hand.

"You're my life, Violet Murphy."

"You're my heart, Hoka Nishimura."

EPILOGUE

Six months later - Hoka
"We'll be here." I sighed, pretending to be calm as Alessandro Benetti started to freak out on the other end of the line. "I've got my own damn plane, Sandro, for fuck sakes. I will not rush her, especially not now."

I was not calm; I was taking my beautiful wife all the way to Chicago to both seal the alliance between the Italian and the *yakuza,* but also for him to introduce Violet as a Benetti to his syndicate.

Violet Murphy-Benetti-Nishumira—talk about a mouthful. But for me, her name was much simpler... *Mine*. Violet was *mine,* and I was hers.

"We'll be there. I'll text you when we leave." I hung up before he could add something more.

"My brother's giving you a hard time?"

I swirled around to find my beautiful wife standing under the threshold of the library, ready to go.

"He's stressing like a bride on her wedding day."

"Is he?" She raised her eyebrows with a playful smile. "I don't remember being the nervous one at our wedding."

"Fine! He's nervous like a mafia boss on his wedding day."

"That's more like it." She laughed and walked toward me, wrapping her arms around my neck as I wrapped mine around her back to kiss her.

I married her as soon as I was able to walk after being shot, and I missed Jiro immensely. He was supposed to have been my best man, but life decided otherwise.

Thanks to the deal with the Italians, all the people who were looking at us wrong now kissed her feet.

"How's our boy?" I asked, resting my hand on the small swell of her belly.

I was still in awe of our child growing peacefully inside her. We were a little apprehensive, especially based on our history, but she was now five months pregnant and the doctor was very confident.

She rested her hand on top of mine. "Our boy is the reason I'm late. Nothing fits me anymore."

"But you're still so small." My eyes fell on her swollen breast and my cock stirred. "Well, not everywhere."

"Oh no, no. I know that look. We can't afford that look right now."

"I love you. I desire you. Can you blame me?"

"No, I can't, but Sandro will kill you if we're late. He loves me, but you...?"

I growled, thrusting my hips against her, making her feel my growing cock.

"Damn it, Hoka," she moaned as she broke our embrace and took a step back. "You're forcing me to be the reasonable one when I'm the one horny filled with hormones."

"I love your hormones," I replied suggestively, taking a step toward her. She'd been really craving sex for the past few weeks. She was seeking me every chance she got and I was way too happy to indulge. I took her on every flat surface and would fuck her until my dick fell off.

"I tell you what. We'll get on that plane, and I'll let you have your way with me during the four-hour flight."

I grinned. "I love your way of compromising, wife. I knew there was a reason I married you."

She extended her hand toward me. "Let's go, husband."

I grabbed her hand and intertwined our fingers as we walked toward the door.

I thanked the ancestors every day for granting me this gift. For allowing me to feel complete and loved, and for the opportunity to be loved.

Violet Murphy was my damnation, my redemption, and above all, my life.

Six years later- Violet

I took a deep breath, stepping out of the house. It was late, despite the sun still being high in the sky.

We spent six weeks every year in Japan, where Hoka could fully be my husband and father of our children, leaving the mafia boss behind.

The loud giggle of our son closely followed Hoka's deep laugh, made me laugh too as I went down the path to the lake.

"Mama!" he squealed as he saw me reach the shore.

I look at two of my favorite men in the world in the lake. My beautiful husband and my son, who was wrapped on his father's back like a little monkey.

"Mama, I saw the monster!" he said, bouncing with excitation.

"Did you?" I raised an eyebrow at Hoka, who gave me a sheepish smile.

I knew that telling Yuko the story about the dragon would lead to hours and hours of searching in the lake.

"You will need to resume your search tomorrow, baby. Granny is running you a bath and dinner will be ready soon."

"Mama..." he whined, using the force of his puppy-dog eyes on me.

I shook my head. That boy was just as charming as his father. He was the spitting image of Hoka when he'd been a child. Same dark hair and sharp face, but his eyes were all mine.

"I'll need to take photos to show Uncle Sandro."

"Tomorrow, son," Hoka replied, swimming back to shore. "Mom said we were done, and you remember what we said."

"We always do what mommy says because she knows best."

"Exactly."

Yuko stepped off his father's back and ran to the towel I held open for him.

I wrapped it around him and rubbed his arms. I kissed the top of his head before I said, "Go on. Granny is waiting, and Sara is, too."

Yuko ran up the path, and once he disappeared up the hill, I turned toward my husband who was walking lazily toward me, all wet and magnificent.

He'd been mine for six years, and I still loved and desired him as much as before. No, that was a lie—I desired him more, I loved him more. Every time I saw him play pirates with our six-year-old son or have a tea party with our four-year-old daughter, I loved him even more. My Hoka always treated me as if I was the most precious gift in the world. Even now, while I was pregnant with our third child, he still treated the situation with the same awe he had during my first and second pregnancy.

"Hello, beautiful wife." He stopped in front of me. "Do you like what you see?"

I smiled. "I always do."

"What would you say about taking this dress off and letting me have my way with you in the lake?"

"I don't know..." I trailed off, already unbuttoning the dress and letting it fall to the ground, standing there completely naked, feeling even sexier in my pregnant state. "Your mother will keep our children occupied."

"Oh, you had it all planned, vixen!" He took off his shorts, showing me his hard cock. He extended his hand to me. "Come on, wife. Let me introduce you to the monster in the lake."

I took his hand and intertwined our fingers. "I know this monster intimately; I love him inside me."

He let out a feral growl as we stepped into the lake.

Hoka Nishimura had many things—my heaven, my hell, and above all, my heart.

The end...For now

Alessandro Benetti's story will be coming soon in **Her Heartless Savior**.

HER RUTHLESS WARRIOR

ABOUT R.G. ANGEL

I'm a trained lawyer, world traveler, coffee addict, cheese aficionado, avid book reviewer and blogger.

I consider myself as an 'Eclectic romantic' as I love to devour every type of romance and I want to write romance in every sub-genre I can think of.

When I'm not busy doing all my lawyerly mayhem, and because I'm living in rainy (yet beautiful) Britain, I mostly enjoy indoor activities such as reading, watching TV, playing with my crazy puppies and writing stories I hope will make you dream and will bring you as much joy as I had writing them.

If you want to know any of the latest news join my reader group R.G.'s Angels on Facebook or subscribe to my newsletter!

Keep calm and read on!
R.G. Angel

Also by

R.G. Angel

The Patricians series
Bittersweet Legacy
Bittersweet Revenge
Bittersweet Truth
Bittersweet Love (Coming soon)
The Cosa Nostra series

The Dark King (Prequel Novella)

Broken Prince

Twisted Knight

Cruel King
Standalones
Lovable
The Tragedy of Us

The Bargain

Acknowledgments

Thank you to my street team, bloggers and readers for helping me promote this book.

Her Ruthless Warrior had been quite an emotional book to write and I was exceptionally nervous to share it with the world. I really tried to explore all the aspects of love and loss as respectfully as I could and I hope you enjoyed Hoka and Violet's journey as much asI enjoyed writing it.

A special shout out to Webtoon stories *Midnight Poppy Land* by LilyDusk and *My dear cold-blooded King* by Lifelight for being my ray of light as I wrote this story. You helped me keep the inspiration intact.

Printed in Great Britain
by Amazon